PENGUIN BOOKS

OUR VILLAGE

Mary Russell Mitford was born at Alresford, Hampshire, on 16 December 1787. She won a £20,000 lottery at the age of ten, but the extravagances of her father eventually reduced her to poverty. In 1820 she went to live in a small cottage at Three Mile Cross, on the road between Reading and Basingstoke, which was her home for more than thirty years. Her one luxury was her flower-garden, which she tended with loving care. Before she died in 1855, she had written a number of sketches, which originally appeared in the *Lady's Magazine*. The best of these have been collected to create this volume.

Anne Scott-James has known and loved village life since childhood, when she walked and cycled and searched for wild flowers among the very same Berkshire and Hampshire woods and lanes immortalized by Miss Mitford. She was educated at St Paul's Girls' School and Somerville College, Oxford, where she was a classical scholar. She then went into journalism, where she was at one time editor of *Harper's Bazaar* and later columnist for the *Daily Mail*. She now specializes in garden writing and is the author, among other books, of *Down to Earth*, *Sissinghurst*, *The Cottage Garden* and *The Pleasure Garden*, which was illustrated by her late husband, Osbert Lancaster.

Mary Russell Mitford

Our Village

Sketches of Rural Character and Scenery

Edited with an
Introduction by Anne Scott-James

PENGUIN BOOKS

Penguin Books Ltd, Harmondsworth, Middlesex, England
Viking Penguin Inc., 40 West 23rd Street, New York, New York 10010, USA
Penguin Books Australia Ltd, Ringwood, Victoria, Australia
Penguin Books Canada Ltd, 2801 John Street, Markham, Ontario, Canada L3R 1B4
Penguin Books (NZ) Ltd, 182–190 Wairau Road, Auckland 10, New Zealand

First published in five volumes 1824–32
This selection, based on the text from the 1835 edition, with illustrations from the 1879
edition, published in Penguin Books 1987

Introduction and selection copyright © Anne Scott-James, 1987
All rights reserved

Filmset in 10/12pt Linotron Sabon by
Rowland Phototypesetting Ltd
Bury St Edmunds, Suffolk
Made and printed in Great Britain by
Cox & Wyman Ltd, Reading

CONTENTS

Contents

Introduction

Mary Russell Mitford was born in 1787 at Alresford, Hampshire, a county which, with neighbouring Berkshire, was to be her background all her life. But Miss Mitford was anything but a country mouse. The only child of well-born parents, intellectual and witty, an ardent Whig, a fluent linguist, she circulated among celebrities all her life and was at one time literally the toast of London; in 1814 no less a person than the Duke of Kent proposed her health at an evening party, and it was drunk with 'a flourish of drums and trumpets from the Duke's band'. Amiable and adaptable by nature, Miss Mitford was equally at home in the castles of her grand relations in the north of England and in the cottages of the Berkshire villages she loved so well. Her range of interests varied from politics to wild flowers, from the London theatre to village cricket. She knew both wealth and poverty. Though a maiden lady who never travelled abroad, she was broad-minded, even unshockable, a daughter of the eighteenth century and the Regency rather than a Victorian though she lived until 1855.

There was, however, a dark side to Miss Mitford's life, a very dark side indeed, which she never, until late in life, when bowed down by hard work and poverty, admitted even to herself: she had a deplorable father. Dr George Mitford was descended from an aristocratic Northumberland family, and married a substantial heiress in 1785, Mary Russell of the Bedford family, the only surviving child of a rich Hampshire rector. Mrs Mitford was ten years older than her husband, an affectionate and well-educated woman, but plain to look at and docile to the point of stupidity.

Dr Mitford was a ne'er-do-well, almost a scoundrel, who speculated, gambled at cards, coursed greyhounds, drank a bit, and ruined his family three times over, running quickly through his own modest fortune and his wife's large one, and finally squandering the handsome sum of £20,000 that his small daughter, by an amazing fluke, won in a lottery when she was ten.

Starting life in her mother's comfortable country house at Alresford, with a splendid library and 'a large old-fashioned garden, full of old-fashioned flowers, stocks, honeysuckles and pinks', Miss Mitford came to know the miseries of bailiffs and dispossession, duns at the door, furniture in the street, squalid lodgings and poky cottages, and, in later life, the threat of total penury, which was averted only by the power of her pen. The first Mitford upheaval came in about 1793, when the family had to sell the Alresford house, with all their books and furniture, and leave for a series of lodgings.

However, Dr Mitford (a medical graduate of Edinburgh University though he never bothered to practise) had magical charm. He was clever, handsome and amusing, with a wide circle of political friends, and both his wife and his daughter adored him. They fretted at his extravagance but, in all their anxieties, they never *blamed* him. His daughter's great love for him, filial at first, became almost maternal before she was twenty. She wrote to him frequently (for he was usually in London while his wife and daughter were in the country), addressing him as 'My dear boy', 'My little boy', 'My dear son and heir', or even 'My beloved ittey boy', admonishing him mildly, as though he were a schoolboy who had overspent at the tuckshop, for not paying the pressing debts which were causing them the depths of humiliation. Miss Mitford never married, nor seems to have fallen even mildly in love, for Dr Mitford filled the place in her affection of father, lover and son.

Miss Mitford's literary ability was revealed very young. She was a precocious child who could read when she was three, and there is a fascinating miniature of her at this age, showing a fat child with a lopsided little face and the knowing gaze of a friendly gnome. (She remained short, fat and plain all her life, but was later admired for her beautiful grey eyes, sweet voice and charm of manner.) From the ages of ten to fifteen she attended a first-class

London boarding-school run by a M St Quintin, a French émigré, and was a prize pupil, learning fluent French and Italian, astronomy and some Latin as well as the usual arts subjects, and becoming a passionate reader. In letters home she discussed Homer and Virgil, compared Pope with Dryden, reported that she was reading Metastasio and Tasso in Italian. She wrote very grown-up letters to her parents, as though they were her contemporaries, and they answered in kind. Visitors, social engagements, family plans were discussed with freedom, and she once complained that an aunt who visited her at school had a 'hypocritical drawl'. When she was ten, and the family finances were at a low ebb, she chose a lottery ticket which brought her father his third fortune, and he immediately bought a dilapidated Elizabethan house and farm, Graseley Court, in Berkshire. He pulled down the house and rebuilt it in the Georgian style, renaming it Bertram House, after Bertram Castle, the family seat in Northumberland. The Mitfords moved into this stately home in 1804, but Dr Mitford increasingly left his wife and Mary to their own country devices and spent his time in the coffee-houses of London.

In 1806, when she was eighteen, Miss Mitford had her first taste of high society among the landed gentry, for Dr Mitford took his clever daughter on a tour of Northumberland, visiting the great houses of his relatives. Miss Mitford thoroughly enjoyed herself, writing enthusiastically to her mother every few days. Anyone who knows Miss Mitford only from *Our Village* should read her spirited account in letters home of the dinners and balls she attended, the castles and gardens she visited, and the great ladies and gentlemen with whom she easily made friends. (She was a prolific letter-writer all her life, and most of her letters, which are always lively and often brilliant, survive.)[1] When the round of visits was over, her volatile father disappeared without warning, leaving her in Northumberland alone with nowhere to go. He turned up in Reading, and for once she was obliged to reproach

---

[1] A selection in three volumes, edited by the Rev. A. G. L'Estrange, was published in 1870, under the title *The Life of Mary Russell Mitford Related in a Selection from her Letters to her Friends.*

him, writing: 'I now implore you to return, and I call upon mamma's sense of propriety to send you here directly. Little did I suspect that my father, my dear, beloved father, would desert me in this manner, at this distance from home. Everyone is surprised.'

When restored to Bertram House, Miss Mitford divided her time between a busy social life, her quiet country pursuits, and her reading and letter-writing. She dearly loved the wild life of Hampshire and Berkshire, and went on long walks in search of wild flowers. (She wrote later: 'Nothing can be more vulgar than my taste in flowers, for which I have a passion. I like scarcely any but the common ones. First and best I love violets, and primroses, and cowslips, and wood anemones, and the whole train of field flowers.') She also liked gardening, and took care of a number of pets, including her father's greyhounds and pointers, though she took no interest in horses and did not ride. Her favourite occupation of all was to lie on a sofa reading, and her range of interests was wide. She devoured the newspaper as a zealous radical (two of her heroes were Charles James Fox and William Cobbett, a family friend). 'Busy as I was yesterday', she wrote to her father in 1809, 'I found time to read the newspaper. If it were not physically, as well as morally, impossible for Sheridan to blush, I should say that his face should glow with shame during the next month for his slavish speech on Friday. The vile degenerate Whig!' She also read novels, plays, poetry and the classical authors, and once mastered fifty-five volumes in a single month. On sorties to London, she went to theatres, balls, art exhibitions and public trials, and met her father's political friends at dinner parties. She was known as 'the clever Miss Mitford', and her conversation was considered delightful.

At about this time, Miss Mitford began to write herself and quickly rose above the amateur ranks to become a professional. She began with poetry, and her first volume was published in 1810, when she was twenty-two. It sold well in England, and even better in America, and from this time on a steady flow of poems and, some ten years later, of plays and essays poured from her pen, bringing in a creditable and much-needed income. Miss Mitford was a marvellous letter-writer – I would put her among the great ones – and a delightful essayist, but her poetry, in trite rhyming couplets, is almost unreadable today, nor have her plays, on heroic historical themes, much to offer the modern reader. But they were successful at the time, on both sides of the Atlantic.

Miss Mitford was thoroughly self-assured about her work and sent copies of her books to celebrities known and unknown to her. She dedicated her first volume to the Honourable William Herbert, after toying with the idea of Lord Holland, and was not above literary lobbying. 'Ten thousand thanks for the management of the Reviews' she wrote to her father when the book was published.

In this same year, 1810, Miss Mitford met one of her father's friends, Sir William Elford, with whom she began a correspondence which lasted for more than twenty years. Sir William was nearly forty years her senior, and perhaps she found in him the reliable qualities which her father lacked. He was a distinguished man who lived in Devonshire, an MP, painter and exhibitor at the Royal Academy, a Fellow of the Royal Society and Recorder of Plymouth. To him she confided, in beautiful classic prose, warmed by humour and affection, her thoughts on all the things she cared for, from nightingales to political reform. Much literary criticism went into these letters to her elderly friend, most of it shrewd and witty, as in her comments on historical fiction:

> Everyone who reads the description of Gothic costume in Walter Scott, and of Turkish habits in Lord Byron, must be convinced by their very elaborateness and detail that they tell of things new both to them and their readers – things of which they know but little. All their panoply of love of war, their Turkish boudoirs and their Gothic drinking-halls, cups, amulets, rosaries, mazers and all, are set down as part of the fiction; and we never find out that so it might have been, till some old gentleman is kind enough to tell us so in a note. But every touch of costume, every minute stroke of manners in Homer, comes on us at once with the clearness, the freshness, and the loveliness of truth.

But sometimes she was wildly astray. She found Jane Austen lacking in elegance, and thought Elizabeth Bennet in *Pride and Prejudice* vulgar, and unworthy of the delectable Mr Darcy. Perhaps she was at first a little jealous of Jane Austen, whom she grew to admire in later life.

In spite of her London triumphs, it was the country which delighted her most. 'I am generally so happy everywhere', she wrote, 'that I was never quite sure of it myself, till, during the latter part of my stay in town, the sight of a rose, the fragrance of a honeysuckle, and even the trees in Kensington Gardens excited nothing but fruitless wishes for our own flowers and our peaceful woodlands.'

Poor Miss Mitford! The happy years at Bertram House were not to last very long. In spite of her hard work and the excellent sales of her poetry, Bertram House had to be sold in 1820, for Dr Mitford had been speculating wildly. The family moved into a labourer's cottage scarcely bigger than a cabin at Three Mile Cross, one mile away, and from this time on Miss Mitford had to support them all. She was at first cheerful about it. The new cottage was near her favourite walks, she was planting a new garden, she had her dear pet animals, but even for this humble standard of living, her income was not enough. She began to write plays – the first to be performed was *Julian*, in 1823, with the famous actor, William Macready, in the title part – and also sketches for the *Lady's Magazine*, which multiplied the circulation of an obscure journal. These were published in book form in 1824, the first of five volumes, under the title *Our Village*. It was to become her most famous and enduring work.

Our Village was a favourite book in our family when I was a child, and reading it first at the age of perhaps eleven or twelve, I loved it for illuminating the country as I knew it. Berkshire happened to be the English county I knew best, and many of Miss Mitford's experiences were exactly my own – picking baskets of violets, driving in a trap, making friends with the village boys, searching the fields and woods inch by inch for unusual flowers. The local fortune-teller, the pedantic schoolmaster, the village Lothario, the rat-catcher, were all people I knew. Miss Mitford's village shop was like our village shop, 'repository of bread, shoes, tea, cheese, tape, ribands and bacon; for everything in short, except the one particular thing which you happen to want at the moment, and will be sure not to find'.

On reading *Our Village* (quite often) in later life, I saw what sophistication lies behind the simple subjects. Miss Mitford never moralizes. The vicissitudes of her life had taught her to accept all kinds of people. The bad boy of the village was likely to be her favourite, if he was amusing, and ill behaviour was rarely followed by nemesis. Indeed, in the only tragic story in this book, 'The Chalk Pit', the victims of disaster are innocent and good. Pomposity was one of the few qualities she could not endure, and pretentiousness annoyed her – she wrote witheringly about a pretty little house which new owners were trying to upgrade into a fashionable residence.

It was her long experience as a professional writer which fashioned the perfection of her prose. I am not going to quote here, for the writing can be enjoyed on every page that follows. Every sentence is lucid, every sketch well-shaped, each one an almost pictorial glimpse of some small scene in village life. In 1821 she wrote to Sir William Elford: 'I have always had a preference for close, shut-in scenes, both in a landscape and in nature, and prefer the end of a woody lane, with a rustic bridge over a little stream, or a bit of an old cottage or farmhouse, with a porch and a vine and clustered chimneys peeping out amongst trees, to any prospect that I ever saw in my life.'

J. C. Squire, writing about *Our Village*, chose 'Frost and Thaw' and 'The First Primrose', as his favourite essays, 'in which she united the detail of Richard Jefferies with a quiet perfection of prose all her own'. James Agate preferred 'A Country Cricket Match' for its wit, quoting these sardonic lines: 'an unnatural coalition between a High Church curate and an evangelical gentleman-farmer drove our lads from the Sunday evening practice' (they went to the public-house instead), and the positively racy 'I must squeeze the account of our grand achievements into as little compass as Cowley, when he crammed the names of eleven of his mistresses into the narrow space of four eight-syllable lines.'

This was strong meat for the readers of the *Lady's Magazine*, but from Miss Mitford anything was acceptable.

My own favourite sketch is 'A Visit to Lucy', a former maid now married and living at a distance, for, reading it, I relive my childhood. The ladies go for a three-mile walk through the woods in spring to a spot well-known to them for its lilies of the valley, finding on the way windflowers and wood-sorrel, Solomon's seal and woodruff, and carpets of orchids. She plans to transplant some of the lilies in the autumn, and writes wisely about the difficulty of transplanting wild flowers (now, of course, largely forbidden). She was a knowledgeable gardener and found that if you move wild flowers to a garden spot, seemingly the same as to soil and situation, they often die.

Five volumes of *Our Village* were published between 1824 and 1832, all best-sellers, and admired by other writers, among them Charles Lamb, Wordsworth, Mrs Trollope and Elizabeth Barrett (later Browning). Some thought her private letters superior to her published sketches, and I agree with them, but she explained that she could not write for the general reader with the same uninhibited freedom as to friends. It must be added that *Our Village* is not only about Three Mile Cross, but is an amalgam of many villages; Miss Mitford did not wish her characters to be too easily identified, and possibly hurt.

From the 1820s onwards, Miss Mitford's life was increasingly one of struggle as she poured out books and plays to support her parents. Her much-loved mother died in 1830, but her father, who became tyrannical with old age, lived until 1842. He demanded every possible delicacy and comfort and round-the-clock attention from his daughter. She had to play cribbage or read to him day and night and became exhausted reading him every line of the newspaper, once 'ten or twelve columns of news from India'. But she still loved him – 'we are the whole world to each other' – and her letters were still cheerful, for there were many compensations. She found new friends and correspondents in John Ruskin, Charles Kingsley and Elizabeth Barrett, whom she met in 1836 and who became very dear to her. Her garden was a delight, with its greenhouse crammed with flowers, especially geraniums. Her fame was gratifying, and she was still a literary lion on her rare visits to London.

But the double strain of writing for money and nursing her father began to tell on her health and by 1837 there were signs of real distress. She suffered constant nausea and pain (probably arthritis), and success extorted its penalty in the shape of begging and even abusive letters from importunate strangers who occasionally besieged her home. In 1837 she wrote to Lord Melbourne asking if he could get her a state pension, and £100 a year was granted. However, the debts still piled up, and she wrote: 'I have not bought a bonnet, a cloak, a gown, hardly a pair of gloves, for four years.' When at last the old man died, she was almost broken in health and very poor; her father's debts amounted to £1,500. Loyal friends opened a fund to pay them off and Queen Victoria, to her great credit, sent an anonymous subscription.

Miss Mitford's last years were easier. Her health picked up, she resumed her country walks, went to concerts and lectures, and wrote to her friends with the old animation. In 1850, when the cottage at Three Mile Cross was crumbling past repair, she moved to a larger and more comfortable cottage at Swallowfield, a few miles away, taking her library of 6,000 books and her favourite garden plants.

In her last years she wrote increasingly to friends in the clergy, read the Gospels and thought much about God. She had always been a member of the Church of England, but was not particularly religious and perhaps not fully a believer. A little time before she died she wanted to take the sacrament but was too honest to receive it until she felt she could do so with total faith. She delayed for some weeks, then received it, and was comforted. She died on 10 January, 1855, and wrote to a friend only three days earlier: 'It had pleased Providence to preserve to me my calmness of mind, clearness of intellect, and also my power of reading by day and by night; and, which is still more, my love of poetry and literature, my cheerfulness, and my enjoyment of little things. This very day, not only my common pensioners, the dear robins, but a saucy troop of sparrows, and a little shining bird of passage, whose name I forget, have all been pecking at once at their tray of breadcrumbs outside the window.'

Miss Mitford was a woman of large intellect whose genius was to chronicle small things.

ANNE SCOTT-JAMES

Our Village

OF all situations for a constant residence, that which appears to me most delightful is a little village far in the country; a small neighbourhood, not of fine mansions finely peopled, but of cottages and cottage-like houses, 'messuages or tenements', as a friend of mine calls such ignoble and nondescript dwellings, with inhabitants whose faces are as familiar to us as the flowers in our garden; a little world of our own, close-packed and insulated like ants in an anthill, or bees in a hive, or sheep in a fold, or nuns in a convent, or sailors in a ship; where we know everyone, are known to everyone, interested in everyone, and authorized to hope that everyone feels an interest in us. How pleasant it is to slide into these true-hearted feelings from the kindly and unconscious influence of habit, and to learn to know and to love the people about us, with all their peculiarities, just as we learn to know and to love the nooks and turns of the shady lanes and sunny commons that we pass every day! Even in books I like a confined locality, and so do the critics when they talk of the unities. Nothing is so tiresome as to be whirled half over Europe at the chariot wheels of a hero, to go to sleep at Vienna, and awaken at Madrid; it produces a real fatigue, a weariness of spirit. On the other hand, nothing is so delightful as to sit down in a country village in one of Miss Austen's delicious novels, quite sure before we leave it to become intimate with every spot and every person it contains; or to ramble with Mr White over his own parish of Selborne,[1] and form a friendship with the fields and coppices, as

[1] White's *Natural History and Antiquities of Selborne*; one of the most fascinating books ever written. I wonder that no naturalist has adopted the same plan.

well as with the birds, mice and squirrels, who inhabit them; or to sail with Robinson Crusoe to his island, and live there with him, and his goats, and his Man Friday – how much we dread any newcomers, any fresh importation of savage or sailor! We never sympathize for a moment in our hero's want of company, and are quite grieved when he gets away. Or to be shipwrecked with Ferdinand on that other lovelier island – the island of Prospero, and Miranda, and Caliban, and Ariel, and nobody else, none of Dryden's exotic inventions – that is best of all. And a small neighbourhood is as good in sober waking reality as in poetry or prose; a village neighbourhood, such as this Berkshire hamlet in which I write; a long, straggling, winding street, at the bottom of a fine eminence, with a road through it, always abounding in carts, horsemen and carriages, and lately enlivened by a stage-coach

from B— to S—, which passed through about ten days ago, and will, I suppose, return some time or other. There are coaches of all varieties nowadays: perhaps this may be intended for a monthly diligence, or a fortnight fly. Will you walk with me through our village, courteous reader? The journey is not long. We will begin at the lower end, and proceed up the hill.

The tidy, square, red cottage on the right hand, with the long well-stocked garden by the side of the road, belongs to a retired publican, from a neighbouring town; a substantial person, with a comely wife; one who piques himself on independence and idleness, talks politics, reads newspapers, hates the minister, and cries out for reform. He introduced into our peaceful vicinage the rebellious innovation of an illumination on the Queen's acquittal. Remonstrance and persuasion were in vain; he talked of liberty and broken windows – so we all lighted up. Oh! how he shone that night with candles, and laurel, and white bows, and gold paper, and a transparency (originally designed for a pocket-handkerchief) with a flaming portrait of her Majesty, hatted and feathered, in red ochre. He had no rival in the village, that we all acknowledged; the very bonfire was less splendid; the little boys reserved their best crackers to be expended in his honour, and he gave them full sixpence more than anyone else. He would like an illumination once a month; for it must not be concealed that, in spite of gardening, of newspaper reading, of jaunting about in his little cart, and frequenting both church and meeting, our worthy neighbour begins to feel the weariness of idleness. He hangs over his gate, and tries to entice passengers to stop and chat; he volunteers little jobs all round, smokes cherry trees to cure the blight, and traces and blows up all the wasp nests in the parish. I have seen a great many wasps in our garden today, and shall enchant him with the intelligence. He even assists his wife in her sweepings and dustings. Poor man! He is a very respectable person, and would be a very happy one, if he would add a little employment to his dignity. It would be the salt of life to him.

Next to his house, though parted from it by another long garden with a yew arbour at the end, is the pretty dwelling of the shoemaker, a pale, sickly looking, black-haired man, the very model of sober industry. There he sits in his little shop, from early morning till late at night. An earthquake would hardly stir him: the illumination did not. He stuck immoveably to his last, from the first lighting up, through the long blaze and the slow decay, till his large solitary candle was the only light in the place. One cannot conceive anything more perfect than the contempt which the man of transparencies and the man of shoes must have felt for each other on that evening. There was at least as much vanity in the sturdy industry as in the strenuous idleness, for our shoemaker is a man of substance: he employs three journeymen, two lame, and one a dwarf, so that his shop looks like a hospital; he has purchased the lease of his commodious dwelling – some even say that he has bought it out and out; and he has only one pretty daughter, a light, delicate, fair-haired girl of fourteen, the champion, protectress, and playfellow of every brat under three years old, whom she jumps, dances, dandles, and feeds all day long. A very attractive person is that child-loving girl. I have never seen anyone in her station who possessed so thoroughly that undefinable charm, the lady-look. See her on a Sunday in her simplicity and her white frock, and she might pass for an earl's daughter. She likes flowers too, and has a profusion of white stocks under her window, as pure and delicate as herself.

The first house on the opposite side of the way is the blacksmith's; a gloomy dwelling, where the sun never seems to shine; dark and smoky within and without, like a forge. The blacksmith is a high officer in our little state, nothing less than a constable. But, alas! alas! when tumults arise, and the constable is called for, he will commonly be found in the thickest of the fray. Lucky would it be for his wife and her eight children if there were no public-house in the land; an inveterate inclination to enter those bewitching doors is Mr Constable's only fault.

Next to this official dwelling is a spruce brick tenement, red, high and narrow, boasting, one above another, three sash-windows, the only sash-windows in the village, with a clematis on one side and a rose on the other, tall and narrow like itself. The slender mansion has a fine genteel look. The little parlour seems made for Hogarth's old maid and her stunted footboy; for tea and card-parties – it would just hold one table; for the rustle of faded silks, and the splendour of old china; for the delight of four-by-honours, and a little snug quiet scandal between the deals; for affected gentility and real starvation. This should have been its destiny; but fate has been unpropitious: it belongs to a plump, merry, bustling dame, with four fat, rosy, noisy children, the very essence of vulgarity and plenty.

Then comes the village shop, like other village shops, multifarious as a bazaar; a repository for bread, shoes, tea, cheese, tape, ribands and bacon; for everything, in short, except the one particular thing which you happen to want at the moment, and will be sure not to find. The people are civil and thriving, and frugal withal; they have let the upper part of their house to two young women (one of them is a pretty blue-eyed girl), who teach little children their ABC, and make caps and gowns for their mammas – parcel schoolmistress, parcel mantua-maker. I believe they find adorning the body a more profitable vocation than adorning the mind.

Divided from the shop by a narrow yard, and opposite the shoemaker's, is a habitation of whose inmates I shall say nothing. A cottage, no, a miniature house, with many additions, little odds

and ends of places, pantries and what not; all angles, and of a charming in-and-outness; a little bricked court before one half, and a little flower yard before the other; the walls, old and weather-stained, covered with hollyhocks, roses, honeysuckles, and a great apricot tree; the casements full of geraniums (ah, there is our superb white cat peeping out from amongst them); the closets (our landlord has the assurance to call them rooms) full of contrivances and corner cupboards; and the little garden behind full of common flowers, tulips, pinks, larkspurs, peonies, stocks and carnations, with an arbour of privet, not unlike a sentry box, where one lives in a delicious green light, and looks out on the gayest of all gay flowerbeds. That house was built on purpose to show in what an exceeding small compass comfort may be packed. Well, I will loiter there no longer.

The next tenement is a place of importance, the Rose Inn; a whitewashed building, retired from the road behind its fine swinging sign, with a little bow-window room coming out on one side, and forming, with our stable on the other, a sort of open square, which is the constant resort of carts, waggons and return chaises. There are two carts there now, and mine host is serving them with beer in his eternal red waistcoat. He is a thriving man and portly, as his waistcoat attests, which has been twice let out within this twelvemonth. Our landlord has a stirring wife, a hopeful son, and a daughter, the belle of the village; not so pretty as the fair nymph of the shoe shop, and far less elegant, but ten times as fine; all curl papers in the morning, like a porcupine, all curls in the afternoon, like a poodle, with more flounces than curl papers, and more lovers than curls. Miss Phœbe is fitter for town than country; and, to do her justice, she has a consciousness of that fitness, and turns her step townwards as often as she can. She is gone to B— today with her last and principal lover, a recruiting serjeant – a man as tall as Serjeant Kite, and as impudent. Some day or other he will carry off Miss Phœbe.

In a line with the bow-window room is a low garden wall, belonging to a house under repair: the white house opposite the collar-maker's shop, with four lime trees before it, and a waggon-load of bricks at the door. That house is the plaything of a wealthy, well-meaning, whimsical person, who lives about a mile off. He has a passion for brick and mortar, and, being too wise to meddle with his own residence, diverts himself with altering and re-altering, improving and re-improving, doing and undoing here. It is a perfect Penelope's web. Carpenters and bricklayers have been at work for these eighteen months, and yet I sometimes stand and wonder whether anything has really been done. One exploit in last June was, however, by no means equivocal. Our good neighbour fancied that the limes shaded the rooms, and made them dark (there was not a creature in the house but the work-men), so he had all the leaves stripped from every tree. There they stood, poor miserable skeletons, as bare as Christmas under the glowing midsummer sun. Nature revenged herself, in her own sweet and gracious manner: fresh leaves sprang out, and at nearly Christmas the foliage was as brilliant as when the outrage was committed.

Next door lives a carpenter, 'famed ten miles round, and worthy all his fame'. Few cabinet-makers surpass him, with his excellent wife, and their little daughter Lizzy, the plaything and queen of the village, a child three years old according to the register, but six in size and strength and intellect, in power and in self-will. She manages everybody in the place, her schoolmistress included; turns the wheeler's children out of their own little cart, and makes them draw her; seduces cakes and lollipops from the very shop window; makes the lazy carry her, the silent talk to her, the grave romp with her; does anything she pleases; is absolutely irresistible. Her chief attraction lies in her exceeding powers of loving, and her firm reliance on the love and indulgence of others. How impossible it would be to disappoint the dear little girl when she runs to meet you, slides her pretty hand into yours, looks up gladly in your face, and says, 'Come!' You must go: you cannot help it. Another part of her charm is her singular beauty. Together with a good deal of the character of Napoleon, she has something of his square, sturdy, upright form, with the finest limbs in the world, a complexion purely English, a round, laughing face, sunburnt and rosy, large merry blue eyes, curling brown hair, and a wonderful play of countenance. She has the imperial attitudes too, and loves to stand with her hands behind her, or folded over her bosom: and sometimes, when she has a little touch of shyness, she clasps them together on the top of her head, pressing down her shining curls, and looking so exquisitely pretty! Yes, Lizzy is queen of the village! She has but one rival in her dominions, a certain white greyhound called Mayflower, much her friend, who resembles her in beauty and strength, in playfulness, and almost in sagacity, and reigns over the animal world as she over the human. They are both coming with me, Lizzy and Lizzy's 'pretty May'.

We are now at the end of the street; a cross-lane, a ropewalk, shaded with limes and oaks, and a cool clear pond overhung with elms, lead us to the bottom of the hill. There is still one house round the corner, ending in a picturesque wheeler's shop. The dwelling-house is more ambitious. Look at the fine flowered window-blinds, the green door with the brass knocker, and the somewhat prim but very civil person, who is sending off a labouring man with sirs and curtsies enough for a prince of the blood. Those are the curate's lodgings – apartments his landlady would call them. He lives with his own family four miles off, but once or twice a week he comes to his neat little parlour to write sermons, to marry, or to bury, as the case may require. Never were better or kinder people than his host and hostess; and there is a reflexion of clerical importance about them, since their connexion with the Church, which is quite edifying – a decorum, a gravity, a solemn politeness. Oh, to see the worthy wheeler carry the gown after his lodger on a Sunday, nicely pinned up in his wife's best handkerchief; or to hear him rebuke a squalling child or a squabbling woman! The curate is nothing to him. He is fit to be perpetual churchwarden.

We must now cross the lane into the shady ropewalk. That pretty white cottage opposite, which stands straggling at the end of the village in a garden full of flowers, belongs to our mason, the shortest of men, and his handsome, tall wife. He, a dwarf, with the voice of a giant; one starts when he begins to talk as if he were shouting through a speaking-trumpet; she, the sister, daughter, and grand-daughter, of a long line of gardeners, and no contemptible one herself. It is very magnanimous in me not to hate her; for she beats me in my own way, in chrysanthemums, and dahlias, and the like gauds. Her plants are sure to live; mine have a sad trick of dying, perhaps because I love them, 'not wisely, but too well', and kill them with over-kindness. Half-way up the hill is another detached cottage, the residence of an officer, and his beautiful family. That eldest boy, who is hanging over the gate, and looking with such intense childish admiration at my Lizzy, might be a model for a Cupid.

How pleasantly the road winds up the hill, with its broad green borders and hedgerows so thickly timbered! How finely the evening sun falls on that sandy excavated bank, and touches the farmhouse on the top of the eminence! And how clearly defined and relieved is the figure of the man who is just coming down! It is poor John Evans, the gardener – an excellent gardener till about ten years ago, when he lost his wife, and became insane. He was sent to St Luke's, and dismissed as cured; but his power was gone and his strength. He could no longer manage a garden, nor submit to the restraint, nor encounter the fatigue of regular employment, so he retreated to the workhouse, the pensioner and factotum of the village, amongst whom he divides his services. His mind often wanders, intent on some fantastic and impracticable plan, and lost to present objects; but he is perfectly harmless, and full of a childlike simplicity, a smiling contentedness, a most touching gratitude. Everyone is kind to John Evans, for there is that about him which must be loved; and his unprotectedness, his utter defencelessness, have an irresistible claim on every better feeling. I know nobody who inspires so deep and tender a pity; he improves all around him. He is useful, too, to the extent of his little power; will do anything, but loves gardening best, and still piques himself on his old arts of pruning fruit trees, and raising cucumbers. He is the happiest of men just now, for he has the management of a melon-bed – a melon-bed! – fie! What a grand pompous name was that for three melon plants under a hand-light! John Evans is sure that they will succeed. We shall see: as the chancellor said, 'I doubt.'

We are now on the very brow of the eminence, close to the Hill House and its beautiful garden. On the outer edge of the paling, hanging over the bank that skirts the road, is an old thorn – such a thorn! The long sprays covered with snowy blossoms, so graceful, so elegant, so lightsome, and yet so rich! There only wants a pool under the thorn to give a still lovelier reflexion, quivering and trembling, like a tuft of feathers, whiter and greener than the life, and more prettily mixed with the bright blue sky. There should indeed be a pool; but on the dark grass plat, under the high bank, which is crowned by that magnificent plume, there is something that does almost as well – Lizzy and Mayflower in the midst of a game at romps, 'making a sunshine in the shady place'; Lizzy rolling, laughing, clapping her hands, and glowing like a rose; Mayflower playing about her like summer lightning, dazzling the eyes with her sudden turns, her leaps, her bounds, her attacks, and her escapes. She darts round the lovely little girl with the same momentary touch that the swallow skims over the water, and has exactly the same power of flight, the same matchless ease and strength and grace. What a pretty picture they would make; what a pretty foreground they do make to the real landscape! The road winding down the hill with a slight bend, like that in the High Street at Oxford; a waggon slowly ascending, and a horseman passing it at a full trot – (ah! Lizzy, Mayflower will certainly desert you to have a gambol with that bloodhorse!); half-way down, just at the turn, the red cottage of the lieutenant, covered with vines, the very image of comfort and content; farther down, on the opposite side, the small white dwelling of the little mason; then the limes and the ropewalk; then the village street, peeping through the trees, whose clustering tops hide all but the chimneys, and various roofs of the houses, and here and there some angle of a wall; farther on, the elegant town of B—, with its fine old church towers and spires; the whole view shut in by a range of chalky hills; and over every part of the picture, trees so profusely scattered that it appears like a woodland scene, with glades and villages intermixed. The trees are of all kinds and all hues, chiefly the finely shaped elm, of so bright and deep a green, the tips of whose high, outer branches drop down with such a crisp and garland-like richness, and the oak, whose stately form is just now so splendidly adorned by the sunny colouring of the young leaves.

Turning again up the hill, we find ourselves on that peculiar charm of English scenery: a green common divided by the road; the right side fringed by hedgerows and trees, with cottages and farmhouses irregularly placed, and terminated by a double avenue of noble oaks; the left, prettier still, dappled by bright pools of water, and islands of cottages and cottage-gardens, and sinking gradually down to cornfields and meadows, and an old farm-house, with pointed roofs and clustered chimneys, looking out from its blooming orchard, and backed by woody hills. The common is itself the prettiest part of the prospect; half-covered with low furze, whose golden blossoms reflect so intensely the last beams of the setting sun, and alive with cows and sheep, and two sets of cricketers: one of young men, surrounded by spectators, some standing, some sitting, some stretched on the grass, all taking a delightful interest in the game; the other, a merry group of little boys, at a humble distance, for whom even cricket is scarcely lively enough, shouting, leaping, and enjoying themselves to their hearts' content. But cricketers and country boys are too important persons in our village to be talked of merely as figures in the landscape. They deserve an individual introduction – an essay to themselves – and they shall have it. No fear of forgetting the good-humoured faces that meet us in our walks every day.

Hannah

THE prettiest cottage on our village green is the little dwelling of Dame Wilson. It stands in a corner of the common, where the hedgerows go curving off into a sort of bay, round a clear bright pond, the earliest haunt of the swallow. A deep, woody, green lane, such as Hobbema or Ruysdael might have painted; a lane that hints of nightingales, forms one boundary of the garden, and a sloping meadow the other; whilst the cottage itself, a low, thatched, irregular building, backed by a blooming orchard, and covered with honeysuckle and jessamine, looks like the chosen abode of snugness and comfort. And so it is.

Dame Wilson was a respected servant in a most respectable family, where she passed all the early part of her life, and which she quitted only on her marriage with a man of character and industry, and of that peculiar universality of genius which forms, what is called in country phrase, a handy fellow. He could do any sort of work; was thatcher, carpenter, bricklayer, painter, gardener, gamekeeper, 'everything by turns, and nothing long'. No job came amiss to him. He killed pigs, mended shoes, cleaned clocks, doctored cows, dogs and horses, and even went as far as bleeding and drawing teeth in his experiments on the human subject. In addition to these multifarious talents, he was ready, obliging, and unfearing; jovial withal, and fond of good fellowship; and endowed with a promptness of resource, which made him the general adviser of the stupid, the puzzled and the timid. He was universally admitted to be the cleverest man in the parish; and his death, which happened about ten years ago, in consequence of standing in the water, drawing a pond for one neighbour, at a time when he was overheated by loading hay for another, made quite a gap in our village commonwealth.

John Wilson had no rival, and has had no successor: for the Robert Ellis, whom certain youngsters would fain exalt to a co-partnery of fame, is simply nobody – a bellringer, a ballad-singer, a troller of profane catches, a fiddler, a bruiser, a loller on ale-house benches, a teller of good stories, a mimic, a poet! What is all this to compare with the solid parts of John Wilson? Whose clock hath Robert Ellis cleaned? Whose windows hath he mended? Whose dog hath he broken? Whose pigs hath he ringed? Whose pond hath he fished? Whose hay hath he saved? Whose cow hath he cured? Whose calf hath he killed? Whose teeth hath he drawn? Whom hath he bled? Tell me that, irreverent whipsters! No! John Wilson is not to be replaced. He was missed by the whole parish; and most of all, he was missed at home.

His excellent wife was left the sole guardian and protector of two fatherless girls: one an infant at her knee, the other a pretty handy lass about nine years old. Cast thus upon the world, there must have been much to endure, much to suffer; but it was borne with a smiling patience, a hopeful cheeriness of spirit, and a decent pride, which seemed to command success as well as respect in their struggle for independence. Without assistance of any sort, by needlework, by washing and mending lace and fine linen, and other skilful and profitable labours, and by the produce of her orchard and poultry, Dame Wilson contrived to maintain herself and her children in their old comfortable home. There was no visible change: she and the little girls were as neat as ever; the house had still within and without the same sunshiny cleanliness; and the garden was still famous over all other gardens for its cloves, and stocks and double wallflowers. But the sweetest flower of the garden, the joy and pride of her mother's heart, was her daughter Hannah. Well might she be proud of her!

At sixteen, Hannah Wilson was, beyond a doubt, the prettiest girl in the village, and the best. Her beauty was quite in a different style from the common country rosebud – far more choice and rare. Its chief characteristic was modesty. A light youthful figure, exquisitely graceful and rapid in all its movements; springy, elastic and buoyant as a bird, and almost as shy; a fair innocent face, with downcast blue eyes, and smiles and blushes coming and going almost with her thoughts; a low soft voice, sweet even in its monosyllables; a dress remarkable for neatness and propriety, and borrowing from her delicate beauty an air of superiority not its own – such was the outward woman of Hannah.

Her mind was very like her person: modest, graceful, gentle, affectionate, grateful and generous above all. The generosity of the poor is always a very real and fine thing; they give what they want; and Hannah was of all poor people the most generous. She loved to give; it was her pleasure, her luxury. Rosy-cheeked apples, plums with the bloom on them, nosegays of cloves and blossomed myrtle – these were offerings which Hannah delighted to bring to those whom she loved, or those who had shown her kindness; whilst to such of her neighbours as needed other attentions than fruit and flowers, she would give her time, her assistance, her skill; for Hannah inherited her mother's dexterity in feminine employments, with something of her father's versatile power. Besides being an excellent laundress, she was accomplished in all the arts of the needle, millinery, dressmaking and plain work; a capital cutter-out, an incomparable mender, and endowed with a gift of altering, which made old things better than new. She had no rival at *rifacimento*, as half the turned gowns on the common can witness. As a dairy woman, and a rearer of pigs and poultry, she was equally successful: none of her ducks and turkeys ever died of neglect or carelessness, or, to use the phrase of the poultry yard on such occasions, of 'ill luck'. Hannah's fowls never dreamed of sliding out of the world in such an ignoble way; they all lived to be killed, to make a noise at their deaths as chickens should do. She was also a famous 'scholar'; kept accounts, wrote bills, read letters, and answered them; was a trusty accomptant, and a safe confidante.

There was no end to Hannah's usefulness or Hannah's kindness, and her prudence was equal to either. Except to be kind or useful, she never left her home; attended no fairs, or revels, or mayings; went nowhere but to church: and seldom made a nearer approach to rustic revelry than by standing at her own garden gate on a Sunday evening, with her little sister in her hand, to look at the lads and lasses on the green. In short, our village beauty had fairly reached her twentieth year without a sweetheart, without the slightest suspicion of her having ever written a love letter on her own account; when, all on a sudden, appearances changed. She was missing at the 'accustomed gate'; and one had seen a young man go into Dame Wilson's; and another had descried a trim elastic figure walking, not unaccompanied, down the shady lane. Matters were quite clear, Hannah had gotten a lover; and, when poor little Susan, who, deserted by her sister, ventured to peep rather nearer to the gay group, was laughingly questioned on the subject, the hesitating 'No', and the half 'Yes', of the smiling child, were equally conclusive.

Since the new marriage act,[1] we who belong to country magistrates, have gained a priority over the rest of the parish in matrimonial news. We (the privileged) see on a workday the names which the sabbath announces to the generality. Many a blushing awkward pair hath our little lame clerk (a sorry Cupid!) ushered in between dark and light to stammer and hacker, to bow and curtsey, to sign or make a mark, as it pleases Heaven.

One Saturday, at the usual hour, the limping clerk made his appearance; and, walking through our little hall, I saw a fine athletic young man, the very image of health and vigour, mental and bodily, holding the hand of a young woman, who with her head half buried in a geranium in the window was turning bashfully away, listening, and yet not seeming to listen, to his tender whispers. The shrinking grace of that bending figure was not to be mistaken. 'Hannah!' She went aside with me, and a rapid series of questions and answers conveyed the story of the courtship.

'William was,' said Hannah, 'a journeyman hatter in B—. He had walked over one Sunday evening to see the cricketing, and then he came again. Her mother liked him. Everybody liked her William – and she had promised – she was going – was it wrong?'

---

[1] It is almost unnecessary to observe, that this little story was written during the short life of that whimsical experiment in legislation.

'Oh no! And where are you to live?' 'William has got a room in B—. He works for Mr Smith, the rich hatter in the market-place, and Mr Smith speaks of him – oh, so well! But William will not tell me where our room is. I suppose in some narrow street or lane, which he is afraid I shall not like, as our common is so pleasant. He little thinks – anywhere –' She stopped suddenly; but her blush and her clasped hand finished the sentence, 'anywhere with him!' 'And when is the happy day?' 'On Monday fortnight, Madam,' said the bridegroom elect, advancing with the little clerk to summon Hannah to the parlour, 'the earliest day possible.' He drew her arm through his, and we parted.

The Monday fortnight was a glorious morning; one of those rare November days, when the sky and the air are soft and bright as in April. 'What a beautiful day for Hannah!' was the first exclamation of the breakfast table. 'Did she tell you where they should dine?' 'No, Ma'am; I forgot to ask.' 'I can tell you,' said the master of the house, with somewhat of good-humoured import-ance in his air, somewhat of the look of a man, who having kept a secret as long as it was necessary, is not sorry to get rid of the burthen. 'I can tell you: in London.' 'In London?' 'Yes. Your little favourite has been in high luck. She has married the only son of one of the best and richest men in B—, Mr Smith the great hatter. It is quite a romance,' continued he. 'William Smith walked over one Sunday evening to see a match at cricket. He saw our pretty Hannah, and forgot to look at the cricketers. After having gazed his fill, he approached to address her, and the little damsel was off like a bird. William did not like her the less for that, and thought of her the more. He came again and again; and at last contrived to tame this wild dove, and even to get the *entrée* of the cottage. Hearing Hannah talk is not the way to fall out of love with her. So William, at last finding his case serious, laid the matter before his father, and requested his consent to the marriage. Mr Smith was at first a little startled: but William is an only son, and an excellent son; and, after talking with me, and looking at Hannah (I believe her sweet face was the more eloquent advocate of the two), he relented; and having a spice of his son's romance, finding that he had not mentioned his situation in life, he made a point of its being kept secret till the wedding-day. We have managed the business of settlements; and William, having discovered that his fair bride has some curiosity to see London (a curiosity, by the bye, which I suspect she owes to you or poor Lucy), intends taking her thither for a fortnight. He will then bring her home to one of the best houses in B——, a fine garden, fine furniture, fine clothes, fine servants, and more money than she will know what to do with. Really, the surprise of Lord E.'s farmer's daughter, when, thinking she had married his steward, he brought her to Burleigh, and installed her as its mistress, could hardly have been greater. I hope the shock will not kill Hannah though, as is said to have been the case with that poor lady.' 'Oh no! Hannah loves her husband too well. Anywhere with him!'

And I was right. Hannah has survived the shock. She is returned to B——, and I have been to call on her. I never saw anything so delicate and bride-like as she looked in her white gown and her lace mob, in a room light and simple, and tasteful and elegant, with nothing fine except some beautiful greenhouse plants. Her reception was a charming mixture of sweetness and modesty, a little more respectful than usual, and far more shamefaced! Poor thing! Her cheeks must have pained her! But this was the only difference. In everything else she is still the same Hannah, and has lost none of her old habits of kindness and gratitude. She was making a handsome matronly cap, evidently for her mother, and spoke, even with tears, of her new father's goodness to her and to Susan. She would fetch the cake and wine herself, and would gather, in spite of all remonstrance, some of her choicest flowers as a parting nosegay. She did, indeed, just hint at her troubles with visitors and servants – how strange and sad it was! – seemed distressed at ringing the bell, and visibly shrank from the sound of a double knock. But, in spite of these calamities, Hannah is a happy woman. The double rap was her husband's; and the glow on her cheek, and the smile of her lips and eyes when he appeared, spoke more plainly than ever, 'Anywhere with him!'

Walks in the Country
Frost

JANUARY 23rd. At noon today I and my white greyhound, Mayflower, set out for a walk into a very beautiful world, a sort of silent fairyland, a creation of that matchless magician – the hoar frost. There had been just snow enough to cover the earth and all its colours with one sheet of pure and uniform white, and just time enough since the snow had fallen to allow the hedges to be freed of their fleecy load, and clothed with a delicate coating of rime. The atmosphere is deliciously calm: soft, even mild, in spite of the thermometer; no perceptible air, but a stillness that might almost be felt; the sky, rather grey than blue, throwing out in bold relief the snow-covered roofs of our village, and the rimy trees that rise above them, and the sun shining dimly as through a veil, giving a pale fair light, like the moon, only brighter. There was a silence, too, that might become the moon, as we stood at our little gate looking up the quiet street; a sabbath-like pause of work and play, rare on a workday. Nothing was audible but the pleasant hum of frost, that low monotonous sound, which is perhaps the nearest approach that life and nature can make to absolute silence. The very waggons as they come down the hill along the beaten track of crisp yellowish frost-dust, glide along like shadows; even May's bounding footsteps, at her height of glee and of speed, fall like snow upon snow.

But we shall hear noise enough presently: May has stopped at Lizzy's door! And Lizzy, as she sat on the window-sill, with her bright rosy face laughing through the casement, has seen her and disappeared. She is coming. No! The key is turning in the door, and sounds of evil omen issue through the keyhole – sturdy 'let me outs', and 'I will goes', mixed with shrill cries on May and on me from Lizzy, piercing through a low continuous harangue, of which the prominent parts are apologies, chilblains, sliding, broken bones, lollipops, rods and gingerbread from Lizzy's careful mother. 'Don't scratch the door, May! Don't roar so, my Lizzy! We'll call for you as we come back.' – 'I'll go now! Let me out! I will go!' are the last words of Miss Lizzy. Mem. Not to spoil that child – if I can help it. But I do think her mother might have let the poor little soul walk with us today. Nothing worse for children than coddling. Nothing better for chilblains than exercise. Besides, I don't believe she has any – and as to breaking her bones in sliding, I don't suppose there's a slide on the common. These murmuring cogitations have brought us up the hill, and half-way across the light and airy common, with its bright expanse of snow and its clusters of cottages, whose turf-fires send such wreaths of smoke sailing up the air, and diffuse such aromatic fragrance around. And now comes the delightful sound of childish voices, ringing with glee and merriment almost from beneath our feet. Ah, Lizzy, your mother was right! They are shouting from that deep, irregular pool, all glass now, where, on two long, smooth, liny slides, half a dozen ragged urchins are slipping along in tottering triumph. Half a dozen steps bring us to the bank right above them. May can hardly resist the temptation of joining her friends, for most of the varlets are of her acquaintance, especially the rogue who leads the slide – he with the brimless hat, whose bronzed complexion and white flaxen hair, reversing the usual lights and shadows of the human countenance, give so strange and foreign a look to his flat and comic features. This hobgoblin, Jack Rapley by name, is May's great crony; and she stands on the brink of the steep irregular descent, her black eyes fixed full upon him, as if she intended him the favour of jumping on his head. She does; she is down, and upon him; but Jack Rapley is not easily to be knocked off his feet. He saw her coming, and in the moment of her leap sprung dexterously off the slide on the rough ice, steadying himself by the shoulder of the next in the file, which unlucky follower, thus unexpectedly checked in his career, fell plump backwards, knocking down the rest of the line like a nest of card houses. There is no harm done; but there they lie, roaring, kicking, sprawling, in every attitude of comic distress, whilst Jack Rapley and Mayflower, sole authors of this calamity, stand apart from the throng, fondling, and coquetting, and complimenting each other, and very visibly laughing, May in her black eyes, Jack in his wide close-shut mouth, and his whole monkey-face, at their comrades' mischances. I think, Miss May, you may as well come up again, and leave Master Rapley to fight your battles. He'll get out of the scrape. He is a rustic wit – a sort of Robin Goodfellow – the sauciest, idlest, cleverest, best-natured boy in the parish; always foremost in mischief, and always ready to do a good turn. The sages of our village predict sad things of Jack Rapley, so that I am sometimes a little ashamed to confess, before wise people, that I have a lurking predilection for him (in common with other naughty ones), and that I like to hear him talk to May, almost as well as she does. 'Come, May!' and up she springs, as light as a bird. The road is gay now; carts and post-chaises, and girls in red cloaks, and, afar off, looking almost like a toy, the coach. It meets us fast and soon. How much happier the walkers look than the riders, especially the frost-bitten gentleman, and the shivering lady with the invisible face, sole passengers of that commodious machine! Hooded, veiled, and bonneted as she is, one sees from her attitude how miserable she would look uncovered.

Another pond, and another noise of children. More sliding? Oh no! This is a sport of higher pretension. Our good neighbour, the lieutenant, skating, and his own pretty little boys, and two or three other four-year-old elves, standing on the brink in an ecstasy of joy and wonder. Oh what happy spectators! And what a happy performer! They admiring, he admired, with an ardour and sincerity never excited by all the quadrilles, and the spread-eagles of the Seine and the Serpentine. He really skates well though, and I am glad I came this way; for, with all the father's feelings sitting gaily at his heart, it must still gratify the pride of skill to have one spectator at that solitary pond who has seen skating before.

Now we have reached the trees – the beautiful trees! – never so beautiful as today. Imagine the effect of a straight and regular double avenue of oaks, nearly a mile long, arching overhead, and closing into perspective like the roof and columns of a cathedral, every tree and branch encrusted with the bright and delicate congelation of hoar frost, white and pure as snow, delicate and defined as carved ivory. How beautiful it is, how uniform, how various, how filling, how satiating to the eye and to the mind – above all, how melancholy! There is a thrilling awfulness, an intense feeling of simple power in that naked and colourless beauty, which falls on the earth like the thoughts of death – death pure, and glorious, and smiling – but still death. Sculpture has always the same effect on my imagination, and painting never. Colour is life.

We are now at the end of this magnificent avenue, and at the top of a steep eminence commanding a wide view over four counties – a landscape of snow. A deep lane leads abruptly down the hill; a mere narrow cart track, sinking between high banks clothed with fern, and furze, and low broom crowned with luxuriant hedgerows, and famous for their summer smell of thyme. How lovely these banks are now – the tall weeds and the gorse fixed and stiffened in the hoar frost, which fringes round the bright prickly holly, the pendent foliage of the bramble, and the deep orange leaves of the pollard oaks! Oh, this is rime in its loveliest form! And there is still a berry here and there on the holly, 'blushing in its natural coral' through the delicate tracery, still a stray hip or haw for the birds, who abound here always. The poor birds, how tame they are, how sadly tame! There is the beautiful and rare crested wren, 'that shadow of a bird', as White of Selborne calls it, perched in the middle of the hedge, nestling as it were amongst the cold bare boughs, seeking, poor pretty thing, for the warmth it will not find. And there, farther on just under the bank, by the slender runlet, which still trickles between its transparent fantastic margin of thin ice, as if it were a thing of life; there, with a swift, scudding motion, flits, in short low flight, the gorgeous kingfisher, its magnificent plumage of scarlet and blue flashing in the sun, like the glories of some tropical bird. He is come for water to this little spring by the hillside – water which even his long bill and slender head can hardly reach, so nearly do the fantastic forms of those garland-like icy margins meet over the tiny stream beneath. It is rarely that one sees the shy beauty so close or so long: and it is pleasant to see him in the grace and beauty of his natural liberty, the only way to look at a bird.

We used, before we lived in a street, to fix a little board outside the parlour window, and cover it with breadcrumbs in the hard weather. It was quite delightful to see the pretty things come and feed, to conquer their shyness, and do away their mistrust. First came the more social tribes: 'the robin redbreast and the wren', cautiously, suspiciously, picking up a crumb on the wing, with the little keen bright eye fixed on the window; then they would stop for two pecks; then stay till they were satisfied. The shyer birds, tamed by their example, came next; and at last one saucy fellow of a blackbird – a sad glutton, he would clear the board in two minutes – used to tap his yellow bill against the window for more. How we loved the fearless confidence of that fine frank-hearted creature! And surely he loved us. I wonder the practice is not more general.

'May! May! Naughty May!' She has frightened away the kingfisher; and now, in her coaxing penitence, she is covering me with snow. 'Come, pretty May! It is time to go home.'

Thaw

JANUARY 28th. We have had rain, and snow, and frost, and rain again; four days of absolute confinement. Now it is a thaw and a flood; but our light, gravelly soil, and country boots, and country hardihood, will carry us through. What a dripping comfortless day it is! Just like the last days of November: no sun, no sky, grey or blue; one low, overhanging, dark, dismal cloud, like London smoke. Mayflower is out coursing, too, and Lizzy gone to school. Never mind. Up the hill again! Walk we must. Oh, what a watery world to look back upon! Thames, Kennet, Loddon – all overflowed; our famous town, inland once, turned into a sort of Venice; C— Park converted into an island; and the long range of meadows, from B— to W—, one huge unnatural lake, with trees growing out of it. Oh, what a watery world! I will look at it no longer. I will walk on. The road is alive again. Noise is re-born. Waggons creak, horses splash, carts rattle, and pattens paddle through the dirt with more than their usual clink. The common has its old fine tints of green and brown, and its old variety of inhabitants: horses, cows, sheep, pigs and donkeys. The ponds are unfrozen, except where some melancholy piece of melting ice floats sullenly on the water; and cackling geese and gabbling ducks have replaced the lieutenant and Jack Rapley. The avenue is chill and dark, the hedges are dripping, the lanes knee-deep, and all nature is in a state of 'dissolution and thaw'.

A Great Farmhouse

THESE are bad times for farmers. I am sorry for it. Independently of all questions of policy, as a mere matter of taste and of old association, it was a fine thing to witness the hearty hospitality, and to think of the social happiness of a great farmhouse. No situation in life seemed so richly privileged; none had so much power for good and so little for evil; it seemed a place where pride could not live, and poverty could not enter. These thoughts pressed on my mind the other day, on passing the green sheltered lane, overhung with trees like an avenue, that leads to the great farm at M—, where, ten or twelve years ago, I used to spend so many pleasant days. I could not help advancing a few paces up the lane, and then turning to lean over the gate, seemingly gazing on the rich undulating valley, crowned with woody hills, which, as I stood under the dark and shady arch, lay bathed in the sunshine before me, but really absorbed in thoughts of other times, in recollections of the old delights of that delightful place, and of the admirable qualities of its owners. How often I had opened the gate, and how gaily, certain of meeting a smiling welcome, and what a picture of comfort it was!

Passing up the lane, we used first to encounter a thick solid suburb of ricks, of all sorts, shapes and dimensions. Then came the farm, like a town: a magnificent series of buildings, stables, cart houses, cow houses, granaries and barns, that might hold half the corn of the parish, placed at all angles towards each other, and mixed with smaller habitations for pigs, dogs and poultry. They formed, together with the old substantial farmhouse, a sort of amphitheatre, looking over a beautiful meadow, which swept greenly and abruptly down into fertile enclosures, richly set with hedgerow timber, oak, and ash, and elm. Both the meadow and the farmyard swarmed with inhabitants of the earth and of the air: horses, oxen, cows, calves, heifers, sheep and pigs; beautiful greyhounds, all manner of poultry, a tame goat and a pet donkey.

The master of this land of plenty was well-fitted to preside over it: a thick, stout man, of middle height, and middle-aged, with a healthy, ruddy, square face, all alive with intelligence and good humour. There was a lurking jest in his eye, and a smile about the corners of his firmly closed lips that gave assurance of good fellowship. His voice was loud enough to have hailed a ship at sea without the assistance of a speaking-trumpet, wonderfully rich and round in its tones, and harmonizing admirably with his bluff, jovial visage. He wore his dark shining hair combed straight over his forehead, and had a trick, when particularly merry, of stroking it down with his hand. The moment his hand approached his head, out flew a jest.

Besides his own great farm, the business of which seemed to go on like machinery, always regular, prosperous and unfailing, besides this and two or three constant stewardships, and a perpetual succession of arbitrations, in which, such was the influence of his acuteness, his temper, and his sturdy justice, that he was often named by both parties, and left to decide alone, in addition to these occupations, he was a sort of standing overseer and churchwarden. He ruled his own hamlet like a despotic monarch, and took a prime minister's share in the government of the large parish to which it was attached; and one of the gentlemen whose estates he managed, being the independent member for an independent borough, he had every now and then a contested election on his shoulders. Even that did not discompose him. He had always leisure to receive his friends at home, or to visit them abroad; to take journeys to London, or make excursions to the seaside; was as punctual in pleasure as in business, and thought being happy and making happy as much the purpose of his life as getting rich.

His great amusement was coursing. He kept several brace of capital greyhounds, so high-blooded that I remember when five of them were confined in five different kennels on account of their ferocity. The greatest of living painters once called a greyhound, 'the line of beauty in perpetual motion'. Our friend's large dogs were a fine illustration of this remark. His old dog, Hector, for instance, for whom he refused a hundred guineas – what a superb dog was Hector! – a model of grace and symmetry, necked and crested like an Arabian, and bearing himself with a stateliness and gallantry which showed some 'conscience of his worth'. He was the largest dog I ever saw, but so finely proportioned that the most determined fault-finder could call him neither too long nor too heavy. There was not an inch too much of him. His colour was the purest white, entirely unspotted, except that his head was very regularly and richly marked with black. Hector was certainly a perfect beauty. But the little bitches, on which his master piqued himself still more, were not in my poor judgment so admirable. They were pretty, little, round, graceful things, sleek and glossy, and for the most part milk-white, with the smallest heads, and the most dove-like eyes that were ever seen. There was a peculiar sort of innocent beauty about them, like that of a roly-poly child. They were as gentle as lambs, too; all the evil spirit of the family evaporated in the gentlemen. But, to my thinking, these pretty creatures were fitter for the parlour than the field. They were strong, certainly, excellently loined, cat-footed, and chested like a war horse; but there was a want of length about them – a want of room, as the coursers say; something a little, a very little inclining to the clumsy; a dumpiness, a pointer look. They went off like an arrow from a bow; for the first hundred yards nothing could stand against them; then they began to flag, to find their weight too much for their speed, and to lose ground from the shortness of the stroke. Up-hill, however, they were capital. There their compactness told. They turned with the hare and lost neither wind nor way in the sharpest ascent.

I shall never forget one single-handed course of our good friend's favourite little bitch Helen, on W— hill. All the coursers were in the valley below, looking up to the hillside as on a moving picture. I suppose she turned the hare twenty times on a piece of greensward not much bigger than an acre, and as steep as the roof of a house. It was an old hare, a famous hare, one that had baffled half the dogs in the country; but she killed him; and then, though almost as large as herself, took it up in her mouth, brought it to her master, and laid it down at his feet. Oh how pleased he was! And what a pleasure it was to see his triumph! He did not always find W— hill so fortunate. It is a high, steep hill, of a conical shape, encircled by a mountain road winding up to the summit like a corkscrew – a deep road dug out of the chalk, and fenced by high mounds on either side. The hares always make for this hollow way, as it is called, because it is too wide for a leap, and the dogs lose much time in mounting and descending the sharp acclivities. Very eager dogs, however, will sometimes dare the leap, and two of our good friend's favourite greyhounds perished in the attempt in two following years. They were found dead in the hollow way. After this he took a dislike to distant coursing meetings, and sported chiefly on his own beautiful farm.

His wife was like her husband, with a difference, as they say in heraldry. Like him in looks, only thinner and paler; like him in voice and phrase, only not so loud; like him in merriment and good humour; like him in her talent of welcoming and making happy, and being kind; like him in cherishing an abundance of pets, and in getting through with marvellous facility an astounding quantity of business and pleasure. Perhaps the quality in which they resembled each other most completely was the happy ease and serenity of behaviour, so seldom found amongst people of the middle rank, who have usually a best manner and a worst, and whose best (that is, the studied, the company manner) is so very much the worst. She was frankness itself; entirely free from prickly defiance, or bristling self-love. She never took offence or gave it; never thought of herself or of what others would think of her; had never been afflicted with the besetting sins of her station, a dread of the vulgar, or an aspiration after the genteel. Those 'words of fear' had never disturbed her delightful heartiness.

Her pets were her cows, her poultry, her bees and her flowers; chiefly her poultry, almost as numerous as the bees, and as various as the flowers. The farmyard swarmed with peacocks, turkeys, geese, tame and wild ducks, fowls, guinea-hens, and pigeons; besides a brood or two of favourite bantams in the green court before the door, with a little ridiculous strutter of a cock at their head, who imitated the magnificent demeanour of the great Tom of the barnyard, just as Tom in his turn copied the fierce bearing of that warlike and terrible biped, the he-turkey. I am the most in the world afraid of a turkey-cock, and used to steer clear of the turkey as often as I could. Commend me to the peaceable vanity of that jewel of a bird, the peacock, sweeping his gorgeous tail along the grass, or dropping it gracefully from some low-boughed tree, whilst he turns round his crested head with the air of a birth-day belle, to see who admires him. What a glorious creature it is! How thoroughly content with himself and with all the world!

Next to her poultry our good farmer's wife loved her flower-garden; and indeed it was of the very first water, the only thing about the place that was fine. She was a real, genuine florist: valued pinks, tulips, and auriculas, for certain qualities of shape and colour, with which beauty has nothing to do; preferred black ranunculuses, and gave into all those obliquities of a triple refined taste by which the professed florist contrives to keep pace with the vagaries of the bibliomaniac. Of all odd fashions, that of dark, gloomy, dingy flowers appears to me the oddest. Your true *connoisseurs* now shall prefer a deep puce hollyhock, to the gay pink blossoms which cluster round that splendid plant like a pyramid of roses. So did she. The nomenclature of her garden was more distressing still. One is never thoroughly sociable with flowers till they are naturalized as it were, christened, provided with decent, homely, well-wearing English names. Now her plants had all sorts of heathenish appellations, which, no offence to her learning, always sounded wrong.

I liked the bees' garden best – the plot of ground immediately round their hives, filled with common flowers for their use, and literally 'redolent of sweets'. Bees are insects of great taste in every way, and seem often to select for beauty as much as for flavour. They have a better eye for colour than the florist. The butterfly is also a *dilettante*. Rover though he be, he generally prefers the blossoms that become him best. What a pretty picture it is, on a sunshiny autumn day, to see a bright spotted butterfly, made up of gold and purple and splendid brown, swinging on the rich flower of the china aster!

To come back to our farm. Within doors everything went as well as without. There were no fine misses sitting before the piano, and mixing the alloy of their new-fangled tinsel with the old sterling metal; nothing but an only son excellently brought up; a fair slim youth, whose extraordinary and somewhat pensive elegance of mind and manner was thrown into fine relief by his father's loud hilarity, and harmonized delightfully with the smiling kindness of his mother. His Spensers and Thomsons, too, looked well amongst the hyacinths and geraniums that filled the windows of the little snug room in which they usually sat; a sort of afterthought, built at an angle from the house, and looking into the farmyard. It was closely packed with favourite armchairs, favourite sofas, favourite tables, and a sideboard decorated with the prize cups and collars of the greyhounds, and generally loaded with substantial work-baskets, jars of flowers, great pyramids of home-made cakes, and sparkling bottles of gooseberry wine, famous all over the country. The walls were covered with portraits of half a dozen greyhounds, a brace of spaniels, as large as life, an old pony, and the master and mistress of the house in half-length. She as unlike as possible, prim, mincing, delicate, in lace and satin; he so staringly and ridiculously like that when the picture fixed its good-humoured eyes upon you as you entered the room, you were almost tempted to say, 'How d'ye do?' Alas! The portraits are now gone, and the originals. Death and distance have despoiled that pleasant home. The garden has lost its smiling mistress; the greyhounds their kind master; and new people, new manners, and new cares, have taken possession of the old abode of peace and plenty – the great farmhouse.

Lucy

ABOUT a twelvemonth ago, we had the misfortune to lose a very faithful and favourite female servant; one who has spoiled us for all others. Nobody can expect to meet with two Lucys. We all loved Lucy – poor Lucy! She did not die, she only married; but we were so sorry to part with her that her wedding, which was kept at our house, was almost as tragical as a funeral, and from pure regret and affection we sum up her merits, and bemoan our loss, just as if she had really departed this life.

Lucy's praise is a most fertile theme; she united the pleasant and amusing qualities of a French soubrette, with the solid excellence of an Englishwoman of the old school, and was good by contraries. In the first place, she was exceedingly agreeable to look at; remarkably pretty. She lived in our family eleven years; but, having come to us very young, was still under thirty, just in full bloom, and a very brilliant bloom it was. Her figure was rather tall and rather large, with delicate hands and feet, and a remarkable ease and vigour in her motions. I never saw any woman walk so fast or so well. Her face was round and dimpled, with sparkling grey eyes, black eyebrows and eyelashes, a profusion of dark hair, very red lips, very white teeth, and a complexion that entirely took away the look of vulgarity which the breadth and flatness of her face might otherwise have given. Such a complexion, so pure, so finely grained, so healthily fair, with such a sweet rosiness, brightening and varying like her dancing eyes whenever she spoke or smiled! When silent, she was almost pale; but, to confess the truth, she was not often silent. Lucy liked talking, and everybody liked to hear her talk. There is always great freshness and originality in an uneducated and quick-witted person, who surprises one continually by unsuspected knowledge or amusing ignorance; and Lucy had a real talent for conversation. Her light and pleasant temper, her cleverness, her universal kindness, and the admirable address, or, rather, the excellent feeling, with which she contrived to unite the most perfect respect with the most cordial and affectionate interest, gave a singular charm to her prattle. No confidence or indulgence, and she was well-tried with both, ever made her forget herself for a moment. All our friends used to loiter at the door or in the hall to speak to Lucy, and they miss her, and ask for her, as if she were really one of the family. She was not less liked by her equals. Her constant simplicity and right-mindedness kept her always in her place with them as with us; and her gaiety and good humour made her a most welcome visitor in every shop and cottage around.

She had another qualification for village society – she was an incomparable gossip, had a rare genius for picking up news, and great liberality in its diffusion. Births, deaths, marriages, casualties, quarrels, battles, scandal – nothing came amiss to her. She could have furnished a weekly paper from her own stores of facts without once resorting for assistance to the courts of law or the two houses of parliament. She was a very charitable reporter, too; threw her own sunshine into the shady places, and would hope and doubt as long as either was possible. Her fertility of intelligence was wonderful; and so early! Her news had always the bloom on it; there was no being beforehand with Lucy. It was a little mortifying when one came prepared with something very recent and surprising, something that should have made her start with astonishment, to find her fully acquainted with the story, and able to furnish you with twenty particulars that you had never heard of. But this evil had its peculiar compensation. By Lucy's aid I passed with everybody, but Lucy herself, for a woman of great information, an excellent authority, an undoubted reference in all matters of gossip. Now I lag miserably behind the time; I never hear of a death till after the funeral, nor of a wedding till I read it in the papers; and, when people talk of reports and rumours, they undo me. I should be obliged to run away from the tea-tables, if I had not taken the resolution to look wise and say nothing, and live on my old reputation. Indeed, even now, Lucy's fund is not entirely exhausted; things have not quite done happening. I know nothing new; but my knowledge of bygone passages is absolute; I can prophesy past events like a gipsy.

Scattered amongst her great merits, Lucy had a few small faults, as all persons should have. She had occasionally an aptness to take an offence where none was intended, and then the whole house bore audible testimony to her displeasure: she used to scour through half a dozen doors in a minute, for the mere purpose of banging them after her. She had rather more fears than were quite convenient of ghosts and witches, and thunder, and earwigs, and various other real and unreal sights and sounds, and thought nothing of rousing half the family, in the middle of the night, at the first symptom of a thunderstorm, or an apparition. She had a terrible genius for music, and a tremendous powerful shrill high voice. Oh! her door-clapping was nothing to her singing! It rang through one's head like the screams of a peacock. Lastly, she was a sad flirt; she had about twenty lovers whilst she lived with us, probably more, but upwards of twenty she acknowledged. Her master, who watched with great amusement this uninterrupted and intricate succession of favourites, had the habit of calling her by the name of the reigning beau – Mrs Charles, Mrs John, Mrs Robert – so that she has answered in her time to as many masculine appellations as would serve to supply a large family with a 'commodity of good names'. Once he departed from this custom, and called her 'Jenny Denison'. On her inquiring the reason, he showed her 'Old Mortality', and asked if she could not guess. 'Dear me,' said she, 'why Jenny Denison had only two!' Amongst Lucy's twenty were three one-eyed lovers, like the three one-eyed calendars in the *Arabian Nights*. They were much about the same period, nearly contemporaries, and one of them had nearly carried off the fair Helen. If he had had two eyes, his success would have been certain. She said yes and no, and yes again; he was a very nice young man. But that one eye – that unlucky one eye – and the being rallied on her three calendars. There was no getting over that one eye. She said no, once more, and stood firm.

And yet the pendulum might have continued to vibrate many

times longer, had it not been fixed by the athletic charms of a gigantic London tailor, a superb man, really; black-haired, black-eyed, six feet high, and large in proportion. He came to improve the country fashions, and fixed his shop-board in a cottage so near us that his garden was only divided from our lawn by a plantation full of acacias and honeysuckles, where 'the air smelt wooingly'. It followed, of course, that he should make love to Lucy, and that Lucy should listen. All was speedily settled; as soon as he should be established in a good business, which, from his incomparable talent at cutting out, nobody could doubt, they were to be married. But they had not calculated on the perversity of country taste. He was too good a workman; his suits fitted over well; his employers missed certain accustomed awkwardnesses and redundancies which passed for beauties. Besides, the stiffness and tightness which distinguished the new coat of the *ancien régime* were wanting in the make of this daring innovator. The shears of our Bond Street cutter were as powerful as the wooden sword of Harlequin; he turned his clowns into gentlemen, and their brother clodhoppers laughed at them, and they were ashamed. So the poor tailor lost his customers and his credit; and, just as he had obtained Lucy's consent to the marriage, he walked off one fair morning, and was never heard of more. Lucy's absorbing feeling on this catastrophe was astonishment, pure unmixed astonishment! One would have thought that she considered fickleness as a female privilege, and had never heard of a man deserting a woman in her life. For three days she could only wonder; then came great indignation, and a little, a very little grief, which showed itself not so much in her words, which were chiefly such disclaimers as 'I don't care!' 'Very lucky!' 'Happy escape!' and so on, as in her goings and doings, her aversion to the poor acacia grove, and even to the sight and smell of honeysuckles, her total loss of memory and, above all, in the distaste she showed to new conquests. She paid her faithless suitor the compliment of remaining loverless for three weary months; and even when she relented a little, she admitted no fresh adorer, nothing but an old hanger-on; one not quite discarded during the tailor's reign; one who had dangled after her during the long courtship of the three calendars; one who was the handiest and most complaisant of wooers, always ready to fill up any interval, like a book, which can be laid aside when company comes in, and resumed a month afterwards at the very page and line where the reader left off. I think it was an affair of amusement and convenience on both sides, Lucy never intended to marry this commodious stopper of love-gaps; and he, though he courted her for ten mortal years, never made a direct offer, till after the banns were published between her and her present husband: then, indeed, he said he was sorry – he had hoped – was it too late? And so forth. Ah! his sorrow was nothing to ours, and, when it came to the point, nothing to Lucy's. She cried every day for a fortnight, and had not her successor in office, the new housemaid, arrived, I do really believe that this lover would have shared the fate of the many successors to the unfortunate tailor.

I hope that her choice has been fortunate: it is certainly very different from what we all expected. The happy man had been a neighbour (not on the side of the acacia trees), and on his removal to a greater distance the marriage took place. Poor dear Lucy! Her spouse is the greatest possible contrast to herself: ten years younger at the very least; well-looking but with no expression good or bad, I don't think he could smile if he would, assuredly he never tries; well-made, but as stiff as a poker; I dare say he never ran three yards in his life; perfectly steady, sober, honest and industrious; but so young, so grave, so dull! One of your 'demure boys', as Falstaff calls them, 'that never come to proof'. You might guess a mile off that he was a schoolmaster from the swelling pomposity of gait, the solemn decorum of manner, the affectation of age and wisdom, which contrast so oddly with his young, unmeaning face. The moment he speaks you are certain. Nobody but a village pedagogue ever did or ever could talk like Mr Brown, ever displayed such elaborate politeness, such a study of phrases, such choice words and long words, and fine words and hard words! He speaks by the book, the spelling-book, and is civil after the fashion of the Polite Letter-writer. He is so entirely without tact that he does not in the least understand the impression produced by his wife's delightful manners, and interrupts her perpetually to speechify and apologize, and explain and amend.

He is fond of her, nevertheless, in his own cold, slow way, and proud of her, and grateful to her friends, and a very good kind of young man altogether; only that I cannot quite forgive him for taking Lucy away in the first place, and making her a schoolmistress in the second. She a schoolmistress, a keeper of silence, a maintainer of discipline, a scolder, a punisher! Ah! She would rather be scolded herself; it would be a far lighter punishment. Lucy likes her vocation as little as I do. She has not the natural love of children which would reconcile her to the evils they cause; and she has a real passion for cleanliness, a fiery spirit of dispatch, which cannot endure the dust and litter created by the little troop on the one hand, or their tormenting slowness and stupidity on the other. She was the quickest and neatest of workwomen, piqued herself on completing a shirt or a gown sooner and better than seemed possible, and was scandalized at finding such talents degraded to the ignoble occupations of tacking a quarter of a yard of hemming for one, pinning half a seam for another, picking out the crooked stitching of a third, and working over the weak irregular burst-out buttonhole of a fourth.

When she first went to S— she was strongly tempted to do all the work herself. 'The children would have liked it,' said she, 'and really I don't think the mothers would have objected; they care for nothing but marking. There are seven girls now in the school working samplers to be framed. Such a waste of silk, and time, and trouble! I said to Mrs Smith, and Mrs Smith said to me.' Then she recounted the whole battle of the samplers, and her defeat; and then she sent for one which, in spite of her declaration that her girls never finished anything, was quite completed (probably with a good deal of her assistance) and of which, notwithstanding her rational objection to its uselessness, Lucy was not a little proud. She held it up with great delight, pointed out all the beauties, selected her own favourite parts, especially a certain square rosebud, and the landscape at the bottom, and finally pinned it against the wall, to show the effect that it would have when framed. Really, that sampler was a superb thing in its way. First came a plain pink border; then a green border, zig-zag; then a crimson, wavy; then a brown, of a different and more complicated zig-zag; then the alphabet, great and small, in every colour of the rainbow, followed by a row of figures flanked on one side by a flower, name unknown, tulip, poppy, lily, something orange or scarlet, or orange-scarlet; on the other by the famous rosebud; then divers sentences, religious and moral. Lucy was quite provoked with me for not being able to read them; I dare say she thought in her heart that I was as stupid as any of her scholars! But never was MS so illegible, not even my own, as the print-work of that sampler – then, last and finest, the landscape, in all its glory. It occupied the whole narrow line at the bottom, and was composed with great regularity. In the centre was a house of a bright scarlet, with yellow windows, a green door and a blue roof; on one side, a man with a dog; on the other, a woman with a cat – this is Lucy's information; I should never have guessed that there was any difference, except in colour, between the man and the woman, the dog and the cat; they were in form, height, and size, alike to a thread; the man grey, the woman pink, his attendant white, and hers black. Next to these figures, on either side, rose two fir-trees from two red flowerpots, nice little round bushes of a bright green intermixed with brown stitches, which Lucy explained, not to me: 'Don't you see the fir-cones, Sir? Don't you remember how fond she used to be of picking them up in her little basket at the dear old place? Poor thing, I thought of her all the time that I was working them! Don't you like the fir-cones?' After this, I looked at the landscape almost as loving as Lucy herself.

With all her dislike to keeping school, the dear Lucy seems happy. In addition to the merciful spirit of conformity, which shapes the mind to the situation, whatever that may be, she has many sources of vanity and comfort – her house above all. It is a very respectable dwelling, finely placed on the edge of a large common, close to a highroad, with a pretty flower-court before it, shaded by four horse chestnuts cut into arches, a sashed window on either side of the door, and on the door a brass knocker, which, being securely nailed down, serves as a quiet peaceable handle for all goers, instead of the importunate and noisy use for which it was designed. Jutting out at one end of the court is a small stable; retiring back at the other, a large schoolroom, and behind, a yard for children, pigs, and poultry, a garden and an arbour. The inside is full of comfort; miraculously clean and orderly for a village school, and with a little touch of very allowable finery, in the gay window-curtains, the cupboard full of pretty china, the handsome chairs, the bright mahogany table, the shining tea-urn and brilliant tea-tray that decorate the parlour. What a pleasure it is to see Lucy presiding in that parlour, in all the glory of her honest affection and warm hospitality, making tea for the three guests whom she loves best in the world, vaunting with courteous pride her home-made bread and her fresh butter, yet thinking nothing good enough for the occasion; smiling and glowing, and looking the very image of beautiful happiness. Such a moment almost consoles us for losing her.

Lucy's pleasure is in her house; mine is in its situation. The common on which it stands is one of a series of heathy hills, or rather a high tableland, pierced in one part by a ravine of marshy ground filled with alder bushes, growing larger and larger as the valley widens, and at last mixing with the fine old oaks of the forest of P—. Nothing can be more delightful than to sit on the steep brow of the hill, amongst the fragrant heath flowers, the bluebells, and the wild thyme, and look upon the sea of trees spreading out beneath us; the sluggish water just peeping from amid the alders, giving brightly back the bright blue sky; and, farther down, herds of rough ponies, and of small stunted cows, the wealth of the poor, coming up from the forest. I have sometimes seen two hundred of these cows together, each belonging to a different person, and distinguishing and obeying the call of its milker.

All the boundaries of this heath are beautiful. On one side is the hanging coppice, where the lily of the valley grows so plentifully amongst broken ridges and fox earths, and the roots of pollard trees. On another are the immense fir plantations of Mr B—, whose balmy odour hangs heavily in the air, or comes sailing on the breeze like smoke across the landscape. Farther on, beyond the pretty parsonage house, with its short avenue, its fishponds, and the magnificent poplars, which form a landmark for many miles round, rise the rocklike walls of the old city of S—, one of the most perfect Roman remains now existing in England. The wall can be traced all round, rising sometimes to a height of twenty feet, over a deep narrow slip of meadowland, once the ditch, and still full of aquatic flowers. The ground within rises level with the top of the wall, which is of grey stone, crowned with the finest forest trees, whose roots seem interlaced with the old masonry, and covered with wreaths of ivy, brambles, and a hundred other trailing plants. Close by one of the openings, which mark the site of the gates, is a graduated terrace, called by antiquaries the Amphitheatre, which commands a rich and extensive view, and is backed by the village church, and an old farmhouse – the sole buildings in that once populous city, whose streets are now traced only by the blighted and withered appearance of the ripening corn. Roman coins and urns are often ploughed up there, and it is a favourite haunt of the lovers of 'hoar antiquity'. But the beauty of the place is independent even of its noble associations. The very heart expands in the deep verdure and perfect loneliness of that narrow winding valley, fenced on one side by steep coppices or its own tall irregular hedge, on the other by the venerable craglike wall, whose proud coronet of trees, its jutting ivy, its huge twisted thorns, its briery festoons, and the deep caves where the rabbits burrow make the old bulwark seem no work of man, but a majestic piece of nature. As a picture it is exquisite. Nothing can be finer than the mixture of those varied greens, so crisp and lifelike, with the crumbling grey stone; nothing more perfectly in harmony with the solemn beauty of the place than the deep cooings of the wood-pigeons, who abound in the walls. I know no pleasure so intense, so soothing, so apt to bring sweet tears into the eyes, or to awaken thoughts that 'lie too deep for tears', as a walk round the old city on a fine summer evening. A ride to S— was always delightful to me, even before it became the residence of Lucy; it is now my prime festival.

Walks in the Country
The First Primrose

MARCH 6th. Fine March weather: boisterous, blustering, much wind and squalls of rain; and yet the sky, where the clouds are swept away, deliciously blue, with snatches of sunshine, bright, and clear, and healthful, and the roads, in spite of the slight glittering showers, crisply dry. Altogether the day is tempting, very tempting. It will not do for the dear common, that windmill of a walk; but the close sheltered lanes at the bottom of the hill, which keep out just enough of the stormy air and let in all the sun, will be delightful. Past our old house, and round by the winding lanes, and the workhouse, and across the Lea, and so into the turnpike road again – that is our route for today. Forth we set,

Mayflower and I, rejoicing in the sunshine, and still more in the wind, which gives such an intense feeling of existence, and, cooperating with brisk motion, sets our blood and our spirits in a glow. For mere physical pleasure, there is nothing perhaps equal to the enjoyment of being drawn, in a light carriage, against such a wind as this, by a blood-horse at his height of speed. Walking comes next to it; but walking is not quite so luxurious nor so spiritual, not quite so much what one fancies of flying or being carried above the clouds in a balloon.

Nevertheless, a walk is a good thing, especially under this southern hedgerow, where nature is just beginning to live again: the periwinkles, with their starry blue flowers, and their shining myrtle-like leaves, garlanding the bushes; woodbines and elder trees pushing out their small swelling buds; and grasses and mosses springing forth in every variety of brown and green. Here we are at the corner where four lanes meet, or rather where a passable road of stones and gravel crosses an impassable one of beautiful but treacherous turf, and where the small white farm-house, scarcely larger than a cottage, and the well-stocked rick-yard behind, tell of comfort and order, but leave all unguessed the great riches of the master. How he became so rich is almost a puzzle; for, though the farm be his own, it is not large; and though prudent and frugal on ordinary occasions, farmer Barnard is no miser. His horses, dogs and pigs are the best kept in the parish. May herself, although her beauty be injured by her fatness, half envies the plight of his bitch Fly; his wife's gowns and shawls cost as much again as any shawls or gowns in the village; his dinner parties (to be sure they are not frequent) display twice the ordinary quantity of good things – two couples of ducks, two dishes of green peas, two turkey poults, two gammons of bacon, two plum puddings; moreover, he keeps a single-horse chaise, and has built and endowed a Methodist chapel. Yes, he is the richest man in these parts. Everything prospers with him. Money drifts about him like snow. He looks like a rich man. There is a sturdy squareness of face and figure; a good-humoured obstinacy; a civil importance. He never boasts of his wealth, or gives himself undue airs; but nobody can meet him at market or vestry without finding out immediately that he is the richest man there. They have no child to all this money; but there is an adopted nephew, a fine, spirited lad, who may, perhaps, some day or other, play the part of a fountain to the reservoir.

Now turn up the wide road till we come to the open common, with its park-like trees, its beautiful stream, wandering and twisting along, and its rural bridge. Here we turn again, past that other white farmhouse, half hidden by the magnificent elms which stand before it. Ah! riches dwell not there; but there is found the next best thing – an industrious and light-hearted poverty.

Twenty years ago, Rachel Hilton was the prettiest and merriest lass in the country. Her father, an old gamekeeper, had retired to a village ale-house, where his good beer, his social humour, and his black-eyed daughter, brought much custom. She had lovers by the score; but Joseph White, the dashing and lively son of an opulent farmer, carried off the fair Rachel. They married and settled here, and here they live still, as merrily as ever, with fourteen children of all ages and sizes, from nineteen years to nineteen months, working harder than any people in the parish, and enjoying themselves more. I would match them for labour and laughter against any family in England. She is a blithe jolly dame, whose beauty has amplified into comeliness: he is tall, and thin, and bony, with sinews like whipcord, a strong lively voice, a sharp weather-beaten face, and eyes and lips that smile and brighten when he speaks into a most contagious hilarity. They are very poor, and I often wish them richer; but I don't know – perhaps it might put them out.

Quite close to farmer White's is a little ruinous cottage, whitewashed once, and now in a sad state of betweenity, where dangling stockings and shirts, swelled by the wind, drying in a neglected garden, give signal of a washerwoman. There dwells, at present in single blessedness, Betty Adams, the wife of our sometimes gardener. I never saw anyone who so much reminded me in person of that lady whom everybody knows, Mistress Meg Merrilies: as tall, as grizzled, as stately, as dark, as gipsy-looking, bonneted and gowned like her prototype, and almost as oracular. Here the resemblance ceases. Mrs Adams is a perfectly honest,

industrious, painstaking person, who earns a good deal of money by washing and charring, and spends it in other luxuries than tidiness – in green tea, and gin and snuff. Her husband lives in a great family, ten miles off. He is a capital gardener, or rather he would be so, if he were not too ambitious. He undertakes all things, and finishes none. But a smooth tongue, a knowing look and a great capacity of labour carry him through. Let him but like his ale and his master, and he will do work enough for four. Give him his own way, and his full quantum, and nothing comes amiss to him.

Ah, May is bounding forward! Her silly heart leaps at the sight of the old place – and so, in good truth, does mine. What a pretty place it was, or rather, how pretty I thought it! I suppose I should have thought any place so where I had spent eighteen happy years. But it was really pretty. A large, heavy, white house, in the simplest style, surrounded by fine oaks and elms, and tall massy

43

plantations shading down into a beautiful lawn, by wild over-grown shrubs, bowery acacias, ragged sweet-briers, promontories of dogwood, and Portugal laurel, and bays overhung by laburnum and bird-cherry; a long piece of water letting light into the picture, and looking just like a natural stream, the banks as rude and wild as the shrubbery, interspersed with broom, and furze, and bramble, and pollard oaks covered with ivy and honeysuckle; the whole enclosed by an old mossy park paling, and terminating in a series of rich meadows, richly planted. This is an exact description of the home which, three years ago, it nearly broke my heart to leave. What a tearing up by the root it was. I have pitied cabbage-plants and celery, and all transplantable things ever since; though, in common with them, and with other vegetables, the first agony of the transportation being over, I have taken such firm and tenacious hold of my new soil, that I would not for the world be pulled up again, even to be restored to the old beloved ground – not even if its beauty were undiminished, which is by no means the case. For in those three years it has thrice changed masters, and every successive possessor has brought the curse of improvement upon the place; so that between filling up the water to cure dampness, cutting down trees to let in prospects, planting to keep them out, shutting up windows to darken the inside of the house (by which means one end looks precisely as an eight of spades would do that should have the misfortune to lose one of his corner pips) and building colonnades to lighten the out, added to a general clearance of pollards, and brambles, and ivy, and honey-suckles, and park palings, and irregular shrubs, the poor place is so transmogrified that, if it had its old looking-glass, the water, back again, it would not know its own face. And yet I love to haunt round about it: so does May. Her particular attraction is a certain broken bank, full of rabbit burrows, into which she insinuates her long pliant head and neck, and tears her pretty feet by vain scratchings; mine is a warm, sunny hedgerow, in the same remote field, famous for early flowers. Never was a spot more variously flowery: primroses yellow, lilac white, violets of either hue, cowslips, oxlips, arums, orchises, wild hyacinths, ground-ivy, pansies, strawberries, heart's-ease formed a small part of the flora of that wild hedgerow. How profusely they covered the sunny open slope under the weeping birch, 'the lady of the woods', and how often have I started to see the early innocent brown snake, who loved the spot as well as I did, winding along the young blossoms, or rustling amongst the fallen leaves. There are primrose leaves already, and short green buds, but no flowers; not even in that furze cradle so full of roots, where they used to blow as in a basket. No, my May, no rabbits, no primroses! We may as well get over the gate into the woody winding lane, which will bring us home again.

Here we are, making the best of our way between the old elms that arch so solemnly overhead, dark and sheltered even now. They say that a spirit haunts this deep pool – a white lady without a head. I cannot say that I have seen her, often as I have paced this lane at deep midnight to hear the nightingales, and look at the glow-worms. But there, better and rarer than a thousand ghosts, dearer even than nightingales or glow-worms, there is a primrose, the first of the year – a tuft of primroses, springing in yonder

sheltered nook from the mossy roots of an old willow, and living again in the clear bright pool. Oh, how beautiful they are – three fully blown, and two bursting buds! How glad I am I came this way! They are not to be reached. Even Jack Rapley's love of the difficult and the unattainable would fail him here: May herself could not stand on that steep bank. So much the better. Who would wish to disturb them? There they live in their innocent and fragrant beauty, sheltered from the storms, and rejoicing in the sunshine, and looking as if they could feel their happiness. Who would disturb them? Oh, how glad I am, I came this way home!

Cousin Mary

ABOUT four years ago, passing a few days with the highly educated daughters of some friends in this neighbourhood, I found domesticated in the family a young lady, whom I shall call as they called her, Cousin Mary. She was about eighteen, not beautiful, perhaps, but lovely certainly to the fullest extent of that loveliest word – as fresh as a rose; as fair as a lily; with lips like winter berries, dimpled, smiling lips; and eyes of which nobody could tell the colour, they danced so incessantly in their own gay light. Her figure was tall, round and slender; exquisitely well-proportioned it must have been for in all attitudes (and in her innocent gaiety, she was scarcely ever two minutes in the same), she was grace itself. She was, in short, the very picture of youth, health and happiness. No one could see her without being prepossessed in her favour. I took a fancy to her the moment she entered the room; and it increased every hour in spite of, or rather perhaps for, certain deficiencies, which caused poor Cousin Mary to be held exceedingly cheap by her accomplished relatives.

She was the youngest daughter of an officer of rank, dead long ago; and his sickly widow, having lost by death, or by that other death, marriage, all her children but this, could not, from very fondness, resolve to part with her darling for the purpose of acquiring the commonest instruction. She talked of it indeed, now and then, but she only talked; so that, in this age of universal education, Mary C. at eighteen exhibited the extraordinary phenomenon of a young woman of high family, whose acquirements were limited to reading, writing, needlework, and the first rules of arithmetic. The effect of this let-alone system, combined with a careful seclusion from all improper society, and a perfect liberty in her country rambles, acting upon a mind of great power and activity, was the very reverse of what might have been predicted. It had produced not merely a delightful freshness and originality of manner and character, a piquant ignorance of those things of which one is tired to death, but also knowledge, positive, accurate and various knowledge. She was, to be sure, wholly unaccomplished; knew nothing of quadrilles, though her every motion was dancing; nor a note of music, though she used to warble like a bird sweet snatches of old songs, as she skipped up and down the house; nor of painting, except as her taste had been formed by a minute acquaintance with nature into an intense feeling for art. She had that real extra sense, an eye for colour, too, as well as an ear for music. Not one in twenty – not one in a hundred – of our sketching and copying ladies could love and appreciate a picture where there was colour and mind, a picture by Claude, or by our English Claudes, Wilson and Hoffland, as she could, for she loved landscape best because she understood it best – it was a portrait of which she knew the original. Then her needle was in her hands almost a pencil. I never knew such an embroideress. She would sit 'printing her thoughts on lawn', till the delicate creation vied with the snowy tracery, the fantastic carving of hoar frost, the richness of Gothic architecture, or of that which so much resembles it, the luxuriant fancy of old point lace. That was her only accomplishment, and a rare artist she was – muslin and net were her canvas. She had no French either, not a word; no Italian; but then her English was racy, unhackneyed, proper to the thought to a degree that only original thinking could give. She had not much reading, except of the Bible and Shakespeare and Richardson's novels, in which she was learned; but then her powers of observation were sharpened and quickened, in a very unusual degree, by the leisure and opportunity afforded for their development at a time of life when they are most acute. She had nothing to distract her mind. Her attention was always awake and alive. She was an excellent and curious naturalist merely because she had gone into the fields with her eyes open; and knew all the details of rural management, domestic or agricultural, as well as the peculiar habits and modes of thinking of the peasantry, simply because she had lived in the country, and made use of her ears. Then she was fanciful, recollective, new; drew her images from the real objects, not from their shadows in books. In short, to listen to her, and the young ladies her companions, who, accomplished to the height, had trodden the education-mill till they all moved in one step, had lost sense in sound, and ideas in words, was enough to make us turn masters and governesses out of doors, and leave our daughters and grand-daughters to Mrs C.'s system of non-instruction. I should have liked to meet with another specimen, just to ascertain whether the peculiar charm and advantage arose from the quick and active mind of this fair ignorant, or was really the natural and inevitable result of the training. But, alas! To find more than one unaccomplished young lady, in this accomplished age, is not to be hoped for. So I admired and envied; and her fair kinswomen pitied and scorned, and tried to teach; and Mary, never made for a learner, and as full of animal spirits as a schoolboy in the holidays, sang, and laughed and skipped about from morning till night.

It must be confessed, as a counterbalance to her other perfections, that the dear Cousin Mary was, as far as great natural modesty and an occasional touch of shyness would let her, the least in the world of a romp! She loved to toss about children, to jump over stiles, to scramble through hedges, to climb trees; and some of her knowledge of plants and birds may certainly have arisen from her delight in these boyish amusements. And which of us has not found that the strongest, the healthiest, and most flourishing acquirement has arisen from pleasure or accident, has been in a manner self-sown, like an oak of the forest? Oh, she was a sad romp; as skittish as a wild colt, as uncertain as a butterfly, as uncatchable as a swallow! But her great personal beauty, the charm, grace and lightness of her movements and, above all, her evident innocence of heart were bribes of indulgence which no one could withstand. I never heard her blamed by any human being. The perfect unrestraint of her attitudes, and the exquisite symmetry of her form, would have rendered her an invaluable study for a painter. Her daily doings would have formed a series of pictures. I have seen her scudding through a shallow rivulet with her petticoats caught up just a little above the ankle, like a young Diana, and a bounding, skimming, enjoying motion, as if native to the element, which might have become a naiad. I have seen her on the topmost rung of a ladder, with one foot on the roof of a house, flinging down the grapes that no one else had nerve enough to reach, laughing and garlanded, and crowned with vine leaves like a bacchante.

But the prettiest combination of circumstances under which I ever saw her was driving a donkey cart up a hill, one sunny windy day in September. It was a gay party of young women, some walking, some in open carriages of different descriptions, bent to see a celebrated prospect from a hill called the Ridges. The ascent was by a steep, narrow lane, cut deeply between sandbanks, crowned with high, feathery hedges. The road and its picturesque banks lay bathed in the golden sunshine, whilst the autumnal sky, intensely blue, appeared at the top as through an arch. The hill was so steep that we had all dismounted and had left our different vehicles in charge of the servants below; but Mary, to whom, as incomparably the best charioteer, the conduct of a certain nondescript machine, a sort of donkey curricle, had fallen, determined to drive a delicate little girl, who was afraid of the walk, to the top of the eminence. She jumped out for the purpose, and we followed, watching and admiring her as she won her way up the hill; now tugging at the donkeys in front, with her bright face towards them and us, and springing along backwards; now pushing the chaise from behind; now running by the side of her steeds, patting and caressing them; now soothing the half-frightened child; now laughing, nodding, and shaking her little whip at us; darting about like some winged creature; till at last she stopped at the top of the ascent, and stood for a moment on the summit, her straw bonnet blown back and held on only by the strings; her brown hair playing on the wind in long natural ringlets; her complexion becoming every moment more splendid from exertion, redder and whiter; her eyes and her smile brightening and dimpling: her figure, in its simple white gown, strongly relieved by the deep blue sky, and her whole form seeming to dilate before our eyes. There she stood under the arch formed by two meeting elms, a Hebe, a

Psyche, a perfect goddess of youth and joy. The Ridges are very fine things altogether, especially the part to which we were bound – a turfy, breezy spot, sinking down abruptly like a rock into a wild foreground of heath and forest, with a magnificent command of distant objects. But we saw nothing that day like the figure on the top of the hill.

After this I lost sight of her for a long time. She was called suddenly home by the dangerous illness of her mother, who, after languishing for some months, died; and Mary went to live with a sister much older than herself, and richly married, in a manufacturing town, where she languished in smoke, confinement, dependence and display (for her sister was a match-making lady, a manœuvrer) for about a twelvemonth. She then left her house and went into Wales – as a governess! Imagine the astonishment caused by this intelligence amongst us all; for I myself, though admiring the untaught damsel almost as much as I loved her, should certainly never have dreamed of her as a teacher. However, she remained in the rich baronet's family where she had commenced her employment. They liked her apparently – there she was; and again nothing was heard of her for many months, until, happening to call on the friends at whose house I had originally met her, I espied her fair blooming face, a rose amongst roses, at the drawing-room window, and instantly, with the speed of light, was met and embraced by her at the hall door.

There was not the slightest perceptible difference in her deportment. She still bounded like a fawn, and laughed and clapped her hands like an infant. She was not a day older, or graver, or wiser, since we parted. Her post of tutoress had at least done *her* no harm, whatever might have been the case with her pupils. The more I looked at her the more I wondered; and, after our mutual expressions of pleasure had a little subsided, I could not resist the temptation of saying, 'So you are really a governess?' 'Yes.' 'And you continue in the same family? 'Yes.' 'And you like your post?' 'O yes! yes!' 'But, my dear Mary, what could induce you to go?' 'Why, they wanted a governess, so I went.' 'But what could induce them to keep you?' The perfect gravity and earnestness with which this question was put set her laughing, and the laugh was echoed back from a group at the end of the room, which I had not before noticed — an elegant man, in the prime of life, showing a portfolio of rare prints to a fine girl of twelve, and a rosy boy of seven, evidently his children. 'Why did they keep me? Ask them,' replied Mary, turning towards them with an arch smile. 'We kept her to teach her ourselves,' said the young lady. 'We kept her to play cricket with us,' said her brother. 'We kept her to marry,' said the gentleman, advancing gaily to shake hands with me. 'She was a bad governess, perhaps; but she is an excellent wife — that is her true vocation.' And so it is. She is, indeed, an excellent wife; and assuredly a most fortunate one. I never saw happiness so sparkling or so glowing; never saw such devotion to a bride, or such fondness for a step-mother, as Sir W.S. and his lovely children show to the sweet Cousin Mary.

Walks in the Country
Violeting

MARCH 27th. It is a dull, grey morning, with a dewy feeling in the air; fresh, but not windy; cool, but not cold; the very day for a person newly arrived from the heat, the glare, the noise and the fever of London to plunge into the remotest labyrinths of the country, and regain the repose of mind, the calmness of heart, which has been lost in that great Babel. I must go violeting – it is a necessity – and I must go alone. The sound of a voice, even my Lizzy's, the touch of Mayflower's head, even the bounding of her elastic foot, would disturb the serenity of feeling which I am trying to recover. I shall go quite alone, with my little basket, twisted like a bee-hive, which I love so well, because *she* gave it to me, and kept sacred to violets and to those whom I love; and I shall get out of the high-road the moment I can. I would not meet anyone just now, even of those whom I best like to meet.

Ha! Is not that group – a gentleman on a bloodhorse, a lady keeping pace with him so gracefully and easily – see how prettily her veil waves in the wind created by her own rapid motion! – and that gay, gallant boy, on the gallant white Arabian, curveting at their side, but ready to spring before them every instant – is not that chivalrous-looking party Mr and Mrs M. and Dear B.? No! The servant is in a different livery. It is some of the ducal family, and one of their young Etonians. I may go on. I shall meet no one now; for I have fairly left the road and am crossing the Lea by one of those wandering paths, amidst the gorse, and the heath, and the low broom, which the sheep and lambs have made – a path turfy, elastic, thymy, and sweet, even at this season.

We have the good fortune to live in an unenclosed parish, and may thank the wise obstinacy of two or three sturdy farmers, and the lucky unpopularity of a ranting madcap lord of the manor, for preserving the delicious green patches, the islets of wilderness amidst cultivation, which form, perhaps, the peculiar beauty of English scenery. The common that I am passing now – the Lea, as it is called – is one of the loveliest of these favoured spots. It is a little sheltered scene, retiring, as it were, from the village; sunk amidst higher lands, hills would be almost too grand a word; edged on one side by one gay high-road, and intersected by another; and surrounded by a most picturesque confusion of meadows, cottages, farms and orchards; with a great pond in one corner, unusually bright and clear, giving a delightful cheerfulness and daylight to the picture. The swallows haunt that pond; so do the children. There is a merry group round it now; I have seldom seen it without one. Children love water; clear, bright, sparkling water; it excites and feeds their curiosity; it is motion and life.

The path that I am treading leads to a less lively spot, to that large, heavy building on one side of the common, whose solid wings, jutting out far beyond the main body, occupy three sides of a square and give a cold shadowy look to the court. On one side is a gloomy garden, with an old man digging in it, laid out in straight, dark beds of vegetables, potatoes, cabbages, onions, beans; all earthy and mouldy as a newly dug grave. Not a flower or flowering shrub! Not a rose tree or currant bush! Nothing but for sober melancholy use. Oh, how different from the long irregular slips of the cottage-gardens, with their gay bunches of polyanthuses and crocuses, their wallflowers sending sweet odours through the narrow casement, and their gooseberry trees bursting into a brilliancy of leaf, whose vivid greenness has the effect of a blossom on the eye! Oh, how different! On the other side of this gloomy abode is a meadow of that deep, intense emerald hue, which denotes the presence of stagnant water, surrounded by willows at regular distances, and like the garden, separated from the common by a wide moat-like ditch. That is the parish workhouse. All about it is solid, substantial, useful – but so dreary! So cold! So dark! There are children in the court, and yet all is silent. I always hurry past that place as if it were a prison. Restraint, sickness, age, extreme poverty, misery, which I have no power to remove or alleviate – these are the ideas, the feelings, which the sight of those walls excites; yet, perhaps, if not certainly, they contain less of that extreme desolation than the morbid fancy is apt to paint. There will be found order, cleanliness, food, clothing, warmth, refuge for the homeless, medicine and attendance for the sick, rest and sufficiency for old age, and sympathy, the true and active sympathy which the poor show to the poor, for the unhappy. There may be worse places than a parish workhouse – and yet I hurry past it. The feeling, the prejudice, will not be controlled.

The end of the dreary garden edges off into a close sheltered lane, wandering and winding, like a rivulet, in gentle 'sinuosities' (to use a word once applied by Mr Wilberforce to the Thames at Henley), amidst green meadows, all alive with cattle, sheep and beautiful lambs, in the very spring and pride of their tottering prettiness, or fields of arable land, more lively still, with troops of stooping bean-setters, women and children, in all varieties of costume and colour; and ploughs and harrows, with their whistling boys and steady carters, going through, with a slow and plodding industry, the main business of this busy season.

What work bean-setting is! What a reverse of the position assigned to man to distinguish him from the beasts of the field! Only think of stooping for six, eight, ten hours a day, drilling holes in the earth with a little stick, and then dropping in the beans one by one. They are paid according to the quantity they plant; and some of the poor women used to be accused of clumping them – that is to say, of dropping more than one bean into a hole. It

seems to me, considering the temptation, that not to clump is to be at the very pinnacle of human virtue.

Another turn in the lane, and we come to the old house standing amongst the high elms – the old farmhouse, which always, I don't know why, carries back my imagination to Shakespeare's days. It is a long, low, irregular building, with one room, at an angle from the house, covered with ivy, fine white-veined ivy; the first floor of the main building, projecting and supported by oaken beams, and one of the windows below, with its old casement and long narrow panes, forming the half of a shallow hexagon. A porch, with seats in it, surmounted by a pinnacle, pointed roofs and clustered chimneys, complete the picture. Alas! It is little else but a picture! The very walls are crumbling to decay under a careless landlord and a ruined tenant.

Now a few yards farther, and I reach the bank. Ah! I smell them already – their exquisite perfume steams and lingers in this moist heavy air. Through this little gate, and along the green south bank of this green wheatfield, and they burst upon me, the lovely violets, in tenfold loveliness! The ground is covered with them, white and purple, enamelling the short dewy grass, looking but the more vividly coloured under the dull, leaden sky. There they lie by hundreds, by thousands. In former years I have been used to watch them from the tiny green bud, till one or two stole into bloom. They never came on me before in such a sudden and luxuriant glory of simple beauty – and I do really owe one pure and genuine pleasure to feverish London! How beautifully they are placed, too, on this sloping bank, with the palm branches waving over them, full of early bees, and mixing their honeyed scent with the more delicate violet odour! How transparent and smooth and lusty are the branches, full of sap and life! And there, just by the old mossy root, is a superb tuft of primroses, with a yellow butterfly hovering over them, like a flower floating on the air. What happiness to sit on this tufty knoll, and fill my basket with the blossoms! What a renewal of heart and mind! To inhabit such a scene of peace and sweetness is again to be fearless, gay and gentle as a child. Then it is that thought becomes poetry, and feeling religion. Then it is that we are happy and good. Oh, that my whole life could pass so, floating on blissful and innocent sensation, enjoying in peace and gratitude the common blessings of nature, thankful above all for the simple habits, the healthful temperament, which render them so dear! Alas! Who may dare expect a life of such happiness? But I can at least snatch and prolong the fleeting pleasure, can fill my basket with pure flowers, and my heart with pure thoughts; can gladden my little home with their sweetness; can divide my treasures with one, a dear one, who cannot seek them; can see them when I shut my eyes; and dream of them when I fall asleep.

The Talking Lady

BEN JONSON has a play called *The Silent Woman*, who turns out, as might be expected, to be no woman at all – nothing, as Master Slender said, but 'a great lubberly boy'; thereby, as I apprehend, discourteously presuming that a silent woman is a nonentity. If the learned dramatist, thus happily prepared and predisposed, had happened to fall in with such a specimen of female loquacity as I have just parted with, he might, perhaps, have given us a pendant to his picture in the Talking Lady. Pity but he had! He would have done her justice, which I could not at any time, least of all now; I am too much stunned, too much like one escaped from a belfry on a coronation day. I am just resting from the fatigue of four days' hard listening – four snowy, sleety, rainy, days – days of every variety of falling weather, all of them too bad to admit the possibility that any petticoated thing, were she as hardy as a Scotch fir, should stir out – four days chained by 'sad civility' to that fireside, once so quiet, and again, cheering thought, again I trust to be so, when the echo of that visitor's incessant tongue shall have died away.

The visitor in question is a very excellent and respectable elderly lady, upright in mind and body, with a figure that does honour to her dancing-master, a face exceedingly well-preserved, wrinkled and freckled but still fair, and an air of gentility over her whole person, which is not the least affected by her out-of-fashion garb. She could never be taken for anything but a woman of family, and perhaps she could as little pass for any other than an old maid. She took us in her way from London to the west of England: and being, as she wrote, 'not quite well, not equal to much company, prayed that no other guest might be admitted, so that she might have the pleasure of our conversation all to herself' (*Ours!* As if it were possible for any of us to slide in a word edgewise!) 'and especially enjoy the gratification of talking over old times with the master of the house, her countryman'. Such was the promise of her letter, and to the letter it has been kept. All the news and scandal of a large county forty years ago, and a hundred years before, and ever since; all the marriages, deaths, births, elopements, lawsuits and casualties of her own times, her father's, grandfather's, great-grandfather's, nephews' and grand-nephews', has she detailed with a minuteness, an accuracy, a prodigality of learning, a profuseness of proper names, a pedantry of locality, which would excite the envy of a county historian, a king-at-arms, or even a Scotch novelist. Her knowledge is astonishing; but the most astonishing part of all is how she came by that knowledge. It should seem, to listen to her, as if, at some time of her life, she must have listened herself; and yet her countryman declares that in the forty years he has known her, no such event has occurred; and she knows new news, too! It must be intuition.

The manner of her speech has little remarkable. It is rather old-fashioned and provincial, but perfectly ladylike, low and gentle, and not seeming so fast as it is; like the great pedestrians, she clears her ground easily, and never seems to use any exertion; yet 'I would my horse had the speed of her tongue, and so good a continuer.' She will talk you sixteen hours a day for twenty days together, and not deduct one poor five minutes for halts and baiting time. Talking, sheer talking, is meat and drink and sleep to her. She likes nothing else. Eating is a sad interruption. For the tea-table she has some toleration; but dinner, with its clatter of plates and jingle of knives and forks, dinner is her abhorrence. Nor are the other common pursuits of life more in her favour. Walking exhausts the breath that might be better employed. Dancing is a noisy diversion, and singing is worse. She cannot endure any music, except the long, grand, dull concerto, which nobody thinks of listening to. Reading and chess she classes together as silent barbarisms, unworthy of a social and civilized people. Cards, too, have their faults; there is a rivalry, a mute eloquence in those four aces, that leads away the attention.

Besides, partners will sometimes scold; so she never plays at cards; and upon the strength of this abstinence had very nearly passed for *serious*, till it was discovered that she could not abide a long sermon. She always looks out for the shortest preacher, and never went to above one Bible Meeting in her life. 'Such speeches!' quoth she. 'I thought the men never meant to have done. People have great need of patience.' Plays, of course, she abhors, and operas, and mobs, and all things that will be heard, especially children; though for babies, particularly when asleep, for dogs and pictures, and such silent intelligences as serve to talk of and to talk to, she has a considerable partiality; and an agreeable and gracious flattery to the mammas and other owners of these pretty dumb things is a very usual introduction to her miscellaneous harangues. The matter of these orations is inconceivably various. Perhaps the local and genealogical anecdotes, the sort of supplement to the history of —shire, may be her strongest point; but she shines almost as much in medicine and housewifery. Her medical dissertations savour a little of that particular branch of the science called quackery. She has a specific against almost every disease to which the human frame is liable; and is terribly prosy and unmerciful in her symptoms. Her cures kill. In housekeeping, her notions resemble those of other verbal managers: full of economy and retrenchment, with a leaning towards reform, though she loves so well to declaim on the abuses in the cook's department that I am not sure that she would very heartily thank any radical who should sweep them quite away. For the rest, her system sounds very finely in theory, but rather fails in practice. Her receipts would be capital, only that some way or other, they do not eat well; her preserves seldom keep; and her sweet wines are sure to turn sour.

These are certainly her favourite topics; but any one will do. Allude to some anecdote of the neighbourhood, and she forthwith treats you with as many parallel passages as are to be found in an air with variations. Take up a new publication, and she is equally at home there; for, though she knows little of books, she has, in the course of an up-and-down life, met with a good many authors, and teases and provokes you by telling of them precisely what you do not care to hear, the maiden names of their wives and the Christian names of their daughters, and into what families their sisters and cousins married, and in what towns they have lived, what streets, and what numbers. Boswell himself never drew up the table of Dr Johnson's Fleet Street courts with greater care than she made out to me the successive residences of P. P. Esq., author of a tract on the French Revolution, and a pamphlet on the Poor Laws. The very weather is not a safe subject. Her memory is a perpetual register of hard frosts, and long droughts, and high winds, and terrible storms, with all the evils that followed in their train, and all the personal events connected with them, so that if you happen to remark that clouds are come up, and you fear it may rain, she replies, 'Ay, it is just such a morning as three and thirty years ago, when my poor cousin was married – you remember my cousin Barbara – she married so and so, the son of so and so.' And then comes the whole pedigree of the bridegroom; the amount of the settlements, and the reading and signing them overnight; a description of the wedding-dresses, in the style of Sir Charles Grandison, and how much the bride's gown cost per yard; the names, residences, and a short subsequent history of the bridesmaids and men, the gentleman who gave the bride away, and the clergyman who performed the ceremony, with a learned antiquarian digression relative to the church; then the setting out in procession; the marriage; the kissing; the crying; the breakfasting; the drawing the cake through the ring; and, finally, the bridal excursion, which brings us back again at an hour's end to the starting-post – the weather – and the whole story of the sopping, the drying, the clothes-spoiling, the cold-catching, and all the small evils of a summer shower. By this time it rains, and she sits down to a pathetic see-saw of conjectures on the chance of Mrs Smith's having set out for her daily walk, or the possibility that Dr Brown may have ventured to visit his patients in his gig, and the certainty that Lady Green's new housemaid would come from London on the outside of the coach.

With all this intolerable prosing, she is actually reckoned a pleasant woman! Her acquaintance in the great manufacturing town where she usually resides is very large, which may partly account for the misnomer. Her conversation is of a sort to bear dividing. Besides, there is, in all large societies, an instinctive sympathy, which directs each individual to the companion most congenial to his humour. Doubtless her associates deserve the old French compliment, '*Ils ont tous un grand talent pour le silence.*' Parcelled out amongst some seventy or eighty, there may even be some savour in her talk. It is the *tête-à-tête* that kills, or the small fireside circle of three or four, where only one can speak, and all the rest must seem to listen – *seem!* did I say? – must listen in good earnest. Hotspur's expedient in a similar situation of crying 'Hem! Go to,' and marking not a word, will not do here: compared to her, Owen Glendower was no conjurer. She has the eye of a hawk, and detects a wandering glance, an incipient yawn, the slightest movement of impatience; the very needle must be quiet. If a pair of scissors do but wag, she is affronted, draws herself up, breaks off in the middle of a story, of a sentence, of a word, and the unlucky culprit must, for civility's sake, summon a more than Spartan fortitude, and beg the torturer to resume her torments – 'That, that is the unkindest cut of all!' I wonder, if she happened to have married, how many husbands she would have talked to death. It is certain that none of her relations are long-lived, after she comes to reside with them. Father, mother, uncle, sister, brother, two nephews and one niece, all these have successively passed away, though a healthy race, and with no visible disorder, except – but we must not be uncharitable. They might have died, though she had been born dumb: 'It is an accident that happens every day.' Since the decease of her last nephew, she attempted to form an establishment with a widow lady, for the sake, as they both said, of the comfort of society. But – strange miscalculation! – she was a talker, too! They parted in a week.

And we have also parted. I am just returned from escorting her to the coach, which is to convey her two hundred miles westward; and I have still the murmur of her *adieux* resounding in my ears, like the indistinct hum of the air on a frosty night. It was curious to see how, almost simultaneously, these mournful *adieux* shaded into cheerful salutations of her new comrades, the passengers in the mail. Poor souls! Little does the civil young lad who made way for her, or the fat lady, his mamma, who with pains and incon-venience made room for her, or the grumpy gentleman in the opposite corner, who, after some dispute, was at length won to admit her dressing-box, little do they suspect what is to befall them. Two hundred miles! And she never sleeps in a carriage! Well, patience be with them, and comfort and peace! A pleasant journey to them! And to her all happiness! She is a most kind and excellent person, one for whom I would do anything in my poor power – ay, even were it to listen to her another four days.

A Country Cricket Match

I DOUBT if there be any scene in the world more animating or delightful than a cricket match. I do not mean a set match at Lord's Ground for money, hard money, between a certain number of gentlemen and players, as they are called – people who make a trade of that noble sport, and degrade it into an affair of bettings, and hedgings, and cheatings, it may be, like boxing or horse-racing. Nor do I mean a pretty fête in a gentleman's park, where one club of cricketing dandies encounter another such club, and where they show off in graceful costume to a gay marquee of admiring belles, who condescend so to purchase admiration, and while away a long summer morning in partaking cold collations, conversing occasionally, and seeming to understand the game; the whole being conducted according to ballroom etiquette, so as to be exceedingly elegant and exceedingly dull. No! The cricket that I mean is a real solid old-fashioned match between neighbouring parishes, where each attacks the other for honour and a supper, glory and half a crown a man. If there be any gentlemen amongst them, it is well; if not, it is so much the better.

Your gentleman cricketer is in general rather an anomalous

character. Elderly gentlemen are obviously good for nothing; and young beaux are, for the most part, hampered and trammelled by dress and habit – the stiff cravat, the pinched-in waist, the dandy-walk – oh, they will never do for cricket! Now, our country lads, accustomed to the flail or the hammer (your blacksmiths are capital hitters), have the free use of their arms; they know how to move their shoulders; and they can move their feet too – they can run. Then they are so much better made, so much more athletic, and yet so much lissomer, to use a Hampshire phrase, which deserves at least to be good English. Here and there, indeed, one meets with an old Etonian, who retains his boyish love for that game which formed so considerable a branch of his education: some even preserve their boyish proficiency. But in general it wears away like the Greek, quite as certainly, and almost as fast; a few years of Oxford, or Cambridge, or the Continent, are sufficient to annihilate both the power and the inclination.

No! A village match is the thing, where our highest officer, our conductor (to borrow a musical term), is but a little farmer's second son; where a day-labourer is our bowler, and a blacksmith our long-stop; where the spectators consist of the retired cricketers, the veterans of the green, the careful mothers, the girls, and all the boys of two parishes, together with a few amateurs, little above them in rank, and not at all in pretension; where laughing and shouting, and the very ecstasy of merriment and good humour prevail; such a match, in short, as I attended yesterday, at the expense of getting twice wet through, and as I would attend tomorrow at the certainty of having that ducking doubled.

For the last three weeks, our village has been in a state of great excitement, occasioned by a challenge from our north-western neighbours, the men of B—, to contend with us at cricket. Now we have not been much in the habit of playing matches. Three or four years ago, indeed, we encountered the men of S—, our neighbours south-by-east, with a sort of doubtful success, beating them on our own ground, whilst they in the second match returned the compliment on theirs. This discouraged us. Then an unnatural coalition between a High Church curate and an evangelical gentleman-farmer drove our lads from the Sunday evening practice, which, as it did not begin before both services were concluded, and as it tended to keep the young men from the ale-house, our magistrates had winked at, if not encouraged. The sport therefore had languished until the present season, when, under another change of circumstances, the spirit began to revive. Half a dozen fine active lads, of influence amongst their comrades, grew into men and yearned for cricket; an enterprising publican gave a set of ribands; his rival, mine host of the Rose, an out-doer by profession, gave two; and the clergyman and his lay ally, both well-disposed and good-natured men, gratified by the submission to their authority, and finding, perhaps, that no great good resulted from the substitution of public-houses for out-of-door diversions, relaxed. In short the practice recommenced, and the hill was again alive with men and boys, and innocent merriment; but farther than the riband matches amongst ourselves nobody dreamed of going, till this challenge – we were modest, and doubted our own strength. The B— people, on the other hand, must have been braggers born, a whole parish of gasconaders. Never was such boasting! Such crowing! Such ostentatious display of practice! Such mutual compliments from man to man, bowler to batter, batter to bowler! It was a wonder they did not challenge all England. It must be confessed that we were a little astounded; yet we firmly resolved not to decline the combat; and one of the most spirited of the new growth, William Grey by name, took up the glove in a style of manly courtesy that would have done honour to a knight in the days of chivalry. 'We were not professed players,' he said; 'being little better than schoolboys, and scarcely older. But, since they had done us the honour to challenge us, we would try our strength. It would be no discredit to be beaten by such a field.'

Having accepted the wager of battle, our champion began forthwith to collect his forces. William Grey is himself one of the finest youths that one shall see – tall, active, slender and yet strong, with a piercing eye full of sagacity, and a smile full of good humour; a farmer's son by station, and used to hard work as farmers' sons are now, liked by everybody, and admitted to be an excellent cricketer. He immediately set forth to muster his men,

remembering with great complacency that Samuel Long, a bowler, *comme il y en a peu*, the very man who had knocked down
nine wickets, had beaten us, bowled us out at the fatal return
match some years ago at S—, had luckily, in a remove of a quarter
of a mile last Lady Day, crossed the boundaries of his old parish,
and actually belonged to us. Here was a stroke of good fortune!
Our captain applied to him instantly! and he agreed at a word.
Indeed Samuel Long is a very civilized person. He is a middle-aged
man, who looks rather old amongst our young lads, and whose
thickness and breadth give no token of remarkable activity. But he
is very active, and so steady a player! So safe! We had half gained
the match when we had secured him. He is a man of substance,
too, in every way; owns one cow, two donkeys, six pigs, and geese
and ducks beyond count; dresses like a farmer, and owes no man a
shilling; and all this from pure industry, sheer day-labour. Note
that your good cricketer is commonly the most industrious
man in the parish; the habits that make him such are precisely
those which make a good workman – steadiness, sobriety and
activity – Samuel Long might pass for the beau ideal of the two
characters. Happy were we to possess him!

Then we had another piece of good luck. James Brown, a
journeyman blacksmith and a native, who, being of a rambling
disposition, had roamed from place to place for half a dozen
years, had just returned to settle with his brother at another corner
of our village, bringing with him a prodigious reputation in
cricket and in gallantry – the gay Lothario of the neighbourhood.
He is said to have made more conquests in love and in cricket than
any blacksmith in the county. To him also went the indefatigable
William Grey, and he also consented to play. No end to our good
fortune!

Another celebrated batter, called Joseph Hearne, had likewise
recently married into the parish. He worked, it is true, at the A—
mills, but slept at the house of his wife's father in our territories.
He also was sought and found by our leader. But he was grand and
shy; made an immense favour of the thing; courted courting and
then hung back: 'Did not know that he could be spared; had
partly resolved not to play again – at least not this season; thought

it rash to accept the challenge; thought they might do without him –' 'Truly I think so, too,' said our spirited champion; 'we will not trouble you, Mr Hearne.'

Having thus secured two powerful auxiliaries, and rejected a third, we began to reckon and select the regular native forces. Thus ran our list: William Grey, 1. Samuel Long, 2. James Brown, 3. George and John Simmons, one capital, the other so-so, – an uncertain hitter, but a good fieldsman, 5. Joel Brent, excellent, 6. Ben Appleton – here was a little pause. Ben's abilities at cricket were not completely ascertained; but then he was so good a fellow, so full of fun and waggery! No doing without Ben. So he figured in the list, 7. George Harris – a short halt there, too! Slowish – slow but sure. I think the proverb brought him in, 8. Tom Coper – oh, beyond the world, Tom Coper! the red-headed gardening lad, whose left-handed strokes send *her* (a cricket-ball, like that other moving thing, a ship, is always of the feminine gender), send her spinning a mile, 9. Harry Willis, another blacksmith, 10.

We had now ten of our eleven, but the choice of the last occasioned some demur. Three young Martins, rich farmers of the neighbourhood, successively presented themselves and were all rejected by our independent and impartial general for want of merit – *cricketal* merit. 'Not good enough,' was his pithy answer. Then our worthy neighbour, the half-pay lieutenant, offered his services – he, too, though with some hesitation and modesty, was refused. 'Not quite young enough,' was his sentence. John Strong, the exceeding long son of our dwarfish mason, was the next candidate. A nice youth, everybody likes John Strong, and a willing, but so tall and so limp, bent in the middle – a thread-paper, six feet high! We were all afraid that, in spite of his name, his strength would never hold out. 'Wait till next year, John,' quoth William Grey, with all the dignified seniority of twenty speaking to eighteen. 'Coper's a year younger,' said John. 'Coper's a foot shorter,' replied William: so, John retired; and the eleventh man remained unchosen, almost to the eleventh hour. The eve of the match arrived, and the post was still vacant, when a little boy of fifteen, David Willis, brother to Harry, admitted by accident to the last practice, saw eight of them out, and was voted in by acclamation.

That Sunday evening's practice (for Monday was the important day) was a period of great anxiety, and, to say the truth, of great pleasure. There is something strangely delightful in the innocent spirit of party. To be one of a numerous body, to be authorized to say *we*, to have a rightful interest in triumph or defeat, is gratifying at once to social feeling and to personal pride. There was not a ten-year-old urchin, or a septuagenarian woman in the parish, who did not feel an additional importance, a reflected consequence, in speaking of 'our side'. An election interests in the same way; but that feeling is less pure. Money is there, and hatred, and politics, and lies. Oh, to be a voter, or a voter's wife, comes nothing near the genuine and hearty sympathy of belonging to a parish, breathing the same air, looking on the same trees, listening to the same nightingales! Talk of a patriotic elector! Give me a parochial patriot, a man who loves his parish! Even we, the female partisans, may partake the common ardour. I am sure I did. I never, though tolerably eager and enthusiastic at all times, remember being in a more delicious state of excitation than on the eve of that battle. Our hopes waxed stronger and stronger. Those of our players, who were present, were excellent. William Grey got forty notches off his own bat; and that brilliant hitter, Tom Coper, gained eight from two successive balls. As the evening advanced, too, we had encouragement of another sort. A spy, who had been dispatched to reconnoitre the enemy's quarters, returned from their practising ground, with a most consolatory report. 'Really,' said Charles Grover, our intelligencer, a fine old steady judge, one who had played well in his day, 'they are no better than so many old women. Any five of ours would beat their eleven.' This sent us to bed in high spirits.

Morning dawned less favourably. The sky promised a series of deluging showers, and kept its word, as English skies are wont to do on such occasions; and a lamentable message arrived at the headquarters from our trusty comrade Joel Brent. His master, a great farmer, had begun the hay harvest that very morning, and Joel, being as eminent in one field as in another, could not be spared. Imagine Joel's plight! The most ardent of all our eleven! A knight held back from the tourney! A soldier from the battle! The poor swain was inconsolable. At last, one who is always ready to do a good-natured action, great or little, set forth to back his petition; and, by dint of appealing to the public spirit of our worthy neighbour and the state of the barometer, talking alternately of the parish honour and thunder showers, of lost matches and sopped hay, he carried his point, and returned triumphantly with the delighted Joel.

In the meantime, we became sensible of another defalcation. On calling over our roll, Brown was missing; and the spy of the preceding night, Charles Grover, the universal scout and messenger of the village, a man who will run half a dozen miles for a pint of beer, who does errands for the very love of the trade, who, if he had been a lord, would have been an ambassador, was instantly dispatched to summon the truant. His report spread general consternation. Brown had set off at four o'clock in the morning to play in a cricket match at M——, a little town twelve miles off, which had been his last residence. Here was desertion! Here was treachery! Here was treachery against that goodly state, our parish! To send James Brown to Coventry was the immediate resolution; but even that seemed too light a punishment for such lelinquency. Then how we cried him down! At ten on Sunday night (for the rascal had actually practised with us, and never said a word of his intended disloyalty) he was our faithful mate, and the best player (take him for all in all) of the eleven. At ten in the morning he had run away, and we were well rid of him; he was no batter compared with William Grey or Tom Coper; not fit to wipe the shoes of Samuel Long, as a bowler; nothing of a scout to John Simmons; the boy David Willis was worth fifty of him:

> I trust we have within our realm
> Five hundred good as he,

was the universal sentiment. So we took tall John Strong, who, with an incurable hankering after the honour of being admitted, had kept constantly with the players, to take the chance of some such accident – we took John for our *pis aller*. I never saw anyone prouder than the good-humoured lad was of this not very flattering piece of preferment.

John Strong was elected, and Brown sent to Coventry; and, when I first heard of his delinquency, I thought the punishment only too mild for the crime. But I have since learned the secret history of the offence (if we could know the secret histories of all offences, how much better the world would seem than it does now!) and really my wrath is much abated. It was a piece of gallantry, of devotion to the sex, or rather a chivalrous obedience to one chosen fair. I must tell my readers the story.

Mary Allen, the prettiest girl of M—, had, it seems, revenged upon our blacksmith the numberless inconstancies of which he stood accused. He was in love over head and ears, but the nymph was cruel. She said no, and no, and no, and poor Brown, three times rejected, at last resolved to leave the place, partly in despair, and partly in that hope which often mingles strangely with a lover's despair – the hope that when he was gone he should be missed. He came home to his brother's accordingly; but for five weeks he heard nothing from, or of, the inexorable Mary, and was glad to beguile his own 'vexing thoughts', by endeavouring to create in his mind an artificial and factitious interest in our cricket match – all unimportant as such a trifle must have seemed to a man in love. Poor James, however, is a social and warm-hearted person, not likely to resist a contagious sympathy. As the time for the play advanced, the interest which he had at first affected became genuine and sincere: and he was really, when he left the ground on Sunday night, almost as enthusiastically absorbed in the event of the next day as Joel Brent himself. He little foresaw the new and delightful interest which awaited him at home, where on the moment of his arrival his sister-in-law and confidante presented him with a *billet* from the lady of his heart. It had, with the usual delay of letters sent by private hands, in that rank of life, loitered on the road, in a degree inconceivable to those who are accustomed to the punctual speed of the post, and had taken ten days for its twelve-mile journey. Have my readers any wish to see this *billet-doux?* I can show them (but in strict confidence) a literal copy. It was addressed:

> For mistur jem browne
> blaxmith by
> S.

The inside ran thus:

> Mistur browne this is to Inform yew that oure parish plays bramley men next monday is a week, i think we shall lose without yew. from your humbell servant to command
> MARY ALLEN

Was there ever a prettier relenting? A summons more flattering, more delicate, more irresistible? The precious epistle was un-dated; but, having ascertained who brought it, and found, by cross-examining the messenger, that the Monday in question was the very next day, we were not surprised to find that *Mistur browne* forgot his engagement to us, forgot all but Mary and Mary's letter, and set off at four o'clock the next morning to walk twelve miles, and play for her parish, and in her sight. Really, we must not send James Brown to Coventry – must we? Though if, as his sister-in-law tells our damsel Harriet he hopes to do, he should bring the fair Mary home as his bride, he will not greatly care how little we say to him. But he must not be sent to Coventry – True Love forbid!

At last we were all assembled, and marched down to H— common, the appointed ground, which, though in our dominions, according to the map, was the constant practising place of our opponents, and *terra incognita* to us. We found our adversaries on the ground as we expected, for our various delays had hindered us from taking the field so early as we wished; and, as soon as we had settled all preliminaries, the match began.

But alas! I have been so long settling my preliminaries that I have left myself no room for the detail of our victory, and must squeeze the account of our grand achievements into as little compass as Cowley, when he crammed the names of eleven of his mistresses into the narrow space of four eight-syllable lines. *They* began the warfare – these boastful men of B—. And what think you, gentle reader, was the amount of their innings? These challengers, the famous eleven, how many did they get? Think! Imagine! Guess! You cannot? Well! They got twenty-two, or, rather, they got twenty; for two of theirs were short notches, and would never have been allowed, only that, seeing what they were made of, we and our umpires were not particular. They should have had twenty more, if they had chosen to claim them. Oh, how well we fielded! And how well we bowled! Our good play had quite as much to do with their miserable failure as their bad. Samuel Long is a slow bowler, George Simmons a fast one, and the change from Long's lobbing to Simmons' fast balls, posed them completely. Poor simpletons! They were always wrong, expecting the slow for the quick, and the quick for the slow. Well, we went in. And what were our innings? Guess again! Guess! A hundred and sixty-nine! In spite of soaking showers, and wretched ground, where the ball would not run a yard, we headed them by a hundred and forty-seven; and then they gave in, as well they might. William Grey pressed them much to try another innings. 'There was so much chance,' as he courteously observed, 'in cricket, that advantageous as our position seemed, we might, very possibly, be overtaken. The B— men had better try.' But they were beaten sulky, and would not move, to my great disappointment; I wanted to prolong the pleasure of success. What a glorious sensation it is to be for five hours together winning – winning – winning! Always feeling what a whist-player feels when he takes up four honours, seven trumps! Who would think that a little bit of leather and two pieces of wood had such a delightful and delighting power?

The only drawback on my enjoyment was the failure of the pretty boy, David Willis, who injudiciously put in first, and playing for the first time in a match amongst men and strangers, who talked to him, and stared at him, was seized with such a fit of shame-faced shyness, that he could scarcely hold his bat, and was bowled out without a stroke, from actual nervousness. 'He will come of that,' Tom Coper says. I am afraid he will. I wonder whether Tom had ever any modesty to lose. Our other modest lad,

John Strong, did very well; his length told in fielding, and he got good fame. Joel Brent, the rescued mower, got into a scrape, and out of it again; his fortune for the day. He ran out his mate, Samuel Long, who, I do believe, but for the excess of Joel's eagerness, would have stayed in till this time, by which exploit he got into sad disgrace; and then he himself got thirty-seven runs, which redeemed his reputation. William Grey made a hit which actually lost the cricket-ball. We think she lodged in a hedge, a quarter of a mile off, but nobody could find her. And George Simmons had nearly lost his shoe, which he tossed away in a passion, for having been caught out, owing to the ball glancing against it. These, together with a very complete somersault of Ben Appleton, our long-stop, who floundered about in the mud, making faces and attitudes as laughable as Grimaldi, none could tell whether by accident or design, were the chief incidents of the scene of action.

Amongst the spectators nothing remarkable occurred, beyond the general calamity of two or three drenchings, except that a form, placed by the side of a hedge, under a very insufficient shelter, was knocked into the ditch, in a sudden rush of the cricketers to escape a pelting shower, by which means all parties shared the fate of Ben Appleton, some on land and some by water; and that, amidst the scramble, a saucy gipsy of a girl contrived to steal from the knee of the demure and well-apparelled Samuel Long, a smart handkerchief, which his careful dame had tied around it, to preserve his new (what is the mincing feminine word?) – his new – inexpressibles; thus reversing the story of Desdemona, and causing the new Othello to call aloud for his handkerchief, to the great diversion of the company. And so we parted; the players retired to their supper, and we to our homes; all wet through, all good-humoured, and all happy – except the losers.

Today we are happy, too. Hats, with ribands in them, go glancing up and down; and William Grey says, with a proud humility, 'We do not challenge any parish; but if we be challenged, we are ready.'

An Old Bachelor

THERE is no effect of the subtle operation of the association of ideas more universal and more curious than the manner in which the most trivial circumstances recall particular persons to our memory. Sometimes these glances of recollection are purely pleasurable. Thus I have a double liking for May Day, as being the birthday of a dear friend whose fair idea bursts upon me with the first sunbeam of that glad morning; and I can never hear certain airs of Mozart and Handel without seeming to catch an echo of that sweetest voice in which I first learned to love them. Pretty often, however, the point of association is less elegant, and occasionally it is tolerably ludicrous. We happened today to have for dinner a couple of wild ducks, the first of the season; and as the master of the house, who is so little of an epicure that I am sure he would never while he lived, out of its feathers, know a wild duck from a tame, whilst he, with a little affectation of science, was squeezing the lemon and mixing cayenne pepper with the gravy, two of us exclaimed in a breath, 'Poor Mr Sidney!' 'Ay,' rejoined the squeezer of lemons, 'poor Sidney! I think he would have allowed that these ducks were done even to half a turn.' And then he told the story more elaborately to a young visitor, to whom Mr Sidney was unknown – how, after eating the best parts of a couple of wild ducks, which all the company pronounced to be the finest and best dressed wild ducks ever brought to table, that judicious critic in the gastronomic art limited the too sweeping praise by gravely asserting that the birds were certainly excellent, and that the cookery would have been excellent also, had they not been roasted half a turn too much. Mr Sidney has been dead these fifteen years; but no wild ducks have ever appeared on our homely board without recalling that observation. It is his memorable saying; his one good thing.

Mr Sidney was, as might be conjectured, an epicure; he was also an old bachelor, a clergyman, and senior fellow of — College, a post which he had long filled, being, although only a second son, so well provided for that he could afford to reject living after living in expectation of one favourite rectory, to which he had taken an early fancy from the pleasantness of the situation and the imputed salubrity of the air. Of the latter quality, indeed, he used to give an instance, which, however satisfactory as confirming his prepossession, could hardly have been quite agreeable, as preventing him from gratifying it; namely, the extraordinary and provoking longevity of the incumbent, who at upwards of ninety gave no sign of decay, and bade fair to emulate the age of old Parr.

Whilst waiting for the expected living, Mr Sidney, who disliked a college residence, built himself a very pretty house in our neighbourhood, which he called his home; and where he lived, as much as a love of Bath and Brighton and London and lords would let him. He counted many noble families amongst his near connexions, and passed a good deal of his time at their country seats – a life for which he was by character and habit peculiarly fitted.

In person he was a tall, stout, gentlemanly man, 'about fifty, or by'r lady inclining to threescore,' with fine features, a composed gravity of countenance and demeanour, a bald head most accurately powdered, and a very graceful bow – quite the pattern of an elderly man of fashion. His conversation was in excellent keeping with the calm imperturbability of his countenance, and the sedate gravity of his manner – smooth, dull, commonplace, exceedingly safe, and somewhat imposing. He spoke so little that people really fell into the mistake of imagining that he thought; and the tone of decision with which he would advance some second-hand opinion, was well calculated to confirm the mistake. Gravity was certainly his chief characteristic, and yet it was not a clerical gravity either. He had none of the generic marks of his profession. Although perfectly decorous in life and word and thought, no stranger ever took Mr Sidney for a clergyman. He never did any duty anywhere, that ever I heard of, except the agreeable duty of saying grace before dinner! And even that was often performed by some lay host, in pure forgetfulness of his guest's ordination. Indeed, but for the direction of his letters, and an eye to — Rectory, I am persuaded that the circumstance might have slipped out of his own recollection.

His quality of old bachelor was more perceptible. There lurked under all his polish, well covered, but not concealed, the quiet selfishness, the little whims, the precise habits, the primness and priggishness of that disconsolate condition. His man Andrews, for instance, valet, groom, and bodyservant abroad; butler, cook, caterer, and major-domo at home; tall, portly, powdered, and black-coated as his master, and like him in all things but the knowing pigtail which stuck out horizontally above his shirt-collar, giving a ludicrous dignity to his appearance; Andrews, who, constant as the dial pointed nine, carried up his chocolate and shaving-water, and regular as 'the chimes at midnight', prepared his white-wine whey; who never forgot his gouty shoe in travelling (once for two days he had a slight touch of that gentlemanly disorder), and never gave him the newspaper un-aired; to whom could this jewel of a valet, this matchless piece of clockwork belong, but an old bachelor? And his little dog Viper, unparagoned of terriers, black, sleek, sharp and shrewish, who would beg and sneeze and fetch and carry like a Christian; eat olives and sweetmeats and mustard, drink coffee and wine and liqueurs; who but an old bachelor could have taught Viper his multifarious accomplishments?

Little Viper was a most useful person in his way; for although Mr Sidney was a very creditable acquaintance to meet on the king's highway (your dull man, if he rides well, should never think of dismounting), or even on the level ground of a carpet, in the crowd of a large party; yet, when he happened to drop in to take a family dinner, a pretty frequent habit of his when in the country, then Viper's talents were inestimable in relieving the *ennui* occa-sioned by that grave piece of gentility his master, 'not only *dull* in himself, but the cause of *dulness* in others'. Anything to pass away the heavy hours, till whist or piquet relieved the female world from his intolerable silence.

In other respects these visits were sufficiently perplexing. Every housewife can tell what a formidable guest is an epicure who comes to take pot-luck – how sure it is to be bad luck, especially when the unfortunate hostess lives five miles from a market town. Mr Sidney always came unseasonably, on washing-day or Saturday, or the day before a great party. So sure as we had a scrap dinner, so sure came he. My dear mother, who, with true benevolence and hospitality, cared much for her guest's comfort, and nothing for her own pride, used to grieve over his discomfiture, and try all that could be done by potted meats and omelettes, and little things tossed up on a sudden to amend the bill of fare. But cookery is an obstinate art, and will have its time; however you may force the component parts, there is no forcing a dinner. Mr Sidney had the evil habit of arriving just as the last bell rang; and in spite of all the hurry-scurry in the kitchen department, the new niceties and the old homely dishes were sure to disagree. There was a total want of keeping. The kickshaws were half raw, the solids were mere rags; the vegetables were cold; the soup was scalding; no shallots to the rump steaks; no mushrooms with the broiled chicken; no fish; no oysters; no ice; no pineapple. Poor Mr Sidney! He must have had a great regard for us to put up with our bad dinners.

Perhaps the chance of a rubber had something to do with his visits to our house. If there be such a thing as a ruling passion, the love of whist was his. Cards were not merely the amusement, but the business, of his life. I do not mean as a money-making speculation; for although he belonged to a fashionable club in London, and to every card-meeting of decent gentility within reach of his country home, he never went beyond a regular moderate stake, and could not be induced to bet even by the rashest defyer of calculation, or the most provoking undervaluer of his play. It always seemed to me that he regarded whist as far too important and scientific a pursuit to be degraded into an affair of gambling. It had in his eyes all the dignity of a study; an acquirement equally gentlemanly and clerical. It was undoubtedly his test of ability. He had the value of a man of family and a man of the world for rank, and wealth, and station, and dignities of all sorts. No human being entertained a higher respect for a king, a prince, a prime minister, a duke, a bishop, or a lord. But these were conventional feelings. His genuine and unfeigned veneration was reserved for him who played a good rubber, a praise he did not easily give. He was a capital player himself, and held all his country competitors, except one, in supreme and undisguised contempt, which they endured to admiration. I wonder they did not send him to Coventry. He was the most disagreeable partner in the world, and nearly as unpleasant an adversary; for he not only enforced the Pythagorean law of science, which makes one hate whist so, but used to distribute quite impartially to everyone at table little disagreeable observations on every card they played. It was not scolding, or grumbling, or fretting; one has a sympathy with those expressions of feeling, and at the worst can scold again; it was a smooth, polite commentary on the errors of the party, delivered in the calm tone of undoubted superiority with which a great critic will sometimes take a small poet, or a batch of poets, to task in a review. How the people could bear it! But the world is a good-natured world, and does not like a man the less for treating it scornfully.

So passed six evenings out of the seven with Mr Sidney; for it was pretty well-known that, on the rare occurrence of his spending a day at home without company, his factotum Andrews used to have the honour of being beaten by his master in a snug game at double dumby! But what he did with himself on Sunday occasioned me some speculation. Never in my life did I see him take up a book, although he sometimes talked of Shakespeare and Milton, and Johnson and Burke, in a manner which proved that he had heard of such things; and as to the newspaper, which he did read, that was generally conned over long before night! Besides, he never exhibited spectacles, and I have a notion that he could not read newspaper type at night without them. How he could possibly get through the after-coffee hours on a Sunday puzzled me long. Chance solved the problem. He came to call on us after church, and agreed to dine and sleep at our house. The moment tea was over, without the slightest apology or attempt at conversation, he drew his chair to the fire, set his feet on the fender, and fell fast asleep in the most comfortable and orderly manner possible. It was evidently a weekly habit. Every sense and limb seemed composed to it. Viper looked up in his face, curled himself round on the hearth-rug, and went to sleep too; and Andrews, just as the clock struck twelve, came in to wake him, that he might go to bed. It was clearly an invariable custom; a settled thing.

His house and grounds were kept in the neatest manner possible. There was something even disagreeable in the excessive nicety, the Dutch preciseness of the shining gravel walks, the smooth shaven turf of the lawn, and the fine sifted mould of the shrubberies. A few dead leaves or scattered flowers, even a weed or two, anything to take away from the artificial toy-like look of the place, would have been an improvement. Mr Sidney, however, did not think so. He actually caused his gardener to remove those littering plants called roses and gum cistuses. Other flowers fared little better. No sooner were they in bloom, than he pulled them up for fear they should drop.

Indoors, matters were still worse. The rooms and furniture were very handsome, abounding in the luxurious Turkish carpets, the sofas, easy chairs, and ottomans, which his habits required; and yet I never in my life saw any house which looked less comfortable. Everything was so constantly in its place, so provokingly in order, so full of naked nicety, so thoroughly old-bachelorish. No work! No books! No music! No flowers. But for those two things of life, Viper and a sparkling fire, one might have thought the place uninhabited. Once a year, indeed, it gave signs of animation, in the shape of a Christmas party. That was Mr Sidney's shining time. Nothing could exceed the smiling hospitality of the host, or the lavish profusion of the entertainment. It breathed the very spirit of a welcome, splendidly liberal; and little Viper frisked and bounded, and Andrews's tail vibrated (I was going to say wagged) with cordiality and pleasure. Andrews, on these occasions, laid aside his 'customary black', in favour of a blue coat and a white silk court waistcoat, with a light running pattern of embroidery and silver spangles, assumed to do honour to his master and the company. How much he enjoyed the applause which the wines and the cookery elicited from the gentlemen; and how anxiously he would direct the ladies' attention to a MS collection of riddles, the compilation of some deceased countess, laid on the drawing-room table for their amusement between dinner and tea. Once, I remember, he carried his attention so far as to produce a gone-by toy, called a bandalore, for the recreation of myself and another little girl, admitted by virtue of the Christmas holidays to this annual festival. Poor Andrews! I am convinced that he considered the entertainment of the visitors quite as much his affair as his master's; and certainly they both succeeded. Never did parties pass more pleasantly. On those evenings Mr Sidney even forgot to find fault at whist.

At last, towards the end of a severe winter, during which he had suffered much from repeated colds, the rectory of — became vacant, and our worthy neighbour hastened to take possession. The day before his journey he called on us in the highest spirits, anticipating a renewal of health and youth in this favourite spot, and approaching nearer than I had ever heard him to a jest on the subject of looking out for a wife. Married or single, he made us promise to visit him during the ensuing summer. Alas! Long before the summer arrived, our poor friend was dead. He had waited for this living thirty years; he did not enjoy it thirty days.

The Talking Gentleman

THE lords of the creation, who are generally (to do them justice) tenacious enough of their distinctive and peculiar faculties and powers, have yet by common consent made over to the females the single gift of loquacity. Every man thinks and says that every woman talks more than he: it is the creed of the whole sex, the debates and law reports notwithstanding. And every masculine eye that has scanned my title, has already, I doubt not, looked to the *errata*, suspecting a mistake in the gender; but it is their misconception, not my mistake. I do not (Heaven forbid!) intend to impugn or abrogate our female privilege; I do not dispute that we do excel, generally speaking, in the use of the tongue; I only mean to assert that one gentleman does exist (whom I have the pleasure of knowing intimately), who stands pre-eminent and unrivalled in the art of talking, unmatched and unapproached by man, woman, or child. Since the decease of my poor friend, the Talking Lady, who dropped down speechless in the midst of a long story about nine weeks ago, and was immediately known to be dead by her silence, I should be at a loss where to seek a competitor to contend with him in a race of words, and I should be still more puzzled to find one that can match him in wit, pleasantry, or good humour.

My friend is usually called Harry L., for, though a man of substance, a lord of land, a magistrate, a field officer of militia, nobody ever dreamed of calling him Mister or Major, or by any such derogatory title – he is and will be all his life plain Harry, the name of universal goodwill. He is indeed the pleasantest fellow that lives. His talk (one can hardly call it conversation, as that would seem to imply another interlocutor, something like reciprocity) is an incessant flow of good things, like Congreve's comedies, without a replying speaker, or Joe Miller laid into one; and its perpetual stream is not lost and dispersed by diffusion, but runs in one constant channel, playing and sparkling like a fountain, the delight and ornament of our good town of B—.

Harry L. is a perfect example of provincial reputation, of local fame. There is not an urchin in the town that has not heard of him, nor an old woman that does not chuckle by anticipation at his approach. The citizens of B— are as proud of him as the citizens of Antwerp were of the Chapeau de Paille, and they have the advantage of the luckless Flemings in the certainty that their boast is not to be purchased. Harry, like the Flemish beauty, is native to the spot; for he was born at B—, educated at B—, married at B—, though, as his beautiful wife brought him a good estate in a distant part of the country, there seemed at that epoch of his history some danger of his being lost to our ancient borough. But he is a social and gregarious animal; so he leaves his pretty place in Devonshire to take care of itself, and lives here in the midst of a hive. His tastes are not at all rural. He is no sportsman, no farmer, no lover of strong exercise. When at B—, his walks are quite regular; from his own house, on one side of the town, to a gossip-shop called 'literary', on the other, where he talks and reads newspapers, and others read newspapers and listen. Thence he proceeds to another house of news, similar in kind, though differing in name, in an opposite quarter, where he and his hearers undergo the same process, and then he returns home, forming a pretty exact triangle of about half a mile. This is his daily exercise, or rather his daily walk; of exercise he takes abundance, not only in talking (though that is nearly as good to open the chest as the dumb-bells), but also in a general restlessness and fidgetiness of person, the result of his ardent and nervous temperament, which can hardly endure repose of mind or body. He neither gives rest nor takes it. His company is, indeed, in one sense (only one) fatiguing. Listening to him tires you like a journey. You laugh till you are forced to lie down. The medical gentlemen of the place are aware of this, and are accustomed to exhort delicate persons to abstain from Harry's society, just as they caution them against temptations in point of amusement or of diet – pleasant but dangerous. Choleric gentlemen should also avoid him, and such as love to have the last word; for, though never provoked himself, I cannot deny that he is occasionally tolerably provoking, in politics especially (and he is an ultra-liberal, quotes Cobbett, and goes rather too far). In politics he loves to put his antagonist in a fume, and generally succeeds, though it is nearly the only subject on which he ever listens to an answer, chiefly, I believe, for the sake of a reply, which is commonly some trenchant repartee that cuts off the poor answer's head like a razor. Very determined speakers would also do well to eschew his company – though, in general, I never met with any talker to whom other talkers were so ready to give way; perhaps because he keeps them in such incessant laughter that they are not conscious of their silence. To himself, the number of his listeners is altogether unimportant. His speech flows not from vanity, or lust of praise, but from sheer necessity – the reservoir is full, and runs over. When he has no one else to talk to, he can be content with his own company, and talks to himself, being, beyond a doubt, greater in a soliloquy than any man off the stage. Where he is not known, this habit sometimes occasions considerable consternation, and very ridiculous mistakes. He has been taken alternately for an actor, a poet, a man in love, and a man beside himself. Once in particular, at Windsor, he greatly alarmed a philanthropic sentinel, by holding forth at his usual rate whilst pacing the terrace alone; and, but for the opportune arrival of his party, and their assurances that it was only 'the gentleman's way', there was some danger that the benevolent soldier might have been tempted to desert his post to take care of him. Even after this explanation, he gazed with a doubtful eye at our friend, who was haranguing himself in great style, sighed and shook his head, and finally implored us to look well after him till he should be safe off the terrace. 'You see, Ma'am,' observed the philanthropist in scarlet, 'it is an awkward place for anybody troubled with vagaries. Suppose the poor soul should take a fancy to jump over the wall!'

In his externals he is a well-looking gentleman of forty, or thereabout; rather thin, and rather pale, but with no appearance of ill health, nor any other peculiarity, except the remarkable circumstance of the lashes of one eye being white, which gives a singular non-resemblance to his organs of vision. Everyone perceives the want of uniformity, and few detect the cause. Some suspect him of what farriers call a wall eye; some think he squints. He himself talks familiarly of his two eyes, the black and the white, and used to liken them to those of our fine Persian cat (now alas! no more), who had, in common with his feline countrymen, one eye blue as a sapphire, the other as yellow as a topaz. The dissimilarity certainly rather spoils his beauty, but greatly improves his wit – I mean the sense of his wit in others. It arrests attention, and predisposes to laughter; is an outward and visible sign of the comical. No common man has two such eyes. They are made for fun.

In his occupations and pleasures, Harry is pretty much like other provincial gentlemen: loves a rubber, and jests all through, at aces, kings, queens, and knaves, bad cards and good, at winning and losing, scolding and praise; loves a play, at which he out-talks the actors whilst on the stage, to say nothing of the advantage he has over them in the intervals between the acts; loves music, as a good accompaniment to his grand solo; loves a contested election above all. That is his real element – that din and uproar and riot and confusion! To ride that whirlwind and direct that storm is his triumph of triumphs! He would make a great sensation in parliament himself, and a pleasant one. (By the way, he was once in danger of being turned out of the gallery for setting all around him in a roar.) Think what a fine thing it would be for the members to have mirth introduced into the body of the house! to be sure of an honest, hearty, good-humoured laugh every night during the session! Besides, Harry is an admirable speaker, in every sense of the word. Jesting is indeed his forte, because he wills it so to be; and, therefore, because he chooses to play jigs and country dances on a noble organ, even some of his staunchest admirers think he can play nothing else. There is no quality of which men so much grudge the reputation as versatility of talent. Because he is so humorous, they will hardly allow him to be eloquent; and because he is so very witty, find it difficult to account him wise. But let him go where he has not that mischievous fame, or let him bridle his jests and rein in his humour only for one short hour, and he will pass for a most reverend orator – logical, pathetic, and vigorous above all. But how can I wish him to cease jesting even for an hour? Who would exchange the genial fame of good-humoured wit for the stern reputation of wisdom? Who would choose to be Socrates, if with a wish he could be Harry L.?

Walks in the Country
Nutting

SEPTEMBER 26th. One of those delicious autumnal days, when the air, the sky, and the earth, seem lulled into a universal calm, softer and milder even than May. We sallied forth for a walk, in a mood congenial to the weather and the season, avoiding, by mutual consent, the bright and sunny common, and the gay highroad, and stealing through shady unfrequented lanes, where we were not likely to meet anyone, not even the pretty family procession which in other years we used to contemplate with so much interest – the father, mother, and children, returning from the wheatfield, the little ones laden with bristling, close-tied bunches of wheat-ears, their own gleanings, or a bottle and a basket which had contained their frugal dinner, whilst the mother would carry her babe hushing and lulling it, and the father and an elder child trudged after with the cradle, all seeming weary, and all happy. We shall not see such a procession as this today; for the harvest is nearly over, the fields are deserted, the silence may almost be felt. Except the wintry notes of the redbreast, nature herself is mute. But how beautiful, how gentle, how harmonious, how rich! The rain has preserved to the herbage all the freshness and verdure of spring, and the world of leaves has lost nothing of its midsummer brightness, and the harebell is on the banks, and the woodbine in the hedges, and the low furze, which the lambs cropped in the spring, has burst again into its golden blossoms.

All is beautiful that the eye can see, perhaps the more beautiful for being shut in with a forest-like closeness. We have no prospect in this labyrinth of lanes, crossroads, mere cart-ways, leading to the innumerable little farms into which this part of the parish is divided. Uphill or down, these quiet woody lanes scarcely give us a peep at the world, except when, leaning over a gate, we look into one of the small enclosures, hemmed in with hedgerows, so closely set with growing timber that the meady opening looks almost like a glade in a wood, or when some cottage, planted at a corner of one of the little greens formed by the meeting of these cross-ways, almost startles us by the unexpected sight of the dwellings of men in such a solitude. But that we have more of hill and dale, and that our crossroads are excellent in their kind, this side of our parish would resemble the description given of La Vendée, in Madam Laroche-Jacquelin's most interesting book.[1] I am sure if wood can entitle a country to be called Le Bocage, none can have a better right to the name. Even this pretty snug farmhouse on the hillside, with its front covered with the rich vine, which goes wreathing up to the very top of the clustered chimney, and its sloping orchard full of fruit – even this pretty quiet nest can hardly peep out of its leaves.

Ah! They are gathering in the orchard harvest. Look at that young rogue in the old mossy apple tree – that great tree, bending with the weight of its golden-rennets – see how he pelts his little sister beneath, with apples as red and as round as her own cheeks, while she, with her outstretched frock, is trying to catch them, and laughing and offering to pelt again as often as one bobs against her. And look at that still younger imp, who, as

---

[1] An almost equally interesting account of that very peculiar and interesting scenery, may be found in *The Maid of La Vendée*, an English novel, remarkable for its simplicity and truth of painting, written by Mrs Le Noir, the daughter of Christopher Smart, and inheritrix of much of his talent. Her works deserve to be better known.

grave as a judge, is creeping on hands and knees under the tree, picking up the apples as they fall so deedily,[1] and depositing them so honestly in the great basket on the grass, already fixed so firmly and opened so widely, and filled almost to overflowing by the brown rough fruitage of the golden-rennet's next neighbour, the russeting. And see that smallest urchin of all, seated apart in infantine state on the turfy bank, with that toothsome piece of deformity a crumpling in each hand, now biting from one sweet hard juicy morsel, and now from another. Is not that a pretty English picture? And then, farther up the orchard, that bold hardy lad, the eldest-born, who has scaled (Heaven knows how!) the tall, straight upper branch of that great pear tree, and is sitting there as securely and as fearlessly, in as much real safety and apparent danger, as a sailor on the topmast. Now he shakes the tree with a mighty swing that brings down a pelting shower of stony bergamots, which the father gathers rapidly up, whilst the mother can hardly assist for her motherly fear, a fear which only spurs the spirited boy to bolder ventures. Is not that a pretty picture?

And they are such a handsome family too, the Brookers. I do not know that there is any gipsy blood, but there is the true gipsy complexion, richly brown, with cheeks and lips so deeply red, black hair curling close to their heads in short crisp rings, white shining teeth – and such eyes! That sort of beauty entirely eclipses your mere roses and lilies. Even Lizzy, the prettiest of fair children, would look poor and watery by the side of Willy Brooker, the sober little personage who is picking up the apples with his small chubby hands, and filling the basket so orderly, next to his father the most useful man in the field. 'Willy!' He hears without seeing; for we are quite hidden by the high bank, and a spreading hawthorn bush that overtops it, though between the lower branches and the grass we have found a convenient peephole.

[1] *Deedily* – I am not quite sure that this word is good English; but it is genuine Hampshire, and is used by the most correct of female writers, Miss Austen. It means (and it is no small merit that it has no exact synonym) anything done with a profound and plodding attention, an action which engrosses all the powers of mind and body.

'Willy!' The voice sounds to him like some fairy dream, and the black eyes are raised from the ground with sudden wonder, the long, silky eyelashes thrown back till they rest on the delicate brow, and a deeper blush is burning on those dark cheeks, and a smile is dimpling about those scarlet lips. But the voice is silent now, and the little quiet boy, after a moment's pause, is gone coolly to work again. He is indeed a most lovely child. I think some day or other he must marry Lizzy; I shall propose the match to their respective mammas. At present the parties are rather too young for a wedding – the intended bridegroom being, as I should judge, six, or thereabout, and the fair bride barely five – but at least we might have a betrothment after the royal fashion, there could be no harm in that. Miss Lizzy, I have no doubt, would be as demure and coquettish as if ten winters more had gone over her head, and poor Willy would open his innocent black eyes, and wonder what was going forward. They would be the very Oberon and Titania of the village, the fairy king and queen.

Ah! Here is the hedge along which the periwinkle wreathes and twines so profusely, with its evergreen leaves shining like the myrtle, and its starry blue flowers. It is seldom found wild in this part of England; but when we do meet with it, it is so abundant and so welcome, the very robin redbreast of flowers, a winter friend. Unless in those unfrequent frosts which destroy all vegetation, it blossoms from September to June, surviving the last lingering cranesbill, forerunning the earliest primrose, hardier even than the mountain daisy, peeping out from beneath the snow, looking at itself in the ice, smiling through the tempests of life, and yet welcoming and enjoying the sunbeams. Oh, to be like that flower!

The little spring that has been bubbling under the hedge all along the hillside, begins, now that we have mounted the eminence and are imperceptibly descending, to deviate into a capricious variety of clear, deep pools and channels, so narrow and so choked with weeds that a child might overstep them. The hedge has also changed its character. It is no longer the close compact vegetable wall of hawthorn, and maple, and brier-roses, intertwined with bramble and woodbine, and crowned with large elms or thickly set saplings. No! The pretty meadow which rises high above us, backed and almost surrounded by a tall coppice, needs no defence on ourside but its own steep bank, garnished with tufts of broom, with pollard oaks wreathed with ivy, and here and there with long patches of hazel overhanging the water. 'Ah, there are still nuts on that bough!' And in an instant my dear companion, active and eager and delighted as a boy, has hooked down with his walking-stick one of the lissome hazel stalks, and cleared it of its tawny clusters, and in another moment he has mounted the bank, and is in the midst of the nuttery, now transferring the spoil from the lower branches into that vast variety of pockets which gentlemen carry about them, now bending the tall tops into the lane, holding them down by main force, so that I might reach them and enjoy the pleasure of collecting some of the plunder myself. A very great pleasure he knew it would be. I doffed my shawl, tucked up my flounces, turned my straw bonnet into a basket, and began gathering and scrambling for, manage it how you may, nutting is scrambling work, those boughs, however tightly you may grasp them by the younger fragrant twigs and the bright green leaves, will recoil and burst away; but there is a pleasure even in that. So on we go, scrambling and gathering with all our might and all our glee. Oh what an enjoyment! All my life long I have had a passion for that sort of seeking which implies finding (the secret, I believe, of the love of field sports, which is in man's mind a natural impulse), therefore I love violeting; therefore, when we had a fine garden, I used to love to gather strawberries, and cut asparagus, and above all, to collect the filberts from the shrubberies. But this hedgerow nutting beats that sport all to nothing. That was a make-believe thing, compared with this; there was no surprise, no suspense, no unexpectedness – it was as inferior to this wild nutting as the turning out of a bag-fox is to unearthing the fellow, in the eyes of a staunch fox-hunter.

Oh, what an enjoyment this nut-gathering is! They are in such abundance that it seems as if there were not a boy in the parish, nor a young man, nor a young woman – for a basket of nuts is the universal tribute of country gallantry; our pretty damsel Harriet has had at least half a dozen this season – but no one has found out these. And they are so full too, we lose half of them from over-ripeness; they drop from the socket at the slightest motion. If we lose, there is one who finds. May is as fond of nuts as a squirrel, and cracks the shell and extracts the kernel with equal dexterity. Her white glossy head is upturned now to watch them as they fall. See how her neck is thrown back like that of a swan, and how beautifully her folded ears quiver with expectation, and how her quick eye follows the rustling noise, and her light feet dance and pat the ground, and leap up with eagerness, seeming almost sustained in the air, just as I have seen her when Brush is beating a hedgerow, and she knows from his questing that there is a hare afoot. See, she has caught that nut just before it touched the water; but the water would have been no defence – she fishes them from the bottom, she delves after them amongst the matted grass, even my bonnet, how beggingly she looks at that! 'Oh what a pleasure nutting is! Is it not, May? But the pockets are almost full, and so is the basket-bonnet, and that bright watch the sun says it is late; and after all it is wrong to rob the poor boys – is it not, May?' May shakes her graceful head denyingly, as if she understood the question. 'And we must go home now – must we not? But we will come nutting again some time or other – shall we not, my May?'

A Walk through the Village

WHEN I had the honour about two years ago of presenting our little village to that multiform and most courteous personage, the Public, I hinted, I think, that it had a trick of standing still, of remaining stationary, unchanged and unimproved in this most changeable and improving world. This habit, whether good or evil, it had retained so pertinaciously that, except that it is two years older, I cannot point out a single alteration which has occurred in our street. I was on the point of paying the inhabitants the same equivocal compliment – and really I almost may – for setting aside the inevitable growth of the younger members of our community, and a few more grey hairs and wrinkles amongst the elder, I see little change. We are the same people, the same generation, neither richer, nor wiser, nor better, nor worse. Some, to be sure, have migrated; and one or two have died; and some – but we had better step out into the village and look about us.

It is a pleasant lively scene this May morning, with the sun shining so gaily on the irregular rustic dwellings, intermixed with their pretty gardens; a cart and a waggon watering (it would be more correct, perhaps, to say *beering*) at the Rose; Dame Wheeler, with her basket and her brown loaf, just coming from the bakehouse; the nymph of the shoeshop feeding a large family of goslings at the open door – they are very late this year, those noisy little geese; two or three women in high gossip dawdling up the street; Charles North the gardener, with his blue apron and a ladder on his shoulder, walking rapidly by; a cow and a donkey browsing the grass by the wayside; my white greyhound, May-flower, sitting majestically in front of her own stable; and ducks, chickens, pigs and children, scattered over all.

A pretty scene! Rather more lopping of trees, indeed, and clipping of hedges, along the highroad, than one quite admires; but then that identical turnpike-road, my ancient despair, is now so perfect and so beautiful a specimen of Macadamization, that one even learns to like tree-lopping and hedge-clipping for the sake of such smooth ways. It is simply the best road in England, so says our surveyor, and so say I. The three miles between us and B— are like a bowling-green. By the way I ought perhaps to mention, as something like change in our outward position, that this little hamlet of ours is much nearer to that illustrious and worshipful town than it used to be. Not that our quiet street hath been guilty of the unbecoming friskiness of skipping from place to place, but that our ancient neighbour, whose suburbs are sprouting forth in all directions, hath made a particularly strong shoot towards us, and threatens some day or other to pay us a visit bodily. The good town has already pushed the turnpike-gate half a mile nearer to us, and is in a fair way to overleap that boundary and build on, till the buildings join ours, as London has done by Hampstead or Kensington. What a strange figure our rude and rustical habitations would cut ranged by the side of some staring red row of newly erected houses, each as like the other as two drops of water, with courts before and behind, a row of poplars opposite, and a fine new name. How different we should look in our countless variety of nooks and angles, our gardens, and arbours, and lime trees, and pond! But this union of town and country will hardly happen in my time, let B— enlarge as it may. We shall certainly lend no assistance, for our boundaries still continue exactly the same.

The first cottage – Ah! Here is the post-cart coming up the road at its most respectable rumble, that cart, or rather caravan, which so much resembles a house upon wheels, or a show of the smaller kind at a country fair. It is now crammed full of passengers, the driver just protruding his head and hands out of the vehicle, and the sharp clever boy, who in the occasional absence of his father, officiates as deputy, perched like a monkey on the roof. 'Any letters today?' And that question, always so interesting, being unsatisfactorily answered, I am at leisure to return to our survey.

A Walk through the Village

The first cottage is that erst inhabited by Mr and Mrs H., the retired publican and his good wife. They are gone; I always thought we were too quiet for them; and his eyes being quite recovered, he felt the weariness of idleness more than ever. So they returned to W——, where he has taken a comfortable lodging next door to their old and well-frequented Inn, the Pie and Parrot, where he has the pleasure every evening of reading the newspaper, and abusing the ministers, amongst his old customers, himself a customer; as well as of lending his willing aid in waiting and entertaining on fair days and market days, at pink-feasts and melon-feasts, to the great solace of mine host, and the no small perplexity of the guests, who, puzzled between the old landlord and the new, hardly know to whom to pay their reckoning, or which to call to account for a bad tap – a mistake which our sometime neighbour, happier than he has been since he left the *Bar*, particularly enjoys. His successor here is an industrious person, by calling a seedsman, as may be collected by the heaps of pea and bean seed, clover and vetches, piled tier above tier against the window.

The little white cottage down the lane, which stands so prettily, backed by a tall elm wood, has also lost its fair inmate, Sally Wheeler, who , finding that Joel continued constant to our pretty Harriet, and was quite out of hope, was suddenly forsaken by the fit of dutifulness which brought her to keep her deaf grandmother company, and returned to service. Dame Wheeler has however a companion, in a widow of her own standing, appointed by the parish to live with, and take care of her. A nice tidy old woman is Dame Shearman; pity that she looks so frumpish; her face seems fixed in one perpetual scold. It was not so when she lived with her sister on the Lea, then she was a light-hearted merry chatterer, whose tongue ran all day long – and that's the reason of her cross look now! Mrs Wheeler is as deaf as a post, and poor Mrs Shearman is pining of a suppression of speech. Fancy what it is for a woman, especially a talking woman, to live without a listener! Forced either to hold her peace, or, when that becomes impossible, to talk to one to whose sense words are as air! La Trappe is nothing to this tantalization; besides, the Trappists were men. No wonder that poor Dame Shearman looks cross.

The blacksmith's! No change in that quarter; except a most astonishing growth amongst the children. George looks quite a man, and Betsy, who was just like a blue-eyed doll, with her flaxen curls, and her apple-blossom complexion, the prettiest fairy that ever was seen, now walks up to school every morning with her work-bag and her spelling-book, and is really a great girl. They are a fine family from the eldest to the youngest.

The shoemaker's! – not much to talk of there; no funeral! – and (which disappoints my prediction) no wedding! My pretty neighbour has not yet made her choice. She does wisely to look about her. A belle and an heiress – I dare say she'll have a hundred pounds to her portion – and still in her teens, has some right to be nice. Besides, what would all the mammas, whose babies she nurses, and all the children whom she spoils, do without her? No sparing the shoemaker's fair daughter! She must not marry yet these half-dozen years!

The shop! All prosperous, tranquil and thriving; another little one coming; an idle apprentice run away – more of him anon; and

a civil journeyman hired in his room. An excellent exchange! Jesse is a very agreeable person. He is the politician of the village since we have lost Mr H., and, as he goes every day into B— in his paper cap to carry our country bread, he is sure to bring home the latest intelligence of all sorts, especially of canvassing and electioneering. Jesse has the most complete collection of squibs in the country, and piques himself on his skill in detecting the writers. He will bestow as many guesses, and bring forward as many proofs, on occasion of a hand-bill signed 'Fair Play', or a song subscribed 'True Blue', as ever were given to that abiding riddle, the authorship of Junius – and very likely come as near the mark.

Ah, the dear home! A runaway there, too! I may as well tell the story now, although very sorry to have to record so sad an act of delinquency of my clients, the boys, as an elopement from our own premises.

Henry Hamilton – that ever a parish boy, offspring of a tailor and a cook-maid, should have an appellation so fitted to the hero of a romance! Henry Hamilton had lived with us for three years and upwards as man of all work, part waterer of my geraniums, sole feeder of May, the general favourite and factotum of the family. Being an orphan with no home but the workhouse, no friend but the overseer, at whose recommendation he was engaged, he seemed to belong to us in an especial manner, to have a more than common claim on protection and kindness. Henry was just the boy to discover and improve this feeling – quick, clever, capable, subtle and supple; exceedingly agreeable in manner, and pleasant in appearance. He had a light, pliant form, with graceful delicate limbs, like a native Indian; a dark but elegant countenance, sparkling with expression; and a remarkable variety and versatility of talent. Nothing came amiss to him. In one week he hath been carpenter, blacksmith, painter, tinker, glazier, tailor, cobbler and wheelwright. These were but a few of his multifarious accomplishments; he would beat Harriet at needlework, and me in gardening. All the parish was in the habit of applying to him on emergency, and I never knew him decline a job in my life. He hath mended a straw bonnet and a smoke-jack, cleaned a clock, constructed a donkey-cart, and dressed a doll.

With all these endowments, Henry was scarcely so good a servant as a duller boy. Besides that he undertook so many things that full half of them were of necessity left unfinished, he was generally to seek when wanted and, after sending a hue and cry round the neighbourhood, would be discovered at the black-smith's or the collar-maker's, intently occupied on some devices of his own. Then he had been praised for invention, till he thought it necessary to display that brilliant quality on all occasions, by which means we, who are exceedingly simple, old-fashioned, matter-of-fact people, were constantly posed by new-fangled novelties, which nobody but the artist could use, or quips and quiddities of no use whatever. Thus we had fastenings for boxes that would not open, and latches for gates that refused to shut, bellows of a new construction that no mortal could blow, and traps that caught fingers instead of rats; May was nearly choked by an improved slip, and my white camellia killed outright by an infallible wash for insects.

Notwithstanding these mishaps, we all liked Henry. His master liked his sportmanship, his skill and boldness in riding, and the zeal with which he would maintain the honour of his own dogs, right or wrong; his mistress liked his civility and good humour; Harriet felt the value of his alert assistance; and I had a real respect for his resource. In the village he was less a favourite; he looked down upon the other boys, and the men, although amused by his cleverness, looked down upon him.

At last he unfortunately met with a friend of his own age in a clever apprentice, who arrived at our neighbour the baker's from the good town of B——. This youngster, 'for shortness called' Bill, was a thorough town boy – you might see at a glance that he had been bred in the streets. He was a bold, sturdy lad, with a look compounded of great impudence and a little slyness, and manners although characterized by the former of these amiable qualities. His voice was a shout, his walk a swagger, and his knock at the door a bounce that threatened to bring the house about our ears. The very first time that I saw him, he was standing before our court with a switch in his hand, with which he was alternately menacing May, who, nothing daunted, returned his attack by an incessant bark, and demolishing a superb crown imperial. Never was a more complete *mauvais sujet*.

This audacious urchin most unfortunately took a great fancy to Henry, which Henry, caught by the dashing assurance of his manner, most unluckily returned. They became friends after the fashion of Orestes and Pylades, or Damon and Pythias, fought for each other, lied for each other, and, finally, ran away with each other. The reason for Bill's evasion was manifest, his conduct having been such that his master had been compelled to threaten him with Bridewell and the treadmill; but why Henry, who, although his invention had latterly taken a decided bent towards that branch of ingenuity called mischief, might still have walked quietly out of the street door with a good character in his pocket, should choose to elope from the garret window, is best known to himself. Off they set upward, that is to say, Londonward, the common destination of your country youths who sally forth to try their fortune. Forth they set, and in about a week they were followed by a third runaway, a quiet, simple, modest-looking lad, a sort of hanger-on to the other two, and an apprentice to our worthy neighbour the carpenter. Poor Ned! We were sorry for him. He was of some promise as a cricketer (by the way, Bill never went near the ground, which I always thought a bad sign); Ned would really have made a good cricketer, not a brilliant hitter, but an excellent stopper of the ball; one of your safe, steady players, whom there is no putting out. Nobody ever dreamt of his running away. We all knew that he was a little idle, and that he was a sort of follower of Bill's – But Ned to decamp! He must have gone out of pure imitation, just as geese waddle into a pond in single file, or as one sheep or pig will follow another through a gap in the hedge – sheer imitation! A notable example of the harm that one town-bred youth will work in a country village! Go he did, and back he is come, poor fellow! Thin as a herring, and ragged as a colt, a mere moral to tag a tale withal. He has not had a day's work since he left his good master, nor, to judge from his looks, a sufficient meal. His account of the other two worthies is just what I expected. Henry, after many ups and downs (during one of which he was within half an inch of being a soldier, that is to say, he *did* enlist, and wanted only that much of the standard), is now in a good place, and likely to do well. His *fidus Achates*, Bill, has disappeared from London as he did from the country. No one knows what has become of him. For my own part, I never looked for any good from a lad, who, to say nothing of his graver iniquities, kept away from the cricket ground, thrashed my flowers, and tried to thrash May.

The flourishing and well-accustomed Rose Inn has lost its comely mistress, a harmless, blameless, kindly-tempered woman, with a pleasant smile, and a gentle voice, who withered suddenly in the very strength and pride of womanhood, and died lamented by high and low. She is succeeded in the management of that respectable hostelry by two light-footed and light-hearted lasses of twelve and thirteen, who skip about after their good, bustling father with an officious civility that the guests find irresistible, and conduct the housekeeping with a frugality and forethought beyond their years.

The white house, with the limes in front, has also lost, though not by death, our good vicar and his charming family. They have taken possession of their own pretty dwelling; and their removal has given me an opportunity of becoming intimately acquainted with all the crooks and turnings, the gates, ponds, and pollards, of the vicarage lane; a walk which, on that event, I suddenly discovered to be one of the prettiest in the neighbourhood.

Ah! Here is Lizzy, half leaning, half riding, on the gate of her own court, looking very demure, and yet quite ripe for a frolic. Lizzy has in some measure outgrown her beauty; which desirable possession does very often run away from a young lady at six years old, and come back again at twelve. I think that such will be the case here. She is still a very nice little girl, quick, clever, active and useful; goes to school; cooks upon occasion her father's dinner; and is beyond all comparison the handiest little waiting woman in the parish. She is waiting now to speak to her playmate and companion, the wheelwright's daughter, who with all her mother's attentive politeness is running down the street with an umbrella and her clogs, to fence their lodger, Mrs Hay, from the ill effects of a summer shower. I think that we have had about a dozen drops of rain, and where they came from no mortal can guess, for there is not a cloud in the sky; but there goes little Mary with a grave civility, a curtsying earnestness, that would be quite amusing in so young a child, if the feeling that dictated the attention were not so good and so real, and the object so respectable.

Mrs Hay is a widow, a slight, delicate, elderly person, in a well-preserved black silk gown, a neat quiet bonnet never in fashion, nor ever wholly out, snow-white stockings, and a handsome grey shawl – her invariable walking-costume. She makes no visits; cultivates no acquaintance; and seldom leaves her neat quiet room, except to glide into church on a Sunday, and to take a short walk on some fine spring morning. No one knows precisely what Mrs Hay's station has been, but everybody feels that she is an object of interest and respect.

Now up the hill! past the white cottage of the little mason, whiter than ever, for it has just been beautified; past the darker but still prettier dwelling of the lieutenant, mantled with sweet-brier and honeysuckles, and fruit trees of all sorts; one turn to look at the landscape so glowingly bright and green, with its affluence of wood dappled with villages, and gentlemen's seats, the wide spreading town of B— lying in the distance with its spires and towers, the Thames and the Kennet, winding along their lines of light like glittering serpents, and the O— hills rising beyond; one glance at that glorious prospect, and here we are at the top of the hill, on the open common, where the air is so fresh and pure, and the sun shines so gaily on the golden furze.

Did I say that there were no alterations in our village? Could I so utterly forget the great doings on the top of the hill, where, by dint of whitening, and sash-windowing, and fresh-dooring, the old ample farmhouse has become a very genteel-looking residence? Or the cottage on the common opposite, or rather the two cottages, which have, by a similar transmogrification, been laid into one, and now form, with their new cart shed, their double garden, and their neat paling, so pretty and comfortable a home for the respectable mistress of the little village school and her industrious husband? How could I forget that cottage, whose inhabitants I see so often and like so well?

Mr Moore is the greatest market-gardener in the parish; and leads his donkey chaise through the street every summer afternoon, vending fruit and vegetables, and followed by a train of urchins of either sex. Some who walk boldly up to the cart, halfpenny customers, who ask questions and change their minds, balance between the merits of cherries and gooseberries, and gravely calculate under what form of fruit they may get most eating for their money.[1] These are the rich. Others, the shy, who stand aloof, are pennyless elves, silent petitioners, who wait about with longing looks, till some child-loving purchaser, or Mr Moore himself, unable to withstand those pleading eyes, flings them a dole, and gives them the double delight of the fruit and the scramble.

The dear cricket ground! Even at this hour there are boys loitering about that beloved scene of evening pastime, not quite playing, but idling and lounging, and looking as if they longed to play. My friend the little Hussar, with his blue jacket and his immoveable gravity, is the quietest of the party, and Ben Kirby, youngest brother of Joe, by far the noisiest. Joe no longer belongs to the boys' side, having been promoted to play with the men; and Ben has succeeded to his post as chief and leader of the youngsters. Joe is a sort of person to make himself happy anywhere, but I suspect that he has not at present gained much pleasure by the exchange. It is always a very equivocal advantage when a person is removed from the first place in one class, to the lowest in the rank just above; and in the present instance poor Joe seems to me to have gained little by his preferment, except the honour of being

[1] It is amusing to see how very early poor children become acquainted with the rate of exchange between the smaller denominations of coin and the commodities – such as cakes, nuts and gingerbread – which they purchase. No better judge of the currency question than a country brat of three years old. Lizzy, before she could speak plain, was so knowing in cakes and halfpence that it was a common amusement with the people at the shop where she dealt to try to cheat her, and watch her excessive anger when she detected the imposition. She was sure to find them out, and was never pacified till she had all that was due to her.

fag general to the whole party. His feelings must be something like those of a provincial actor transplanted to the London boards, who finds himself on the scene of his ambition indeed, but playing Richmond instead of Richard, Macduff instead of Macbeth. Joe, however, will doubtless work his way up, and in the meantime Ben fills his abdicated throne with eminent ability.

Jem Eusden, his quondam rival, is lost to the cricket ground altogether. He is gone forth to see the world. An uncle of his mother's, a broker by profession, resident in Shoe Lane, came into this neighbourhood to attend a great auction, and was so caught by Jem's scholarship that he carried him off to London and placed him with a hosier in Cheapside, where he is to this hour engaged in tying up gloves and stockings, and carrying out parcels. His grand-uncle describes him as much improved by the removal; and his own letters to Ben (for since they have been parted they are become great friends) confirm the assertion. He writes by every opportunity, full as often, I should think, as once a quarter; and his letters give by far the best accounts of the Lord Mayor's day, as well as of the dwarfs, giants, and other monsters on show in London, of any that arrive in these parts. He is critical on the Christmas pantomimes, descriptive on the panoramas, and his narrative on the death of the elephant (whose remains his good kinsman the broker took him to visit) was so pathetic that it made the whole village cry. All the common is in admiration of Jem's genius, always excepting his friend Ben Kirby, who laughs at everything, even his correspondent's letters, and hath been heard to insinuate that the most eloquent morceaux are 'bits out of newspapers'. Ben is a shrewd wag and a knowing; but in this instance I think that he is mistaken. I hold Jem's flights for original, and suspect that the young gentleman will turn out literary.

Walks in the Country
The Copse

APRIL 18th. Sad wintry weather; a north-east wind; a sun that puts out one's eyes, without affording the slightest warmth; dryness that chaps lips and hands like a frost in December; rain that comes chilling and arrowy like hail in January; nature at a dead pause; no seeds up in the garden; no leaves out in the hedgerows; no cowslips swinging their pretty bells in the fields; no nightingales in the dingles; no swallows skimming round the great pond; no cuckoos (that ever I should miss that rascally sonneteer) in any part! Nevertheless there is something of a charm in this wintery spring, this putting back of the seasons. If the flower-clock must stand still for a month or two, could it choose a better time than that of the primroses and violets? I never remember (and for such gauds my memory, if not very good for aught of wise or useful, may be trusted) such an affluence of the one or such a duration of the other. Primrosy is the epithet which this year will retain in my recollection. Hedge, ditch, meadow, field, even the very paths and highways, are set with them; but their chief *habitat* is a certain copse, about a mile off, where they are spread like a carpet, and where I go to visit them rather oftener than quite comports with the dignity of a lady of mature age. I am going thither this very afternoon, and May and her company are going too.

This Mayflower of mine is a strange animal. Instinct and imitation make in her an approach to reason which is sometimes almost startling. She mimics all that she sees us do, with the dexterity of a monkey, and far more of gravity and apparent purpose; cracks nuts and eats them; gathers currants and severs them from the stalk with the most delicate nicety; filches and munches apples and pears; is as dangerous in an orchard as a schoolboy; smells to flowers; smiles at meeting; answers in a pretty lively voice when spoken to (sad pity that the language should be unknown), and has greatly the advantage of us in a conversation, inasmuch as our meaning is certainly clear to her. All this, and a thousand amusing prettinesses (to say nothing of her canine feat of bringing her game straight to her master's feet, and refusing to resign it to any hand but his) does my beautiful greyhound perform untaught, by the mere effect of imitation and sagacity. Well, May, at the end of the coursing season, having lost Brush, our old spaniel, her great friend, and the blue greyhound Mariette, her comrade and rival, both of which fourfooted worthies were sent out to keep for the summer, began to find solitude a weary condition, and to look abroad for company. Now it so happened that the same suspension of sport, which had reduced our little establishment from three dogs to one, had also dispersed the splendid kennel of a celebrated courser in our neighbourhood, three of whose finest young dogs came home to 'their walk' (as the sporting phrase goes) at the collar-maker's in our village. May, accordingly, on the first morning of her solitude (she had never taken the slightest notice of her neighbours before, although they had sojourned in our street upwards of a fortnight), bethought herself of the timely resource offered to her by the vicinity of these canine *beaux*, and went up boldly and knocked at their stable door, which was already very commodiously on the half-latch. The three dogs came out with much alertness and gallantry, and May, declining apparently to enter their territories, brought them off to her own. This manœuvre has been repeated every day, with one variation; of the three dogs, the first a brindle, the second a yellow, and the third a black, the two first only are now admitted to walk or consort with her, and the last, poor fellow, for no fault that I can discover except May's caprice, is driven away not only by the fair lady, but even by his old companions – is, so to say, sent to Coventry. Of her two permitted followers, the yellow gentleman, Saladin by name, is decidedly the favourite. He is indeed, May's shadow, and will walk with me whether I choose or not. It is quite impossible to get rid of him

unless by discarding Miss May also; and to accomplish a walk in the country without her would be like an adventure of Don Quixote without his faithful 'squire Sancho.

So forth we set, May and I, and Saladin and the brindle: May and myself walking with the sedateness and decorum befitting our sex and age (she is five years old this grass, rising six); the young things, for the soldan and the brindle are (not meaning any disrespect) little better than puppies, frisking and frolicking as best pleased them.

Our route lay for the first part along the sheltered quiet lanes which lead to our old habitation; a way never trodden by me without peculiar and home-like feelings; full of the recollections, the pains and pleasures of other days. But we are not to talk sentiment now – even May would not understand that maudlin language. We must get on. What a wintry hedgerow this is for the eighteenth of April! Primrosy to be sure, abundantly spangled with those stars of the earth – but so bare, so leafless, so cold! The wind whistles through the brown boughs as in winter. Even the early elder shoots, which do make an approach to springiness, look brown, and the small leaves of the woodbine, which have also ventured to peep forth, are of a sad purple, frost-bitten, like a dairy-maid's elbows on a snowy morning. The very birds, in this season of pairing and building, look chilly and uncomfortable, and their nests! 'Oh Saladin! Come away from the hedge! Don't you see that what puzzles you and makes you leap up in the air is a redbreast's nest? Don't you see the pretty speckled eggs? Don't you hear the poor hen calling as it were for help? Come here this moment, sir!' And by good luck Saladin (who for a paynim has tolerable qualities) comes, before he has touched the nest, or before his playmate the brindle, the less manageable of the two, has espied it.

Now we go round the corner and cross the bridge, where the common, with its clear stream winding between clumps of elms, assumes so park-like an appearance. Who is this approaching so slowly and majestically, this square bundle of petticoat and cloak, this road-waggon of a woman! It is, it must be Mrs Sally Mearing, the completest specimen within my knowledge of farmeresses (may I be allowed that innovation in language?) as they were. It can be nobody else.

Mrs Sally Mearing, when I first became acquainted with her, occupied, together with her father (a superannuated man of ninety), a large farm very near our former habitation. It had been anciently a great manor-farm or court-house, and was still a stately substantial building, whose lofty halls and spacious chambers gave an air of grandeur to the common offices to which they were applied. Traces of gilding might yet be seen on the panels which covered the walls, and on the huge carved chimney-pieces which rose almost to the ceilings; and the marble tables and the inlaid oak staircase still spoke of the former grandeur of the court. Mrs Sally corresponded well with the date of her mansion, although she troubled herself little with its dignity. She was thoroughly of the old school, and had a most comfortable contempt for the new: rose at four in winter and summer, breakfasted at six, dined at eleven in the forenoon, supped at five, and was regularly in bed before eight, except when the hay-time or the harvest imperiously required her to sit up till sunset – a necessity to which she submitted with no very good grace. To a deviation from these hours, and to the modern iniquities of white aprons, cotton stockings and muslin handkerchiefs (Mrs Sally herself always wore check, black worsted, and a sort of yellow compound which she was wont to call *susy*), together with the invention of drill plough and thrashing machines, and other agricultural novelties, she failed not to attribute all the mishaps or misdoings of the whole parish. The last-mentioned discovery especially aroused her indignation. Oh! to hear her descant on the merits of the flail, wielded by a stout right arm, such as she had known in her youth (for by her account there was as great a deterioration in bones and sinews as in the other implements of husbandry), was enough to make the very inventor break his machine. She would even take up her favourite instrument, and thrash the air herself, by way of illustrating her argument, and, to say truth, few men in these degenerate days could have matched the stout, brawny, muscular limb which Mrs Sally displayed at sixty-five.

In spite of this contumacious rejection of agricultural improvements, the world went well with her at Court Farm. A good landlord, an easy rent, incessant labour, unremitting frugality and excellent times ensured a regular, though moderate, profit; and she lived on, grumbling and prospering, flourishing and complaining, till two misfortunes befell her at once – her father died, and her lease expired. The loss of her father, although a bedridden man, turned of ninety, who could not in the course of nature have been expected to live long, was a terrible shock to a daughter, who was not so much younger as to be without fears for her own life, and who had beside been so used to nursing the good old man, and looking to his little comforts, that she missed him as a mother would miss an ailing child. The expiration of the lease was a grievance and a puzzle of a different nature. Her landlord would have willingly retained his excellent tenant, but not on the terms on which she then held the land, which had not varied for fifty years; so that poor Mrs Sally had the misfortune to find rent rising and prices sinking both at the same moment – a terrible solecism in political economy. Even this, however, I believe she would have endured rather than have quitted the house where she was born, and to which all her ways and notions were adapted, had not a priggish steward, as much addicted to improvement and reform as she was to precedent and established usages, insisted on binding her by lease to spread a certain number of loads of chalk on every field. This tremendous innovation, for never had that novelty in manure whitened the crofts and pightles of Court Farm, decided her at once. She threw the proposals into the fire, and left the place in a week.

Her choice of a habitation occasioned some wonder, and much amusement in our village world. To be sure, upon the verge of seventy, an old maid may be permitted to dispense with the more rigid punctilio of her class, but Mrs Sally had always been so tenacious on the score of character, so very a prude, so determined an avoider of the 'men folk' (as she was wont contemptuously to call them), that we all were conscious of something like astonishment on finding that she and her little handmaid had taken up their abode in one end of a spacious farmhouse belonging to the bluff old bachelor, George Robinson, of the Lea. Now farmer Robinson was quite as notorious for his aversion to petticoated things as Mrs Sally for her hatred to the unfeathered bipeds who wear doublet and hose, so that there was a little astonishment in that quarter too, and plenty of jests, which the honest farmer speedily silenced by telling all who joked on the subject that he had given his lodger fair warning that, let people say what they would, he was quite determined not to marry her; so that if she had any views that way, it would be better for her to go elsewhere. This declaration, which must be admitted to have been more remarkable for frankness than civility, made, however, no ill impression on Mrs Sally. To the farmer's she went, and at his house she lives still, with her little maid, her tabby cat, a decrepit sheepdog, and much of the lumber of Court Farm, which she could not find in her heart to part from. There she follows her old ways and her old hours, untempted by matrimony, and unassailed (as far as I hear) by love or by scandal, with no other grievance than an occasional dearth of employment for herself and her young lass (even pewter dishes do not always want scouring), and now and then a twinge of the rheumatism.

Here she is, that good relique of the olden time, for, in spite of her whims and prejudices, a better and a kinder woman never lived – here she is, with the hood of her red cloak pulled over her close black bonnet, of that silk which once (it may be presumed) was fashionable, since it is still called mode, and her whole stout figure huddled up in a miscellaneous and most substantial covering of thick petticoats, gowns, aprons, shawls and cloaks, a weight which it requires the strength of a thrasher to walk under – here she is, with her square honest visage, and her loud frank voice. And we hold a pleasant disjointed chat of rheumatisms and early chickens, bad weather and hats with feathers in them – the last exceedingly sore subject being introduced by poor Jane Davis (a cousin of Mrs Sally), who, passing us in a beaver bonnet on her road from school, stopped to drop her little curtsy, and was soundly scolded for her civility. Jane, who is a gentle, humble, smiling lass, about twelve years old, receives so many rebukes from her worthy relative, and bears them so meekly, that I should not wonder if they were to be followed by a legacy: I sincerely wish they may. Well, at last we said goodbye; when, on inquiring my destination, and hearing that I was bent to the ten-acre copse (part of the farm which she ruled so long), she stopped me to tell a dismal story of the two sheep-stealers who sixty years ago were found hidden in that copse, and only taken after great difficulty and resistance, and the maiming of a peace officer. 'Pray don't go there, Miss! For mercy's sake don't be so venturesome? Think if they should kill you!' were the last words of Mrs Sally.

Many thanks for her care and kindness! But, without being at all foolhardy in general, I have no great fear of the sheep-stealers of sixty years ago. Even if they escaped hanging for that exploit, I should greatly doubt their being in case to attempt another. So on we go: down the short shady lane, and out on the pretty retired green, shut in by fields and hedgerows, which we must cross to reach the copse. How lively this green nook is today, half covered with cows and horses and sheep! And how glad these frolicsome greyhounds are to exchange the hard gravel of the high road for this pleasant short turf, which seems made for their gambols! How beautifully they are at play, chasing each other round and round in lessening circles, darting off at all kinds of angles, crossing and recrossing May, and trying to win her sedateness into a game at romps, turning round on each other with gay defiance, pursuing the cows and the colts, leaping up as if to catch the crows in their flight; all in their harmless and innocent . . . 'Ah wretches! villains! rascals! four-footed mischiefs! canine plagues! Saladin! Brindle!' They are after the sheep – 'Saladin, I say!' They have actually singled out that pretty spotted lamb – 'Brutes, if I catch you! Saladin, Brindle!' We shall be taken up for sheep-stealing presently ourselves. They have chased the poor little lamb into a ditch and are mounting guard over it, standing at bay. 'Ah wretches, I have you now! For shame, Saladin! Get away, Brindle! See how good May is. Off with you, brutes! For shame! For shame!' And brandishing a handkerchief, which could hardly be an efficient instrument of correction, I succeeded in driving away the two puppies, who after all meant nothing more than play, although it was somewhat rough, and rather too much in the style of the old fable of the boys and the frogs. May is gone after them, perhaps to scold them; for she has been as grave as a judge during the whole proceeding, keeping ostentatiously close to me, and taking no part whatever in the mischief.

The poor little pretty lamb! Here it lies on the bank quite motionless, frightened I believe to death, for certainly those villains never touched it. It does not stir. Does it breathe? Oh yes, it does! It is alive, safe enough. Look, it opens its eyes, and, finding the coast clear and its enemies far away, it springs up in a moment and gallops to its dam, who has stood bleating the whole time at a most respectful distance. Who would suspect a lamb of so much simple cunning? I really thought the pretty thing was dead – and now how glad the ewe is to recover her curling, spotted little one! How fluttered they look! Well! This adventure has flurried me too; between fright and running, I warrant you my heart beats as fast as the lamb's.

Ah! here is the shameless villain Saladin, the cause of the commotion, thrusting his slender nose into my hand to beg pardon and make up! 'Oh wickedest of soldans! Most iniquitous pagan! Soul of a Turk!' But there is no resisting the good-humoured creature's penitence. I must pat him.'There! there! Now we will go to the copse, I am sure we shall find no worse malefactors than ourselves – shall we, May? And the sooner we get out of sight of the sheep the better; for Brindle seems meditating another attack. *Allons, messieurs*, over this gate, across this meadow, and here is the copse.'

How boldly that superb ash tree with its fine silver bark rises from the bank, and what a fine entrance it makes with the holly beside it, which also deserves to be called a tree! But here we are in the copse. Ah! only one half of the underwood was cut last year, and the other is at its full growth: hazel, brier, woodbine, bramble, forming one impenetrable thicket, and almost uniting with the lower branches of the elms, and oaks, and beeches, which rise at regular distances overhead. No foot can penetrate that dense and thorny entanglement; but there is a walk all round by the side of the wide sloping bank, walk and bank and copse carpeted with primroses, whose fresh and balmy odour impregnates the very air. Oh how exquisitely beautiful! And it is not the primroses only, those gems of flowers, but the natural mosaic of which they form a part: that network of ground-ivy, with its lilac blossoms and the subdued tint of its purplish leaves, those rich mosses, those enamelled wild hyacinths, those spotted arums, and above all those wreaths of ivy, linking all those flowers together with chains of leaves more beautiful than blossoms, whose white veins seem swelling amidst the deep green or splendid brown – it is the whole earth that is so beautiful! Never surely were primroses so richly set, and never did primroses better deserve such a setting. There they are of their own lovely yellow, the hue to which they have given a name, the exact tint of the butterfly that overhangs them (the first I have seen this year! can spring really be coming at last?) – sprinkled here and there with tufts of a reddish purple, and others of the purest white, as some accident of soil affects that strange and inscrutable operation of nature, the colouring of flowers. Oh how fragrant they are, and how pleasant it is to sit in this sheltered copse, listening to the fine creaking of the wind amongst the branches, the most unearthly of sounds, with this gay tapestry under our feet, and the wood-pigeons flitting from tree to tree, and mixing the deep note of love with the elemental music.

Yes! spring is coming. Wood-pigeons, butterflies and sweet flowers all give token of the sweetest of the seasons. Spring is coming. The hazel stalks are swelling and putting forth their pale tassels; the satin palms with their honeyed odours are out on the willow, and the last lingering winter berries are dropping from the hawthorn, and making way for the bright and blossomy leaves.

The Touchy Lady

ONE of the most unhappy persons whom it has been my fortune to encounter is a pretty woman of thirty, or thereabout, healthy, wealthy and of good repute, with a fine house, a fine family and an excellent husband. A solitary calamity renders all these blessings of no avail – the gentlewoman is touchy. This affliction has given a colour to her whole life. Her biography has a certain martial dignity, like the history of a nation; she dates from battle to battle, and passes her days in an interminable civil war.

The first person who, long before she could speak, had the misfortune to offend the young lady was her nurse; then in quick succession four nursery maids, who were turned away, poor things! because Miss Anne could not abide them; then her brother Harry, by being born, and diminishing her importance; then three governesses; then two writing-masters; then one music-mistress; then a whole school. On leaving school, affronts multiplied of course; and she has been in a constant miff with servants, tradespeople, relations and friends ever since; so that although really pretty (at least she would be so if it were not for a standing frown and a certain watchful defying look in her eyes), decidedly clever and accomplished and particularly charitable, as far as giving money goes (your ill-tempered woman has often that redeeming grace), she is known only by her one absorbing quality of touchiness, and is dreaded and hated accordingly by everyone who has the honour of her acquaintance.

Paying her a visit is one of the most formidable things that can be imagined, one of the trials which in a small way demand the greatest resolution. It is so difficult to find what to say. You must make up your mind to the affair as you do when going into a shower bath. Differing from her is obviously pulling the string; and agreeing with her too often or too pointedly is nearly as bad; she then suspects you of suspecting her infirmity, of which she has herself a glimmering consciousness, and treats you with a sharp touch of it accordingly. But what is there that she will not suspect? Admire the colours of a new carpet, and she thinks you are looking at some invisible hole; praise the pattern of a morning cap, and she accuses you of thinking it too gay. She has an ingenuity of perverseness which brings all subjects nearly to a level. The mention of her neighbours is evidently *taboo*, since it is at least twenty to one but she is in a state of affront with nine-tenths of them; her own family are also *taboo* for the same reason. Books are particularly unsafe. She stands vibrating on the pinnacle where two fears meet, ready to be suspected of blue-stockingism on the one hand, or of ignorance and frivolity on the other, just as the work you may chance to name happens to be recondite or popular; nay, sometimes the same production shall excite both feelings. 'Have you read Hajji Baba,' said I to her one day last winter, 'Hajji Baba the Persian?' 'Really, Ma'am, I am no orientalist.' 'Hajji Baba the clever Persian tale?' continued I, determined not to be daunted. 'I believe, Miss M.,' rejoined she, 'that you think I have nothing better to do than to read novels.' And so she snip-snaps to the end of the visit. Even the Scotch novels, which she does own to reading, are no resource in her desperate case. There we are shipwrecked on the rocks of taste. A difference there is fatal. She takes to those delicious books as personal property, and spreads over them the prickly shield of her protection in the same spirit with which she appropriates her husband and her children; is huffy if you prefer Guy Mannering to the Antiquary, and quite jealous if you presume to praise Jeanie Deans; thus cutting off his Majesty's lieges from the most approved topic of discussion among civilized people, a neutral ground as open and various as the weather, and far more delight-ful. But what did I say? The very weather is with her no prudent word. She pretends to skill in that science of guesses commonly called weather-wisdom, and a fog, or a shower, or a thunder-storm, or the blessed sun himself, may have been rash enough to contradict her bodements and put her out of humour for the day.

Her own name has all her life long been a fertile source of misery to this unfortunate lady. Her maiden name was Smythe, Anne Smythe. Now Smythe, although perfectly genteel and unexceptionable to look at, a pattern appellation on paper, was, in speaking, no way distinguished from the thousands of common Smiths who cumber the world. She never heard that 'word of fear', especially when introduced to a new acquaintance, without looking as if she longed to spell it. Anne was bad enough; people had housemaids of that name, as if to make a confusion; and her grandmamma insisted on omitting the final *e*, in which important vowel was seated all it could boast of elegance or dignity; and once a brother of fifteen, the identical brother Harry, an Etonian, a pickle, one of that order of clever boys who seem born for the torment of their female relatives, 'foredoomed their *sister's* soul to cross', actually went so far as to call her Nancy! She did not box his ears, although how near her tingling fingers' ends approached to that consummation it is not my business to tell. Having suffered so much from the perplexity of her equivocal maiden name, she thought herself most lucky in pitching on the thoroughly well-looking and well-sounding appellation of Morley for the rest of her life. Mrs Morley – nothing could be better. For once there was a word that did not affront her. The first alloy to this satisfaction was her perceiving on the bridal cards, Mr and Mrs B. Morley, and hearing that close to their future residence lived a rich bachelor uncle, till whose death that fearful diminution of her consequence, the Mrs B. must be endured. Mrs B.! The brow began to wrinkle – but it was the night before the wedding, the uncle had made some compensation for the crime of being born thirty years before his nephew in the shape of a superb set of emeralds and, by a fortunate mistake, she had taken it into her head that B., in the present case, stood for Basil, so that the loss of dignity being compensated by an increase of elegance, she bore the shock pretty well. It was not till the next morning during the ceremony that the full extent of her misery burst upon her, and she found that B. stood not for Basil, but for Benjamin. Then the veil fell off; then the full horror of her situation, the affront of being a Mrs Benjamin, stared her full in the face; and certainly but for the accident of her being struck dumb by indignation, she never would have married a man so ignobly christened. Her fate has been even worse than then appeared probable; for her husband, an exceedingly popular and convivial person, was known all over his own county by the familiar diminutive of his ill-omened appellation; so that she found herself not merely a Mrs Benjamin, but a Mrs Ben, the wife of a Ben Morley, Junior, Esq. (for the peccant uncle was also godfather and namesake), the future mother of a Ben Morley the third. Oh, the Miss Smith, the Ann, even the Nancy, shrunk into nothing when compared with that short word.

Neither is she altogether free from misfortunes on her side of the house. There is a terrible *mésalliance* in her own family. Her favourite aunt, the widow of an officer with five portionless children, became one fair morning the wife of a rich mercer in Cheapside, thus at a stroke gaining comfort and losing caste. The manner in which this affected poor Mrs Ben Morley is inconceivable. She talked of the unhappy connexion, as aunts are wont to talk when nieces get paired at Gretna Green, wrote a formal renunciation of the culprit, and has considered herself insulted ever since if any one mentions a silk gown in her presence. Another affliction, brought on her by her own family, is the production of a farce by her brother Harry (born for her plague) at Covent Garden Theatre. The farce was damned, as the author (a clever young Templar) declares most deservedly. He bore the catastrophe with great heroism; and celebrated its downfall by venting sundry good puns and drinking an extra bottle of claret; leaving to Anne, sister Anne, the pleasant employment of fuming over his discomfiture – a task which she performed *con amore*. Actors, manager, audience and author, seventeen newspapers and three magazines had the misfortune to displease her on this occasion; in short the whole town. Theatres and newspapers, critics and the drama have been banished from her conversation ever since. She would as lieve talk of a silk-mercer.

Next after her visitors, her correspondents are to be pitied; they had need look to their Ps and Qs, their spelling and their station-ery. If you write a note to her, be sure that the paper is the best double post, hot-pressed and gilt-edged; that your pen is in good order; that your 'dear Madams' have a proper mixture of regard and respect; and that your folding and sealings are unexception-able. She is of a sort to faint at the absence of an envelope, and to die of a wafer. Note, above all, that your address be perfect; that your *to* be not forgotten; that the offending *Benjamin* be omitted; and that the style and title of her mansion, SHAWFORD MANOR HOUSE, be set forth in full glory. And, when this is achieved, make up your mind to her taking some inexplicable affront after all. Thrice fortunate would he be who could put twenty words together without affronting her. Besides, she is great at a scornful reply, and shall keep up a quarrelling correspondence with any lady in Great Britain. Her letters are like challenges; and, but for the protection of the petticoat, she would have fought fifty duels, and have been either killed or quieted long ago.

If her husband had been of her temper, she would have brought him into twenty scrapes, but he is as unlike her as possible: a good-humoured, rattling creature, with a perpetual festivity of temper and a propensity to motion and laughter, and all sorts of merry mischief, like a schoolboy in the holidays, which felicitous personage he resembles bodily in his round, ruddy, handsome face, his dancing black eyes, curling hair, and light, active figure, the youngest man that ever saw forty. His pursuits have the same happy juvenility. In the summer he fishes and plays cricket; in the winter he hunts and courses; and what with grouse and par-tridges, pheasants and woodcocks, wood-pigeons and flappers, he contrives pretty tolerably to shoot all the year round. Moreover, he attends revels, races, assizes and quarter-sessions; drives stage-coaches, patronizes plays, is steward to concerts, goes to every dance within forty miles, and talks of standing for the county; so that he has no time to quarrel with his wife or for her, and affronts her twenty times an hour simply by giving her her own way.

To the popularity of this universal favourite, for the restless sociability of his temper is invaluable in a dull country neighbour-hood, his wife certainly owes the toleration which bids fair to render her incorrigible. She is fast approaching to the melancholy condition of a privileged person, one put out of the pale of civilized society. People have left off being angry with her, and begin to shrug up their shoulders, and say it is her way, a species of placability which only provokes her the more. For my part, I have too great a desire to obtain her good opinion to think of treating her in so shabby a manner; and as it is morally certain that we shall never be friends whilst we visit, I intend to try the effect of non-intercourse, and to break with her outright. If she reads this article, which is very likely, for she is addicted to new publications, and thinks herself injured if a book be put into her hands with the leaves cut — if she reads only half a page she will inevitably have done with me for ever. If not, there can hardly be any lack of a sufficient quarrel in her company; and then, when we have ceased to speak or to curtsy, and fairly sent each other to Coventry, there can be no reason why we should not be on as civil terms as if the one lived at Calcutta, and the other at New York.

Walks in the Country
The Wood

APRIL 20th. Spring is actually come now, with the fulness and almost the suddenness of a northern summer. Today is completely April — clouds and sunshine, wind and showers; blossoms on the trees, grass in the fields, swallows by the pond, snakes in the hedgerows, nightingales in the thickets, and cuckoos everywhere. My young friend Ellen G. is going with me this evening to gather wood-sorrel. She never saw that most elegant plant, and is so delicate an artist that the introduction will be a mutual benefit; Ellen will gain a subject worthy of her pencil, and the pretty weed will live — no small favour to a flower almost as transitory as the gum cistus — duration is the only charm which it wants, and that Ellen will give it. The weather is, to be sure, a little threatening, but we are not people to mind the weather when we have an object in view. We shall certainly go in quest of the wood-sorrel, and will take May, provided we can escape May's followers; for, since the adventure of the lamb, Saladin has had an affair with a gander, furious in defence of his goslings, in which rencontre the gander came off conqueror; and as geese abound in the wood to which we are going (called by the country people the Pinge), and the victory may not always incline to the right side, I should be very sorry to lead the Soldan to fight his battles over again. We will take nobody but May.

So saying, we proceeded on our way through winding lanes, between hedgerows tenderly green, till we reached the hatch-gate, with the white cottage beside it, embosomed in fruit trees, which forms the entrance to the Pinge, and in a moment the whole scene was before our eyes.

'Is not this beautiful, Ellen?' The answer could hardly be other than a glowing, rapid 'Yes!' A wood is generally a very pretty place; but this wood – Imagine a smaller forest, full of glades and sheep-walks, surrounded by irregular cottages with their bloom-ing orchards, a clear stream winding about the brakes and a road intersecting it, and giving life and light to the picture; and you will have a faint idea of the Pinge. Every step was opening a new point of view, a fresh combination of glade, and path, and thicket. The accessories too were changing every moment. Ducks, geese, pigs and children, giving way, as we advanced into the wood, to sheep and forest ponies; and they again disappearing as we became more entangled in its mazes, till we heard nothing but the song of the nightingale, and saw only the silent flowers.

What a piece of fairyland! The tall elms overhead just bursting into tender, vivid leaf, with here and there a hoary oak or a silver-barked beech; every twig swelling with the brown buds, and yet not quite stripped of the tawny foliage of autumn; tall hollies and hawthorn beneath, with their crisp, brilliant leaves mixed with the white blossoms of the sloe, and woven together with garlands of woodbines and wild-briers – what a fairyland!

Primroses, cowslips, pansies and the regular open-eyed white blossom of the wood anemone (or to use the more elegant Hampshire name, the windflower) were set under our feet as thick as daisies in a meadow; but the pretty weed that we came to seek was coyer and Ellen began to fear that we had mistaken the place or the season. At last she had herself the pleasure of finding it under a brake of holly: 'Oh look! look! I am sure that this is the wood-sorrel! Look at the pendant white flower, shaped like a snowdrop and veined with purple streaks, and the beautiful trefoil leaves folded like a heart – some, the young ones, so vividly, yet tenderly green that the foliage of the elm and the hawthorn would show dully at their side; others of a deeper tint and lined, as it were, with a rich and changeful purple! Don't you see them?' pursued my dear young friend, who is a delightful piece of life and sunshine, and was half-inclined to scold me for the calmness with which, amused by her enthusiasm, I stood listening to her ardent exclamations. 'Don't you see them? Oh how beautiful! And in what quantity! What profusion! See how the dark shade of the holly sets off the light and delicate colouring of the flower! And see that other bed of them springing from the rich moss in the roots of that old beech tree! Pray let us gather some. Here are baskets.' So, quickly and carefully we began gathering, leaves, blossoms, roots and all, for the plant is so fragile that it will not brook separation; quickly and carefully we gathered, encountering divers petty misfortunes in spite of all our care, now caught by the veil in a holly bush, now hitching our shawls in a bramble, still gathering on, in spite of scratched fingers, till we had nearly filled our baskets and began to talk of our departure.

'But where is May? May! May! No going home without her. May! Here she comes galloping, the beauty!' (Ellen is almost as fond of May as I am.) 'What has she got in her mouth? That rough, round, brown substance which she touches so tenderly? What can it be? A bird's nest? Naughty May?'

'No! As I live, a hedgehog! Look, Ellen, how it has coiled itself into a thorny ball! Off with it, May! Don't bring it to me!' And May, somewhat reluctant to part with her prickly prize, however troublesome of carriage, whose change of shape seemed to me to have puzzled her sagacity more than any event I ever witnessed, for in general she has perfectly the air of understanding all that is going forward – May at last dropped the hedgehog; continuing, however, to pat it with her delicate cat-like paw, cautiously and daintily applied, and caught back suddenly and rapidly after every touch, as if her poor captive had been a red-hot coal. Finding that these pats entirely failed in solving the riddle (for the hedgehog shammed dead, like the lamb the other day, and appeared entirely motionless), she gave him so spirited a nudge with her pretty black nose that she not only turned him over, but sent him rolling some little way along the turfy path – an operation which that sagacious quadruped endured with the most perfect passiveness, the most admirable non-resistance. No wonder that May's discernment was at fault. I, myself, if I had not been aware of the trick, should have said that the ugly rough thing which she was trundling along, like a bowl or a cricket-ball, was an inanimate substance, some-thing devoid of sensation and of will. At last my poor pet, thoroughly perplexed and tired out, fairly relinquished the contest, and came slowly away, turning back once or twice to look at the object of her curiosity, as if half inclined to return and try the event of another shove. The sudden flight of a wood-pigeon effectually diverted her attention; and Ellen amused herself by fancying how the hedgehog was scuttling away, till our notice was also attracted by a very different object.

We had nearly threaded the wood and were approaching an open grove of magnificent oaks on the other side when sounds, other than of nightingales, burst on our ear, the deep and frequent strokes of the woodman's axe; and emerging from the Pinge we discovered the havoc which that axe had committed. Above twenty of the finest trees lay stretched on the velvet turf. There they lay in every shape and form of devastation: some, bare trunks stripped ready for the timber carriage, with the bark built up in long piles at the side; some with the spoilers busy about them, stripping, hacking, hewing; others with their noble branches, their brown and fragrant shoots all fresh as if they were alive – majestic corpses, the slain of today! The grove was like a field of battle. The young lads who were stripping the bark, the very children who were picking up the chips seemed awed and silent, as if conscience that death was around them. The nightingales sang faintly and interruptedly – a few low frightened notes like a requiem.

Ah! Here we are at the very scene of murder, the very tree that they are felling; they have just hewn round the trunk with those slaughtering axes, and are about to saw it asunder. After all it is a fine and thrilling operation, as the work of death usually is. Into how grand an attitude was that young man thrown as he gave the final strokes round the root; and how wonderful is the effect of that supple and apparently powerless saw, bending like a riband, and yet overmastering that giant of the woods, conquering and overthrowing that thing of life! Now it has passed half through the trunk, and the woodman has begun to calculate which way the tree will fall; he drives a wedge to direct its course – now a few more movements of the noiseless saw; and then a larger wedge. See how the branches tremble! Hark how the trunk begins to crack! Another stroke of the huge hammer on the wedge, and the tree quivers, as with a mortal agony, shakes, reels, and falls. How slow, and solemn, and awful it is! How like to death, to human death in its grandest form! Cæsar in the Capitol, Seneca in the bath, could not fall more sublimely than that oak.

Even the Heavens seem to sympathize with the devastation. The clouds have gathered into one thick, low canopy, dark and vapoury as the smoke which overhangs London; the setting sun is just gleaming underneath with a dim and bloody glare, and the crimson rays spreading upward with a lurid and portentous grandeur, a subdued and dusky glow, like the light reflected on the sky from some vast conflagration. The deep flush fades away, and the rain begins to descend; and we hurry homeward rapidly, yet sadly, forgetful alike of the flowers, the hedgehog, and the wetting, thinking and talking only of the fallen tree.

A Visit to Lucy

LUCY, who in her single state bore so striking a resemblance to Jenny Dennison in the number and variety of her lovers, continues to imitate that illustrious original in her married life, by her dexterous and excellent management, of which I have been lately an amused and admiring witness. Not having seen her for a long time, tempted by the fineness of the day, the first day of summer, and by the pleasure of carrying to her a little housewifely present from her sometime mistress, we resolved to take a substantial luncheon at two o'clock, and drive over to drink tea with her at five, such being, as we well knew, the fashionable visiting hour at S—.

The day was one glow of sunshine, and the road wound through a beautiful mixture of hill, and dale, and rich woodland, clothed in the brightest foliage, and thickly studded with gentlemen's seats, and prettier cottages, their gardens gay with the blossoms of the plum and the cherry, tossing their snowy garlands across the deep blue sky. So we journeyed on through pleasant villages and shady lanes till we emerged into the opener and totally different scenery of M— Common; a wild district, always picturesque and romantic, but not peculiarly brilliant, and glowing with the luxuriant orange flowers of the furze in its height of bloom, stretching around us like a sea of gold, and loading the very air with its rich almond odour. Who would have believed that this brown, barren, shaggy heath could have assumed such splendour, such majesty? The farther we proceeded, the more beautiful it appeared, the more gorgeous, the more brilliant. Whether climbing up the steep bank, and mixing with the thick plantation of dark firs; or chequered with brown heath and green turf on the open plain, where the sheep and lambs were straying; or circling round the pool covered with its bright white flowers; or edging the dark morass inlaid with the silky tufts of the cotton grass; or creeping down the deep dell where the alders grow; or mixing by the roadside with the shining and varied bark, now white, now purplish, and the light tremulous leaves of the feathery birch tree – in every form or variety this furze was beauty itself. We almost lamented to leave it, as we wound down the steep hill of M— West End, that most picturesque village, with its long open sheds for broom and faggot-making; its little country inn, the Red Lion; its pretty school just in the bottom, where the clear stream comes bubbling over the road, and the romantic foot-bridge is flung across; and with cottages straggling up the hill on the opposite ascent, orchards backed by meadows, and the light wreaths of smoke sailing along the green hillside, the road winding amidst all, beside another streamlet, whose deep, rust-coloured scum gives token of a chalybeate spring.

Even this sweet and favourite scene, which, when I would think of the perfection of village landscape, of a spot to live and die in, rises unbidden before my eyes, this dear and cherished picture, which I generally leave so reluctantly, was hurried over now, so glad were we to emerge once more from its colder colouring into the full glory of the waving furze on S— common, brighter even than that of M— which we left behind us. Even Lucy's house was unheeded till we drove up to the door, and found, to our great satisfaction, that she was at home.

The three years that have elapsed since her marriage have changed the style of her beauty. She is grown very fat, and rather coarse; and having moreover taken to loud speaking (as I apprehend a village schoolmistress must do in pure self-defence, that her voice may be heard in the *mêlée*), our airy sparkling soubrette, although still handsome, has been transmuted somewhat suddenly into a bustling merry country dame, looking her full age, if not a little older. It is such a transition as a rosebud experiences when turned into a rose, such as might befal the pretty coquette mistress Anne Page when she wedded master Fenton, and became one of the merry wives of Windsor. Lucy, however, in her dark gown and plain cap (for her dress hath undergone as much alteration as her person), her smiles and her rosiness, is still as fair a specimen of country comeliness as heart can desire.

We found her very busy, superintending the operations of a certain she-tailor, a lame woman, famous for buttonholes, who travels from house to house in that primitive district, making and repairing men's gear, and who was at that moment endeavouring to extract a smart waistcoat for our friend the schoolmaster out of a remnant of calico and blemished waistcoat-piece, which had been purchased at half-price for his behoof by his frugal helpmate. The more material parts of the cutting-out had been effected before my arrival, considerably at the expense of the worthy pedagogue's comfort, although to the probable improvement of his shape; for certainly the new fabric promised to be at least an inch smaller than the pattern. That point, however, had been by dint of great ingenuity satisfactorily adjusted, and I found the lady of the shears and the lady of the rod in the midst of a dispute on the question of buttons, which the tailoress insisted must be composed of metal or mother of pearl, or anything but covered moulds, inasmuch as there would be no stuff left to cover them; whilst Lucy on her side insisted that there was plenty, that anything (as all the world knew) would suffice to cover buttons if people were clever and careful, and that certain most diminutive and irregular scraps, which she gathered from the table and under it, and displayed with great ostentation, were amply sufficient for the purpose. 'If the pieces are not big enough,' continued she, 'you have nothing to do but to join them.' And as Lucy had greatly the advantage both in loudness of voice and fluency of thought and word over the itinerant sempstress, who was a woman of slow quiet speech, she carried her point in the argument most triumphantly, although whether the unlucky waistcoat-maker will succeed in stretching her materials so as to do the impossible remains to be proved, the button question being still undecided when I left S—.

Her adversary being fairly silenced, Lucy laid aside her careful thoughts and busy looks; and leaving the poor woman to her sewing and stitching, and a little tidy lass (a sort of half-boarder, who acts half as servant, half as pupil) to get all things ready for tea, she prepared to accompany me to a pleasant coppice in the neighbourhood, famous for wild lilies of the valley, to the love of which delicate flower, she, not perhaps quite unjustly, partly attributed my visit.

Nothing could be more beautiful than the wood where they are found, which we reached by crossing first the open common, with its golden waves of furze, and then a clover field intensely green, deliciously fresh and cool to the eye and the tread. The copse was just in its pleasantest state, having luckily been cut last year, and being too thinly clothed with timber to obstruct the view. It goes sloping down a hill, till it is lost in the green depths of P— Forest, with an abruptness of descent that resembles a series of terraces or rather ledges, so narrow that it is sometimes difficult to find a space on which to walk. The footing is the more precarious, as even the broader paths are intersected and broken by hollows and caves, where the ground has given way and been undermined by fox earths. On the steepest and highest of these banks, in a very dry unsheltered situation, the lily of the valley grows so profusely that the plants almost cover the ground with their beautiful broad leaves, and the snowy white bells, which envelope the most delicate of odours. All around grow the fragile wind-flowers, pink as well as white; the coral blossoms of the whortleberry; the graceful wood-sorrel; the pendent drops of the stately Solomon's seal, which hang like waxen tassels under the full and regular leaves; the bright wood-vetch; the unobtrusive woodruff, whose scent is like new hay, and which retains and communicates it when dried; and lastly, those strange freaks of nature the orchises, where the portrait of an insect is so quaintly depicted in a flower. The bee orchis abounds also in the Mapledurham woods – those woods where whilome flourished the two stately but unlovely flowers Martha and Teresa Blount of *Popish* fame, and which are still in the possession of their family. But, although it is found at Mapledurham as well as in these copses of north Hampshire, yet, in the little slip of Berks which divides Hants from Oxfordshire, I have never been able to discover it.

The locality of flowers is a curious puzzle. The field tulip, for instance, through whose superb pendent blossoms chequered with puce and lilac the sun shines as gloriously as through stained glass, and which, blended with a still more elegant white variety covers whole acres of the Kennet meadows, can by no process be coaxed into another habitation, however apparently similar in situation and soil. Treat them as you may, they pine and die and disappear. The duke of Marlborough only succeeded in naturalizing them at White-knights by the magnificent operation of transplanting half an acre of meadow, grass and earth and all, to the depth of two feet! And even there they seem dwindling. The wood-sorrel, which I was ambitious of fixing in the shrubberies of our old place, served me the provoking trick of living a year or two, and bearing leaves but never flowers; and that far rarer but less beautiful plant, the field-star of Bethlehem, a sort of large hyacinth of the hue of the mistletoe, which, in its pale and shadowy stalk and blossom, has something to me awful, unearthly, ghastly, mystical, druidical, used me still worse, not only refusing to grow in a corner of our orchard where I planted it, but vanishing from the spot where I procured the roots, although I left at least twenty times as many as I took.

Nothing is so difficult to tame as a wild flower; and wisely so, for they generally lose much of their characteristic beauty by any change of soil or situation. That very wood-sorrel now, which I coveted so much, I saw the other day in a greenhouse! By what chance my fellow amateur persuaded that swamp-loving, cold-braving, shade-seeking plant to blossom in the very region of light, and heat, and dryness, I cannot imagine; but there it was in full bloom, as ugly a little abortion as ever showed its poor face, smaller far than in its native woods, the flowers unveined and colourless, and bolt upright, the leaves full spread and stiff – no umbrella fold! No pendant grace! No changing hue! None but a lover's eye would have recognized the poor beauty of the woods in the faded prisoner of the greenhouse. No caged bird ever underwent such a change. I will never try to domesticate that pretty blossom again – content to visit it in its own lovely haunts, the bed of moss or the beech-root sofa.

The lily of the valley we may perhaps try to transplant. The garden is its proper home; it seems thrown here by accident; we cannot help thinking it an abasement, a condescension. The lily must be transportable. For the present, however, we were content to carry away a basket of blossoms, reserving till the autumn our design of peopling a shady border in our own small territories, the identical border where in summer our geraniums flourish, with that simplest and sweetest of flowers.

We then trudged back to Lucy's to tea, talking by the way of old stories, old neighbours, and old friends – mixed on her part with a few notices of her new acquaintances, lively, shrewd, and good humoured as usual. She is indeed a most agreeable and delightful person; I think the lately developed quality at which I hinted in my opening remarks, the slight tinge of Jenny Dennisonism, only renders her conversation more piquant and individualized, and throws her merits into sharper relief. We talked of old stories and new, and soon found she had lost none of her good gifts in gossipry; of her thousand and one lovers, about whom, although she has quite left off coquetry, she inquired with a kindly interest; of our domestic affairs, and above all of her own. She has no children – a circumstance which I sometimes think she regrets; I do not know why, except that my dear mother having given her on her marriage, amongst a variety of parting gifts, a considerable quantity of baby things, she probably thinks it a pity that they should not be used. And yet the expensiveness of children might console her on the one hand, and the superabundance of them with which she is blessed in schooltime on the other. Indeed, she has now the care of a charity Sunday-school, in addition to her workday labours – a circumstance which has by no means altered her opinion of the inefficacy and inexpediency of general education.

I suspect that the irregularity of payment is one cause of her dislike to the business; and yet she is so ingenious a contriver in the matter of extracting money's worth from those who have no money that we can hardly think her unreasonable in requiring the *hen-tailor* to cover buttons out of nothing. Where she can get no cash, she takes the debt in kind; and, as most of her employers are in that predicament, she lives in this respect like the Loochooans, who never heard of a currency. She accommodates herself to this state of things with admirable facility. She has sold her cow because she found she could be served with milk and butter by the wife of a small farmer who has four children at her school; and has parted with her poultry and pigs, and left off making bread, because the people of both shops are customers to her husband in his capacity of shoemaker, and she gets bread, and eggs, and bacon, for nothing. On the same principle, she has commenced brewing because the maltster's son and daughter attend her seminary, and she procured three new barrels, coolers, tubs, etc. from a cooper who was in debt to her husband for shoes. 'Shoes', or 'children', is indeed the constant answer to the civil notice which one is accustomed to take of any novelty in the house. 'Shoes' produced the commodious dressing-table and washing-stand, coloured like rosewood, which adorn her bed-chamber; 'children' were the source of the good-as-new roller and wheel-barrow which stand in the court; and to 'shoes and children' united are they indebted for the excellent double hedgerow of grubbed wood which she took me to see in returning from the copse – 'a brand (as she observed) snatched out of the fire; for the poor man who owed them the money must break, and had nothing useful to give them except this wood, which was useless to him, as he had not money to get it grubbed up. If he holds on till the autumn,' continued Lucy, 'we shall have a good crop of potatoes from the hedgerow. We have planted them on the chance.' The ornamental part of her territory comes from the same fertile source. Even the thrift which adorns the garden (fit emblem of its mistress!) was a present from the drunken gardener of a gentleman in the neighbourhood. 'He does not pay his little girl's schooling very regularly', quoth she, 'but then he is so civil, poor man! Anything in the garden is at our service.'

'Shoes and children' are the burden of the song. The united professions react on each other in a remarkable manner; shoes bring scholars and scholars consume shoes. The very charity school before mentioned, a profitable concern, of which the payment depends on rich people and not on poor, springs in-directly from a certain pair of purple kid boots, a capital fit (I must do our friend, the pedagogue, the justice to say that he under-stands the use of his awl, no man better!), which so pleased the vicar's lady, who is remarkable for a neat ankle, that she not only gave a magnificent order for herself, and caused him to measure her children, but actually prevailed on her husband to give the appointment of Sunday-schoolmaster to this matchless cordwainer. I should not wonder if, through her powerful patronage, he should one day rise to parish clerk.

Well, the tea and the bread and butter were discussed with the appetite produced by a two hours' ride and a three hours' walk — to say nothing of the relish communicated to our viands by the hearty hospitality of our hostess, who 'gaily pressed and smiled'. And then the present, our ostensible errand, a patchwork quilt, long the object of Lucy's admiration, was given with due courtesy, and received with abundance of pleased and blushing thanks.

At last the evening began to draw in, her husband, who had been absent, returned, and we were compelled to set out home-wards, and rode back with our basket of lilies through a beauti-ful twilight world, inhaling the fragrance of the blossomed furze, listening to the nightingales and talking of Lucy's good management.

Doctor Tubb

EVERY country village has its doctor. I allude to that particular department of the medical world, which is neither physician, nor surgeon, nor apothecary, although it unites the offices of all three; which is sometimes an old man, and sometimes an old woman, but generally an oracle, and always (with reverence be it spoken) a quack. Our village, which is remarkably rich in functionaries adorned with the true official qualities, could hardly be without so essential a personage. Accordingly we have a quack of the highest and most extended reputation in the person of Doctor Tubb, inventor and compounder of medicines, bleeder, shaver and physicker of man and beast.

How this accomplished barber-surgeon came by his fame I do not very well know; his skill he inherited (as I have been told) in the female line, from his great-aunt Bridget, who was herself the first practitioner of the day, the wise woman of the village, and bequeathed to this favourite nephew her blessing, *Culpepper's Herbal*, a famous salve for cuts and chilblains, and a still. This legacy decided his fate. A man who possessed a herbal and could read it without much spelling, who had a still and could use it, had already the great requisites for his calling. He was also blessed with a natural endowment which I take to be at least equally essential to the success of quackery of any sort, especially of medical quackery; namely, a prodigious stock of impudence. Molière's hero, who having had the ill-luck to place the heart on the wrong side (I mean the right), and being reminded of his mistake, says coolly, '*nous avons changé tout cela*', is modesty itself compared with the brazen front of Doctor Tubb. And it tells accordingly. Patients come to him from far and near; he is the celebrated person (*l'homme marquant*) of the place. I myself have heard of him all my life as a distinguished character, although our personal acquaintance is of a comparatively recent date, and began in a manner sufficiently singular and characteristic.

On taking possession of our present abode, about four years ago, we found our garden, and all the gardens of the straggling village street in which it is situated, filled, peopled, infested by a beautiful flower, which grew in such profusion and was so difficult to keep under that (poor pretty thing!) instead of being admired and cherished and watered and supported, as it well deserves to be, and would be if it were rare, it is disregarded, affronted, maltreated, cut down, pulled up, hoed out, like a weed. I do not know the name of this elegant plant, nor have I met with anyone who does; we call it the spicer, after an old naval officer who once inhabited the white house just above, and, according to tradition, first brought the seed from foreign parts. It is a sort of large veronica, with a profusion of white gauzy flowers streaked with red, like the apple blossom. Strangers admire it prodigiously; and so do I – everywhere but in my own garden.

I never saw anything prettier than a whole bed of these spicers, which had clothed the top of a large heap of earth belonging to our little mason by the roadside. Whether the wind had carried the light seed from his garden, or it had been thrown out in the mould, none could tell; but there grew the plants as thick and close as grass in a meadow, and covered with delicate red and white blossoms like a fairy orchard. I never passed without stopping to look at them; and, however accustomed to the work of extirpation in my own territories, I was one day half-shocked to see a man, his pockets stuffed with the plants, two huge bundles under each arm, and still tugging away root and branch. 'Poor pretty flower,' thought I, 'not even suffered to enjoy the waste by the roadside! Chased from the very common of nature, where the thistle and the nettle may spread and flourish! Poor despised flower!' This devastation did not, however, as I soon found, proceed from disrespect; the spicer-gatherer being engaged in sniffing with visible satisfaction to the leaves and stalks of the plant, which (although the blossom is wholly scentless) emit when bruised a very unpleasant odour. 'It has a fine venomous smell,' quoth he in soliloquy, 'and will certainly when stilled be good for something or other.' This was my first sight of Doctor Tubb.

We have frequently met since, and are now well acquainted, although the worthy experimentalist considers me as a rival practitioner, an interloper, and hates me accordingly. He has very little cause. My quackery – for I plead guilty to a little of that aptness to offer counsel in very plain and common cases, which those who live much among poor people, and feel an unaffected interest in their health and comfort, can hardly help – my quackery, being mostly of the cautious, preventive, safe side, common-sense order, stands no chance against the boldness and decision of his all-promising ignorance. He says, 'Do!' I say, 'Do not!' He deals in *stimuli*; I in sedatives; I give medicine, he gives cordial waters. Alack! Alack! When could a dose of rhubarb, even although reinforced by a dole of good broth, compete with a draught of peppermint, a licensed dram! No! No! Doctor Tubb has no cause to fear my practice.

The only patient I ever won from the worthy empiric was his own wife, who had languished under his prescriptions for three mortal years, and at last stole down in the dusk of the evening to hold a private consultation with me. I was not very willing to invade the doctor's territories in my own person, and really feared to undertake a case which had proved so obstinate; I therefore offered her a ticket for the B— dispensary, an excellent charity, which has rescued many a victim from the clutches of our herbalist. But she said that her husband would never forgive such an affront to his skill, he having an especial aversion to the dispensary and its excellent medical staff, whom he was wont to call 'book-doctors'; so that wise measure was perforce abandoned. My next suggestion was more to her taste; I counselled her to 'throw physic to the dogs'; she did so, and by the end of the week she was another woman. I never saw such a cure. Her husband never made such a one in all the course of his practice. By the simple expedient of throwing away his decoctions, she is become as strong and as hearty as I am. NB for fear of misconstruction, it is proper to add, that I do not in the least accuse or suspect the worthy doctor of wishing to get rid of his wife. God forbid! He is a tolerable husband, as times go, and performs no murders but in the way of his profession; indeed, I think he is glad that his wife should be well again; yet he cannot quite forgive the cause of the cure, and continues boldly to assert, in all companies, that it was a newly discovered fomentation of *yarbs*, applied to her by himself about a month before, which produced this surprising recovery; and I really believe that he thinks so. One secret of the implicit confidence which he inspires is that triumphant reliance on his own infallibility with which he is possessed – the secret perhaps of all creators of enthusiasm, from Mahomet and Cromwell to the

> Prevailing poet, whose undoubting mind
> Believ'd the magic wonders that he sang.

As if to make some amends to this prescriber-general for the patient of whom I had deprived him, I was once induced to seek his services medically, or rather surgically, for one of my own family – for no less a person than May, poor pretty May! One November evening, her master being on a coursing visit in Oxfordshire, and May having been left behind as too much fatigued with a recent hard day's work to stand a long dirty journey (note, that a greyhound, besides being exceedingly susceptible of bad weather and watery ways, is a worse traveller than any other dog that breathes; a miserable little pug, or a lady's lap-dog, would, in a progress of fifty miles, tire down the slayer of hares and outrunner of racehorses – May being, as I said, left behind slightly indisposed, the boy who had the care of her, no less a person than the runaway Henry, came suddenly into the parlour to tell me that she was dying. Now May is not only my pet but the pet of the whole house, so that the news spread universal consternation; there was a sudden rush of the female world to the stable, and a general feeling that Henry was right, when poor May was discovered stretched at full length in a stall, with no other sign of life than a tremendous and visible pulsation of the arteries about her chest – you might almost hear the poor heart beat, so violent was the action. 'Bleeding!' – 'She must be bled!' burst simultaneously from two of our corps! And immediately her body-servant the boy, who stood compromising his dignity by a very unmanly shower of tears, vanished, and reappeared in a few seconds, dragging Doctor Tubb by the skirts, who, as it was Saturday night, was exercising his tonsorial functions in the tap-room of the Rose, where he is accustomed to operate hebdominally on half the beards of the parish.

The doctor made his entry apparently with considerable reluctance, enacting for the first and last time in his life the part of *Le Médecin malgré lui*. He held his razor in one hand and a shaving-brush in the other, whilst a barber's apron was tied round the shabby, rusty, out-at-elbow, second-hand, black coat, renewed once in three years, and the still shabbier black breeches, of which his costume usually consists. In spite of my seeming, as I really was, glad to see him, a compliment which from me had at least the charm of novelty, in spite of a very gracious reception, I never saw the man of medicine look more completely astray. He has a pale, meagre, cadaverous face at all times, and a long lank body that seems as if he fed upon his own physic (although it is well known that gin, sheer gin, of which he is by no means sparing, is the only distilled water that finds its way down his throat). But on this night, between fright – for Henry had taken possession of him without even explaining his errand – and shame to be dragged into my presence whilst bearing the *insignia* of the least dignified of his professions, his very wig, the identical brown scratch, which he wears by way of looking professional, actually stood on end. He was followed by a miscellaneous procession of assistants, very kind, very curious, and very troublesome, from that noisy neighbour of ours, the well-frequented Rose inn. First marched mine host, red-waistcoated and jolly as usual, bearing a huge foaming pewter-pot of double X, a sovereign cure for all sublunary ills, and lighted by the limping hostler, who tried in vain to keep pace with the swift strides of his master, and held at arm's length before him a smoky horn lantern, which might well be called dark. Next tripped Miss Phœbe (this misadventure happened before the grand event of her marriage with the patten-maker), with a flaring candle in one hand and a glass of cherry-brandy, reserved by her mother for grand occasions, in the other – *autre remède*! Then followed the motley crew of the tap-room, among whom figured my friend Joel, with a woman's apron tied round his neck, and his chin covered with lather, he having been the identical customer, the very shavee, whose beard happened to be under discussion when the unfortunate interruption occurred.

After the bustle and alarm had in some measure subsided, the doctor marched up gravely to poor May, who had taken no sort of notice of the uproar.

'She must be bled!' quoth I.

'She must be fomented and physicked,' quoth the doctor! And he immediately produced from either pocket a huge bundle of dried herbs (perhaps the identical venomous-smelling spicer), which he gave to Miss Phœbe to make into a decoction *secundum artem*, and a huge horse-ball, which he proceeded to divide into bolusses. Think of giving a horse-ball to my May! 'She must be bled immediately!' said I.

'She must not!' replied the doctor.

'You shall bleed her!' cried Henry.

'I won't!' rejoined the doctor. 'She shall be fo' – *mented* he would have added; but her faithful attendant, thoroughly enraged, screamed out, 'She sha'nt!' And a regular scolding match ensued, during which both parties entirely lost sight of the poor patient, and mine host of the Rose had very nearly succeeded in administering his specific – the double X, which would doubtless have been as fatal as any prescription of licentiate or quack. The worthy landlord had actually forced open her jaws, and was about to pour in the liquor, when I luckily interposed in time to give the ale a more natural direction down his own throat, which was almost as well accustomed to such potations as that of Boniface. He was not at all offended at my rejection of his kindness, but drank to my health and May's recovery with equal goodwill.

In the meantime the tumult was ended by my friend the cricketer, who, seeing the turn which things were taking, and quite regardless of his own plight, ran down the village to the Lea, to fetch another friend of mine, an old gamekeeper, who set us all to rights in a moment, cleared the stable of the curious imperti-nents, flung the horse-ball on the dung-hill, and the decoction into the pond, bled poor May, and turned out the doctor; after which, it is almost needless to say, the patient recovered.

Walks in the Country
The Dell

MAY 2nd. A delicious evening; bright sunshine; light summer air; a sky almost cloudless; and a fresh yet delicate verdure on the hedges and in the fields; an evening that seems made for a visit to my newly discovered haunt, the mossy dell, one of the most beautiful spots in the neighbourhood, which after passing, times out of number, the field which it terminates, we found out about two months ago from the accident of May's killing a rabbit there. May has had a fancy for the place ever since; and so have I.

Thither accordingly we bend our way; through the village; up the hill; along the common; past the avenue; across the bridge; and by the mill. How deserted the road is tonight! We have not seen a single acquaintance, except poor blind Robert, laden with his sack of grass plucked from the hedges, and the little boy that leads him. A singular division of labour! Little Jem guides Robert to the spots where the long grass grows, and tells him where it is most plentiful; and then the old man cuts it close to the roots, and between them they fill the sack, and sell the contents in the village. Half the cows in the street – for our baker, our wheelwright, and our shoemaker has each his Alderney – owe the best part of their maintenance to blind Robert's industry.

Here we are at the entrance of the cornfield which leads to the dell, and which commands so fine a view of the Loddon, the mill, the great farm, with its picturesque outbuildings, and the range of woody hills beyond. It is impossible not to pause a moment at that gate, the landscape, always beautiful, is so suited to the season and the hour – so bright, and gay, and springlike. But May, who has the chance of another rabbit in her pretty head, has galloped forward to the dingle, and poor May, who follows me so faithfully in all my wanderings, has a right to a little indulgence in hers. So to the dingle we go.

At the end of the field, which when seen from the road seems terminated by a thick dark coppice, we come suddenly to the edge of a ravine, on one side fringed with a low growth of alder, birch and willow, on the other mossy, turfy and bare, or only broken by bright tufts of blossomed broom. One or two old pollards almost conceal the winding road that leads down the descent, by the side of which a spring as bright as crystal runs gurgling along. The dell itself is an irregular piece of broken ground, in some parts very deep, intersected by two or three high banks of equal irregularity, now abrupt and bare, and rock-like, now crowned with tufts of the feathery willow or magnificent old thorns. Everywhere the earth is covered by short fine turf, mixed with mosses, soft, beautiful and various, and embossed with the speckled leaves and lilac flowers of the arum, the paler blossoms of the common orchis, the enamelled blue of the wild hyacinth, so splendid in this evening light, and large tufts of oxlips and cowslips rising like nosegays from the short turf.

The ground on the other side of the dell is much lower than the field through which we came, so that it is mainly to the labyrinthine intricacy of these high banks that it owes its singular character of wildness and variety. Now we seem hemmed in by those green cliffs, shut out from all the world, with nothing visible but those verdant mounds and the deep blue sky; now by some sudden turn we get a peep at an adjoining meadow, where the sheep are lying, dappling its sloping surface like the small clouds on the summer heaven. Poor, harmless, quiet creatures, how still they are! Some socially lying side by side; some grouped in threes and fours; some quite apart. Ah! There are lambs amongst them – pretty, pretty lambs! – nestled in by their mothers. Soft, quiet, sleepy things! Not all so quiet, though! There is a party of these young lambs as wide awake as heart can desire; half a dozen of them playing together, frisking, dancing, leaping, butting and crying in the young voice, which is so pretty a diminutive of the full-grown bleat. How beautiful they are with their innocent spotted faces, their mottled feet, their long curly tails, and their light flexible forms, frolicking like so many kittens, but with a gentleness, an assurance of sweetness and innocence, which no kitten, nothing that ever is to be a cat, can have. How complete and perfect is their enjoyment of existence! Ah! Little rogues! Your play has been too noisy; you have awakened your mammas; and two or three of the old ewes are getting up; and one of them marching gravely to the troop of lambs has selected her own, given her a gentle butt, and trotted off; the poor rebuked lamb following meekly, but every now and then stopping and casting a longing look at its playmates; who, after a moment's awed pause, had resumed their gambols; whilst the stately dam every now and then looked back in her turn, to see that her little one was following. At last she lay down, and the lamb by her side. I never saw so pretty a pastoral scene in my life.[1]

---

[1] I have seen one which affected me much more. Walking in the Church Lane with one of the young ladies of the vicarage, we met a large flock of sheep, with the usual retinue of shepherds and dogs. Lingering after them and almost out of sight, we encountered a straggling ewe, now trotting along, now walking, and every now and then stopping to look back, and bleating. A little behind her came a lame lamb, bleating occasionally, as if in answer to its dam, and doing its very best to keep up with her. It was a lameness of both the fore feet; the knees were bent, and it seemed to walk on the very edge of the hoof – on tiptoe, if I may venture such an expression. My young friend thought that the lameness proceeded from original malformation, I am rather of opinion that it was accidental, and that the poor creature was wretchedly footsore. However that might be, the pain and difficulty with which it took every step were not to be mistaken; and the distress and fondness of the mother, her perplexity as the

The Dell

Another turning of the dell gives a glimpse of the dark coppice by which it is backed, and from which we are separated by some marshy, rushy ground, where the springs have formed into a pool, and where the moorhen loves to build her nest. Aye, there is one scudding away now; I can hear her plash into the water, and the rustling of her wings amongst the rushes. This is the deepest part of the wild dingle. How uneven the ground is! Surely these excavations, now so thoroughly clothed with vegetation, must originally have been huge gravel pits; there is no other way of accounting for the labyrinth, for they do dig gravel in such capricious meanders; but the quantity seems incredible. Well! There is no end of guessing! We are getting amongst the springs, and must turn back. Round this corner, where on ledges like fairy terraces the orchises and arums grow, and we emerge suddenly on a new side of the dell, just fronting the small homestead of our good neighbour farmer Allen.

This rustic dwelling belongs to what used to be called in this part of the country 'a little bargain': thirty or forty acres, perhaps, of arable land, which the owner and his sons cultivated themselves, whilst the wife and daughters assisted in the husbandry, and eked out the slender earnings by the produce of the dairy, the poultry yard and the orchard – an order of cultivators now passing rapidly away, but in which much of the best part of the English character, its industry, its frugality, its sound sense, and its kindness might be found. Farmer Allen himself is an excellent specimen, the cheerful venerable old man, with his long white hair, and his bright grey eye, and his wife is a still finer. They have had a hard struggle to win through the world and keep their little

---

flock passed gradually out of sight, the effort with which the poor lamb contrived to keep up a sort of trot, and their mutual calls and lamentations, were really so affecting, that Ellen and I, although not at all larmoyante sort of people, had much ado not to cry. We could not find a boy to carry the lamb, which was too big for us to manage; but I was quite sure that the ewe would not desert it, and as the dark was coming on, we both trusted that the shepherds on folding their flock would miss them and return for them; and so I am happy to say it proved.

property undivided; but good management and good principles and the assistance afforded them by an admirable son, who left our village a poor 'prentice boy, and is now a partner in a great house in London, have enabled them to overcome all the difficulties of these trying times, and they are now enjoying the peaceful evening of a well-spent life as free from care and anxiety as their best friends could desire.

Ah! there is Mr Allen in the orchard, the beautiful orchard, with its glorious garlands of pink and white, its pearly pear-blossoms and coral apple-buds. What a flush of bloom it is! How brightly delicate it appears, thrown into strong relief by the dark house and the weather-stained barn, in this soft evening light. The very grass is strewed with the snowy petals of the pear and the cherry. And there sits Mrs Allen, feeding her poultry, with her three little grand-daughters from London, pretty fairies from three years old to five (only two and twenty months elapsed between the birth of the eldest and the youngest) playing round her feet.

Mrs Allen, my dear Mrs Allen, has been that rare thing a beauty, and although she be now an old woman, I had almost said that she is so still. Why should I not say so? Nobleness of feature and sweetness of expression are surely as delightful in age as in youth. Her face and figure are much like those which are stamped indelibly on the memory of everyone who ever saw that grand specimen of woman – Mrs Siddons. The outline of Mrs Allen's face is exactly the same; but there is more softness, more gentleness, a more feminine composure in the eye and in the smile. Mrs Allen never played Lady Macbeth. Her hair, almost as black as at twenty, is parted on her large fair forehead, and combed under her exquisitely neat and snowy cap, a muslin neck-kerchief, a grey stuff gown, and a white apron complete the picture.

There she sits under an old elder tree, which flings its branches over her like a canopy, whilst the setting sun illumines her venerable figure and touches the leaves with an emerald light; there she sits, placid and smiling, with her spectacles in her hand and a measure of barley on her lap, into which the little girls are dipping their chubby hands and scattering the corn amongst the ducks and chickens with unspeakable glee. But those ingrates, the poultry, don't seem so pleased and thankful as they ought to be; they mistrust their young feeders. All domestic animals dislike children, partly from an instinctive fear of their tricks and their thoughtlessness; partly, I suspect, from jealousy. Jealousy seems a strange tragic passion to attribute to the inmates of the basse-cour, but only look at that strutting fellow of a bantam cock (evidently a favourite), who sidles up to his old mistress with an air half affronted and half tender, turning so scornfully from the barley-corns which Annie is flinging towards him, and say if he be not as jealous as Othello! Nothing can pacify him but Mrs Allen's notice and a dole from her hand. See, she is calling to him and feeding him, and now how he swells out his feathers, and flutters his wings, and erects his glossy neck, and struts and crows and pecks, proudest and happiest of bantams, the pet and glory of the poultry yard!

In the meantime my own pet May, who has all this while been peeping into every hole, and penetrating every nook and winding of the dell, in hopes to find another rabbit, has returned to my side, and is sliding her snake-like head into my hand, at once to invite the caress which she likes so well, and to intimate, with all due respect, that it is time to go home. The setting sun gives the same warning; and in a moment we are through the dell, the field and the gate, past the farm and the mill, and hanging over the bridge that crosses the Loddon river.

What a sunset! How golden! How beautiful! The sun just disappearing, and the narrow liny clouds, which a few minutes ago lay like soft vapoury streaks along the horizon, lighted up with a golden splendour that the eye can scarcely endure, and those still softer clouds which floated above them wreathing and curling into a thousand fantastic forms, as thin and changeful as summer smoke, now defined and deepened into grandeur, and edged with ineffable, insufferable light! Another minute and the brilliant orb totally disappears, and the sky above grows every moment more varied and more beautiful as the dazzling golden lines are mixed with glowing red and gorgeous purple, dappled with small dark specks, and mingled with such a blue as the egg of the hedge-sparrow. To look up at that glorious sky, and then to see that magnificent picture reflected in the clear and lovely Loddon water is a pleasure never to be described and never forgotten. My heart swells and my eyes fill as I write of it, and think of the immeasurable majesty of nature, and the unspeakable goodness of God, who has spread an enjoyment so pure, so peaceful, and so intense before the meanest and the lowliest of His creatures.

Walks in the Country
The Old House at Aberleigh

JUNE 25th. What a glowing glorious day! Summer in its richest prime, noon in its most sparkling brightness, little white clouds dappling the deep blue sky, and the sun, now partially veiled, and now bursting through them with an intensity of light! It would not do to walk today, professedly to walk, we should be frightened at the very sound! And yet it is probable that we may be beguiled into a pretty long stroll before we return home. We are going to drive to the old house at Aberleigh, to spend the morning under the shade of those balmy firs, and amongst those luxuriant rose trees, and by the side of that brimming Loddon river. 'Do not expect us before six o'clock', said I, as I left the house. 'Six at soonest!'

added my charming companion; and off we drove in our little pony chaise, drawn by our old mare, and with the good-humoured urchin, Henry's successor, a sort of younger Scrub, who takes care of horse and chaise, and cow and garden, for our charioteer.

My comrade in this homely equipage was a young lady of high family and higher endowments, to whom the novelty of the thing, and her own naturalness of character and simplicity of taste gave an unspeakable enjoyment. She danced the little chaise up and down as she got into it, and laughed for very glee like a child. Lizzy herself could not have been more delighted. She praised the horse and the driver, and the roads and the scenery, and gave herself fully up to the enchantment of a rural excursion in the sweetest weather of this sweet season. I enjoyed all this too; for the road was pleasant to every sense, winding through narrow lanes, under high elms, and between hedges garlanded with woodbine and rose trees, whilst the air was scented with the delicious fragrance of blossomed beans. I enjoyed it all. But, I believe, my principal pleasure was derived from my companion herself.

Emily I. is a person whom it is a privilege to know. She is quite like a creation of the older poets, and might pass for one of Shakespeare's or Fletcher's women stepped into life; just as tender, as playful, as gentle, and as kind. She is clever too, and has all the knowledge and accomplishments that a carefully conducted education, acting on a mind of singular clearness and ductility, matured and improved by the very best company, can bestow. But one never thinks of her acquirements. It is the charming artless character, the bewitching sweetness of manner, the real and universal sympathy, the quick taste and the ardent feeling, that one loves in Emily. She is Irish by birth, and has in perfection the melting voice and soft caressing accent by which her fair countrywomen are distinguished. Moreover she is pretty – I think her beautiful, and so do all who have heard as well as seen her – but pretty, very pretty, all the world must confess; and perhaps that is a distinction more enviable, because less envied, than the 'palmy state' of beauty. Her prettiness is of the prettiest kind – that of which the chief character is youthfulness. A short but pleasing figure, all grace and symmetry; a fair blooming face, beaming with intelligence and good humour; the prettiest little feet and the whitest hands in the world; such is Emily I.

She resides with her maternal grandmother, a venerable old lady, slightly shaken with the palsy; and when together (and they are so fondly attached to each other that they are seldom parted) it is one of the loveliest combinations of youth and age ever witnessed. There is no seeing them without feeling an increase of respect and affection for both grandmother and grand-daughter – always one of the tenderest and most beautiful of natural connexions – as Richardson knew when he made such exquisite use of it in his matchless book. I fancy that grandmamma Shirley must have been just such another venerable lady as Mrs S., and our sweet Emily. Oh, no! Harriet Byron is not half good enough for her! There is nothing like her in the whole seven volumes.

But here we are at the bridge! Here we must alight! 'This is the Loddon, Emily. Is it not a beautiful river? Rising level with its banks, so clear, and smooth, and peaceful, giving back the verdant landscape and the bright blue sky, and bearing on its pellucid stream the snowy water-lily, the purest of flowers, which sits

enthroned on its own cool leaves, looking chastity itself, like the lady in Comus. That queenly flower becomes the water, and so do the stately swans who are sailing so majestically down the stream, like those who

On St. Mary's lake
Float double, swan and shadow.

We must dismount here, and leave Richard to take care of our equipage under the shade of these trees, whilst we walk up to the house. See there it is! We must cross this stile; there is no other way now.'

And crossing the stile we were immediately in what had been a drive round a spacious park, and still retained something of the character, though the park itself had long been broken into arable fields – and in full view of the Great House, a beautiful structure of James the First's time, whose glassless windows and dilapidated doors form a melancholy contrast with the strength and entireness of the rich and massive front.

The story of that ruin – for such it is – is always to me singularly affecting. It is that of the decay of an ancient and distinguished family, gradually reduced from the highest wealth and station to actual poverty. The house and park, and a small estate around it, were entailed on a distant cousin, and could not be alienated; and the late owner, the last of his name and lineage, after long struggling with debt and difficulty, farming his own lands, and clinging to his magnificent home with a love of place almost as tenacious as that of the younger Foscari, was at last forced to abandon it, retired to a paltry lodging in a paltry town, and died there about twenty years ago, broken-hearted. His successor, bound by no ties of association to the spot, and rightly judging the residence to be much too large for the diminished estate, immediately sold the superb fixtures, and would have entirely taken down the house, if, on making the attempt, the masonry had not been found so solid that the materials were not worth the labour. A great part, however, of one side is laid open, and the splendid chambers, with their carving and gilding, are exposed to the wind and rain – sad memorials of past grandeur! The grounds have been left in a merciful neglect: the park, indeed, is broken up, the lawn mown twice a year like a common hayfield, the grotto mouldering into ruin, and the fishponds choked with rushes and aquatic plants; but the shrubs and flowering trees are un-destroyed, and have grown into a magnificence of size and wildness of beauty, such as we may imagine them to attain in their native forests. Nothing can exceed their luxuriance, especially in the spring, when the lilac, and laburnum, and double-cherry put forth their gorgeous blossoms. There is a sweet sadness in the sight of such floweriness amidst such desolation; it seems the triumph of nature over the destructive power of man. The whole place, in that season more particularly, is full of a soft and soothing melancholy, reminding me, I scarcely know why, of some of the descriptions of natural scenery in the novels of Charlotte Smith, which I read when a girl, and which, perhaps, for that reason hang on my memory.

But here we are, in the smooth grassy ride, on the top of a steep turfy slope descending to the river, crowned with enormous firs and limes of equal growth, looking across the winding waters into a sweet, peaceful landscape of quiet meadows, shut in by distant woods. What a fragrance is in the air from the balmy fir trees and the blossomed limes! What an intensity of odour! And what a murmur of bees in the lime trees! What a coil those little winged people make over our heads! And what a pleasant sound it is! The pleasantest of busy sounds, that which comes associated with all that is good and beautiful – industry and forecast, and sunshine and flowers. Surely these lime trees might store a hundred hives; the very odour is of a honied richness, cloying, satiating.

Emily exclaimed in admiration as we stood under the deep, strong, leafy shadow, and still more when honeysuckles trailed their untrimmed profusion in our path, and roses, really trees, almost intercepted our passage.

'On, Emily! farther yet! Force your way by that jessamine – it will yield; I will take care of this stubborn white rose bough.' 'Take care of yourself! Pray take care,' said my fairest friend; 'let me hold back the branches.' After we had won our way through the strait, at some expense of veils and flounces, she stopped to contemplate and admire the tall graceful shrub, whose long thorny stems, spreading in every direction, had opposed our progress, and now waved their delicate clusters over our heads. 'Did I ever think,' exclaimed she, 'of standing under the shadow of a white rose tree! What an exquisite fragrance! And what a beautiful flower! So pale, and white, and tender, and the petals thin and smooth as silk! What rose is it?' 'Don't you know? Did you never see it before? It is rare now, I believe, and seems rarer than it is, because it only blossoms in very hot summers; but this, Emily, is the musk rose – that very musk rose of which Titania talks, and which is worthy of Shakespeare and of her, is it not? No! do not smell to it; it is less sweet so than other roses; but one cluster in a vase, or even that bunch in your bosom, will perfume a large room, as it does the summer air.' 'Oh! we will take twenty clusters,' said Emily. 'I wish grandmamma were here! She talks so often of a musk rose tree that grew against one end of her father's house. I wish she were here to see this!'

Echoing her wish, and well-laden with musk roses, planted perhaps in the days of Shakespeare, we reached the steps that led to a square summerhouse or banqueting-room, overhanging the river: the under part was a boathouse, whose projecting roof, as well as the walls and the very top of the little tower, was covered with ivy and woodbine, and surmounted by tufted barberries, bird cherries, acacias, covered with their snowy chains, and other pendent and flowering trees. Beyond, rose two poplars of un-rivalled magnitude, towering like stately columns over the dark tall firs, and giving a sort of pillared and architectural grandeur to the scene.

We were now close to the mansion; but it looked sad and desolate, and the entrance, choked with brambles and nettles, seemed almost to repel our steps. The summer-house, the beautiful summer-house was free and open, and inviting, commanding from the unglazed windows, which hung high above the water, a reach of the river terminated by a rustic mill.

There we sat, emptying our little basket of fruit and country cakes, till Emily was seized with a desire of viewing, from the other side of the Loddon, the scenery which had so much

enchanted her. 'I must,' said she, 'take a sketch of the ivied boathouse, and of this sweet room, and this pleasant window. Grandmamma would never be able to walk from the road to see the place itself, but she must see its likeness.' So forth we sallied, not forgetting the dear musk roses.

We had no way of reaching the desired spot but by retracing our steps a mile, during the heat of the hottest hour of the day, and then following the course of the river to an equal distance on the other side; nor had we any materials for sketching, except the rumpled paper which had contained our repast, and a pencil without a point, which I happened to have about me. But these small difficulties are pleasures to gay and happy youth. Regardless of such obstacles, the sweet Emily bounded on like a fawn, and I followed, delighting in her delight. The sun went in, and the walk was delicious; a reviving coolness seemed to breathe over the water, wafting the balmy scent of the firs and limes; we found a point of view presenting the boathouse, the water, the poplars and the mill in a most felicitous combination; the little straw fruit basket made a capital table; and refreshed and sharpened and pointed by our trusty lacquey's excellent knife (your country boy is never without a good knife, it is his prime treasure), the pencil did double duty – first in the skilful hands of Emily, whose faithful and spirited sketch does equal honour to the scene and to the artist, and then in the humbler office of attempting a faint transcript of my own impressions in the following sonnet:

> It was an hour of calmest noon, a day
>   Of ripest summer: o'er the deep blue sky
>   White speckled clouds came sailing peacefully,
> Half-shrouding in a chequer'd veil the ray
> Of the sun, too ardent else – what time we lay
>   By the smooth Loddon, opposite the high
>   Steep bank, which as a coronet gloriously
> Wore its rich crest of firs and lime trees, gay
>
>   With their pale tassels; while from out a bower
> Of ivy (where those column'd poplars rear
>   Their heads) the ruin'd boathouse, like a tower,
> Flung its deep shadow on the waters clear.
>   My Emily! Forget not that calm hour,
> Nor that fair scene, by thee made doubly dear!

The Old Gipsy

WE have few gipsies in our neighbourhood. In spite of our tempting green lanes, our woody dells and heathy commons, the rogues don't take to us. I am afraid that we are too civilized, too cautious; that our sheepfolds are too closely watched; our barnyards too well guarded; our geese and ducks too fastly penned; our chickens too securely locked up; our little pigs too safe in their sty; our game too scarce; our laundresses too careful. In short, we are too little primitive: we have a snug brood of vagabonds and poachers of our own, to say nothing of their regular followers, constables and justices of the peace; we have stocks in the village, and a treadmill in the next town; and therefore we go gipsyless – a misfortune of which every landscape painter, and every lover of that living landscape, the country, can appreciate the extent. There is nothing under the sun that harmonizes so well with nature, especially in her woodland recesses, as that picturesque people, who are, so to say, the wild genus – the pheasants and roebucks of the human race.

Sometimes, indeed, we used to see a gipsy procession passing along the common, like an eastern caravan, men, women, and children, donkeys and dogs; and sometimes a patch of bare earth, strewed with ashes and surrounded by scathed turf, on the broad green margin of some crossroad, would give token of a gipsy halt. But a regular gipsy encampment has always been so rare an event that I was equally surprised and delighted to meet with one in the course of my walks last autumn, particularly as the party was of the most innocent description, quite free from those tall, dark, lean, Spanish-looking men, who it must be confessed, with all my predilection for the caste, are rather startling to meet when alone in an unfrequented path; and a path more solitary than that into which the beauty of a bright October morning had tempted me could not well be imagined.

Branching off from the high road, a little below our village, runs a wide green lane, bordered on either side by a row of young oaks and beeches just within the hedge, forming an avenue, in which, on a summer afternoon, you may see the squirrels disporting from tree to tree, whilst the rooks, their fellow denizens, are wheeling in noisy circles over their heads. The fields sink gently down on each side, so that, being the bottom of a natural winding valley, and crossed by many little rills and rivulets, the turf exhibits even in the dryest summers an emerald verdure. Scarcely anyone passes the end of that lane, without wishing to turn into it; but the way is in some sort dangerous and difficult for foot passengers because the brooklets which intersect it are in many instances bridgeless, and in others bestridden by planks so decayed that it were rashness to pass them; and the nature of the ground, treacherous and boggy, and in many places as unstable as water, renders it for carriages wholly impracticable.

I, however, who do not dislike a little difficulty where there is no absolute danger, and who am moreover almost as familiar with the one only safe track as the heifers who graze there, sometimes venture along this seldom trodden path, which terminates, at the end of a mile and a half, in a spot of singular beauty. The hills become abrupt and woody, the cultivated enclosures cease, and the long narrow valley ends in a little green, bordered on one side by a fine old park, whose mossy paling, overhung with thorns and hollies, comes sweeping round it, to meet the rich coppices which clothe the opposite acclivity. Just under the high and irregular paling, shaded by the birches and sycamores of the park, and by the venerable oaks which are scattered irregularly on the green, is a dark deep pool, whose broken banks, crowned with fern and wreathed with brier and bramble, have an air of wilderness and grandeur that might have suited the pencil of Salvator Rosa.

In this lonely place (for the mansion to which the park belongs has long been uninhabited) I first saw our gipsies. They had pitched their tent under one of the oak trees, perhaps from a certain dim sense of natural beauty, which those who live with nature in the fields are seldom totally without; perhaps because the neighbourhood of the coppices, and of the deserted hall, was favourable to the acquisition of game, and of the little fuel which their hardy habits required. The party consisted only of four: an old crone, in a tattered red cloak and black bonnet, who was stooping over a kettle, of which the contents were probably as savoury as that of Meg Merrilies, renowned in story; a pretty black-eyed girl, at work under the trees; a sun-burned urchin of eight or nine, collecting sticks and dead leaves to feed their out-of-door fire; and a slender lad two or three years older, who lay basking in the sun, with a couple of shabby dogs, of the sort called mongrel, in all the joy of idleness, whilst a grave patient donkey stood grazing hard-by. It was a pretty picture, with its soft autumnal sky, its rich woodiness, its sunshine, its verdure, the light smoke curling from the fire, and the group disposed around it so harmless, poor outcasts! and so happy – a beautiful picture! I stood gazing on it till I was half ashamed to look longer, and came away half afraid that they should depart before I could see them again.

This fear I soon found to be groundless. The old gipsy was a celebrated fortune-teller, and the post having been so long vacant, she could not have brought her talents to a better market. The whole village rang with the predictions of this modern Cassandra – unlike her Trojan predecessor, inasmuch as her prophecies were never of evil. I myself could not help admiring the real cleverness, the genuine gipsy tact with which she adapted her foretellings to the age, the habits, and the known desires and circumstances of her clients.

To our little pet, Lizzy, for instance, a damsel of seven, she predicted a fairing; to Ben Kirby, a youth of thirteen, head batter of the boys, a new cricket-ball; to Ben's sister Lucy, a girl some three years his senior, and just promoted to that ensign of womanhood a cap, she promised a pink top-knot; whilst for Miss Sophia Matthews, our old-maidish schoolmistress, who would be heartily glad to be a girl again, she foresaw one handsome husband, and for the smart widow Simmons, two. These were the

least of her triumphs. George Davis, the dashing young farmer of
the Hill House, a gay sportsman, who scoffed at fortune-tellers and
matrimony, consulted her as to whose greyhound would win the
courser's cup at the beacon meeting: to which she replied, that she
did not know to whom the dog would belong, but that the winner
of the cup would be a white greyhound, with one blue ear, and a
spot on its side, being an exact description of Mr George Davis's
favourite Helen, who followed her master's steps like his shadow,
and was standing behind him at this very instant. This prediction
gained our gipsy half-a-crown; and master Welles, the thriving
thrifty yeoman of the Lea, she managed to win sixpence from his
hard honest frugal hand, by a prophecy that his old brood mare,
called Blackfoot, should bring forth twins; and Ned the blacksmith, who was known to court the tall nursemaid at the mill – she
got a shilling from Ned, simply by assuring him that his wife
should have the longest coffin that ever was made in our wheelwright's shop. A most tempting prediction! ingeniously combin-
ing the prospect of winning and of surviving the lady of his heart –
a promise equally adapted to the hot and cold fits of that ague,
called love; lightening the fetters of wedlock; uniting in a breath
the bridegroom and the widower. Ned was the best pleased of all
her customers, and enforced his suit with such vigour that he and
the fair giantess were asked in church the next Sunday, and
married at the fortnight's end.

No wonder that all the world – that is to say, all our world –
were crazy to have their fortunes told; to enjoy the pleasure of
hearing from such undoubted authority that what they wished to
be should be. Amongst the most eager to take a peep into futurity
was our pretty maid Harriet, although her desire took the not
unusual form of disclamation – 'nothing should induce her to
have her fortune told, nothing upon earth! She never thought of
the gipsy, not she!' And, to prove the fact, she said so at least
twenty times a day. Now Harriet's fortune seemed told already;
her destiny was fixed. She, the belle of the village, was engaged, as
everybody knows, to our village beau, Joel Brent; they were only
waiting for a little more money to marry; and as Joel was already
head carter to our head farmer, and had some prospect of

a bailiff's place, their union did not appear very distant. But Harriet, besides being a beauty, was a coquette, and her affection for her betrothed did not interfere with certain flirtations which came in like Isabella, 'by the bye', and occasionally cast a shadow of coolness between the lovers, which, however, Joel's cleverness and good humour generally contrived to chase away. There had probably been a little fracas in the present instance for, at the end of one of her daily professions of unfaith in gipsies and their predictions, she added, 'that none but fools did believe them; that Joel had had his fortune told, and wanted to treat her to a prophecy – but she was not such a simpleton.'

About half an hour after the delivery of this speech, I happened, in tying up a chrysanthemum, to go to our wood-yard for a stick of proper dimensions, and there, enclosed between the faggot-pile and the coal-shed, stood the gipsy, in the very act of palmistry, conning the lines of fate in Harriet's hand. Never was a stronger contrast than that between the old withered sybil, dark as an Egyptian, with bright laughing eyes, and an expression of keen humour under all her affected solemnity, and our village beauty, tall, and plump, and fair, blooming as a rose, and simple as a dove. She was listening too intently to see me, but the fortune-teller did, and stopped so suddenly that her attention was awakened, and the intruder discovered.

Harriet at first meditated a denial. She called up a pretty innocent unconcerned look; answered my silence (for I never spoke a word) by muttering something about 'coals for the parlour'; and catching up my new-painted green watering-pot, instead of the coal-scuttle, began filling it with all her might, to the unspeakable discomfiture of that useful utensil, on which the dingy dust stuck like bird-lime, and of her own clean apron, which exhibited a curious interchange of black and green on a white ground. During the process of filling the watering-pot, Harriet made divers signs to the gipsy to decamp. The old sybil, however, budged not a foot, influenced probably by two reasons: one, the hope of securing a customer in the newcomer, whose appearance is generally, I am afraid, the very reverse of dignified, rather merry than wise; the other, a genuine fear of passing through the yard gate, on the outside of which a much more imposing person, my greyhound Mayflower, who has a sort of beadle instinct anent drunkards and pilferers, and disorderly persons of all sorts, stood barking most furiously.

This instinct is one of May's remarkable qualities. Dogs are all, more or less, physiognomists and, commonly, pretty determined aristocrats, fond of the fine, and averse to the shabby, distinguishing, with a nice accuracy, the master castes from the pariahs of the world. But May's power of perception is another matter; more, as it were, moral. She has no objection to honest rags; can away with dirt, or age, or ugliness, or any such accident, and, except just at home, makes no distinction between kitchen and parlour. Her intuition points entirely to the race of people commonly called suspicious, on whom she pounces at a glance. What a constable she would have made! What a jewel of a thief-taker! Pity that those four feet should stand in the way of her preferment! she might have risen to be a Bow Street officer. As it is, we make the gift useful in a small way. In the matter of hiring and marketing, the whole village likes to consult May. Many a chap has stared when she has been whistled up to give her opinion as to his honesty; and many a pig bargain has gone off on her veto. Our neighbour, mine host of the Rose, used constantly to follow her judgment in the selection of his lodgers. His house was never so orderly as when under her government. At last he found out that she abhorred tipplers as well as thieves – indeed, she actually barked away three of his best customers; and he left off appealing to her sagacity, since which he has, at different times, lost three silver spoons and a leg of mutton. With everyone else May is an oracle. Not only in the case of wayfarers and vagrants, but also amongst our own people, her fancies are quite a touchstone. A certain hump-backed cobbler, for instance – May cannot abide him, and I don't think he has had so much as a job of heel-piecing to do since her dislike became public. She really took away his character.

Longer than I have taken to relate Mayflower's accomplishments stood we, like the folks in the *Critic*, at a deadlock: May, who probably regarded the gipsy as a sort of rival, an interloper on her oracular domain, barking with the voice of a lioness; the gipsy trying to persuade me into having my fortune told; and I endeavouring to prevail on May to let the gipsy pass. Both attempts were unsuccessful; and the fair consulter of destiny, who had by this time recovered from the shame of her detection, extricated us from our dilemma by smuggling the old woman away through the house.

Of course Harriet was exposed to some raillery, and a good deal of questioning about her future fate, as to which she preserved an obstinate, but evidently satisfied, silence. At the end of three days, however – my readers are, I hope, learned enough in gipsy lore to know that, unless kept secret for three entire days, no prediction can come true – at the end of three days, when all the family except herself had forgotten the story, our pretty soubrette, half-bursting with the long retention, took the opportunity of lacing on my new half-boots to reveal the prophecy. 'She was to see within the week, and this was Saturday, the young man, the real young man, whom she was to marry.' 'Why, Harriet, you know poor Joel.' 'Joel, indeed! The gipsy said that the young man, the real young man, was to ride up to the house dressed in a dark greatcoat (and Joel never wore a greatcoat in his life – all the world knew that he wore smock-frocks and jackets) and mounted on a white horse – and where should Joel get a white horse?' 'Had this real young man made his appearance yet?' 'No; there had not been a white horse past the place since Tuesday; so it must certainly be today.'

A good look-out did Harriet keep for white horses during this fateful Saturday, and plenty did she see. It was the market-day at B—, and team after team came by with one, two, and three white horses; cart after cart, and gig after gig, each with a white steed; Colonel M.'s carriage, with its prancing pair – but still no horseman. At length one appeared; but he had a greatcoat whiter than the animal he rode; another, but he was old farmer Lewington, a married man; a third, but he was little Lord L., a schoolboy, on his Arabian pony. Besides, they all passed the house; and, as the day wore on, Harriet began, alternately, to profess her old infidelity on the score of fortune-telling, and to let out certain apprehensions that, if the gipsy did really possess the power of foreseeing events, and no such horseman arrived, she might possibly be unlucky enough to die an old maid – a fate for which, although the proper destiny of a coquette, our village beauty seemed to entertain a very decided aversion.

At last, just at dusk, just as Harriet, making believe to close our casement shutters, was taking her last peep up the road, something white appeared in the distance coming leisurely down the hill. Was it really a horse? Was it not rather Titus Strong's cow driving home to milking? A minute or two dissipated that fear; it certainly was a horse, and as certainly it had a dark rider. Very slowly he descended the hill, pausing most provokingly at the end of the village, as if about to turn up the vicarage lane. He came on, however, and after another short stop at the Rose, rode up full to our little gate, and catching Harriet's hand as she was opening the wicket, displayed to the half-pleased, half-angry damsel, the smiling triumphant face of her own Joel Brent, equipped in a new greatcoat, and mounted on his master's newly purchased market nag. 'Oh, Joel! Joel! The gipsy! The gipsy!'

A New Married Couple

THERE is no pleasanter country sound than that of a peal of
village bells, as they come vibrating through the air, giving token
of marriage and merriment; nor ever was that pleasant sound
more welcome than on this still, foggy, gloomy November morning, when all nature stood as if at pause; the large drops hanging
on the thatch without falling; the sere leaves dangling on the trees;
the birds mute and motionless on the boughs; turkeys, children,
geese and pigs unnaturally silent; the whole world quiet and
melancholy as some of the enchanted places in the *Arabian
Nights*. That merry peal seemed at once to break the spell, and to
awaken sound, and life, and motion. It had a peculiar welcome,
too, as stirring up one of the most active passions in woman or in
man, and rousing the rational part of creation from the torpor
induced by the season and the weather at the thrilling touch of
curiosity. Never was a completer puzzle. Nobody in our village
had heard that a wedding was expected; no unaccustomed conveyance, from a coach to a wheelbarrow, had been observed
passing up the vicarage lane; no banns had been published in
church; no marriage of gentility, that is to say, of licence, talked
of, or thought of; none of our village beaux had been seen, as
village beaux are apt to be on such occasions, smirking and
fidgety; none of our village belles ashamed and shy. It was the
prettiest puzzle that had occurred since Grace Neville's time; and,
regardless of the weather, half the gossips of the street, in other
words, half the inhabitants, gathered together in knots and
clusters, to discuss flirtations and calculate possibilities.

Still the bells rang merrily on, and still the pleasant game of
guessing continued, until the appearance of a well-known, but

most unsuspected, equipage, descending the hill from the church, and showing dimly through the fog the most unequivocal signs of bridal finery, supplied exactly the solution which all riddles ought to have, adding a grand climax of amazement to the previous suspense – the new married couple being precisely the two most unlikely persons to commit matrimony in the whole neighbourhood; the only two whose names had never come in question during the discussion, both bride and bridegroom having been long considered the most confirmed and resolute old maid and old bachelor to be found in the countryside.

Master Jacob Frost is an itinerant chapman, somewhere on the wrong side of sixty, who traverses the counties of Hants, Berks

and Oxon, with a noisy lumbering cart full of panniers, containing the heterogeneous commodities of fruit and fish, driving
during the summer a regular and profitable barter between the
coast on one side of us and the cherry country on the other. We
who live about midway between these two extreme points of his
peregrination, have the benefit of both kinds of merchandise
going and coming; and there is not a man, woman, or child in the
parish who does not know Master Frost's heavy cart and old grey
mare half a mile off, as well as the stentorian cry of 'Cherries,
crabs, and salmon,' sometimes pickled, and sometimes fresh, with
which he makes the common and village re-echo; for, with an
indefatigable perseverance, he cries his goods along the whole line
of road, picking up customers where a man of less experience
would despair, and so used to utter those sounds while marching
beside his rumbling equipage that it would not be at all surprising
if he were to cry 'Cherries – salmon! Salmon – cherries!' in his
sleep. As to fatigue, that is entirely out of the question. Jacob is a
man of iron: a tall, lean, gaunt figure, all bone and sinew,
constantly clad in a tight brown jacket with breeches to match,
long leather gaiters, and a leather cap; his face and hair tanned by
constant exposure to the weather into a tint so nearly resembling
his vestments that he looks all of a colour, like the statue ghost in
Don Giovanni, although the hue be different from that renowned
spectre – Jacob being a brown man. Perhaps Master Peter in Don
Quixote, him of the ape and the shamoy doublet, were the apter
comparison; or, with all reverence be it spoken, the ape himself.
His visage is spare, and lean, and saturnine, enlivened by a slight
cast in the dexter eye, and diversified by a partial loss of his teeth,
all those on the left hand having been knocked out by a cricket-
ball, which, aided by the before-mentioned obliquity of vision,
gives a peculiar one-sided expression to his physiognomy.

His tongue is well hung and oily, as suits his vocation. No better
man at a bargain than Master Frost – he would persuade you that
brill was turbot, and that black cherries were Maydukes; and yet,
to be an itinerant vender of fish, the rogue hath a conscience. Try
to bate him down, and he cheats you without scruple or mercy;
but put him on his honour, and he shall deal as fairly with you as

the honestest man in Billingsgate. Neither doth he ever impose on children, with whom, in the matter of shrimps, periwinkles, nuts, apples, and such boyish ware, he hath frequent traffic. He is liberal to the urchins; and I have sometimes been amused to see the Wat Tyler and Robin Hood kind of spirit with which he will fling to some wistful, penniless brat, the identical handful of cherries which, at the risk of his character, and his customer, he hath cribbed from the scales, when weighing out a long-contested bargain with some clamorous housewife.

Also he is an approved judge and devoted lover of country sports; attends all pony races, donkey races, wrestling and cricket matches, an amateur and arbiter of the very first water. At every revel or Maying within six miles of his beat, may Master Frost be seen, pretending to the world, and doubtless to his own conscience (for of all lies those that one tells to that stern monitor are the most frequent) that he is only there in the way of business; whilst in reality the cart, and the old white mare, who perfectly understands the affair, may generally be found in happy quietude under some shady hedge; whilst a black sheepdog, his constant and trusty follower, keeps guard over the panniers, Master Frost himself being seated in full state amidst the thickest of the throng, gravest of umpires, most impartial and learned of referees, utterly oblivious of cart and horse, panniers and sheepdog. The veriest old woman that ever stood before a stall, or carried a fruit-basket, would beat our shrewd merchant out of the field on such a day as that; he hath not even time to bestow a dole on his usual pensioners, the children. Unprofitable days to him, of a surety, so far as blameless pleasure can be called unprofitable; but it is worth something to a spectator to behold him in his glory, to see the earnest gravity, the solemn importance with which he will ponder the rival claims of two runners tied in sacks, or two grinners through a horse-collar.

Such were the habits, the business, and the amusements of our old acquaintance Master Frost. Home he had none, nor family, save the old sheepdog, and the old grey horse, who lived, like himself, on the road; for it was his frequent boast that he never entered a house, but ate, drank and slept in the cart, his only dwelling-place. Who would ever have dreamt of Jacob's marrying! And yet he it is that has just driven down the vicarage lane, seated in, not walking beside, that rumbling conveyance, the mare and the sheepdog decked in white satin favours, already somewhat soiled, and wondering at their own finery; himself adorned in a new suit of brown exactly of the old cut, adding by a smirk and a wink to the usual knowingness of his squinting visage. There he goes, a happy bridegroom, perceiving and enjoying the wonder that he has caused, and chuckling over it in low whispers to his fair bride, whose marriage seems to the puzzled villagers more astonishing still.

In one corner of an irregular and solitary green, communicating by intricate and seldom trodden lanes with a long chain of commons, stands a thatched and whitewashed cottage, whose little dovecot windows, high chimneys, and honeysuckled porch, stand out picturesquely from a richly wooded background; whilst a magnificent yew-tree, and a clear bright pond on one side of the house, and a clump of horse chestnuts overhanging some low weather-stained outbuildings on the other, form altogether an assemblage of objects that would tempt the pencil of a landscape painter, if ever painter could penetrate to a nook so utterly obscure. There is no road across the green, but a well-trodden footpath leads to the door of the dwelling, which the sign of the bell suspended from the yew tree, and a board over the door announcing 'Hester Hewit's home-brewed Beer', denote to be a small public-house.

Everybody is surprised to see even the humblest village hostel in such a situation; but the Bell is in reality a house of great resort, not only on account of Hester's home-brewed, which is said to be the best ale in the county, but also because, in point of fact, that apparently lonely and trackless common is the very high-road of the drovers who come from different points of the west to the great mart, London. Seldom would that green be found without a flock of Welsh sheep, footsore and weary, and yet tempted into grazing by the short fine grass dispersed over its surface, or a drove of gaunt Irish pigs sleeping in a corner, or a score of Devonshire cows straggling in all directions, picking the long grass from the surrounding ditches; whilst dog and man, shepherd and drover, might be seen basking in the sun before the porch, or stretched on the settles by the fire, according to the weather and the season.

The damsel who, assisted by an old Chelsea pensioner minus a leg, and followed by a little stunted red-haired parish-girl and a huge tabby cat, presided over this flourishing hostelry, was a spinster of some fifty years standing, with a reputation as upright as her person; a woman of slow speech and civil demeanour, neat, prim, precise and orderly, stiff-starched and strait-laced as any maiden gentlewoman within a hundred miles. In her youth she must have been handsome; even now, abstract the exceeding primness, the pursed-up mouth, and the bolt-upright carriage, and Hester is far from uncomely, for her complexion is delicate, and her features are regular. And Hester, besides her comeliness and her good ale, is well to do in the world, has money in the stocks, some seventy pounds, a fortune in furniture, feather-beds, mattresses, tables, presses and chairs of shining walnut-tree, to say nothing of a store of home-spun linen, and the united wardrobes of three maiden aunts. A wealthy damsel was Hester, and her suitors most probably have exceeded in number and boldness those of any lady in the land. Welsh drovers, Scotch pedlars, shepherds from Salisbury Plain, and pig-drivers from Ireland – all these had she resisted for five and thirty years, determined to live and die 'in single blessedness', and 'leave the world no copy'.

And she it is whom Jacob has won, from Scotchman and Irishman, pig-dealer and shepherd, she who now sits at his side in sober finery, a demure and blushing bride! Who would ever have thought of Hester's marrying! And when can the wooing have been? And how will they go on together? Will Master Frost still travel the country, or will he sink quietly into the landlord of the Bell? And was the match for love or for money? And what will become of the lame ostler? And how will Jacob's sheepdog agree with Hester's cat? These, and a thousand such, are the questions of the village, whilst the bells ring merrily, and the new married couple went peaceably home.

A Quiet Gentlewoman

MY present reminiscence will hardly be of the tenderest sort, since I am about to commemorate one of the oldest bores of my acquaintance, one of the few grievances of my happy youth. The person in question, my worthy friend Mrs Aubrey, was a respectable widow lady, whose daughter having married a relation of my father's just at the time that she herself came to settle in the town near which we resided, constituted exactly that mixture of juxtaposition and family connexion, which must of necessity lead to a certain degree of intimacy, whatever discrepancies might exist in the habits and characters of the parties. We were intimate accordingly; dined with her once a year, drank tea with her occasionally, and called on her every time that the carriage went into W—; visits which she returned in the lump, by a sojourn of at least a month every summer with us at the Lodge. How my dear mother endured this last infliction I cannot imagine; I most undutifully contrived to evade it, by so timing an annual visit, which I was accustomed to pay, as to leave home on the day before her arrival, and return to it the day after her departure, quite content with the share of *ennui* which the morning calls and the tea-drinkings (evils which generally fell to my lot) entailed upon me.

This grievance was the more grievous, inasmuch as it was one of those calamities which do not admit the great solace and consolation to be derived from complaint. Mrs Aubrey, although the most tiresome person under the sun, without an idea, without a word, a mere inert mass of matter, was yet, in the fullest sense of those 'words of fear', a good sort of woman, well-born, well-bred, well-jointured and well-conducted, a perfectly unexceptionable acquaintance. There were some who even envied me my intimacy with this human automaton, this most extraordinary specimen of still life.

In her youth she had been accounted pretty; a fair, sleepy, blue-eyed beauty, languid and languishing, and was much followed by that class of admirers, who like a woman the better, the nearer she approaches to a picture in demeanour as well as in looks.[1] She had, however, with the disparity that so often attends upon matrimony, fallen to the lot of a most vivacious and mercurial country squire, a thorough-paced fox-hunter, whose pranks (some of them more daring than lawful) had obtained for him the cognomen of 'mad Aubrey'; and having had the good fortune to lose this husband in the third year of their nuptials, she had never undergone the fatigue and trouble of marrying another.

When I became acquainted with her, she was a sleek, round, elderly lady, with very small features, very light eyes, invisible eyebrows, and a flaxen wig. She sat all day long on a sofa by the fireside, with her feet canted up on an ottoman; the ingenious machine called a pair of lazy tongs on one side of her, and a small table on the other, provided with everything that she was likely or unlikely to want for the whole morning. The bell-pull was also within reach; but she had an aversion to ringing the bell, a process which involved the subsequent exertion of speaking to the servant when he appeared. The dumb-waiter was her favourite attendant. There she sat, sofa-ridden; so immoveable, that if the fire had been fierce enough to roast her into a fever, as once happened to some exquisitely silly king of Spain, I do think that she would have followed his example, and have stayed quiet, not from etiquette, but from sheer laziness. She was not however unemployed; your very idle people have generally some play-work, the more tedious

[1] One of her lovers, not quite so devoted to quietude in the fair sex, adventured on a gentle admonition. He presented to her a superb copy of the *Castle of Indolence*, and requested her to read it. A few days after, he inquired of her sister if his fair mistress had condescended to look into the book. 'No,' was the answer; 'No, but I read it to her as she lay on the sofa.' The gentleman was a man of sense. He shrugged his shoulders, and six months after married this identical sister.

and useless the better. Hers was knitting with indefatigable perseverance little diamonds in white cotton, destined at some future period to dovetail into a counterpane. The diamonds were striped, and were intended to be sewed together so artistically that the stripes should intersect each other, one row running perpendicularly and the next horizontally, so as to form a regular pattern; a bit of white mosaic, a tessellated quilt.

At this work I regularly found Mrs Aubrey when compelled to the 'sad civility' of a morning call, in which her unlucky visitor had all the trouble of keeping up the conversation. What a trouble it was! Just like playing at battledore by oneself, or singing a duet with one's own single voice; not the lightest tap would mine hostess give to the shuttlecock; not a note would she contribute to the concert. She might almost as well have been born dumb, and but for a few stray noes and yeses, and once in a quarter of an hour some savourless inquiry, she might certainly have passed for such. She would not even talk of the weather. Then her way of listening! One would have wagered that she was deaf. News was thrown away upon her; scandal did not rouse her; the edge of wit fell upon her dulness like the sword of Richard on the pillow of Saladin. There never was such a woman! Her drawing-room, too, lacked all the artificial aids of conversation: no books, no newspapers, no children, no dogs; nothing but Mrs Aubrey and her knitted squares, and an old Persian cat, who lay stretched on the hearth-rug, as impassable as his mistress; a cat so iniquitously quiet that he would neither play, nor purr, nor scratch, nor give any token of existence beyond mere breathing. I don't think, if a mouse had come across him, that he would have condescended to notice it.

Such was the state of things within the room: without, it was nearly as bad. Her house, one of the best in W—, was situated in a new street standing slantways to one of the entrances of the town: a street of great gentility but of little resort, and, above all, no thoroughfare. So that after going to the window to look for a subject, and seeing nothing but the dead-wall of an opposite chapel, we were driven back to the sofa to expatiate for the twentieth time on Selim's beauty, and admire once again the eternal knitting. Oh the horror of those morning visits!

One very great aggravation of the calamity was the positive certainty of finding Mrs Aubrey at home. The gentle satisfaction with which one takes a ticket from one's card-case, after hearing the welcome answer 'my mistress is just walked out!' never befel one at Mrs Aubrey's. She never took a walk, although she did sometimes, moved by the earnest advice of her apothecary, get so far as to talk of doing so. The weather was always too hot, or too cold; or it had been raining; or it looked likely to rain; or the streets were dirty; or the roads were dusty; or the sun shone; or the sun did not shine (either reason would serve – her laziness was much indebted to that bright luminary); or somebody had called; or somebody might call; or (and this I believe was the excuse that she most commonly made to herself) she had not time to walk on account of her knitting, she wanted to get on with that.

The only time that I ever saw her equipped in out-of-door costume was one unexceptionable morning in April, when the sun, the wind, the sky and the earth were all as bright, and sweet, and balmy, as if they had put themselves in order on purpose to receive an unaccustomed visitor. I met her just as she was issuing slowly from the parlour, and enchanted at my good fortune, entreated, with equal truth and politeness, that I might not keep her within. She entered into no contest of civility; but returned with far more than her usual alacrity into the parlour, rung the bell for her maid, sat down on her dear sofa, and was forthwith unclogged, unshawled and unbonneted, seemingly as much rejoiced at the respite, as a schoolboy reprieved from the rod, or a thief from the gallows. I never saw such an expression of relief, of escape from a great evil, on any human countenance. It would have been quite barbarous to have pressed her to take her intended walk; and, moreover, it would have been altogether useless. She had satisfied her conscience with the attempt, and was now set in to her beloved knitting in contented obstinacy. The whole world would not have moved her from that sofa.

She did however exchange evening visits, in a quiet melancholy way, with two or three ladies her near neighbours, to whose houses she was carried in the stately ease of a sedan-chair – for in those days *flies* were not; at which times the knitting was replaced by cassino. Those visits were, if not altogether so silent, yet very nearly as dull as the inflictions of the morning; her companions (if companions they may be called) being for the most part persons of her own calibre, although somewhat more loquacious. They had a beau or two belonging to this West Street coterie, which even beaux failed to enliven; a powdered physician, rather pompous; a bald curate, very prim; and a simpering semi-bald apothecary, who brushed a few straggling locks up to the top of his crown and tried to make them pass for a head of hair. He was by far the most gallant man of the party, and amongst them might almost be reckoned amusing.

So passed the two first years of Mrs Aubrey's residence in W—. The third brought her a guest whose presence was felt as a relief by everybody, perhaps the only woman who could have kept her company constantly, to the equal satisfaction of both parties.

Miss Dale was the daughter of a deceased officer, with a small independence, who boarded in the winter in Charterhouse Square, and passed her summer in visiting her friends. She was what is called a genteel little woman, of an age that seemed to vary with the light and the hour: oldish in the morning, in the evening almost young, always very smartly dressed, very good-humoured, and very lively. Her spirits were really astonishing; how she could not only appear gay, but be gay in such an atmosphere of dulness, still puzzles me to think of. There was no French blood either, which might have accounted for the phenomenon; her paternal grandfather having been in his time high sheriff for the county of Notts – a genuine English country gentleman; and her mother, strange to relate, a renegade Quakeress, expelled from the Society of Friends for the misdemeanour of espousing an officer. Some sympathy might exist there; no doubt the daughter would have been as ready to escape from a community of lawn caps and drab gowns as the mother. Her love of pink ribbons was certainly hereditary; and, however derived, her temper was as thoroughly *couleur de rose* as her cap trimming. Through the long quiet mornings, the formal visits, the slow dull dinners, she preserved one unvarying gaiety, carried the innovation of smiles amongst the insipid gravities of the cassino table; and actually struck up an intermitting flirtation with the apothecary, which I, in my ignorance, expected to find issue in a marriage, and was simple enough to be astonished, when one morning the gentleman brought home a cherry-cheeked bride, almost young enough to be his granddaughter.

The loss of a lover, however, had no effect on Miss Dale's spirits. I have never known anything more enviable than the buoyancy of her temper. She was not by any means too clever for her company, or too well-informed; never shocked their prejudices, or startled their ignorance, nor ever indeed said anything remarkable at all. On the contrary, I think that her talk, if recollected, would seem, although always amiable and inoffensive, somewhat vapid and savourless; but her prattle was so effervescent, so *up* – the cheerfulness was so natural, so real – that contrary to the effect of most sprightly conversation, it was quite contagious and even exhilarated, as much as any thing could exhilarate the sober circle amongst whom she moved.

She had another powerful attraction in her extraordinary pliancy of mind. No sooner had the stagecoach conveyed her safely to the door of the large house in West Street, than all her Charterhouse Square associations vanished from her mind; it seemed as if she had left locked up in her drawers with her winter apparel every idea not West Streetian. She was as if she had lived in W— all her days; had been born there; and there meant to die. She even divested herself of the allowable London pride, which looks down so scornfully on country dignitaries, admired the Mayor, revered the corporation, preferred the powdered physician to Sir Henry Halford, and extolled the bald curate as the most eminent preacher in England, Mr Harness and Mr Benson notwithstanding.

So worthy a denizen of West Street was of course hailed there with great delight. Mrs Aubrey, always in her silent way glad to receive her friends, went so far as to testify some pleasure at the sight of Miss Dale; and the Persian cat, going beyond his mistress in the activity of his welcome, fairly sprang into her lap. The visits grew longer and longer, more and more frequent, and at last, on some diminution of income, ended in her coming regularly to live with Mrs Aubrey, partly as humble companion, partly as friend: a most desirable increase to that tranquil establishment, which was soon after enlarged by the accession of a far more important visitor.

Besides her daughter, whom she would have probably forgotten if our inquiries had not occasionally reminded her that such a person was in existence, Mrs Aubrey had a son in India, who did certainly slip her memory, except just twice a year when letters arrived from Bengal. She herself never wrote to either of her children, nor did I ever hear her mention Mr Aubrey till one day, when she announced, with rather more animation than common, that poor William had returned to England on account of ill health, and that she expected him in W— that evening.

In the course of a few days my father called on the invalid, and we became acquainted. He was an elegant-looking man, in the prime of life, high in the Company's service, and already possessed of considerable wealth. His arrival excited a great sensation in W— and the neighbourhood. It was the eve of a general election, and some speculating aldermen did him the favour of making an attack upon his purse, by fixing on him as a candidate to oppose the popular member; whilst certain equally speculating mammas meditated a more covert attack on his heart, through the charms of their unmarried daughters. Both parties were fated to disappointment; he waved off either sort of address with equal disdain, and had the good luck to get quit of his popularity almost as rapidly as he had acquired it.

Sooth to say, a man with more eminent qualifications for rendering himself disagreeable than were possessed by Mr Aubrey seldom made his appearance in civilized society. He had nothing in common with his good-humoured mother but her hatred of trouble and of talking; and having the misfortune to be very clever and very proud, tall and stately in his person, with a head habitually thrown back, bright black scornful eyes and a cold disdainful smile, did contrive to gratify his own self-love by looking down upon other people more affrontingly than the self-love of the said people could possibly endure. Nobody knew any harm of Mr Aubrey, but nobody could abide him; so that it being perfectly clear that he would have nothing to say, either to the Borough or the young ladies, the attentions offered to him by town and country suddenly ceased; it being to this hour a moot point whether he or the neighbourhood first sent the other to Coventry.

He, on his part, right glad as it seemed to be rid of their officious civility, remained quietly in his mother's house, very fanciful and a little ill; talking between whiles of an intended visit to Leamington or Cheltenham, but as easily diverted from a measure so unsuited to his habits as an abode at a public place, as Mrs Aubrey herself had been from a morning walk. All the summer he lingered at W—, and all the autumn; the winter found him still there; and at last, he declared that he had made up his mind to relinquish India altogether, and to purchase an estate in England.

By this time our little world had become accustomed to his haughty manner, which had the advantage of being equally ungracious to everyone (people will put up with a great deal in good company; it is the insolence which selects its object that gives indelible offence); and a few who had access to him on business, such as lawyers and physicians, speaking in high terms of his intelligence and information, whilst tradesmen of all classes were won by his liberality, Mr Aubrey was in some danger of under-going a second attack of popularity, when he completely destroyed his rising reputation by a measure the most unexpected and astonishing – he married Miss Dale, to the inexpressible affront of every young lady of fashion in the neighbourhood. He actually married Miss Dale, and all W— spoke of her as the artfulest woman that ever wore a wedding-ring, and pitied poor Mrs Aubrey, whose humble companion had thus ensnared her unwary son. Nothing was heard but sympathy for her imputed sufferings on this melancholy occasion, mixed with abuse of the unfortunate bride, whose extraordinary luck in making so brilliant an alliance had caused her popularity to vanish as speedily as her husband's.

With these reports tingling in my ears, I went to pay the wedding visit to Mrs Aubrey, Senior, delighted at the event myself, both as securing much of good to Miss Dale, who was just the person to enjoy the blessings of her lot, and pass lightly over the evil; and as a most proper and fitting conclusion to the airs of her spouse; but a little doubtful how my old acquaintance might take the matter, especially as it involved the loss of her new daughter's company, and must of necessity cause her some little trouble. I was never more puzzled in my life, whether to assume a visage of condolence or of congratulation; and the certainty that her countenance would afford no indication either of joy or sorrow, enhanced my perplexity. I was, however, immediately relieved by the nature of her employment; she was sitting surrounded by sempstresses, at a table covered with knitting and wedding-cake, whilst her maidens were putting together, under her inspection, that labour of her life – the tessellated quilt: the only wedding present by which she could sufficiently compliment her son, or adequately convey her sense of the merits and excellence of his fair bride! Her pleasure in this union was so great that she actually talked about it, presented the cake herself, and poured out with her own hands the wine to be drunk to the health of the new married couple.

Mr Aubrey had purchased a place in Devonshire, and six months after his mother quitted W— to go and live near him. But, poor dear lady, she did not live there – she died. The unsettling, and the journey, and the settling again, terrible operations to one who seemed, like the Turkish women, to have roots to her feet, fairly killed her. She was as unfit to move as a two-year-old cabbage, and drooped, and withered, and dropped down dead of the transplantation. Peace to her memory! The benediction that she would assuredly have preferred to all others. Peace to her ashes!

The Two Valentines

VALENTINE'S DAY is one of great stir and emotion in our little village. In large towns – especially in London – the wicked habit of quizzing has entirely destroyed the romance and illusion of that tender anniversary. But we in the country are, for the most part, uninfected by 'over-wiseness', or 'over-niceness' (to borrow two of Sir Walter Raleigh's quaint but expressive phrases), and are content to keep the gracious festival of love-making and *billets-doux* as simply and confidingly as our ancestors of old. I do not mean to say that every one of our youths and maidens pair on that day, like the 'goldfinch, bullfinch, greenfinch, and all the finches of the grove'. Heaven forbid! Nor that the spirit of fun hath so utterly evaporated from us that we have no display of innocent trick or harmless raillery on that licensed morn: all that I contend for is that, in our parts, some truth may be found lurking amidst the fictions of those annual rhymes – that many a village beau hath so broken the ice of courtship – and that many a village belle hath felt her heart throb, as she glanced at the emblematic scroll, and tried to guess the sender, in spite of the assumed carelessness, the saucy head-tossings, and the pretty poutings, with which she attempted to veil her real interest. In short, there is something like sincerity amongst us, even in a Valentine; as witness the number of wooings begun on the Fourteenth of February, and finished in that usual end of courtships and comedies – a wedding – before Whitsuntide. Our little lame clerk, who keeps a sort of *catalogue raisonné* of marriages, as a companion to the parish-register, computes those that issue from the bursting Valentine-bag of our postman, at not less than three and a half per annum – that is to say, seven between two years.

But, besides the matches which spring, directly or indirectly, from the *billets* commonly called Valentines, there is another superstition connected with the day, which has no small influence on the destinies of our country maidens. They hold that the first man whom they espy in the morning – provided that such man be neither of kin to them, nor married, nor an inmate of the same house – is to pass for their Valentine during the day; and, perhaps (for this is the secret clause which makes the observation import-ant), to prove their husband for life. It is strange how much faith they put in this kind of *sortes virgilianæ* – this turning over the living leaf of destiny; and how much pains they will take to cheat the fates, and see the man they like best first in spite of the stars! One damsel, for instance, will go a quarter of a mile about, in the course of her ordinary avocations, in order to avoid a youth whom she does not fancy; another shall sit within doors, with her eyes shut, half the morning, until she hears the expected voice of the favourite swain; whilst, on their part, our country lads take care to place themselves each in the way of his chosen she; and a pretty lass would think herself overlooked if she had not three or four standing round her door, or sauntering beneath her window, before sunrise.

Now, one of the prettiest girls in our parish is, undoubtedly, Sally North. Pretty is hardly the proper phrase – Sally is a magnificent girl: tall, far above the common height of woman, and large in proportion, but formed with the exactest symmetry, and distinguished by the firm, erect and vigorous carriage, and the light, elastic step, peculiar to those who are early accustomed to walk under burthens. Sally's father is an eminent baker – the most celebrated personage in our village; besides supplying half the next town with genuine country bread, which he carries thither himself in his huge tilted cart, he hath struck into other arts of the oven, and furnishes all the breakfast tables, within five miles, with genuine London rolls. No family of gentility can possibly get through the first meal without them. The rolls, to be sure, are, just like other rolls, very good, and nothing more; but some whim of a great man, or caprice of a fine lady, has put them in fashion; and so Sally walks round the parish every morning, with her great basket, piled to the very brim, poised on her pretty head, now lending it the light support of one slender hand, and now of another; the dancing black eyes, and the bright blushing smile, that flash from under her burthen, as well as the perfect ease and grace with which she trips along, entirely taking away all painful impression of drudgery or toil. She is quite a figure for a painter, is Sally North — and the gipsy knows it. There is a gay, good-humoured consciousness of her power and her beauty, as she passes on her morning round, carolling as merrily as the lark over her head, that makes no small part of her charm. The lass is clever, too — sharp and shrewd in her dealings — and, although sufficiently civil and respectful to her superiors, and never actually wanting in decorum, is said to dismiss the compliments of some of her beaux with a repartee generally *brusque*, and frequently poignant.

Of beaux — between the lacqueys of the houses that she takes in her circuit, and the wayfarers whom she picks up on the road — Sally hath more than a court beauty; and two of them — Mr Thompson, my lord's gentleman, a man of substance and gravity, not much turned of fifty; and Daniel Tubb, one of Sir John's gardeners, a strapping red-haired youth, as comely and merry as herself — were severally recommended, by the old and the young, as fitting matches for the pretty mistress of the rolls. But Sally silenced Mr Thompson's fine speeches by a very stout, sturdy, steady 'No'; and even inflicted a similar sentence (although so mildly, that Daniel did not quite despair) on his young rival; for Sally, who was seventeen last Candlemas Day, had been engaged these three years!

The love affair had begun at the Free School at Aberleigh; and the object of it, by name Stephen Long, was the son of a little farmer in the neighbourhood, and about the same age with his fair mistress. There the resemblance ceased; for Stephen had been as incomparably the shortest and ugliest boy in the school, as Sally was the tallest and prettiest girl — being, indeed, of that stunted and large-headed appearance which betokens a dwarf, and is usually accompanied by features as unpleasant in their expression as they are grotesque in their form. But then he was the head boy;

and, being held up by the master as a miracle of reading, writing and cyphering, was a personage of no small importance at Aberleigh; and Sally being, with all her cleverness, something of a dunce, owed to Stephen much obligation for assistance in the school business. He arranged, cast up, and set in order on the slate, the few straggling figures which poor Sally called her sum; painted over, and reduced to something like form, the misshapen and disjointed letters in her copy-book; learned all her lessons himself, and tried most ineffectually to teach them to her; and, finally, covered her unconquerable want of memory by the loudest and boldest prompting ever heard out of a theatre. Many a rap of the knuckles have Sally North's blunders cost Stephen Long, and vainly did the master admonish him to hold his tongue. Prompt he would, although so incorrigibly stupid was his fair mistress that, even when the words were put into her mouth, she stumbled at repeating them; and Stephen's officious kindness commonly ended in their being punished in company – a consummation, for his share of which the boy was gallant enough to rejoice. She was fully sensible of this flattering devotion, and repaid it, as far as lay in her power, by taking him under her protection at playtimes, in return for the services which he rendered her in school; and, becoming more and more bound to him by a series of mutual good offices, finished by vindicating his ugliness, denying his pedantry, and, when twitted with his dwarfishness, boldly predicting that he would grow. They walked together, talked together, laughed, romped, and quarrelled – in short, it was a decided attachment; and when our village Romeo was taken as an apprentice by a cousin of his mother's, a respectable hosier in Cheapside, it is on record, that his Juliet, the lightest hearted personage in the neighbourhood, cried for an hour, and moped for a day. All the school stood amazed at her constancy!

Stephen, on his side, bore the test of absence, like a knight of Amadis his day. Never was *preux chevalier* so devoted to the lady of his love. Every letter home contained some tender message or fond inquiry; and although the messages became gradually less and less intelligible, as the small pedantry of the country school-

boy ripened into the full-blown affectation of the London apprentice, still Sally was far from quarrelling with a love message on so
small a ground as not understanding it; whilst, however mys-
terious his words might seem, his presents spoke his affection in a
more homely and convincing language. Of such tokens there was
no lack. The very first packet that he sent home, consisting of
worsted mittens for his old grandmother, a pair of cotton hose for
his sister, and a nightcap for his father, contained also a pair of
scarlet garters for Sally; which attention was followed up at every
opportunity by pin-cushions, ribbons, thimbles, needle-cases and
as great a variety of female ware as that with which Autolycus'
basket was furnished. No wonder that Sally, in spite of occasional
flirtations with Daniel Tubb, continued tolerably constant; especially as one of Stephen's sisters, who had been at service in
London, affirmed that he was so much improved as to be one of
the smartest beaux in all Cheapside.

So affairs continued until this identical Valentine's Day. Last
spring, a written Valentine, exceedingly choice in its decorations,
had made its appearance at Master North's; rather out of date, it
must be owned, since, being enclosed in a packet, to save postage,
and sent by an opportunity, as the country phrase goes, it had been
detained, either by accident or waggery, till the First of April. But
this was none of Stephen's fault: there was the Valentine in the
newest London taste, consisting of a raised group of roses and
heart's-ease, executed on a kind of paper cut-work, which, on
being lifted up, turned into a cage, enclosing a dove – tender
emblem! – with all the rapidity of a change in a pantomime. There
the Valentine was – equally known for Stephen's, by the savour of
the verses and the flourish of the signature – the finest specimen of
poetry and penmanship, as my friend the schoolmaster triumphantly asserted, that had ever been seen in Aberleigh. 'The force
of *writing* could no farther go'; so, this year, our 'good apprentice'
determined to come himself to be her personal Valentine, and to
renew, if not complete, their early engagement.

On this determination being announced to Sally, it occasioned
no small perturbation in that fair damsel, equally alarmed at the
mental accomplishments and the personal defects of her constant

swain. In fact, her feeling towards Stephen had been almost as ideal and unsubstantial as the shadow of a rainbow. She liked to think of him when she had nothing better to do; or to talk of him, when she had nothing better to say; or to be puzzled by his verses, or laughed at for his homage; but as a real substantial Valentine, a present wooer, a future husband, and he so ugly, and a poet too – oh dear! she was frightened to think of it! This impression first broke forth to his sister, who communicated the news of his intended arrival, in a variety of questions as to Stephen's height, and size, and shape, and complexion; especially as compared with Daniel Tubb's! and was afterwards displayed to that rustic adorer himself; not by words, indeed, but by the encouraging silence and saucy smile with which she listened to his account of the debarkation of his cockney rival, from the top of the B— stage. 'He's tinier than ever,' quoth Daniel, 'and the smartest dandy that ever was seen. I shall be your Valentine, after all, Sally,' pursued her swain, 'for I could hide him with the shadow of my fist.'

This was Valentine's Eve. Valentine's Morn saw Sally eyeing the two rivals through a peephole in her little check curtain, as they stood side by side on the green, watching for the first glimpse of their divinity. Never was seen such a contrast. Stephen, whose original square dwarfishness had fined down into a miniature dandy – sallow, strutting, and all over small – the very Tom Thumb of apprentices! Daniel, taller, bigger, ruddier and heartier than ever – the actual Goliath of country lads! Never was such a contrast seen. At length, Sally, laughing, blushing, and bridling, sallied forth from the cottage, her huge roll basket, but not as usual filled with rolls, carried, not on her head, but in her hands. 'I'm your Valentine, Sally! Am I not?' exclaimed Daniel Tubb, darting towards her. 'You saw me first; I know you saw me first,' continued the ardent lover, proceeding to claim the salute usual on such occasions. 'Pshaw! Nonsense! Let me alone then, Daniel, can't you?' was the reply of his mistress, advancing to Stephen, who perhaps dazzled by the beauty, perhaps astounded by the height of the fair giantess, remained motionless and speechless on the other side of the road. 'Would you like a ride in my basket this fine morning, Mr Stephen?' said the saucy lass emptying all his gifts, garters, pin-cushions, ribbons, and Valentines from their huge reservoir, and depositing it on the ground at his feet. 'Don't be afraid; I'll be bound to carry you as easily as the little Italian boy carries *his* tray of images. He's not half the weight of the rolls – is he, Daniel?' pursued the unmerciful beauty. 'For my part, I think he has grown shorter. Come, do step in!' And, with the word, the triumphant Daniel lifted up the discomfited beau, placed him safely in the basket, and hoisted the burthen on Sally's head – to the unspeakable diversion of that saucy maiden, and the complete cure of Master Stephen's love. No need, after this, to declare which of the two rivals is Sally North's Valentine. I think, with the little clerk, that they will be married at Whitsuntide, if not before.

A Country Apothecary

ONE of the most important personages in a small country town is the apothecary. He takes rank next after the rector and the attorney, and before the curate; and could be much less easily dispensed with than either of those worthies, not merely as holding 'fate and physic' in his hand, but as the general and, as it were, official, associate, adviser, comforter and friend of all ranks and all ages, of high and low, rich and poor, sick and well. I am no despiser of dignities; but twenty emperors shall be less intensely missed in their wide dominions than such a man as my friend John Hallett in his own small sphere.

The spot which was favoured with the residence of this excellent person was the small town of Hazelby, in Dorsetshire; a pretty little place, where everything seems at a standstill. It was originally built in the shape of the letter T: a long, broad market-place (still so called, although the market be gone) serving for the perpendicular stem, traversed by a straight, narrow, horizontal street to answer for the top line. Not one addition has occurred to interrupt this architectural regularity since. Fifty years ago, a rich London tradesman built, at the west end of the horizontal street, a wide-fronted single house, with two low wings, iron pallisades before, and a fishpond opposite, which still goes by the name of New Place, and is balanced, at the east end of the street, by an erection of nearly the same date, a large, square, dingy mansion enclosed within high walls, inhabited by three maiden sisters, and called, probably by way of nickname, the Nunnery. New Place being on the left of the road, and the Nunnery on the right, the T has now something the air of the italic capital *T*, turned up at one end and down on the other. The latest improvements are the bow-window in the market-place, commanding the pavement both ways, which the late brewer, Andrews, threw out in his snug parlour some twenty years back, and where he used to sit smoking, with the sash up, in summer afternoons, enjoying himself, good man; and the great room at the Swan, originally built by the speculative publican, Joseph Allwright, for an assembly room. That speculation did not answer. The assembly, in spite of canvassing and patronage, and the active exertions of all the young ladies in the neighbourhood, dwindled away and died at the end of two winters. Then it became a club-room for the hunt, but the hunt quarrelled with Joseph's cookery; then a market-room for the farmers, but the farmers (it was in the high-price time) quarrelled with Joseph's wine; then it was converted into the magistrates' room – the Bench, but the Bench and the market went away together, and there was an end of justicing. Then Joseph tried the novel attraction (to borrow a theatrical phrase) of a billiard-table. But, alas! That novelty succeeded as ill as if it had been theatrical; there were not customers enough to pay the marker. At last, it has merged finally in that unconscious receptacle of pleasure and pain, a post-office; although Hazelby has so little to do with traffic of any sort, even the traffic of correspondence, that a saucy mail-coach will often carry on its small bag, and as often forget to call for the London bag in return.

In short, Hazelby is an insignificant place – my readers will look for it in vain in the map of Dorsetshire. It is omitted, poor dear town! left out by the map-maker with as little remorse as a dropped letter! And it is also an old-fashioned place. It has not even a cheap shop for female gear. Everything in the one store which it boasts, kept by Martha Deane, linen-draper and haberdasher, is dear and good, as things were wont to be. You may actually get there thread made of flax, from the gouty, uneven, clumsy, shiny fabric, yclept whited-brown, to the delicate commodity of lisle, used for darning muslin. I think I was never more astonished than when, on asking, from the mere force of habit, for thread, I was presented, instead of the pretty lattice-wound balls or snowy reels of cotton, with which that demand is usually answered, with a whole drawerful of skeins, peeping from their blue papers – such skeins as in my youth a thrifty maiden would draw into the nicely stitched compartments of that silken repository, a housewife, or fold into a congeries of graduated thread-papers, 'fine by degrees, and beautifully less'. The very literature of Hazelby is doled out at the pastry-cook's, in a little one-windowed shop kept by Matthew Wise. Tarts occupy one end of the counter, and reviews the other; whilst the shelves are parcelled out between books, and dolls, and gingerbread. It is a question by which of his trades poor Matthew gains least; he is so shabby, so threadbare, and so starved.

Such a town would hardly have known what to do with a highly informed and educated surgeon, such as one now generally sees in that most liberal profession. My friend, John Hallett, suited it exactly. His predecessor, Mr Simon Shuter, had been a small, wrinkled, spare old gentleman, with a short cough and thin voice, who always seemed as if he needed an apothecary himself. He wore generally a full suit of drab, a flaxen wig of the sort called a Bob Jerom, and a very tight muslin stock; a costume which he had adopted in his younger days in imitation of the most eminent physician of the next city, and continued to the time of his death. Perhaps the cough might have been originally an imitation also, engrafted on the system by habit. It had a most unsatisfactory sound, and seemed more like a trick than a real effort of nature. His talk was civil, prosy and fidgety, much addicted to small scandal, and that kind of news which passes under the denomination of tittle-tattle. He was sure to tell one half of the town where the other drank tea, and recollected the blancmanges and jellies on a supper-table, or described a new gown, with as much science and unction as if he had been used to make jellies and wear gowns in his own person. Certain professional peculiarities might have favoured the supposition. His mode of practice was exactly that popularly attributed to old women. He delighted in innocent remedies – manna, magnesia and camphor julep; never put on a blister in his life; and would sooner, from pure complaisance, let a patient die, than administer an unpalatable prescription.

So qualified, to say nothing of his gifts in tea-drinking, cassino and quadrille (whist was too many for him), his popularity could not be questioned. When he expired, all Hazelby mourned. The lamentation was general. The women of every degree (to borrow a phrase from that great phrasemonger, Horace Walpole) 'cried quarts'; and the procession to the churchyard – that very churchyard to which he had himself followed so many of his patients – was now attended by all of them that remained alive.

It was felt that the successor of Mr Simon Shuter would have many difficulties to encounter. My friend, John Hallett, 'came, and saw, and overcame'. John was what is usually called a rough diamond. Imagine a short, clumsy, stout-built figure, almost as broad as it is long, crowned by a bullet head, covered with shaggy brown hair, sticking out in every direction; the face round and solid, with a complexion originally fair, but dyed red by exposure to all sorts of weather; open good-humoured eyes of a greenish cast, his admirers called them hazel; a wide mouth, full of large white teeth; a cocked-up nose, and a double chin; bearing altogether a strong resemblance to a print which I once saw hanging up in an ale-house parlour, of 'the celebrated divine' (to use the identical words of the legend) 'Doctor Martin Luther'.

The condition of a country apothecary being peculiarly liable to the inclemency of the season, John's dress was generally such as might bid defiance to wind or rain, or snow or hail. If anything, he wrapped up most in the summer, having a theory that people were never so apt to take cold as in hot weather. He usually wore a bearskin great-coat, a silk handkerchief over his cravat, top boots on those sturdy pillars, his legs, a huge pair of overalls, and a hat, which, from the day in which it first came into his possession to that in which it was thrown aside, never knew the comfort of being freed from its oilskin – never was allowed to display the glossy freshness of its sable youth. Poor dear hat! How its vanity (if hats have vanity) must have suffered! For certain its owner had none, unless a lurking pride in his own bluffness and bluntness may be termed such. He piqued himself on being a plain down-right Englishman, and on a voice and address pretty much like his apparel; rough, strong and warm, and fit for all weathers. A heartier person never lived.

In his profession he was eminently skilful, bold, confident and successful. The neighbouring physicians liked to come after Mr Hallett; they were sure to find nothing to undo. And blunt and abrupt as was his general manner, he was kind and gentle in a sickroom; only nervous disorders, the pet diseases of Mr Simon Shuter, he could not abide. He made short work with them; frightened them away, as one does by children when they have the hiccough; or, if the malady were pertinacious and would not go, he fairly turned off the patient. Once or twice, indeed, on such occasions, the patient got the start, and turned him off; Mrs Emery, for instance, the lady's maid at New Place, most delicate and mincing of waiting-gentlewomen, motioned him from her presence; and Miss Deane, daughter of Martha Deane, haberdasher, who, after completing her education at a boarding-school, kept a closet full of millinery in a little den behind her mamma's shop, and was by many degrees the finest lady in Hazelby, was so provoked at being told by him that nothing ailed her that, to prove her weakly condition, she pushed him by main force out of doors.

With these exceptions, Mr Hallett was the delight of the whole town, as well as of all the farmhouses within six miles round. He just suited the rich yeomanry, cured their diseases, and partook of their feasts; was constant at christenings, and a man of prime importance at weddings. A country merrymaking was nothing without 'the Doctor'. He was 'the very prince of good fellows'; had a touch of epicurism, which, without causing any distaste of his own homely fare, made dainties acceptable when they fell in his way; was a most absolute carver; prided himself upon a sauce of his own invention, for fish and game – 'Hazelby sauce' he called it; and was universally admitted to be the best compounder of a bowl of punch in the country.

Besides these rare convivial accomplishments, his gay and jovial temper rendered him the life of the table. There was no resisting his droll faces, his droll stories, his jokes, his tricks, or his laugh – the most contagious cachinnation that ever was heard. Nothing in the shape of fun came amiss to him. He would join in a catch or roar out a solo, which might be heard a mile off; would play at hunt the slipper, or blindman's buff; was a great man in a country dance, and upon very extraordinary occasions would treat the company to a certain remarkable hornpipe, which put the walls in danger of tumbling about their ears, and belonged to him as exclusively as the Hazelby sauce. It was a sort of parody on a *pas seul* which he had once seen at the opera house, in which his face, his figure, his costume, his rich humour, and his strange, awkward, unexpected activity told amazingly. 'The force of frolic could no farther go', than 'the Doctor's hornpipe'. It was the climax of jollity.

But the chief scene of Mr Hallett's gaiety lay out of doors, in a very beautiful spot, called the Down, a sloping upland, about a mile from Hazelby; a side view of which, with its gardens and orchards, its pretty church peeping from amongst lime and yew trees, and the fine piece of water, called Hazelby Pond, it commanded. The Down itself was an extensive tract of land covered with the finest verdure, backed by a range of hills, and surrounded by coppice woods, large patches of which were scattered over the turf, like so many islands on an emerald sea. Nothing could be more beautiful or more impenetrable than these thickets; they were principally composed of birch, holly, hawthorn and maple, woven together by garlands of woodbine, interwreathed and intertwisted by bramble and brier, till even the sheep, although the bits of their snowy fleece left on the bushes bore witness to the attempt, could make no way in the leafy mass. Here and there a huge oak or beech rose towering above the rich underwood; and all around, as far as the eye could pierce, the borders of this natural shrubbery were studded with a countless variety of woodland flowers. When the old thorns were in blossom, or when they were succeeded by the fragrant woodbine and the delicate brier-rose, it was like a garden, if it were possible to fancy any garden so peopled with birds.[1]

The only human habitation on this charming spot was the

---

[1] A circumstance of some curiosity in natural history occurred for several successive years on this Down. There was constantly in one of the thickets a blackbird's nest, of which the young were distinguished by a striking peculiarity. The old birds (probably the same pair) were of the usual sable colour, but the plumage of their progeny was milk-white, as white as a swan, without a single discoloured feather. They were always taken, and sold at high

cottage of the shepherd, old Thomas Tolfrey, who, with his grand-daughter, Jemima, a light pretty maiden of fourteen, tended the flocks on the Down; and the rustic carols of this little lass and the tinkling of the sheep-bells were usually the only sounds that mingled with the sweet songs of the feathered tribes. On May-days and holidays, however, the thickets resounded with other notes of glee than those of the linnet and the wood-lark. Fairs, revels, May games, and cricket matches – all were holden on the Down; and there would John Hallett sit, in his glory, universal umpire and referee of cricketer, wrestler, or back-sword player, the happiest and greatest man in the field. Little Jemima never failed to bring her grandfather's armchair, and place it under the old oak for the good doctor; I question whether John would have exchanged his throne for that of the king of England.

On these occasions he certainly would have been the better for that convenience, which he piqued himself on not needing – a partner. Generally speaking, he really, as he used to boast, did the business of three men; but when a sickly season and a Maying happened to come together, I cannot help suspecting that the patients had the worst of it. Perhaps, however, a partner might not have suited him. He was sturdy and independent to the verge of a fault, and would not have brooked being called to account, or brought to a reckoning by any man under the sun; still less would he endure the thought of that more important and durable co-partnery – marriage. He was a most determined bachelor; and so afraid of being mistaken for a wooer, or incurring the reputation of a gay deceiver that he was as uncivil as his good nature would permit to every unwedded female from sixteen to sixty, and had nearly fallen into some scrapes on that account with the spinsters of the town, accustomed to the soft silkiness of Mr Simon Shuter. But they got used to it – it was the man's way; and there was an indirect flattery in his fear of their charms which the

---

prices to the curious in such freaks of nature. The late bishop of Winchester had a pair of them for a long time in the aviary at Farnham Castle; they were hardy, and the male was a fine song-bird; but all attempts to breed from them failed. They died, 'and left the world no copy'.

maiden ladies, especially the elder ones, found very mollifying; so he was forgiven.

In his shop and his household he had no need either of partner or of wife: the one was excellently managed by an old rheumatic journeyman, slow in speech and of vinegar aspect, who had been a pedagogue in his youth, and now used to limp about with his Livy in his pocket, and growl, as he compounded the medicines, over the bad Latinity of the prescriptions; the other was equally well conducted by an equally ancient housekeeper and a cherry-cheeked niece, the orphan daughter of his only sister, who kept everything within doors in the bright and shining order in which he delighted. John Hallett, notwithstanding the roughness of his aspect, was rather knick-knacky in his tastes; a great patron of small inventions, such as the improved *ne plus ultra* corkscrew, and the latest patent snuffers. He also trifled with horticulture, dabbled in tulips, was a connoisseur in pinks, and had gained a prize for polyanthuses. The garden was under the especial care of his pretty niece, Miss Margaret, a grateful, warm-hearted girl, who thought she never could do enough to please her good uncle, and prove her sense of his kindness. He was indeed as fond of her as if he had been her father, and as kind.

Perhaps there was nothing very extraordinary in his goodness to the gentle and cheerful little girl, who kept his walks so trim and his parlour so neat, who always met him with a smile, and who (last and strongest tie to a generous mind) was wholly dependent on him – had no friend on earth but himself. There was nothing very uncommon in that. But John Hallett was kind to everyone, even where the sturdy old English prejudices, which he cherished as virtues, might seem most likely to counteract his gentler feelings. One instance of his benevolence and of his delicacy shall conclude this sketch.

Several years ago an old French emigré came to reside at Hazelby. He lodged at Matthew Wise's, of whose twofold shop for cakes and novels I have before made honourable mention, in the low three-cornered room, with a closet behind it, which Matthew had the impudence to call his first floor. Little was known of him but that he was a thin, pale, foreign-looking gentleman, who shrugged his shoulders in speaking, took a great deal of snuff, and made a remarkably low bow. The few persons with whom he had any communication spoke with amusement of his bad English, and with admiration of his good humour, and it soon appeared, from a written paper placed in a conspicuous part of Matthew's shop, that he was an Abbé, and that he would do himself the honour of teaching French to any of the nobility or gentry of Hazelby who might think fit to employ him. Pupils dropped in rather slowly: the curate's daughters, and the attorney's son, and Miss Deane the milliner – but she found the language difficult, and left off, asserting that M. l'Abbé's snuff made her nervous. At last poor M. l'Abbé fell ill himself, really ill, dangerously ill, and Matthew Wise went in all haste to summon Mr Hallett. Now Mr Hallett had such an aversion to a Frenchman, in general, as a cat has to a dog; and was wont to erect himself into an attitude of defiance and wrath at the mere sight of the object of his antipathy. He hated and despised the whole nation, abhorred the language, and 'would as lief,' he assured Matthew, 'have been called in to a toad.' He went, however; grew interested in the case, which was difficult and complicated; exerted all his skill, and in about a month accomplished a cure.

By this time he had also become interested in his patient, whose piety, meekness and resignation had won upon him in an extraordinary degree. The disease was gone, but a languor and lowness remained, which Mr Hallett soon traced to a less curable disorder, poverty: the thought of the debt to himself evidently weighed on the poor Abbé's spirits, and our good apothecary at last determined to learn French purely to liquidate his own long bill. It was the drollest thing in the world to see this pupil of fifty, whose habits were so entirely unfitted for a learner, conning his task; or to hear him conjugating the verb *avoir*, or blundering through the first phrases of the easy dialogues. He was a most unpromising scholar, shuffled the syllables together in a manner that would seem incredible, and stumbled at every step of the pronunciation, against which his English tongue rebelled amain. Every now and then he solaced himself with a fluent volley of execrations in his own language, which the Abbé understood well enough to return, after rather a politer fashion, in French. It was a most amusing scene. But the motive! the generous, noble motive! M. l'Abbé, after a few lessons, detected this delicate artifice, and, touched almost to tears, insisted on dismissing his pupil, who, on his side, declared that nothing should induce him to abandon his studies. At last they came to a compromise. The cherry-cheeked Margaret took her uncle's post as a learner, which she filled in a manner much more satisfactory; and the good old Frenchman not only allowed Mr Hallett to administer gratis to his ailments, but partook of his Sunday dinner as long as he lived.

Wheat-hoeing
A Morning Ramble

MAY 3rd. Cold bright weather. All within doors, sunny and chilly; all without, windy and dusty. It is quite tantalizing to see that brilliant sun careering through so beautiful a sky, and to feel little more warmth from his presence than one does from that of his fair but cold sister, the moon. Even the sky, beautiful as it is, has the look of that one sometimes sees in a very bright moonlight night – deeply, intensely blue, with white fleecy clouds driven vigorously along by a strong breeze, now veiling and now exposing the dazzling luminary around whom they sail. A beautiful sky! And, in spite of its coldness, a beautiful world! The effect of this backward spring has been to arrest the early flowers, to which heat is the great enemy; whilst the leaves and the later flowers have, nevertheless, ventured to peep out slowly and cautiously in sunny places, exhibiting, in the copses and hedgerows, a pleasant mixture of March and May. And we, poor chilly mortals, must follow, as nearly as we can, the wise example of the May blossoms, by avoiding bleak paths and open commons, and creeping up the sheltered road to the vicarage – the pleasant sheltered road, where the western sun steals in between two rows of bright green elms, and the east wind is fenced off by the range of woody hills which rise abruptly before us, forming so striking a boundary to the picture.

How pretty this lane is, with its tall elms, just dressed in their young leaves, bordering the sunny path, or sweeping in a semi-circle behind the clear pools, and the white cottages that are scattered along the way. You shall seldom see a cottage hereabout without an accompanying pond, all alive with geese and ducks, at the end of the little garden. Ah! here is Dame Simmons making a most original use of her piece of water, standing on the bank that divides it from her garden, and most ingeniously watering her onion bed with a new mop – now a dip, and now a twirl! Really, I give her credit for the invention. It is as good an imitation of a shower as one should wish to see on a summer day. A squirt is nothing to it!

And here is another break to the tall line of elms – the gate that leads into farmer Thorpe's great enclosures. Eight, ten, fourteen people in this large field, wheat-hoeing. The couple nearest the gate, who keep aloof from all the rest, and are hoeing this furrow so completely in concert, step by step and stroke for stroke, are Jem Tanner and Mabel Green. There is not a handsomer pair in the field or in the village. Jem, with his bright complexion, his curling hair, his clear blue eye, and his trim figure – set off to great advantage by his short jacket and trousers and new straw hat; Mabel, with her little stuff gown, and her white handkerchief and apron, defining so exactly her light and flexible shape, and her black eyes flashing from under a deep bonnet lined with pink, whose reflection gives to her bright dark countenance and dimpled cheeks a glow innocently artificial, which was the only charm that they wanted.

Jem and Mabel are, beyond all doubt, the handsomest couple in the field, and I am much mistaken if each have not a vivid sense of the charms of the other. Their mutual admiration was clear enough in their work; but it speaks still more plainly in their idleness. Not a stroke have they done for these five minutes; Jem, propped on his hoe, and leaning across the furrow, whispering soft nonsense; Mabel, blushing and smiling, now making believe to turn away, now listening, and looking up with a sweeter smile than ever, and a blush that makes her bonnet-lining pale. Ah, Mabel! Mabel! Now they are going to work again – no! – after three or four strokes, the hoes have somehow become entangled, and, without either advancing a step nearer the other, they are playing with these rustic implements as pretty a game at romps – showing off as nice a piece of rural flirtation – as ever was exhibited since wheat was hoed.

Ah, Mabel! Mabel! Beware of farmer Thorpe! He'll see, at a

glance, that little will his corn profit by such labours. Beware, too, Jem Tanner! For Mabel is, in some sort, an heiress: being the real niece and adopted daughter of our little lame clerk, who, although he looks such a tattered ragamuffin that the very grave-diggers are ashamed of him, is well to pass in the world, keeps a scrub pony, indeed he can hardly walk up the aisle, hath a share in the county fire-office, and money in the funds. Mabel will be an heiress despite the tatterdemalion costume of her honoured uncle, which I think he wears out of coquetry that the remarks which might otherwise fall on his miserable person – full as misshapen as that of any hunchback recorded in the *Arabian Nights* – may find a less offensive vent on his raiment. Certain such a figure hath seldom been beheld out of church or in. Yet will Mabel, nevertheless, be a fortune; and, therefore, she must intermarry with another fortune, according to the rule made and provided in such cases; and the little clerk hath already looked her out a spouse, about his own standing – a widower in the next parish, with four children and a squint. Poor Jem Tanner! Nothing will that smart person or that pleasant speech avail with the little clerk; never will he officiate at your marriage to his niece; 'amen' would 'stick in his throat'. Poor things! In what a happy oblivion of the world and its cares, farmer Thorpe and the wheat-hoeing, the squinting shopkeeper and the little clerk, are they laughing and talking at this moment! Poor things! Poor things!

Well, I must pursue my walk. How beautiful a mixture of flowers and leaves is in the high bank under this north hedge –

quite an illustration of the blended seasons of which I spoke. An old irregular hedgerow is always beautiful, especially in the springtime, when the grass, and mosses, and flowering weeds mingle best with the bushes and creeping plants that overhang them. But this bank is, most especially, various and lovely. Shall we try to analyse it? First, the clinging white-veined ivy, which crawls up the slope in every direction, the masterpiece of that rich mosaic; then the brown leaves and the lilac blossoms of its fragrant namesake, the ground-ivy, which grows here so profusely; then the late-lingering primrose; then the delicate wood-sorrel; then the regular pink stars of the cranesbill, with its beautiful leaves; then the golden oxlip and the cowslip, 'cinque-spotted'; then the blue pansy, and the enamelled wild hyacinth; then the bright foliage of the brier-rose, which comes trailing its green wreaths amongst the flowers; then the bramble and the woodbine, creeping round the foot of a pollard oak, with its brown folded leaves; then a verdant mass – the blackthorn, with its lingering blossoms, the hawthorn, with its swelling buds, the bushy maple, the long stems of the hazel, and between them, hanging like a golden plume over the bank, a splendid tuft of the blossomed broom; then, towering high above all, the tall and leafy elms. And this is but a faint picture of this hedge, on the meadowy side of which sheep are bleating, and where, everywhere and there, a young lamb is thrusting its pretty head between the trees.

Who is this approaching? Farmer Thorpe? Yes, of a certainty, it is that substantial yeoman, sallying forth from his substantial farmhouse, which peeps out from between two huge walnut trees on the other side of the road, with intent to survey his labourers in the wheatfield. Farmer Thorpe is a stout, square, sturdy personage of fifty, or thereabout, with a hard, weather-beaten countenance, of that peculiar vermilion, all over alike, into which the action of the sun and wind sometimes tans a fair complexion; sharp, shrewd features, and a keen grey eye. He looks completely like a man who will neither cheat nor be cheated; and such is his character – an upright, downright English yeoman – just always, and kind in a rough way, but given to fits of anger, and filled with an abhorrence of pilfering, and idleness, and trickery of all sorts that makes him strict as a master, and somewhat stern at work-house and vestry. I doubt if he will greatly relish the mode in which Jem and Mabel are administering the hoe in his wheat-drills. He will not reach the gate yet! for his usual steady active pace is turned, by a recent accident, into an unequal, impatient halt, as if he were alike angry with his lameness and the cause. I must speak to him as he passes – not merely as a due courtesy to a good neighbour, but to give the delinquents in the field notice to resume their hoeing; but not a word of the limp – that is a sore subject.

'A fine day, Mr Thorpe!'

'We want rain, ma'am?'

And on, with great civility, but without pausing a moment, he is gone. He'll certainly catch Mabel and her love philandering over his wheat-furrows. Well, that may take its chance! They have his lameness in their favour – only that the cause of that lameness has made the worthy farmer unusually cross. I think I must confide the story to my readers.

Gipsies and beggars do not in general much inhabit our neigh-bourhood; but, about half a mile off, there is a den so convenient for strollers and vagabonds that it sometimes tempts the rogues to a few days' sojourn. It is, in truth, nothing more than a deserted brick-kiln, by the side of a lonely lane. But there is something so smug and comfortable in the old building (always keeping in view gipsy notions of comfort); the blackened walls are so backed by the steep hill on whose side they are built, so fenced from the bleak north-east, and letting in so gaily the pleasant western sun; and the wide, rugged, impassable lane (used only as a road to the kiln, and with that abandoned) is at once so solitary and deserted, and so close to the inhabited and populous world that it seems made for a tribe whose prime requisites in a habitation are shelter, privacy and a vicinity to farmyards.

Accordingly, about a month ago, a pretty strong encampment, evidently gipsies, took up their abode in the kiln. The party consisted of two or three tall, lean, sinister-looking men, who went about the country mending pots and kettles, and driving a small trade in old iron; one or two children unnaturally quiet, the spies of the crew; an old woman, who sold matches and told fortunes; a young woman, with an infant strapped to her back, who begged; several hungry-looking dogs, and three ragged donkeys.

The arrival of these vagabonds spread a general consternation through the village. Gamekeepers and housewives were in equal dismay. Snares were found in the preserves; poultry vanished from the farmyards; a lamb was lost from the Lea; and a damask tablecloth, belonging to the worshipful the mayor of W—, was abstracted from the drying-ground of Rachel Strong, the most celebrated laundress in these parts, to whom it had been sent for the benefit of country washing. No end to the pilfering, and the stories of pilfering! The inhabitants of the kiln were not only thieves in themselves, but the cause of thievery in others. 'The gipsies!' was the answer general to every inquiry for things missing.

Farmer Thorpe, whose dwelling, with its variety of outbuildings, barns, ricks and stables, is only separated by a meadow and a small coppice from the lane that leads to the gipsy retreat, was particularly annoyed by this visitation. Two couple of full-grown ducks, and a whole brood of early chickens, disappeared in one night; and Mrs Thorpe fretted over the loss, and the farmer was indignant at the roguery. He set traps, let loose mastiffs, and put in action all the resources of village police – but in vain. Every night, property went; and the culprits, however strongly suspected, still continued unamenable to the law.

At last, one morning, the great Chanticleer of the farmyard – a cock of a million, with an unrivalled crow, a matchless strut, and plumage all gold and green, and orange, and purple, gorgeous as a peacock, and fierce as a he-turkey – Chanticleer, the pride and glory of the yard, was missing! And Mrs Thorpe's lamentations and her husband's anger redoubled. Vowing vengeance against the gipsies, he went to the door to survey a young blood mare of his own breeding; and as he stood at the gate, now bemoaning Chanticleer, now cursing the gipsies, now admiring the bay filly, his neighbour, Dame Simmons – the identical lady of the mop, who occasionally charred at the house – came to give him the comfortable information that she had certainly heard Chanticleer, she was quite ready to swear to Chanticleer's voice, crowing in the brick-kiln. No time, she added, should be lost, if Farmer Thorpe wished to rescue that illustrious cock, and to punish the culprits, since the gipsies, when she passed the place, were preparing to decamp.

No time *was* lost. In one moment Farmer Thorpe was on the bay filly's unsaddled back, with the halter for a bridle; and, in the next, they were on full gallop towards the kiln. But, alas! alas! 'the more haste the worse speed', says the wisdom of nations. Just as they arrived at the spot from which the procession, gipsies, dogs and donkeys, and Chanticleer in a sack, shrieking most vigorously, were proceeding on their travels, the young blood mare – whether startled at the unusual *cortège*, or the rough ways, or the hideous noise of her old friend, the cock – suddenly reared and threw her master, who lay in all the agony of a sprained ankle, unable to rise from the ground; whilst the whole tribe, with poor Chanticleer their prisoner, marched triumphantly past him, utterly regardless of his threats and imprecations. In this plight was the unlucky farmer discovered, about half an hour afterwards, by his wife, the constable, and a party of his own labourers, who came to give him assistance in securing the culprits; of whom, notwithstanding an instant and active search through the neighbourhood, nothing has yet transpired. We shall hardly see them again in these parts, and have almost done talking of them. The village is returned to its old state of order and honesty; the mayor of W— has replaced his tablecloth, and Mrs Thorpe her cock; and the poor farmer's lame ankle is all that remains to give token of the gipsies.

Here we are at the turning, which, edging round by the coppice, branches off to their sometime den; the other bend to the right leads up a gentle ascent to the vicarage, and that is our way. How fine a view of the little parsonage we have hence, between those arching elms, which enclose it like a picture in a frame! and how pretty a picture it forms, with its three pointed roofs, its snug porch, and its casement windows glittering from amid the china-roses! What a nest of peace and comfort! Farther on, almost at the summit of the hill, stands the old church with its massy tower – a row of superb lime trees running along one side of the churchyard, and a cluster of dark yews shading the other. Few country churches have so much to boast in architectural beauty, or in grandeur of situation.

We lose sight of it as we mount the hill, the lane narrowing and winding between deep banks, surmounted by high hedges, excluding all prospects till we reach the front of the vicarage, and catch across the gate of the opposite field a burst of country the most extensive and the most beautiful – field and village, mansion and cot, town and river, all smiling under the sparkling sun of May, and united and harmonized by the profusion of hedgerow timber in its freshest verdure, giving a rich woodland character to the scene, till it is terminated in the distance by the blue line of the Hampshire hills almost melting into the horizon. Such is the view from the vicarage. But it is too sunny and too windy to stand about out of doors, and time to finish our ramble. Down the hill, and round the corner, and past farmer Thorpe's house, and one glance at the wheat-hoers, and then we will go home.

Ah! It is just as I feared. Jem and Mabel have been parted: they are now at opposite sides of the fields – he looking very angry, working rapidly and violently, and doing more harm than good; she looking tolerably sulky, and just moving her hoe, but evidently doing nothing at all. Farmer Thorpe, on his part, is standing in the middle of the field, observing, but pretending not to observe, the little humours of the separated lovers. There is a lurking smile about the corners of his mouth that bespeaks him more amused than angry. He is a kind person after all, and will certainly make no mischief. I should not even wonder if he espoused Jem Tanner's cause; and, for certain, if anyone can prevail on the little clerk to give up his squinting favourite in favour of true love, farmer Thorpe is the man.

The Chalk Pit

ONE of the most admirable persons whom I have ever known is my friend Mrs Mansfield, the wife of the good vicar of Aberleigh. Her daughters are just what might be expected from girls trained under such a mother. Of Clara, the youngest, I have spoken elsewhere. Ellen, the elder sister, is as delightful a piece of sunshine and gaiety as ever gladdened a country home. One never thinks whether she is pretty, there is such a play of feature, such a light in her dark eye, such an alternation of blush and smile on her animated countenance; for Ellen has her mother's trick of blushing, although her 'eloquent blood' speaks through the medium of a richer and browner skin. One forgets to make up one's mind as to her prettiness; but it is quite certain that she is charming.

She has, in the very highest degree, those invaluable everyday spirits which require no artificial stimuli, no public amusements, no company, no flattery, no praise. Her sprightliness is altogether domestic. Her own dear family, and a few dear friends, are all the listeners she ever thinks of. No one doubts but Ellen might be a wit, if she would; she is saved from that dangerous distinction as much by natural modesty as by a kind and constant consideration for the feelings of others. I have often seen a repartee flashing and laughing in her bright eyes, but seldom, very seldom, heard it escape her lips; never unless quite equally matched and challenged to such a bout of 'bated foils' by some admirer of her playful conversation. They who have themselves that splendid but de- lusive talent can best estimate the merit of such forbearance. Governed as it is in her, it makes the delight of the house, and supplies perpetual amusement to herself and to all about her.

Another of her delightful and delighting amusements is her remarkable skill in drawing flowers. I have never seen any portraits so exactly resembling the originals as her carnations and geraniums. If they could see themselves in her paintings, they might think that it was their own pretty selves in their looking-glass, the water. One reason for this wonderful verisimilitude is that our fair artist never flatters the flowers that sit to her; never puts leaves that ought to be there, but are not there, never makes them hold up their heads unreasonably, or places them in an attitude, or forces them into a group. Just as they are, she sets them down; and if she does make any slight deviation from her models, she is so well-acquainted with their persons and habits, that all is in keeping; you feel that so the plant might have looked. By the way, I do not know any accomplishment that I would more earnestly recommend to my young friends than this of flower-painting. It is a most quiet, unpretending, womanly employment; a great amusement within doors, and a constant pleasure without. The enjoyment of a country walk is much enhanced when the chequered fritillary or the tinted wood anemone are to be sought, and found, and gathered, and made our own; and the dear domestic spots, haunted by

> Retired leisure,
> Who in trim gardens takes his pleasure,

are doubly gardens when the dahlias and china-asters, after flourishing there for their little day, are to re-blossom on paper. Then it supplies such pretty keepsakes, the uncostly remembrances which are so pleasant to give and to take; and, above all, it fosters and sharpens the habit of observation and the love of truth. How much of what is excellent in art, in literature, in conversation, and in conduct, is comprised in that little word!

Ellen had great delight in comparing our sylvan flora with the minute and fairy blossoms of the South Downs, where she had passed the greater part of her life. She could not but admit the superior luxuriance and variety of our woodland plants, and yet she had a good deal to say in favour of the delicate, flowery carpet, which clothes the green hills of Sussex; and in fact was on that point of honour, a little jealous – a little, a very little, the least in the world, touchy. She loved her former abode, the abode of her childhood, with enthusiasm: the downs; the sea, whose sound, as she said, seemed to follow her to her inland home, to dwell within her as it does in the folds of the seashell; and, above all, she loved her old neighbours, high and low. I do not know whether Mrs Mansfield or her daughters returned oftenest to the 'simple annals of the *Sussex* poor'. It was a subject of which they never wearied; and we to whom they came, liked them the more for their clinging and lingering affection for those whom they had left. We received it as a pledge of what they would feel for us when we became better acquainted, a pledge which has been amply redeemed. I flatter myself that Aberleigh now almost rivals their dear old parish; only that Clara, who has been here three years, and is now eighteen, says, very gravely, that 'people as they grow old, cannot be expected to form the very strong local attachments which they did when they were young.' I wonder how old Clara will think herself when she comes to be eight-and-twenty?

Between Ellen's stories and her mother's there is usually a characteristic difference: those of the one being merry, those of the other grave. One occurrence, however, was equally impressed on the mind of either. I shall try to tell it as shortly and simply as it was told to me; but it will want the charm of Mrs Mansfield's touching voice, and of Ellen's glistening eyes.

Towards the bottom of one of the green hills of the parish of Lanton was a large deserted chalk pit; a solemn and ghastly-looking place, blackened in one part by an old lime-kiln, whose ruinous fragments still remained, and in others mossy and weather-stained, and tinted with every variety of colour – green, yellow and brown. The excavation extended far within the sides of the hill, and the edges were fringed by brier, and bramble, and ivy, contrasting strongly with the smooth, level verdure of the turf above, whilst plants of a ranker growth, nettles, docks, and fumatory, sprang up beneath, adding to the wildness and desolation of the scene. The road that led by the pit was little frequented. The place had an evil name; none cared to pass it even in the glare of the noonday sun; and the villagers would rather go a mile about than catch a glimpse of it when the pale moonlight brought into full relief those cavernous white walls, and the dark briers and ivy waved fitfully in the night wind. It was a vague and shuddering feeling. None knew why he feared, or what; but the awe and the avoidance were general, and the owls and the bats remained in undisturbed possession of Lanton chalk pit.

One October day, the lively work of ploughing, and wheat-sowing, and harrowing was going on all at once in a great field just beyond the dreaded spot: a pretty and an interesting scene, especially on sloping ground, and under a gleaming sun throwing an ever-shifting play of light and shadow over the landscape. Towards noon, however, the clouds began to gather, and one of the tremendous pelting showers, peculiar to the coast, came suddenly on. Seedsmen, ploughmen and carters hastened home with their teams, leaving the boys to follow; and they, five in number, set out at their fullest speed. The storm increased apace; and it was evident that their thin jackets and old smock-frocks would be drenched through and through long before they could reach Lanton Great Farm. In this dilemma, James Goddard, a stout lad of fifteen, the biggest and boldest of the party, proposed to take shelter in the chalk pit. Boys are naturally thoughtless and fearless; the real inconvenience was more than enough to counterbalance the imaginary danger, and they all willingly adopted the plan, except one timid child, eight years old, who shrunk and hung back.

Harry Lee was a widow's son. His father, a fisherman, had perished at sea, a few months after the birth of this only child; and his mother, a fond and delicate woman, had reared him delicately and fondly, beyond her apparent means. Night and day had she laboured for her poor Harry; and nothing but a long illness and the known kindness of the farmer in whose service he was placed had induced her to part with him at so early an age.

Harry was, indeed, a sweet and gracious boy, noticed by every stranger for his gentleness and beauty. He had a fair, blooming, open countenance; large, mild, blue eyes, which seemed to ask kindness in every glance; and a quantity of shining, light hair, curling in ringlets round his neck. He was the best reader in Mrs

Mansfield's Sunday-school and only the day before, Miss Clara had given him a dinner to carry home to his mother, in reward of his proficiency: indeed, although they tried to conceal it, Harry was the decided favourite of both the young ladies. James Goddard, under whom he worked, and to whose care he had been tearfully committed by the widow Lee, was equally fond of him, in a rougher way; and in the present instance, seeing the delicate boy shivering between cold and fear at the outside of the pit (for the same constitutional timidity which prevented his entering, hindered him from going home by himself), he caught him up in his arms, brought him in, and deposited him in the snuggest recess, on a heap of dry chalk. 'Well, Harry, is not this better than standing in the wet?' said he kindly, sitting down by his protégé, and sharing with him a huge luncheon of bread and cheese; and the poor child smiled in his face, thanked him, and kissed him, as he had been used to kiss his mother.

Half an hour had passed away in boyish talk, and still the storm continued. At last James Goddard thought that he heard a strange and unaccustomed sound, as of bursting or cracking – an awful and indescribable sound: low, and yet distinctly audible, although the wind and rain were raging, and the boys loud in mirth and laughter. He seemed to feel the sound, as he said afterwards; and was just about to question his companions if they too heard that unearthly noise, when a horseman passed along the road, making signs to them and shouting. His words were drowned in the tempest; James rushed out to inquire his meaning; and in that moment the side of the chalk pit fell in! He heard a crash and a scream – the death scream! – felt his back grazed by the descending mass; and turning round saw the hill rent, as by an earthquake, and the excavation which had sheltered them, filled, piled, heaped up, by the still quivering and gigantic fragments – no vestige left to tell where it was, or where his wretched companions lay buried!

'Harry! Harry! The child! The child!' was his first thought and his first exclamation. 'Help! Instant help!' was the next, and, assisted by the stranger horseman, whose speed had been stayed by the awful catastrophe, the village of Lanton was quickly alarmed, and its inhabitants assembled on the spot. Who may describe that scene! Fathers, brothers, kinsmen, friends, digging literally for life! every nerve quivering with exertion, and yet all exertion felt to be unavailing. Mothers and sisters looking on in agony; and the poor widow Lee, and poor, poor, James Goddard, the self-accuser! A thousand and a thousand times did he crave pardon of that distracted mother, for the peril – the death of her son; for James felt that there could be no hope for the helpless child, and tears, such as no personal calamity could have drawn from the strong-hearted lad, fell fast for his fate. Hour after hour the men of Lanton laboured, and all was in vain. The mass seemed impenetrable, inexhaustible. Towards sunset one boy appeared, crushed and dead; another, who showed some slight signs of life, and who still lives, a cripple; a third dead; and then, last of all, Harry Lee. Alas! Only by his raiment could that fond mother know her child! His death must have been instantaneous. She did not linger long. The three boys were interred together in Lanton churchyard on the succeeding Sabbath; and before the end of the year, the widow Lee was laid by her son.

Whitsun Eve

THE pride of my heart and the delight of my eyes is my garden. Our house, which is in dimensions very much like a bird-cage, and might, with almost equal convenience, be laid on a shelf, or hung up in a tree, would be utterly unbearable in warm weather, were it not that we have a retreat out of doors – and a very pleasant retreat it is. To make my readers fully comprehend it, I must describe our whole territories.

Fancy a small plot of ground with a pretty low irregular cottage at one end; a large granary, divided from the dwelling by a little court running along one side; and a long thatched shed open towards the garden, and supported by wooden pillars on the other. The bottom is bounded, half by an old wall, and half by an old paling, over which we see a pretty distance of woody hills. The house, granary, wall and paling are covered with vines, cherry trees, roses, honeysuckles, and jessamines, with great clusters of tall hollyhocks running up between them; a large elder overhanging the little gate, and a magnificent bay tree, such a tree as shall scarcely be matched in these parts, breaking with its beautiful conical form the horizontal lines of the buildings. This is my garden; and the long pillared shed, the sort of rustic arcade which runs along one side, parted from the flower-beds by a row of rich geraniums, is our out-of-door drawing-room.

I know nothing so pleasant as to sit there on a summer afternoon with the western sun flickering through the great elder tree and lighting up our gay parterres, where flowers and flowering shrubs are set as thick as grass in a field – a wilderness of blossom, interwoven, intertwined, wreathy, garlandy, profuse beyond all profusion, where we may guess that there is such a thing as mould, but never see it. I know nothing so pleasant as to sit in the shade of that dark bower with the eye resting on that bright piece of colour, lighted so gloriously by the evening sun, now catching a glimpse of the little birds as they fly rapidly in and out of their nests – for there are always two or three bird's-nests in the thick tapestry of cherry trees, honeysuckles, and china-roses, which covers our walls; now tracing the gay gambols of the common butterflies as they sport around the dahlias; now watching that rarer moth, which the country people, fertile in pretty names, call the bee-bird;[1] that bird-like insect, which flutters in the hottest days over the sweetest flowers, inserting its long proboscis into the small tube of the jessamine, and hovering over the scarlet blossoms of the geranium, whose bright colour seems reflected on its own feathery breast; that insect which seems so thoroughly a creature of the air, never at rest; always, even when feeding, self-poised, and self-supported, and whose wings, in their ceaseless motion, have a sound so deep, so full, so lulling, so musical. Nothing so pleasant as to sit amid that mixture of the flower and the leaf, watching the bee-bird! Nothing so pretty to look at as my garden! It is quite a picture; only unluckily it resembles a picture in more qualities than one – it is fit for nothing but to look at. One might as well think of walking in a bit of framed canvas. There are walks to be sure – tiny paths of smooth gravel, by courtesy called such – but they are so overhung by roses and lilies, and such gay encroachers; so over-run by convolvulus, and heart's-ease, and mignonette, and other sweet stragglers that, except to edge through them occasionally, for the purposes of planting, or weeding, or watering, there might as well be no paths at all. Nobody thinks of walking in my garden. Even May glides along with a delicate and trackless step, like a swan through the water; and we, its two-footed denizens, are fain to treat it as if it were really a saloon, and go out for a walk towards sunset, just as if we had not been sitting in the open air all day.

What a contrast from the quiet garden to the lively street! Saturday night is always a time of stir and bustle in our village,

---

[1] *Sphinx ligustri*, privet hawk-moth.

and this is Whitsun Eve, the pleasantest Saturday of all the year, when London journeymen and servant lads and lasses snatch a short holiday to visit their families. A short and precious holiday, the happiest and liveliest of any; for even the gambols and merrymakings of Christmas offer but a poor enjoyment, compared with the rural diversions, the Mayings, revels and cricket matches of Whitsuntide.

We ourselves are to have a cricket match on Monday, not played by the men, who, since a certain misadventure with the Beech Hillers, are, I am sorry to say, rather chapfallen, but by the boys, who, zealous for the honour of their parish, and headed by their bold leader, Ben Kirby, marched in a body to our antagonists' ground the Sunday after our melancholy defeat, challenged the boys of that proud hamlet, and beat them out and out on the spot. Never was a more signal victory. Our boys enjoyed this triumph with so little moderation that it had like to have produced a very tragical catastrophe. The captain of the Beech Hill youngsters, a capital bowler, by name Amos Stone, enraged past all bearing by the crowing of his adversaries, flung the ball at Ben Kirby with so true an aim that, if that sagacious leader had not warily ducked his head when he saw it coming, there would probably have been a coroner's inquest on the case, and Amos Stone would have been tried for manslaughter. He let fly with such vengeance that the cricket-ball was found embedded in a bank of clay five hundred yards off, as if it had been a cannon shot. Tom Coper and farmer Thackum, the umpires, both say that they never saw so tremendous a ball. If Amos Stone live to be a man (I mean to say, if he be not hanged first), he'll be a pretty player. He is coming here on Monday with his party to play the return match, the umpires having respectively engaged farmer Thackum that Amos shall keep the peace, Tom Coper that Ben shall give no unnecessary or wanton provocation — a nicely worded and lawyer-like clause, and one that proves that Tom Coper hath his doubts of the young gentleman's discretion; and, of a truth, so have I. I would not be Ben Kirby's surety, cautiously as the security is worded. No! not for a white double dahlia, the present object of my ambition.

This village of ours is swarming tonight like a hive of bees, and all the church bells round are pouring out their merriest peals, as if to call them together. I must try to give some notion of the various figures.

First there is a group suited to Teniers, a cluster of out-of-door customers of the Rose, old benchers of the inn, who sit round a table smoking and drinking in high solemnity to the sound of Timothy's fiddle. Next, a mass of eager boys, the combatants of Monday, who are surrounding the shoemaker's shop, where an invisible hole in their ball is mending by Master Keep himself, under the joint superintendence of Ben Kirby and Tom Coper; Ben showing much verbal respect and outward deference for his umpire's judgment and experience, but managing to get the ball done his own way after all. Whilst outside the shop, the rest of the eleven, the less-trusted commons, are shouting and bawling round Joel Brent, who is twisting the waxed twine round the handles of the bats – the poor bats, which please nobody, which the taller youths are despising as too little and too light, and the smaller are abusing as too heavy and too large. Happy critics! Winning their match can hardly be a greater delight – even if to win it they be doomed! Farther down the street is the pretty black-eyed girl, Sally Wheeler, come home for a day's holiday from B—, escorted by a tall footman in a dashing livery, whom she is trying to curtsy off before her deaf grandmother sees him. I wonder whether she will succeed!

Ascending the hill are two couples of a different description. Daniel Tubb and his fair Valentine, walking boldly along like licensed lovers; they have been asked twice in church, and are to be married on Tuesday; and closely following that happy pair, near each other, but not together, come Jem Tanner and Mabel Green, the poor culprits of the wheat-hoeing. Ah, the little clerk hath not relented! The course of true love doth not yet run smooth in that quarter. Jem dodges along, whistling 'Cherry ripe', pretending to walk by himself, and to be thinking of nobody; but every now and then he pauses in his negligent saunter, and turns round outright to steal a glance at Mabel, who, on her part, is making believe to walk with poor Olive Hathaway, the lame mantua-maker, and even affecting to talk and to listen to that gentle, humble creature, as she points to the wild flowers on the common, and the lambs and children disporting amongst the gorse; but whose thoughts and eyes are evidently fixed on Jem Tanner, as she meets his backward glance with a blushing smile, and half springs forward to meet him; whilst Olive has broken off the conversation as soon as she perceived the preoccupation of her companion, and begun humming, perhaps unconsciously, two or three lines of Burns, whose 'Whistle and I'll come to thee, my love', and 'Gi'e me a glance of thy bonnie black ee', were never better exemplified than in the couple before her. Really, it is curious to watch them, and to see how gradually the attraction of this tantalizing vicinity becomes irresistible, and the rustic lover rushes to his pretty mistress like the needle to the magnet. On they go, trusting to the deepening twilight, to the little clerk's absence, to the good humour of the happy lads and lasses, who are passing and re-passing on all sides; or rather, perhaps, in a happy oblivion of the cross uncle, the kind villagers, the squinting lover, and the whole world. On they trip, linked arm-in-arm, he trying to catch a glimpse of her glowing face under her bonnet, and she hanging down her head and avoiding his gaze with a mixture of modesty and coquetry, which well becomes the rural beauty. On they go, with a reality and intensity of affection, which must overcome all obstacles; and poor Olive follows with an evident sympathy in their happiness, which makes her almost as enviable as they. And we pursue our walk amidst the moonshine and the nightingales, with Jacob Frost's cart looming in the distance, and the merry sounds of Whitsuntide, the shout, the laugh, and the song echoing all around us, like 'noises of the air'.

Our Maying

As party produces party, and festival brings forth festival in higher life, so one scene of rural festivity is pretty sure to be followed by another. The boys' cricket match at Whitsuntide, which was won most triumphantly by our parish, and luckily passed off without giving cause for a coroner's inquest, or indeed without injury of any sort, except the demolition of Amos Stone's new straw hat, the crown of which (Amos's head being fortunately at a distance) was fairly struck out by the cricket-ball; this match produced one between our eleven and the players of the neighbouring hamlet of Whitley; and being patronized by the young lord of the manor and several of the gentry round, and followed by jumping in sacks, riding donkey-races, grinning through horse-collars, and other diversions more renowned for their antiquity than their elegance, gave such general satisfaction that it was resolved to hold a Maying in full form in Whitley wood.

Now this wood of ours happens to be a common of twenty acres, with three trees on it, and the Maying was fixed to be held between hay-time and harvest; but 'what's in a name?' Whitley wood is a beautiful piece of green sward, surrounded on three sides by fields, and farmhouses, and cottages and woody uplands, and on the other by a fine park; and the May house was erected, and the May games held in the beginning of July – the very season of leaves and roses, when the days are at the longest, and the weather at the finest, and the whole world is longing to get out of doors. Moreover, the whole festival was aided, not impeded, by the gentlemen amateurs, headed by that very genial person, our young lord of the manor; whilst the business part of the affair was confided to the well-known diligence, zeal, activity and intelligence of that most popular of village landlords, mine host of the Rose. How could a Maying fail under such auspices? Everybody expected more sunshine and more fun, more flowers and more laughing than ever was known at a rustic merrymaking – and really, considering the manner in which expectation had been raised, the quantity of disappointment has been astonishingly small.

Landlord Sims, the master of the revels, and our very good neighbour, is a portly bustling man, of five-and-forty, or thereabout, with a hale, jovial visage, a merry eye, a pleasant smile and a general air of good fellowship. This last qualification, whilst it serves greatly to recommend his ale, is apt to mislead superficial observers, who generally account him a sort of slenderer Boniface, and imagine that, like that renowned hero of the spigot, Master Sims eats, drinks and sleeps on his own anno domini. They were never more mistaken in their lives: no soberer man than Master Sims within twenty miles! Except for the good of the house, he no more thinks of drinking beer than a grocer of eating figs. To be sure when the jug lags he will take a hearty pull, just by way of example, and to set the good ale a-going. But, in general, he trusts to subtler and more delicate modes of quickening its circulation. A good song, a good story, a merry jest, a hearty laugh and a most winning habit of assentation: these are his implements. There is not a better companion, or a more judicious listener in the county. His pliability is astonishing. He shall say yes to twenty different opinions on the same subject, within the hour; and so honest and cordial does his agreement seem that no one of his customers, whether drunk or sober, ever dreams of doubting his sincerity. The hottest conflict of politics never puzzles him: Whig or Tory, he is both, or either – 'the happy Mercutio, that curses both houses'. Add to this gift of conformity, a cheerful, easy temper, an alacrity of attention, a zealous desire to please, which gives to his duties, as a landlord, all the grace of hospitality and a perpetual civility and kindness, even when he has nothing to gain by them, and no one can wonder at Master Sims's popularity.

After his good wife's death, this popularity began to extend itself in a remarkable manner amongst the females of the neighbourhood; smitten with his portly person, his smooth oily manner, and a certain soft, earnest, whispering voice, which he generally assumes when addressing one of the fairer sex, and which seems to make his very 'How d'ye do' confidential and complimentary. Moreover, it was thought that the good landlord was well to do in the world; and though Betsy and Letty were good little girls, quick, civil, and active, yet, poor things, what could such young girls know of a house like the Rose? All would go to rack and ruin without the eye of a mistress! Master Sims must look out for a wife. So thought the whole female world, and, apparently, Master Sims began to think so himself.

The first fair one to whom his attention was directed, was a rosy, pretty widow, a pastry-cook of the next town, who arrived in our village on a visit to her cousin, the baker, for the purpose of giving confectionery lessons to his wife. Nothing was ever so hot as that courtship. During the week that the lady of pie-crust stayed, her lover almost lived in the oven. One would have thought that he was learning to make the cream-tarts without pepper by which Bedreddin Hassan regained his state and his princess. It would be a most suitable match, as all the parish agreed; the widow, for as pretty as she was (and one sha'n't often see a pleasanter open countenance, or a sweeter smile), being within ten years as old as her suitor, and having had two husbands already. A most proper and suitable match, said everybody; and, when our landlord carried her back to B— in his new-painted green cart, all the village agreed that they were gone to be married, and the ringers were just setting up a peal, when Master Sims returned alone, single, crestfallen, dejected: the bells stopped of themselves, and we heard no more of the pretty pastry-cook. For three months after that rebuff, mine host, albeit not addicted to aversions, testified an equal dislike to women and tartlets, widows and plum-cake. Even poor Alice Taylor, whose travelling basket of lollipops and gingerbread he had whilome patronized, was forbidden the house; and not a bun or a biscuit could be had at the Rose, for love or money.

The fit, however, wore off in time; and he began again to follow the advice of his neighbours, and to look out for a wife, up street and down; whilst at each extremity a fair object presented herself, from neither of whom had he the slightest reason to dread a repetition of the repulse which he had experienced from the blooming widow. The down-street lady was a widow also; the portly, comely relict of our drunken village blacksmith, who, in spite of her joy at her first husband's death, and an old spite at mine host of the Rose, to whose good ale and good company she was wont to ascribe most of the aberrations of the deceased, began to find her shop, her journeymen, and her eight children (six unruly obstreperous pickles of boys, and two tomboys of girls) rather more than a lone woman could manage, and to sigh for a helpmate to ease her of her cares, collect the boys at night, see the girls to school of a morning, break the large imps of running away to revels and fairs, and the smaller fry of bird's-nesting and orchard-robbing, and bear a part in the lectures and chastisements, which she deemed necessary to preserve the young rebels from the bad end which she predicted to them twenty times a day. Master Sims was the coadjutor on whom she had inwardly pitched; and, accordingly, she threw out broad hints to that effect, every time she encountered him, which, in the course of her search for boys and girls, who were sure to be missing at schooltime and bedtime, happened pretty often; and Mr Sims was far too gallant and too much in the habit of assenting to listen unmoved; for really the widow was a fine, tall, comely woman; and the whispers, and smiles, and hand-pressings, when they happened to meet, were becoming very tender; and his admonitions and head-shakings, addressed to the young crew (who, nevertheless, all liked him) quite fatherly. This was his down-street flame.

The rival lady was Miss Lydia Day, the carpenter's sister; a slim, upright maiden, not remarkable for beauty, and not quite so young as she had been, who, on inheriting a small annuity from the mistress with whom she had spent the best of her days, retired to her native village to live on her means. A genteel, demure, quiet personage was Miss Lydia Day; much addicted to snuff and green tea, and not averse from a little gentle scandal—for the rest, a good sort of woman, and *un très bon parti* for Master Sims, who seemed to consider it a profitable speculation, and made love to her whenever she happened to come into his head, which, it must be confessed, was hardly so often as her merits and her annuity deserved. Remiss as he was, he had no lack of encouragement to complain of – for she 'to hear would seriously incline', and put on her best silk, and her best simper, and lighted up her faded complexion into something approaching to a blush, whenever he came to visit her. And this was Master Sims's up-street love.

So stood affairs at the Rose when the day of the Maying arrived; and the double flirtation, which, however dexterously managed, must have been, sometimes, one would think, rather inconvenient to the inamorato, proved on this occasion extremely useful. Each of the fair ladies contributed her aid to the festival: Miss Lydia by tying up sentimental garlands for the May house, and scolding the carpenters into diligence in the erection of the booths; the widow by giving her whole bevy of boys and girls a holiday, and turning them loose on the neighbourhood to collect flowers as they could. Very useful auxiliaries were these light foragers; they scoured the country far and near – irresistible mendicants! pardonable thieves! coming to no harm, poor children, except that little George got a black eye in the tumbling from the top of an acacia tree at the Park, and that Sam (he's a sad pickle is Sam!) narrowly escaped a horse-whipping from the head gardener at the Hall, who detected a bunch of his new rhododendron, the only plant in the county, forming the very crown and centre of the Maypole. Little harm did they do, poor children, with all their pilfery; and when they returned, covered with their flowery loads, like the May Day figure called 'Jack of the Green', they worked at the garlands and the May houses, as none but children ever do work, putting all their young life and their untiring spirit of noise and motion into their pleasant labour. Oh, the din of that building! Talk of the Tower of Babel! That was a quiet piece of masonry compared to the May house of Whitley Wood, with its walls of leaves and flowers, and its canvas booths at either end for refreshments and musicians. Never was known more joyous note of preparation.

The morning rose more quietly, I had almost said more dully, and promised ill for the fête. The sky was gloomy, the wind cold, and the green filled as slowly as a balloon seems to do when one is watching it. The entertainments of the day were to begin with a cricket match (two elevens to be chosen on the ground), and the wickets pitched at twelve o'clock precisely. Twelve o'clock came, but no cricketers, except, indeed, some two or three punctual and impatient gentlemen; one o'clock came, and brought no other reinforcement than two or three more of our young Etonians and Wykhamites – less punctual than their precursors, but not a whit less impatient. Very provoking, certainly, but not very uncommon. Your country cricketer, the peasant, the mere rustic, does love, on these occasions, to keep his betters waiting, if only to display his power; and when we consider that it is the one solitary opportunity in which importance can be felt and vanity gratified, we must acknowledge it to be perfectly in human nature that a few airs should be shown. Accordingly, our best players held aloof. Tom Coper would not come to the ground; Joel Brent came, indeed, but would not play; Samuel Long coquetted – he would and he would not. Very provoking, certainly! Then two young farmers, a tall brother and a short, Hampshire men, cricketers born, whose good humour and love of the game rendered them sure cards, had been compelled to go on business – the one, ten miles south; the other, fifteen north – that very morning. No playing without the Goddards! No sign of either of them on the B— road or the F—. Most intolerably provoking, beyond a doubt! Master Sims tried his best coaxing and his best double X on the recusant players; but all in vain. In short, there was great danger of the match going off altogether; when, about two o'clock, Amos Stone, who was there with the crown of his straw hat sewed in wrong side outward, new thatched, as it were, and who had been set to watch the B— highway, gave notice that something was coming as tall as the Maypole – which something turning out to be the long Goddard, and his brother approaching at the same moment in the opposite direction, hope, gaiety, and good humour revived again; and two elevens, including Amos and another urchin of his calibre, were formed on the spot. •

I never saw a prettier match. The gentlemen, the Goddards, and the boys being equally divided, the strength and luck of the parties were so well-balanced that it produced quite a neck-and-neck race, won only by two notches. Amos was completely the hero of the day, standing out half of his side, and getting five notches at one hit. His side lost – but so many of his opponents gave him their ribbons (have not I said that Master Sims bestowed a set of ribbons?) that the straw hat was quite covered with purple trophies; and Amos, stalking about the ground, with a shy and awkward vanity looked with his decorations like the sole conqueror – the Alexander or Napoleon of the day. The boy did not speak a word; but every now and then he displayed a set of huge white teeth in a grin of inexpressible delight. By far the happiest and proudest personage of that Maying was Amos Stone.

By the time the cricket match was over, the world began to be gay at Whitley Wood. Carts and gigs, and horses and carriages, and people of all sorts, arrived from all quarters; and lastly, 'the blessed sun himself' made his appearance, adding a triple lustre to the scene. Fiddlers, ballad-singers, cake-baskets, Punch, Master Frost, crying cherries, a Frenchman with dancing dogs, a Bavarian woman selling brooms, half a dozen stalls with fruit and frippery, and twenty noisy games of quoits, and bowls, and ninepins, boys throwing at boxes, girls playing at ball, gave to the assemblage the bustle, clatter, and gaiety of a Dutch fair, as one sees it in Teniers' pictures. Plenty of drinking and smoking on the green; plenty of eating in the booths. The gentlemen cricketers, at one end, dining off a round of beef, which made the table totter; the players, at the other, supping off a gammon of bacon; Amos Stone crammed at both; and landlord Sims bustling everywhere with an activity that seemed to confer upon him the gift of ubiquity, assisted by the little light-footed maidens, his daughters, all smiles and curtsies, and by a pretty black-eyed young woman, name unknown, with whom, even in the midst of his hurry, he found time, as it seemed to me, for a little philandering. What would the widow and Miss Lydia have said? But they remained in happy ignorance – the one drinking tea in most decorous primness in a distant marquee, disliking to mingle with so mixed an assembly; the other in full chase after the most unlucky of all her urchins, the boy called Sam, who had gotten into a *démêlé*, with a showman, in consequence of mimicking the wooden gentleman Punch, and his wife Judy, thus, as the showman observed, bringing his exhibition into disrepute.

Meanwhile, the band struck up in the May house, and the dance, after a little demur, was fairly set afloat – an honest English country dance (there had been some danger of waltzing and quadrilling) with ladies and gentlemen at the top, and country lads and lasses at the bottom; a happy mixture of cordial kindness on the one hand, and pleased respect on the other. It was droll though to see the beplumed and beflowered French hats, the silks and the furbelows sailing and rustling amidst the straw bonnets and cotton gowns of the humbler dancers; and not less so to catch a glimpse of the little lame clerk, shabbier than ever, peeping through the canvas opening of the booth, with a grin of ineffable delight, over the shoulder of our vicar's pretty wife. Really, considering that Mabel Green and Jem Tanner were standing together at that moment at the top of the set, so deeply engaged in making love that they forgot when they ought to begin, and that the little clerk must have seen them, I cannot help taking his grin for a favourable omen to those faithful lovers.

Well, the dance finished, the sun went down, and we departed. The Maying is over, the booths carried away, and the May house demolished. Everything has fallen into its old position, except the love affairs of landlord Sims. The pretty lass with the black eyes, who first made her appearance at Whitley wood, is actually staying at the Rose Inn, on a visit to his daughters; and the village talk goes that she is to be the mistress of that thriving hostelry, and the wife of its master. And both her rivals are jealous, after their several fashions – the widow in the tantrums, the maiden in the dumps. Nobody knows exactly who the black-eyed damsel may be, but she's young, and pretty, and civil, and modest; and, without intending to depreciate the merits of either of her competitors, I cannot help thinking that our good neighbour has shown his taste.

The Mole-catcher

THERE are no more delightful or unfailing associations than those afforded by the various operations of the husbandman, and the changes on the fair face of nature. We all know that busy troops of reapers come with the yellow corn, whilst the yellow leaf brings a no less busy train of ploughmen and seedsmen preparing the ground for fresh harvests; that woodbines and wild roses, flaunting in the blossomy hedgerows, give token of the gay bands of haymakers which enliven the meadows; and that the primroses, which begin to unfold their pale stars by the side of the green lanes, bear marks of the slow and weary female processions, the gangs of tired yet talkative bean-setters, who defile twice a day through the intricate mazes of our cross-country roads. These are general associations, as well known and as universally recognized as the union of mince-pies and Christmas. I have one, more private and peculiar, one, perhaps, the more strongly impressed on my mind because the impression may be almost confined to myself. The full flush of violets which, about the middle of March, seldom fails to perfume the whole earth, always brings to my recollection one solitary and silent coadjutor of the husbandman's labours, as unlike a violet as possible – Isaac Bint, the mole-catcher.

I used to meet him every spring, when we lived at our old house, whose park-like paddock, with its finely clumped oaks and elms, and its richly timbered hedgerows, edging into wild, rude, and solemn fir plantations, dark, and rough, and hoary, formed for so many years my constant and favourite walk. Here, especially under the great horse chestnut, and where the bank rose high and naked above the lane, crowned only with a tuft of golden broom;

222

here the sweetest and prettiest of wild flowers, whose very name hath a charm, grew like a carpet under one's feet, enamelling the young green grass with their white and purple blossoms, and loading the air with their delicious fragrance; here I used to come almost every morning, during the violet-tide; and here almost every morning I was sure to meet Isaac Bint.

I think that he fixed himself the more firmly in my memory by his singular discrepancy with the beauty and cheerfulness of the scenery and the season. Isaac is a tall, lean, gloomy personage, with whom the clock of life seems to stand still. He has looked sixty-five for these last twenty years, although his dark hair and beard, and firm manly stride, almost contradict the evidence of his sunken cheeks and deeply lined forehead. The stride is awful: he hath the stalk of a ghost. His whole air and demeanour savour of one that comes from underground. His appearance is 'of the earth, earthy'. His clothes, hands and face are of the colour of the mould in which he delves. The little round traps which hang behind him over one shoulder, as well as the strings of dead moles which embellish the other, are encrusted with dirt like a tombstone; and the staff which he plunges into the little hillocks, by which he traces the course of his small quarry, returns a hollow sound, as if tapping on the lid of a coffin. Images of the churchyard come, one does not know how, with his presence. Indeed he does officiate as assistant to the sexton in his capacity of grave-digger, chosen, as it should seem, from a natural fitness; a fine sense of congruity in good Joseph Reed, the functionary in question, who felt, without knowing why, that, of all men in the parish, Isaac Bint was best fitted to that solemn office.

His remarkable gift of silence adds much to the impression produced by his remarkable figure. I don't think that I ever heard him speak three words in my life. An approach of that bony hand to that earthy leather cap was the greatest effort of courtesy that my daily salutations could extort from him. For this silence, Isaac has reasons good. He hath a reputation to support. His words are too precious to be wasted. Our mole-catcher, ragged as he looks, is the wise man of the village, the oracle of the village inn, foresees the weather, charms away agues, tells fortunes by the stars, and writes notes upon the almanac, turning and twisting about the predictions after a fashion so ingenious that it is a moot point which is oftenest wrong – Isaac Bint, or Francis Moore. In one eminent instance, our friend was, however, eminently right. He had the good luck to prophesy, before sundry witnesses – some of them sober, in the tap-room of the Bell; he then sitting, pipe in mouth, on the settle at the right-hand side of the fire, whilst Jacob Frost occupied the left – he had the good fortune to foretell, on New Year's Day, 1812, the downfall of Napoleon Bonaparte – a piece of soothsayership which has established his reputation, and dumbfounded all doubters and cavillers ever since, but which would certainly have been more striking if he had annually uttered the same prediction, from the same place, from the time that the aforesaid Napoleon became first consul. But this small circumstance is entirely overlooked by Isaac and his admirers, and they believe in him, and he believes in the stars, more firmly than ever.

Our mole-catcher is, as might be conjectured, an old bachelor. Your married man hath more of this world about him – is less, so to say, planet-struck. A thorough old bachelor is Isaac, a contemner and maligner of the sex, a complete and decided woman-hater. Female frailty is the only subject on which he hath ever been known to dilate; he will not even charm away their agues, or tell their fortunes, and, indeed, holds them to be unworthy the notice of the stars.

No woman contaminates his household. He lives on the edge of a pretty bit of woodland scenery, called the Penge, in a snug cottage of two rooms, of his own building, surrounded by a garden cribbed from the waste, well-fenced with quickset, and well-stocked with fruit trees, herbs and flowers. One large apple tree extends over the roof – a pretty bit of colour when in blossom, contrasted with the thatch of the little dwelling, and relieved by the dark wood behind. Although the owner be solitary, his demesne is sufficiently populous. A long row of bee-hives extends along the warmest side of the garden, for Isaac's honey is celebrated far and near; a pig occupies a commodious stye at one corner; and large flocks of ducks and geese (for which the Penge, whose glades are intersected by water, is famous) are generally waiting round a back gate leading to a spacious shed, far larger than Isaac's own cottage, which serves for their feeding and roosting-place. The great tameness of all these creatures – for the ducks and geese flutter round him the moment he approaches, and the very pig follows him like a dog – gives no equivocal testimony of the kindness of our mole-catcher's nature. A circumstance of recent occurrence puts his humanity beyond doubt.

Amongst the probable causes of Isaac's dislike to women, may be reckoned the fact of his living in a female neighbourhood (for the Penge is almost peopled with duck-rearers and goose-crammers of the duck and goose gender), and being himself exceedingly unpopular amongst the fair poultry-feeders of that watery vicinity. He beat them at their own weapons; produced at Midsummer geese fit for Michaelmas; and raised ducks so precocious that the gardeners complained of them as forerunning their vegetable accompaniments: 'panting *peas* toiled after them in vain'. In short, the naiads of the Penge had the mortification to find themselves driven out of B— market by an interloper, and that interloper a man, who had no manner of right to possess any skill in an accomplishment so exclusively feminine as duck-rearing. And being no ways inferior in another female accomplishment, called scolding, to their sister-nymphs of Billingsgate, they set up a clamour and a cackle which might rival the din of their own gooseries at feeding-time, and would inevitably have frightened from the field any competitor less impenetrable than our hero. But Isaac is not a man to shrink from so small an evil as female objurgation. He stalked through it all in mute disdain, looking now at his mole-traps, and now at the stars, pretending not to hear, and very probably not hearing. At first this scorn, more provoking than any retort, only excited his enemies to fresh attacks; but one cannot be always answering another person's silence. The flame which had blazed so fiercely at last burned itself out, and peace reigned once more in the green alleys of Penge wood.

One, however, of his adversaries – his nearest neighbour – still remained unsilenced.

Margery Grover was a very old and poor woman, whom age

and disease had bent almost to the earth; shaken by palsy, pinched by penury, and soured by misfortune – a moving bundle of misery and rags. Two centuries ago she would have been burned for a witch; now she starved and grumbled on the parish allowance; trying to eke out a scanty subsistence by the dubious profits gained from the produce of two geese and a lame gander, once the unmolested tenants of a greenish pool, situated right between her dwelling and Isaac's, but whose watery dominion had been invaded by his flourishing colony.

This was the cause of feud; and although Isaac would willingly, from a mingled sense of justice and of pity, have yielded the point to the poor old creature, especially as ponds are there almost as plentiful as blackberries, yet it was not so easy to control the habits and inclinations of their feathered subjects, who all perversely fancied that particular pool; and various accidents and skirmishes occurred, in which the ill-fed and weak birds of Margery had generally the worst of the fray. One of her early goslings was drowned – an accident which may happen even to water-fowl; and her lame gander, a sort of pet with the poor old woman, injured in his well leg; and Margery vented curses as bitter as those of Sycorax; and Isaac, certainly the most superstitious personage in the parish – the most thorough believer in his own gifts and predictions – was fain to nail a horseshoe on his door for the defence of his property, and to wear one of his own ague charms about his neck for his personal protection.

Poor old Margery! A hard winter came; and the feeble, tottering creature shook in the frosty air like an aspen leaf; and the hovel in which she dwelled – for nothing could prevail on her to try the shelter of the workhouse – shook like herself at every blast. She was not quite alone either in the world or in her poor hut: husband, children and grandchildren had passed away, but one young and innocent being, a great-grandson, the last of her descendants, remained, a helpless dependant on one almost as helpless as himself.

Little Harry Grover was a shrunken, stunted boy, of five years old; tattered and squalid, like his grandame, and, at first sight, presented almost as miserable a specimen of childhood, as Margery herself did of age. There was even a likeness between them; although the fierce blue eye of Margery had, in the boy, a mild appealing look, which entirely changed the whole expression of the countenance. A gentle and a peaceful boy was Harry, and, above all, a useful. It was wonderful how many ears of corn in the autumn, and sticks in the winter, his little hands could pick up! How well he could make a fire, and boil the kettle, and sweep the hearth, and cram the goslings! Never was a handier boy or a trustier; and when the united effects of cold, and age, and rheumatism confined poor Margery to her poor bed, the child continued to perform his accustomed offices: fetching the money from the vestry, buying the loaf at the baker's, keeping house, and nursing the sick woman, with a kindness and thoughtfulness, which none but those who know the careful ways to which necessity trains cottage children would deem credible; and Margery, a woman of strong passions, strong prejudices and strong affections, who had lived in and for the desolate boy, felt the approach of death, embittered by the certainty that the workhouse, always the scene of her dread and loathing, would be the only refuge for the poor orphan.

Death, however, came on visibly and rapidly; and she sent for the overseer to beseech him to put Harry to board in some decent cottage; she could not die in peace until he had promised; the fear of the innocent child's being contaminated by wicked boys and godless women preyed upon her soul; she implored, she conjured. The overseer, a kind but timid man, hesitated, and was beginning a puzzled speech about the bench and the vestry, when another voice was heard from the door of the cottage.

'Margery,' said our friend Isaac, 'will you trust Harry to me? I am a poor man, to be sure; but, between earning and saving, there'll be enough for me and little Harry. 'Tis as good a boy as ever lived, and I'll try to keep him so. Trust him to me, and I'll be a father to him. I can't say more.'

'God bless thee, Isaac Bint! God bless thee!' was all poor Margery could reply.

They were the last words she ever spoke. And little Harry is living with our good mole-catcher, and is growing plump and rosy; and Margery's other pet, the lame gander, lives and thrives with them, too.

Mademoiselle Thérèse

ONE of the prettiest dwellings in our neighbourhood is the Lime Cottage at Burley Hatch. It consists of a small low-browed habitation, so entirely covered with jessamine, honeysuckle, passion-flowers and china-roses as to resemble a bower, and is placed in the centre of a large garden, turf and flowers before, vegetables and fruit trees behind, backed by a superb orchard, and surrounded by a quickset hedge, so thick, and close, and regular as to form an impregnable defence to the territory which it encloses – a thorny rampart, a living and growing *chevaux-de-frise*. On either side of the neat gravel walk, which leads from the outer gate to the door of the cottage, stand the large and beautiful trees to which it owes its name; spreading their strong, broad shadow over the turf beneath, and sending, on a summer afternoon, their rich, spicy fragrance half across the irregular village green, dappled with wood and water, and gay with sheep, cattle and children, which divides them, at the distance of a quarter of a mile, from the little hamlet of Burley, its venerable church and handsome rectory, and its short straggling street of cottages, and country shops.

Such is the habitation of Thérèse de G., an emigrée of distinction, whose aunt having married an English officer, was luckily able to afford her niece an asylum during the horrors of the Revolution, and to secure to her a small annuity and the Lime Cottage after her death. There she has lived for these five-and-thirty years, gradually losing sight of her few and distant foreign connexions, and finding all her happiness in her pleasant home and her kind neighbours – a standing lesson of cheerfulness and contentment.

229

Mademoiselle Thérèse

A very popular person is Mademoiselle Thérèse – popular both with high and low; for the prejudice which the country people almost universally entertain against foreigners, vanished directly before the charm of her manners, the gaiety of her heart, and the sunshine of a temper that never knows a cloud. She is so kind to them too, so liberal of the produce of her orchard and garden, so full of resource in their difficulties, and so sure to afford sympathy if she has nothing else to give, that the poor all idolize Mademoiselle. Among the rich, she is equally beloved. No party is complete without the pleasant Frenchwoman, whose amenity and cheerfulness, her perfect, general politeness, her attention to the old, the poor, the stupid and the neglected, are felt to be invaluable in society. Her conversation is not very powerful either, nor very brilliant; she never says anything remarkable, but then it is so good-natured, so genuine, so unpretending, so constantly up and alive, that one would feel its absence far more than that of a more showy and ambitious talker; to say nothing of the charm which it derives from her language, which is alternately the most graceful and purest French, and the most diverting and absurd broken English – a dialect in which, whilst contriving to make herself perfectly understood both by gentle and simple, she does also contrive, in the course of an hour, to commit more blunders than all the other foreigners in England make in a month.

Her appearance betrays her country almost as much as her speech. She is a French-looking little personage, with a slight, active figure, exceedingly nimble and alert in every movement; a round and darkly complexioned face, somewhat faded and *passée*, but still striking from the laughing eyes, the bland and brilliant smile, and the great mobility of expression. Her features, pretty as they are, want the repose of an English countenance; and her air, gesture, and dress, are decidedly foreign, all alike deficient in the English charm of quietness. Nevertheless, in her youth, she must have been pretty; so pretty that some of our young ladies, scandalized at finding their favourite an old maid, have invented sundry legends to excuse the solecism, and talk of duels fought *pour l'amour de ses beaux yeux*, and of a betrothed lover guillo-tined in the Revolution. And the thing may have been so; although one meets everywhere with old maids who have been pretty, and whose lovers have not been guillotined; and although Mademoiselle Thérèse has not, to do her justice, the least in the world the air of a heroine crossed in love. The thing may be so, but I doubt it much. I rather suspect our fair demoiselle of having been in her youth a little of a flirt. Even during her residence at Burley Hatch hath not she indulged in divers very distant, very discreet, very decorous, but still very evident flirtations? Did not Doctor Abdy, the portly, ruddy schoolmaster of B—, dangle after her for three mortal years, holidays excepted? And did she not refuse him at last? And Mr Foreclose, the thin, withered, wrinkled city solicitor, a man, so to say, smoke-dried, who comes down every year to Burley for the air, did not he do suit and service to her during four long vacations, with the same ill success? Was not Sir Thomas himself a little smitten? Nay, even now, does not the good major, a halting veteran of seventy – but really it is too bad to tell tales out of the parish. All that is certain is that Mademoiselle Thérèse might have changed her name long before now had she so chosen; and that it is most probable that she will never change it at all.

Her household consists of her little maid Betsy, a cherry-cheeked, blue-eyed country lass, brought up by herself, who, with a full clumsy figure, and a fair, innocent, unmeaning countenance, copies, as closely as these obstacles will permit, the looks and gestures of her alert and vivacious mistress, and has even caught her broken English; of a fat lap-dog, called Fido, silky, sleepy, and sedate; and of a beautiful white Spanish ass, called Donnabella, an animal docile and spirited, far beyond the generality of that despised race, who draws her little donkey chaise half the country over, runs to her the moment she sees her, and eats roses, bread and apples from her hand; but who, accustomed to be fed and groomed, harnessed and driven only by females, resists and rebels the moment she is approached by the rougher sex; has overturned more boys, and kicked more men, than any donkey in the kingdom; and has acquired such a character for restiveness amongst the grooms in the neighbourhood that when Mademoiselle Thérèse goes out to dinner, Betsy is fain to go with her to drive Donnabella home again, and to return to fetch her mistress in the evening.

If everybody is delighted to receive this most welcome visitor, so is everybody delighted to accept her graceful invitations, and meet to eat strawberries at Burley Hatch. Oh, how pleasant are those summer afternoons, sitting under the blossomed limes, with the sun shedding a golden light through the broad branches, the bees murmuring overhead, roses and lilies all about us, and the choicest fruit served up in wicker baskets of her own making – itself a picture! The guests looking so pleased and happy, and the kind hostess the gayest and happiest of all. Those are pleasant meetings; nor are her little winter parties less agreeable, when, to two or three female friends assembled round their coffee, she will tell thrilling stories of that terrible Revolution, so fertile in great crimes and great virtues; or gayer anecdotes of the brilliant days preceding that convulsion, the days which Madame de Genlis has described so well, when Paris was the capital of pleasure, and amusement the business of life; illustrating her descriptions by a series of spirited drawings of costumes and characters done by herself, and always finishing by producing a group of Louis Seize, Marie Antoinette, the Dauphin, and Madame Elizabeth, as she had last seen them at Versailles – the only recollection that ever brings tears into her smiling eyes.

Mademoiselle Thérèse's loyalty to the Bourbons was in truth a very real feeling. Her family had been about the court, and she had imbibed an enthusiasm for the royal sufferers natural to a young and a warm heart – she loved the Bourbons, and hated Napoleon with like ardour. All her other French feelings had for some time been a little modified. She was not quite so sure as she had been that France was the only country, and Paris the only city of the world; that Shakespeare was a barbarian, and Milton no poet; that the perfume of English limes was nothing compared to French orange trees; that the sun never shone in England; and that sea-coal fires were bad things. She still, indeed, would occasionally make these assertions, especially if dared to make them; but her faith in them was shaken. Her loyalty to her legitimate king was, however, as strong as ever, and that loyalty had nearly cost us our dear Mademoiselle. After the Restoration, she hastened as fast as steamboat and diligence could carry her to enjoy the delight of seeing once more the Bourbons at the Tuileries; took leave, between smiles and tears, of her friends, and of Burley Hatch, carrying with her a branch of the lime tree, then in blossom, and commissioning her old lover, Mr Foreclose, to dispose of the cottage. But in less than three months, luckily before Mr Foreclose had found a purchaser, Mademoiselle Thérèse came home again. She complained of nobody, but times were altered. The house in which she was born was pulled down; her friends were scattered, her kindred dead; Madame did not remember her (she had probably never heard of her in her life); the king did not know her again (poor man! he had not seen her for these thirty years); Paris was a new city; the French were a new people; she missed the sea-coal fires; and for the stunted orange trees at the Tuileries, what were they compared with the blossomed limes of Burley Hatch!

Lost and Found

ANYBODY may be lost in a wood. It is well for me to have so good an excuse for my wanderings; for I am rather famous for such misadventures, and have sometimes been accused by my kindest friends of committing intentional blunders, and going astray out of malice prepense. To be sure, when in two successive rambles I contrived to get mazed on Burghfield Common, and bewildered in Kibe's Lane, those exploits did seem to overpass the common limits of stupidity. But in a wood, and a strange wood, a new place, a fresh country, untrodden ground beneath the feet, unknown landmarks before the eyes, wiser folks than I might require the silken clue of Rosamond, or the bag of ashes given to Finette Cendron (Anglice, Cinderella) by the good fairy her godmother, to help them home again. Now my luck exceeded even hers of the Glass Slipper, for I found something not unlike the good fairy herself in the pleasant earthly guise of an old friend. But I may as well begin my story.

About two years ago we had the misfortune to lose one of the most useful and popular inhabitants of our village, Mrs Bond the butterwoman. She – for although there was a very honest and hardworking farmer Bond, who had the honour to be Mrs Bond's husband, she was so completely the personage of the family that nobody ever thought of him – she lived on a small dairy-farm, at the other side of the parish, where she had reared ten children in comfort and respectability, contriving in all years, and in all seasons, to look, and to be flourishing, happy, and contented, and to drive her tilted cart twice a week into B—, laden with the richest butter, the freshest eggs and the finest poultry of the county. Never was market-woman so reliable as Mrs Bond, so safe to deal with,

234

or so pleasant to look at. She was a neat comely woman of five-and-forty, or thereabout, with dark hair, laughing eyes, a bright smile, and a brighter complexion – red and white like a daisy. People used to say how pretty she must have been; but I think she was then in the prime of her good looks; just as a full-blown damask rose is more beautiful than the same flower in the bud.

Very pleasant she was to look at, and still pleasanter to talk to; she was so gentle, so cheerful, so respectful, and so kind. Everybody in the village loved Mrs Bond. Even Lizzy and May, the two most aristocratical of its inhabitants, and the most tenacious of the distinctions of rank, would run to meet the butter-cart as if it were a carriage and four. A mark of preference which the good-humoured dairywoman did not fail to acknowledge and confirm by gifts suited to their respective tastes, an occasional pitcher of butter-milk to May, and a stick with cherries tied round it to poor Lizzy.

Nor was Mrs Bond's bounty confined to largesses of so suspicious a nature, as presents to the pets of a good customer. I have never known any human being more thoroughly and universally generous, more delicate in her little gifts, or with so entire an absence of design or artifice in her attentions. It was a prodigality of kindness that seemed never weary of well-doing. What posies of pinks and sweet williams, backed by marjoram and rosemary, she used to carry to the two poor old ladies who lodged at the pastry-cook's at B—! What faggots of lilac and laburnum she would bring to deck the poor widow Hay's open hearth! What baskets of watercresses, the brownest, the bitterest, and the crispest of the year, for our fair neighbour, the nymph of the shoeshop, a delicate girl, who could only be tempted into her breakfast by that pleasant herb! What pots of honey for John Brown's cough! What gooseberries and currants for the baker's little children! And as soon as her great vine ripened, what grapes for everybody! No wonder that when Mrs Bond left the parish, to occupy a larger farm in a distant county, her absence was felt as a misfortune by the whole village; that poor Lizzy inquired after her every day for a week, and that May watched for the tilted cart every Wednesday and Friday for a month or more.

I myself joined very heartily in the general lamentation. But time and habit reconcile us to most privations, and I must confess that, much as I liked her, I had nearly forgotten our good butterwoman until an adventure which befel me last week placed me once more in the way of her ready kindness.

I was on a visit at a considerable distance from home, in one of the most retired parts of Oxfordshire. Nothing could be more beautiful than the situation, or less accessible; shut in amongst woody hills, remote from great towns, with deep chalky roads, almost impassable, and a broad bridgeless river, coming, as if to intercept your steps, whenever you did seem to have fallen into a beaten track. It was exactly the country and the season in which to wander about all day long.

One fair morning I set out on my accustomed ramble. The sun was intensely hot; the sky almost cloudless. I had climbed a long abrupt ascent to enjoy the sight of the magnificent river, winding like a snake amidst the richly clothed hills; the pretty village, with its tapering spire, and the universal freshness and brilliancy of the gay and smiling prospect – too gay perhaps! I gazed till I became dazzled with the glare of the sunshine, oppressed by the very brightness, and turned into a beech wood by the side of the road, to seek relief from the overpowering radiance. These beech woods should rather be called coppices. They are cut down occasionally, and consist of long flexible stems, growing out of the old roots. But they are like no other coppices, or rather none other can be compared with them. The young beechen stems, perfectly free from underwood, go arching and interwining over head, forming a thousand mazy paths, covered by a natural trellis; the shining green leaves, just bursting from their golden sheaths, contrasting with the smooth silvery bark, shedding a cool green light around, and casting a thousand dancing shadows on the mossy flowery path, pleasant to the eye and to the tread, a fit haunt for wood-nymph or fairy. There is always much of interest in the mystery of a wood; the uncertainty produced by the confined boundary; the objects which crowd together, and prevent the eye from penetrating to any distance; the strange flickering mixture of shadow and sunshine; the sudden flight of birds – oh, it was enchanting! I wandered on, quite regardless of time or distance, now admiring the beautiful wood-sorrel which sprang up amongst the old roots, now plucking the fragrant woodruff, now trying to count the countless varieties of woodland moss, till, at length, roused by my foot's catching in a rich trail of the white-veined ivy, which crept, wreathing and interlaced, over the ground, I became aware that I was completely lost, had entirely forsaken all track, and out-travelled all landmarks. The wood was, I knew, extensive, and the ground so tumbled about that every hundred yards presented some flowery slope or broken dell, which added greatly to the picturesqueness of the scenery, but very much diminished my chance of discovery or extrication.

In this emergency, I determined to proceed straight onward, trusting in this way to reach at last one side of the wood, although I could not at all guess which; and I was greatly solaced, after having walked about a quarter of a mile, to find myself crossed by a rude cart track; and still more delighted, on proceeding a short distance farther, to hear sounds of merriment and business – none of the softest, certainly, but which gave token of rustic habitation; and to emerge suddenly from the close wood, amongst an open grove of huge old trees, oaks, with their brown plaited leaves, cherries, covered with snowy garlands, and beeches, almost as gigantic as those of Windsor Park, contrasting, with their enormous trunks and majestic spread of bough, the light and flexible stems of the coppice I had left.

I had come out at one of the highest points of the wood, and now stood on a platform overlooking a scene of extraordinary beauty. A little to the right, in a very narrow valley, stood an old farmhouse, with pointed roofs and porch and pinnacles, backed by a splendid orchard, which lay bathed in the sunshine, exhaling its fresh aromatic fragrance, all one flower. Just under me was a strip of rich meadowland through which a stream ran sparkling, and directly opposite a ridge of hanging coppices, surrounding and crowning, as it were, an immense old chalk pit, which, overhung by bramble, ivy and a hundred pendent weeds, irregular and weather-stained, had an air as venerable and romantic as some grey ruin. Seen in the gloom and stillness of evening, or by the pale glimpses of the moon, it would have required but little aid from the fancy to picture out the broken shafts and mouldering arches of some antique abbey. But, besides that daylight is the sworn enemy of such illusions, my attention was imperiously claimed by a reality of a very different kind. One of the gayest and noisiest operations of rural life – sheep-washing – was going on in the valley below:

> the turmoil that unites
> Clamour of boys with innocent despites
> Of barking dogs, and bleatings from strange fear.
> (WORDSWORTH)

All the inhabitants of the farm seemed assembled in the meadow. I counted a dozen at least of men and boys of all ages, from the stout, sunburned, vigorous farmer of fifty, who presided over the operation, down to the eight-year-old urchin, who, screaming, running, and shaking his ineffectual stick after an eloped sheep, served as a sort of aide-de-camp to the sheepdog. What a glorious scene of confusion it was. What shouting! What scuffling! What glee! Four or five young men and one amazon of a barefooted girl, with her petticoats tucked up to her knees, stood in the water where it was pent between two hurdles, ducking, sousing, and holding down by main force the poor, frightened, struggling sheep, who kicked, and plunged, and bleated, and butted, and in spite of their imputed innocence, would certainly, in the ardour of self-defence, have committed half a dozen homicides, if their power had equalled their inclination. The rest of the party was fully occupied; some in conducting the purified sheep, who showed a strong disposition to go the wrong way, back to their quarters; others in leading the uncleansed part of the flock to their destined ablution, from which they also testified a very ardent and active desire to escape. Dogs, men, boys and girls were engaged in marshalling these double processions, the order of which was constantly interrupted by the out-breaking of some runaway sheep, who turned the march into a pursuit, to the momentary increase of the din, which seemed already to have reached the highest possible pitch.

The only quiet persons in the field were a delicate child of nine years old, and a blooming woman of forty-five – a comely, blooming woman, with dark hair, bright eyes, and a complexion like a daisy, who stood watching the sheep-washers with the happiest smiles, and was evidently the mother of half the lads and lasses in the *mêlée*. It could be, and it was no other than, my friend Mrs Bond and, resolving to make myself and my difficulties known to her, I scrambled down no very smooth or convenient path, and keeping a gate between me and the scene of action, contrived, after sundry efforts, to attract her attention.

Here of course my difficulties ceased. But, if I were to tell how glad she was to see her old neighbour, how full of kind questions and of hospitable cares, how she would cut the great cake intended for the next day's sheep-shearing, would tap her two-year-old currant wine, would gather a whole bush of early honeysuckles, and, finally, would see me home herself, I being, as she observed, rather given to losing my way; if I were to tell all these things, when should I have done? I would rather conclude in the words of an old French fairytale:

> *Je crains déjà d'avoir abusé de la patience du lecteur.*
> *Je finis avant qu'il me dise de finir.*

Lost and Won

'NAY, but my dear Letty –'

'Don't dear Letty me, Mr Paul Holton! Have not the East Woodhay Eleven beaten the Hazelby Eleven for the first time in the memory of man? And is it not entirely your fault? Answer me that, sir! Did not you insist on taking James White's place, when he got that little knock on the leg with the ball last night, though James, poor fellow, maintained to the last that he could play better with one leg than you with two? Did not you insist on taking poor James's place? And did you get a single notch in either innings? And did not you miss three catches – three fair catches – Mr Paul Holton? Might not you twice have caught out John Brown, who, as all the world knows, hits up? And did not a ball from the edge of Tom Taylor's bat come into your hands, absolutely into your hands, and did not you let her go? And did not Tom Taylor after that get forty-five runs in that same innings, and thereby win the game? That a man should pretend to play at cricket, and not be able to hold the ball when he has her in his hands! O, if I had been there!'

'You! – Why Letty!'

'Don't Letty me, Sir! Don't talk to me! I am going home!'

'With all my heart, Miss Letitia Dale! I have the honour, madam, to wish you a good evening.' And each turned away at a smart pace, and the one went westward and the other eastward-ho.

This unlover-like parting occurred on Hazelby Down one fine afternoon in the Whitsun week between a couple whom all Hazelby and Aberleigh to boot, had, for at least a month before, set down as lovers: Letty Dale, the pretty daughter of the jolly old tanner, and Paul Holton, a rich young yeoman, on a visit in the place. Letty's angry speech will sufficiently explain their mutual provocation, although, to enter fully into her feelings, one must be born in a cricketing parish, and sprung of a cricketing family, and be accustomed to rest that very uncertain and arbitrary standard, the point of honour, on beating our rivals and next neighbours in the annual match – for juxtaposition is a great sharpener of rivalry, as Dr Johnson knew when, to please the inhabitants of Plymouth, he abused the good folks who lived at Dock. Moreover, one must be also a quick, zealous, ardent, hot-headed, warm-hearted girl, like Letty; a beauty and an heiress, quite unused to disappointment, and not a little in love. And then we shall not wonder, in the first place, that she should be unreasonably angry, or, in the next, that, before she had walked half a mile, her anger vanished, and was succeeded by tender relentings and earnest wishes for a full and perfect reconciliation.

'He'll be sure to call tomorrow morning,' thought Letty to herself: 'He said he would, before this unlucky cricket-playing. He told me that he had something to say, something particular. I wonder what it can be!' thought poor Letty. 'To be sure, he never has said anything about liking me – but still – and then aunt Judith, and Fanny Wright, and all the neighbours say – However, I shall know tomorrow.'

And home she tripped to the pleasant house by the tan-yard, as happy as if the East Woodhay men had not beaten the men of Hazelby. 'I shall not see him before tomorrow, though,' repeated Letty to herself, and immediately repaired to her pretty flower-garden, the little gate of which opened on a path leading from the Down to the street – a path that, for obvious reasons, Paul was wont to prefer – and began tying up her carnations in the dusk of the evening, and watering her geraniums by the light of the moon until it was so late that she was fain to return, disappointed, to the house, repeating to herself, 'I shall certainly see him tomorrow.'

Far different were the feelings of the chidden swain. Well-a-day for the age of chivalry! The happy times of knights and paladins, when a lecture from a lady's rosy lip, or a buffet from her lily hand, would have been received as humbly and as thankfully as the Benedicite from a mitred abbot, or the accolade from a king's sword! Alas for the days of chivalry! They are gone, and I fear me for ever. For certain, our present hero was not born to revive them.

Paul Holton was a well-looking and well-educated young farmer, just returned from the north, whither he had been sent for agricultural improvement, and now on the look-out for a farm and a wife, both of which he thought he had found at Hazelby, where he had come on the double errand of visiting some distant relations, and letting two or three small houses recently fallen into his possession. As owner of these houses, all situated in the town, he had claimed a right to join the Hazelby Eleven; mainly induced to avail himself of the privilege by the hope of winning favour in the eyes of the ungrateful fair one, whose animated character, as well as her sparkling beauty, had delighted his fancy, and apparently won his heart; until her rude attack on his play armed all the vanity of man against her attractions. Love is more intimately connected with self-love than people are willing to imagine; and Paul Holton's had been thoroughly mortified. Besides, if his fair mistress's character were somewhat too impetuous, his was greatly over-firm. So he said to himself: 'The girl is a pretty girl, but far too much of a shrew for my taming. I am no Petruchio to master this Catherine. "I come to wive it happily in Padua"; and, let her father be as rich as he may, I'll none of her.' And, mistaking anger for indifference – no uncommon delusion in a love quarrel – off he set within the hour, thinking so very much of punishing the saucy beauty that he entirely forgot the possibility of some of the pains falling to his own share.

The first tidings that Letty heard the next morning were that Mr Paul Holton had departed overnight, having authorized his cousin to let his houses, and to decline the large farm, for which he was in treaty; the next intelligence informed her that he was settled in Sussex; and then his relation left Hazelby – and poor Letty heard no more. Poor Letty! Even in a common parting for a common journey, she who stays behind is the object of pity; how much more so when he who goes, goes never to return, and carries with

him the fond affection, the treasured hopes, of a young un-
practised heart:

> And gentle wishes long subdued –
> Subdued and cherish'd long!

Poor, poor Letty!

Three years passed away, and brought much of change to our
country maiden and to her fortunes. Her father, the jolly old
tanner, a kind, frank, thoughtless man, as the cognomen would
almost imply, one who did not think that there were such things as
wickedness and ingratitude under the sun, became bound for a
friend to a large amount. The friend proved a villain, and the jolly
tanner was ruined. He and his daughter now lived in a small
cottage near their former house; and, at the point of time at which
I have chosen to resume my story, the old man was endeavouring
to persuade Letty, who had never attended a cricket match since
the one which she had so much cause to remember, to accompany
him the next day (Whit Tuesday) to see the Hazelby Eleven
again encounter their ancient antagonists, the men of East
Woodhay.

'Pray come, Letty,' said the fond father; 'I can't go without you;
I have no pleasure anywhere without my Letty; and I want to see
this match, for Isaac Hunt can't play on account of the death of his
mother, and they tell me that the East Woodhay men have
consented to our taking in another mate, who practises the new
Sussex bowling – I want to see that new-fangled mode. Do come,
Letty!' And, with a smothered sigh at the mention of Sussex, Letty
consented.

Now old John Dale was not quite ingenuous with his pretty
daughter. He did not tell her what he very well knew himself, that
the bowler in question was no other than their sometime friend,
Paul Holton, whom the business of letting his houses, or some
other cause, not, perhaps, clearly defined even to himself, had
brought to Hazelby on the eve of the match, and whose new
method of bowling (in spite of his former mischances) the Hazelby
Eleven were willing to try. The more so as they suspected, what,
indeed, actually occurred – that the East Woodhayites, who

would have resisted the innovation of the Sussex system of delivering the ball in the hands of anyone else, would have no objection to let Paul Holton, whose bad playing was a standing joke amongst them, do his best or his worst in any way.

Not a word of this did John Dale say to Letty; so that she was quite taken by surprise, when, having placed her father, now very infirm, in a comfortable chair, she sat down by his side on a little hillock of turf, and saw her recreant lover standing amongst a group of cricketers very near, and evidently gazing on her – just as he used to gaze three years before.

Perhaps Letty had never looked so pretty in her life as at that moment. She was simply dressed, as became her fallen fortunes. Her complexion was still coloured, like the apple blossom, with vivid red and white, but there was more of sensibility, more of the heart in its quivering mutability, its alternation of paleness and blushes; the blue eyes were still as bright, but they were oftener cast down; the smile was still as splendid, but far more rare; the girlish gaiety was gone, but it was replaced by womanly sweetness – sweetness and modesty formed now the chief expression of that lovely face, lovelier, far lovelier, than ever. So apparently thought Paul Holton, for he gazed and gazed with his whole soul in his eyes, in complete oblivion of cricket and cricketer, and the whole world. At last he recollected himself, blushed and bowed, and advanced a few steps, as if to address her; but timid and irresolute, he turned away without speaking, joined the party who had now assembled round the wickets, the umpires called 'Play!' and the game began.

East Woodhay gained the toss and went in, and all eyes were fixed on the Sussex bowler. The ball was placed in his hands; and instantly the wicket was down, and the striker out – no other than Tom Taylor, the boast of his parish, and the best batsman in the county. 'Accident, mere accident!' of course, cried East Woodhay; but another, and another followed. Few could stand against the fatal bowling, and none could get notches. A panic seized the whole side. And then, as losers will, they began to exclaim against the system, called it a toss, a throw, a trick; anything but bowling, anything but cricket; railed at it as destroying the grace of the attitude, and the balance of the game; protested against being considered as beaten by such jugglery, and, finally, appealed to the umpires as to the fairness of the play. The umpires, men of conscience, and old cricketers, hummed and hawed, and see-sawed; quoted contending precedents and jostling authorities; looked grave and wise, whilst even their little sticks of office seemed vibrating in puzzled importance. Never were judges more sorely perplexed. At last they did as the sages of the bench often do in such cases – reserved the point of law, and desired them to 'play out the play'. Accordingly, the match was resumed; only twenty-seven notches being gained by the East Woodhayians in their first innings, and they entirely from the balls of the old Hazelby bowler, James White.

During the quarter of an hour's pause which the laws allow, the victorious man of Sussex went up to John Dale, who had watched him with a strange mixture of feeling, delighted to hear the stumps rattle, and to see opponent after opponent throw down his bat and walk off, and yet much annoyed at the new method by which the object was achieved. 'We should not have called this cricket in my day,' said he, 'and yet it knocks down the wickets gloriously, too.' Letty, on her part, had watched the game with unmingled interest and admiration: 'He knew how much I liked to see a good cricketer,' thought she; yet still, when that identical good cricketer approached, she was seized with such a fit of shyness – call it modesty – that she left her seat and joined a group of young women at some distance.

Paul looked earnestly after her, but remained standing by her father, inquiring with affectionate interest after his health, and talking over the game and the bowling. At length he said, 'I hope that I have not driven away Miss Letitia.'

'Call her Letty, Mr Holton,' interrupted the old man; 'plain Letty. We are poor folks now, and have no right to any other title than our own proper names, old John Dale and his daughter Letty. A good daughter she has been to me,' continued the fond father; 'for when debts and losses took all that we had – for we paid to the uttermost farthing, Mr Paul Holton, we owe no man a shilling! when all my earnings and savings were gone, and the house over our head – the house I was born in, the house she was born in – I loved it the better for that! Taken away from us, then she gave up the few hundreds she was entitled to in right of her blessed mother to purchase an annuity for the old man, whose trust in a villain had brought her to want.'

'God bless her!' interrupted Paul Holton.

'Ay, and God will bless her,' returned the old man solemnly. 'God will bless the dutiful child, who despoiled herself of all to support her old father!'

'Blessings on her dear generous heart!' again ejaculated Paul; 'and I was away and knew nothing of this!'

'I knew nothing of it myself until the deed was completed,' rejoined John Dale. 'She was just of age, and the annuity was purchased and the money paid before she told me; and a cruel kindness it was to strip herself for my sake; it almost broke my heart when I heard the story. But even that was nothing,' continued the good tanner, warming with his subject, 'compared with her conduct since. If you could but see how she keeps the house, and how she waits upon me; her handiness, her cheerfulness, and all her pretty ways and contrivances to make me forget old times and old places. Poor thing! She must miss her neat parlour and the flower-garden she was so fond of, as much as I do my tan-yard and the great hall; but she never seems to think of them, and never has spoken a hasty word since our misfortunes, for all you know, poor thing! She used to be a little quick-tempered!'

'And I knew nothing of this!' repeated Paul Holton, as, two or three of their best wickets being down, the Hazelby players summoned him to go in. 'I knew nothing of all this!'

Again all eyes were fixed on the Sussex cricketer, and at first he seemed likely to verify the predictions and confirm the hopes of the most malicious of his adversaries, by batting as badly as he had bowled well. He had not caught sight of the ball; his hits were weak, his defence insecure, and his mates began to tremble and his opponents to crow. Every hit seemed likely to be the last; he missed a leg ball of Ned Smith's; was all but caught out by Sam Newton; and East Woodhay triumphed, and Hazelby sat quaking; when a sudden glimpse of Letty, watching him with manifest anxiety, recalled her champion's wandering thoughts. Gathering himself up he stood before the wicket another man; knocked the ball hither and thither to the turnpike, the coppice, the pond; got three, four, five at a hit; baffled the slow bowler James Smith, and the fast bowler Tom Taylor; got fifty-five notches off his own bat; stood out all the rest of his side; and so handled the adverse party when they went in that the match was won at a single innings, with six-and-thirty runs to spare.

Whilst his mates were discussing their victory, Paul Holton again approached the father and daughter, and this time she did not run away. 'Letty, dear Letty,' said he; 'three years ago I lost the cricket match and you were angry, and I was a fool. But Letty, dear Letty, this match is won; and if you could but know how deeply I have repented, how earnestly I have longed for this day! The world has gone well with me, Letty, for these three long years. I have wanted nothing but the treasure which I myself threw away, and now, if you would but let your father be my father, and my home your home! If you would but forgive me, Letty!'

Letty's answer is not upon record; but it is certain that Paul Holton walked home from the cricket ground that evening with old John Dale hanging on one arm, and John Dale's pretty daughter on the other; and that a month after the bells of Hazelby church were ringing merrily in honour of one of the fairest and luckiest matches that ever cricketer lost and won.

Walks in the Country
The Shaw

SEPTEMBER 9th. A bright sunshiny afternoon. What a comfort it is to get out again – to see once more that rarity of rarities, a fine day! We English people are accused of talking overmuch of the weather; but the weather, this summer, has forced people to talk of it. Summer! did I say? Oh! season most unworthy of that sweet, sunny name! Season of coldness and cloudiness, of gloom and rain! A worse November! For in November the days are short; and shut up in a warm room, lighted by that household sun, a lamp, one feels through the long evenings comfortably independent of the out-of-door tempests. But though we may have, and did have, fires all through the dog-days, there is no shutting out daylight; and sixteen hours of rain, pattering against the windows and dripping from the eaves – sixteen hours of rain, not merely audible but visible, for seven days in the week – would be enough to exhaust the patience of Job or Grizzel; especially if Job were a farmer, and Grizzel a country gentlewoman. Never was known such a season! Hay swimming, cattle drowning, fruit rotting, corn spoiling! And that naughty river, the Loddon, who never can take Puff's advice, and 'keep between its banks', running about the country, fields, roads, gardens and houses like mad! The weather would be talked of. Indeed, it was not easy to talk of anything else. A friend of mine having occasion to write me a letter thought it worth abusing in rhyme, and bepommelled it through three pages of Bath Guide verse; of which I subjoin a specimen:

> Aquarius surely *reigns* over the world,
> And of late he his water-pot strangely has twirled;
> Or he's taken a cullender up by mistake,
> And unceasingly dips it in some mighty lake;

The Shaw

Though it is not in Lethe – for who can forget
The annoyance of getting most thoroughly wet?
It must be in the river called Styx, I declare,
For the moment it drizzles it makes the men swear.
'It did rain tomorrow', is growing good grammar;
Vauxhall and camp-stools have been brought to the hammer;
A pony-gondola is all I can keep,
And I use my umbrella and pattens in sleep:
Row out of my window, whene'er 'tis my whim
To visit a friend, and just ask, 'Can you swim?'

So far my friend.[1] In short, whether in prose or in verse, everybody railed at the weather. But this is over now. The sun has come to dry the world; mud is turned into dust; rivers have retreated to their proper limits; farmers have left off grumbling; and we are about to take a walk, as usual, as far as the Shaw, a pretty wood about a mile off. But one of our companions being a stranger to the gentle reader, we must do him the honour of an introduction.

Dogs, when they are sure of having their own way, have sometimes ways as odd as those of the unfurred, unfeathered animals, who walk on two legs, and talk, and are called rational. My beautiful white greyhound, Mayflower,[2] for instance, is as whimsical as the finest lady in the land. Amongst her other fancies,

---

[1] This friend of mine is a person of great quickness and talent, who, if she were not a beauty and a woman of fortune – that is to say, if she were prompted by either of those two powerful *stimuli*, want of money or want of admiration, to take due pains – would inevitably become a clever writer. As it is, her notes and *jeux d'esprit* struck off *à trait de plume*, have great point and neatness. Take the following *billet*, which formed the label to a closed basket, containing the ponderous present alluded to, last Michaelmas Day:

> To Miss M.
> When this you see
> Remember me,
> Was long a phrase in use;
> And so I send
> To you, dear friend,
> My proxy. 'What?' 'A goose!'

[2] Dead, alas, since this was written!

she has taken a violent affection for a most hideous stray dog, who made his appearance here about six months ago, and contrived to pick up a living in the village, one can hardly tell how. Now appealing to the charity of old Rachael Strong, the launderess – a dog-lover by profession; now winning a meal from the light-footed and open-hearted lasses at the Rose; now standing on his hindlegs, to extort by sheer beggary a scanty morsel from some pair of 'drouthy cronies', or solitary drover, discussing his dinner or supper on the ale-house bench; now catching a mouthful, flung to him in pure contempt by some scornful gentleman of the shoulder-knot, mounted on his throne, the coach-box, whose notice he had attracted by dint of ugliness; now sharing the commons of Master Keep the shoemaker's pigs; now succeeding to the reversion of the well-gnawed bone of Master Brown the shopkeeper's fierce house-dog; now filching the skim-milk of Dame Wheeler's cat. Spat at by the cat; worried by the mastiff; chased by the pigs; screamed at by the dame; stormed at by the shoemaker; flogged by the shopkeeper; teased by all the children, and scouted by all the animals of the parish – but yet living through his griefs, and bearing them patiently, 'for sufferance is the badge of all his tribe'; and even seeming to find, in an occasional full meal, or a gleam of sunshine, or a whisp of dry straw on which to repose his sorry carcase, some comfort in his disconsolate condition.

In this plight was he found by May, the most high-blooded and aristocratic of greyhounds; and from this plight did May rescue him; invited him into her territory, the stable; resisted all attempts to turn him out; reinstated him there, in spite of maid and boy, and mistress and master; wore out everybody's opposition, by the activity of her protection, and the pertinacity of her self-will; made him sharer of her bed and of her mess; and, finally, established him as one of the family as firmly as herself.

Dash – for he has even won himself a name amongst us; before, he was anonymous – Dash is a sort of a kind of a spaniel; at least there is in his mongrel composition some sign of that beautiful race. Besides his ugliness, which is of the worst sort – that is to say, the shabbiest – he has a limp on one leg that gives a peculiarly one-sided awkwardness to his gait; but independently of his great merit in being May's pet, he has other merits which serve to account for that phenomenon, being, beyond all comparison, the most faithful, attached, and affectionate animal that I have ever known; and that is saying much. He seems to think it necessary to atone for his ugliness by extra good conduct, and does so dance on his lame leg, and so wag his scrubby tail, that it does anyone who has a taste for happiness good to look at him – so that he may now be said to stand on his own footing. We are all rather ashamed of him when strangers come in the way, and think it necessary to explain that he is May's pet; but amongst ourselves, and those who are used to his appearance, he has reached the point of favouritism in his own person. I have, in common with wiser women, the feminine weakness of loving whatever loves me – and, therefore, I like Dash. His master has found out that he is a capital finder, and in spite of his lameness will hunt a field or beat a cover with any spaniel in England – and, therefore, *he* likes Dash. The boy has fought a battle, in defence of his beauty, with another boy, bigger than himself, and beat his opponent most handsomely – and, therefore, *he* likes Dash; and the maids like him, or pretend to like him, because we do – as is the fashion of that pliant and imitative class. And now Dash and May follow us everywhere, and are going with us to the Shaw, as I said before – or rather to the cottage by the Shaw, to bespeak milk and butter of our little dairy-woman, Hannah Bint; a housewifely occupation, to which we owe some of our pleasantest rambles.

And now we pass the sunny, dusty village street – who would have thought, a month ago, that we should complain of sun and dust again! – and turn the corner where the two great oaks hang so beautifully over the clear deep pond, mixing their cold green shadows with the bright blue sky, and the white clouds that flit over it: and loiter at the wheeler's shop, always picturesque, with its tools, and its work, and its materials, all so various in form, and so harmonious in colour; and its noisy, merry workmen, hammering and singing, and making a various harmony also. The shop is rather empty today, for its usual inmates are busy on the green beyond the pond – one set building a cart, another painting a wagon. And then we leave the village quite behind, and proceed slowly up the cool, quiet lane, between tall hedgerows of the darkest verdure, overshadowing banks green and fresh as an emerald.

Not so quick as I expected, though – for they are shooting here today, as Dash and I have both discovered; he with great delight, for a gun to him is as a trumpet to a war-horse; I with no less annoyance, for I don't think that a partridge itself, barring the accident of being killed, can be more startled than I at that abominable explosion. Dash has certainly better blood in his veins than anyone would guess to look at him. He even shows some inclination to elope into the fields, in pursuit of those noisy iniquities. But he is an orderly person after all, and a word has checked him.

Ah! Here is a shriller din mingling with the small artillery – a shriller and more continuous. We are not yet arrived within sight of Master Weston's cottage, snugly hidden behind a clump of elms; but we are in full hearing of Dame Weston's tongue, raised as usual to scolding-pitch. The Westons are new arrivals in our neighbourhood, and the first thing heard of them was a complaint from the wife to our magistrate of her husband's beating her: it was a regular charge of assault – an information in full form. A most piteous case did Dame Weston make of it, softening her voice for the nonce into a shrill tremulous whine, and exciting the mingled pity and anger – pity towards herself, anger towards her husband – of the whole female world, pitiful and indignant as the female world is wont to be on such occasions. Every woman in the parish railed at Master Weston; and poor Master Weston was summoned to attend the Bench on the ensuing Saturday, and answer the charge; and such was the clamour abroad and at home that the unlucky culprit, terrified at the sound of a warrant and a constable, ran away, and was not heard of for a fortnight.

At the end of that time he was discovered, and brought to the Bench; and Dame Weston again told her story, and, as before, on the full cry. She had no witnesses, and the bruises of which she made complaint had disappeared, and there were no women present to make common cause with the sex. Still, however, the general feeling was against Master Weston; and it would have gone hard with him when he was called in, if a most unexpected witness had not risen up in his favour. His wife had brought in her arms a little girl about eighteen months old, partly perhaps to move compassion in her favour; for a woman with a child in her arms is always an object that excites kind feelings. The little girl had looked shy and frightened, and had been as quiet as a lamb during her mother's examination; but she no sooner saw her father, from whom she had been a fortnight separated, than she clapped her hands, and laughed, and cried, 'Daddy! Daddy!' – and sprang into his arms, and hung round his neck, and covered him with kisses – again shouting, 'Daddy, come home! Daddy! Daddy!' – and finally nestled her little head in his bosom, with a fulness of contentment, an assurance of tenderness and protection, such as no wife-beating tyrant ever did inspire, or ever could inspire, since the days of King Solomon. Our magistrates acted in the very spirit of the Jewish monarch: they accepted the evidence of nature, and dismissed the complaint. And subsequent events have fully justified their decision; Mistress Weston proving not only renowned for the feminine accomplishment of scolding (tongue-banging, it is called in our parts, a compound word which deserves to be Greek), but is actually herself addicted to administering the conjugal discipline, the infliction of which she was pleased to impute to her luckless husband.

Now we cross the stile, and walk up the fields to the Shaw. How beautifully green this pasture looks! And how finely the evening sun glances between the boles of that clump of trees, beech, and ash, and aspen! And how sweet the hedgerows are with woodbine and wild scabious, or, as the country people call it, the gipsy-rose! Here is little Dolly Weston, the unconscious witness, with cheeks as red as a real rose, tottering up the path to meet her father. And here is the carroty-polled urchin, George Coper, returning from work, and singing, 'Home! sweet home!' at the top of his voice; and then, when the notes prove too high for him, continuing the air in a whistle, until he has turned the impassable corner; then taking up again the song and the words, 'Home! sweet home!' and looking as if he felt their full import, ploughboy though he be.

And so he does; for he is one of a large, an honest, a kind, and an industrious family, where all goes well, and where the poor ploughboy is sure of finding cheerful faces and coarse comforts – all that he has learned to desire. Oh, to be as cheaply and as thoroughly contented as George Coper! All his luxuries, a cricket match! All his wants satisfied in 'Home! sweet home!'

Nothing but noises today! They are clearing farmer Brooke's great bean-field, and crying the 'Harvest Home!' in a chorus before which all other sounds – the song, the scolding, the gunnery – fade away, and become faint echoes. A pleasant noise is that! Though, for one's ears' sake,

one makes some haste to get away from it. And here, in happy time, is that pretty wood, the Shaw, with its broad pathway, its tangled dingles, its nuts and its honeysuckles; and, carrying away a faggot of those sweetest flowers, we reach Hannah Bint's, of whom, and of whose doings, we shall say more another time.

NOTE. Poor Dash is also dead. We did not keep him long, indeed I believe that he died of the transition from starvation to good feed, as dangerous to a dog's stomach and to most stomachs, as the less agreeable change from good feed to starvation. He has been succeeded in place and favour by another Dash, not less amiable in demeanour, and far more creditable in appearance, bearing no small resemblance to the pet spaniel of my friend Master Dinely. Let not the unwary reader opine that in assigning the same name to several individuals I am acting as an humble imitator of the inimitable writer who has given immortality to the Peppers and the Mustards, on the one hand; or showing a poverty of invention or a want of acquaintance with the bead-roll of canine appellations on the other. I merely, with my usual scrupulous fidelity, take the names as I find them. The fact is that half the handsome spaniels in England are called Dash, just as half the tall footmen are called Thomas. The name belongs to the species. Sitting in an open carriage one day last summer at the door of a farmhouse where my father had some business, I saw a noble and beautiful animal of this kind lying in great state and laziness on the steps, and felt an immediate desire to make acquaintance with him. My father, who had had the same fancy, had patted him, and called him 'poor fellow' in passing, without eliciting the smallest notice in return. 'Dash!' cried I at a venture, 'good Dash! Noble Dash;' and up he started in a moment, making but one spring from the door into the gig. Of course I was right in my guess. The gentleman's name was Dash.

Walks in the Country
Hannah Bint

THE SHAW, leading to Hannah Bint's habitation, is as I perhaps have said before, a very pretty mixture of wood and coppice; that is to say, a track of thirty or forty acres covered with fine growing timber – ash, and oak, and elm – very regularly planted; and interspersed here and there with large patches of underwood, hazel, maple, birch, holly and hawthorn, woven into almost impenetrable thickets by long wreaths of the bramble, the briony, and the brier-rose, or by the pliant and twisting garlands of the wild honeysuckle. In other parts, the Shaw is quite clear of its bosky undergrowth, and clothed only with large beds of feathery fern, or carpets of flowers, primroses, orchises, cowslips, ground-ivy, cranesbill, cotton-grass, Solomon's seal and forget-me-not, crowded together with a profusion and brilliancy of colour, such as I have rarely seen equalled even in a garden. Here the wild hyacinth really enamels the ground with its fresh and lovely purple; there:

> On aged roots, with bright green mosses clad,
> Dwells the wood-sorrel, with its bright thin leaves
> Heart-shaped and triply folded, and its root
> Creeping like beaded coral; whilst around
> Flourish the copse's pride, anemones,
> With rays like golden studs on ivory laid
> Most delicate; but touched with purple clouds,
> Fit crown for April's fair but changeful brow.

The variety is much greater than I have enumerated, for the ground is so unequal, now swelling in gentle ascents, now dimpling into dells and hollows, and the soil so different in different parts, that the sylvan flora is unusually extensive and complete.

The season is, however, now too late for this floweriness; and except the tufted woodbines, which have continued in bloom during the whole of this lovely autumn, and some lingering garlands of the purple wild vetch, wreathing round the thickets, and uniting with the ruddy leaves of the bramble, and the pale festoons of the briony, there is little to call one's attention from the grander beauties of the trees: the sycamore, its broad leaves already spotted; the oak, heavy with acorns; and the delicate shining rind of the weeping birch, 'the lady of the woods', thrown out in strong relief from a background of holly and hawthorns, each studded with coral berries, and backed with old beeches, beginning to assume the rich tawny hue, which makes them perhaps the most picturesque of autumnal trees, as the transparent freshness of their young foliage is undoubtedly the choicest ornament of the forest in spring.

A sudden turn round one of these magnificent beeches brings us to the boundary of the Shaw and, leaning upon a rude gate, we look over an open space of about ten acres of ground, still more varied and broken than that which we have passed, and surrounded on all sides by thick woodland. As a piece of colour, nothing can be well finer. The ruddy glow of the heath flower, contrasting, on the one hand, with the golden-blossomed furze; on the other, with a patch of buckwheat, of which the bloom is not past, although the grain be ripening, the beautiful buckwheat, whose transparent leaves and stalks are so brightly tinged with vermilion, while the delicate pink-white of the flower, a paler persicaria, has a feathery fall, at once so rich and so graceful, and a fresh and reviving odour, like that of birch trees in the dew of a May evening. The bank that surmounts this attempt at cultivation is crowned with the late foxglove and the stately mullein; the pasture of which so great a part of the waste consists, looks as green as an emerald; a clear pond, with the bright sky reflected in it, lets light into the picture; the white cottage of the keeper peeps from the opposite coppice; and the vine-covered dwelling of

Hannah Bint rises from amidst the pretty garden, which lies bathed in the sunshine around it.

The living and moving accessories are all in keeping with the cheerfulness and repose of the landscape. Hannah's cow grazing quietly beside the keeper's pony; a brace of fat pointer puppies holding amicable intercourse with a litter of young pigs; ducks, geese, cocks, hens and chickens scattered over the turf; Hannah herself sallying forth from the cottage-door, with her milk-bucket in her hand, and her little brother following with the milking-stool.

My friend, Hannah Bint, is by no means an ordinary person. Her father, Jack Bint (for in all his life he never arrived at the dignity of being called John — indeed in our parts, he was commonly known by the cognomen of London Jack), was a drover of high repute in his profession. No man, between Salisbury Plain and Smithfield, was thought to conduct a flock of sheep so skilfully through all the difficulties of lanes and commons, streets and highroads, as Jack Bint, aided by Jack Bint's famous dog, Watch; for Watch's rough, honest face, black, with a little white about the muzzle, and one white ear, was as well-known at fairs and markets, as his master's equally honest and weather-beaten visage. Lucky was the dealer that could secure their services: Watch being renowned for keeping a flock together better than any shepherd's dog on the road; Jack, for delivering them more punctually, and in better condition. No man had a more thorough knowledge of the proper night stations, where good feed might be procured for his charge, and good liquor for Watch and himself; Watch, like other sheepdogs, being accustomed to live chiefly on bread and beer. His master, although not averse to a pot of good double X, preferred gin; and they who plod slowly along, through wet and weary ways, in frost and in fog, have undoubtedly a stronger temptation to indulge in that cordial and reviving stimulus than we water-drinkers, sitting in warm and comfortable rooms, can readily imagine. For certain, our drover could never resist the gentle seduction of the gin-bottle, and being of a free, merry, jovial temperament, one of those persons commonly called good fellows, who like to see others happy in the same way with themselves, he was apt to circulate it at his own expense, to the great improvement of his popularity, and the great detriment of his finances.

All this did vastly well whilst his earnings continued proportionate to his spendings, and the little family at home were comfortably supported by his industry; but when a rheumatic fever came on, one hard winter, and finally settled in his limbs, reducing the most active and hardy man in the parish to the state of a confirmed cripple, then his reckless improvidence stared him in the face; and poor Jack, a thoughtless, but kind, creature, and a most affectionate father, looked at his three motherless children with the acute misery of a parent, who has brought those whom he loves best in the world to abject destitution. He found help, where he probably least expected it, in the sense and spirit of his young daughter, a girl of twelve years old.

Hannah was the eldest of the family, and had, ever since her mother's death, which event had occurred two or three years before, been accustomed to take the direction of their domestic concerns, to manage her two brothers, to feed the pigs and the poultry, and to keep house during the almost constant absence of her father. She was a quick clever lass, of a high spirit, a firm temper, some pride, and a horror of accepting parochial relief, which is every day becoming rarer amongst the peasantry, but which forms the surest safeguard to the sturdy independence of the English character. Our little damsel possessed this quality in perfection; and when her father talked of giving up their comfortable cottage, and removing to the workhouse, whilst she and her brothers must go to service, Hannah formed a bold resolution, and, without disturbing the sick man by any participation of her hopes and fears, proceeded after settling their trifling affairs to act at once on her own plans and designs.

Careless of the future as the poor drover had seemed, he had yet kept clear of debt, and by subscribing constantly to a benefit club, had secured a pittance that might at least assist in supporting him during the long years of sickness and helplessness to which he was doomed to look forward. This his daughter knew. She knew, also, that the employer in whose service his health had suffered so severely was a rich and liberal cattle-dealer in the neighbourhood, who would willingly aid an old and faithful servant, and had, indeed, come forward with offers of money. To assistance from such a quarter Hannah saw no objection. Farmer Oakley and the parish were quite distinct things. Of him, accordingly, she asked, not money, but something much more in his own way: 'a cow! any cow! old or lame, or what not, so that it were a cow! She would be bound to keep it well; if she did not, he might take it back again. She even hoped to pay for it by and by, by instalments, but that she would not promise!' and partly amused, partly interested, by the child's earnestness, the wealthy yeoman gave her, not as a purchase, but as a present, a very fine young

Alderney. She then went to the lord of the manor, and, with equal knowledge of character, begged his permission to keep her cow on the Shaw Common. 'Farmer Oakley had given her a fine Alderney, and she would be bound to pay the rent, and keep her father off the parish, if he would only let it graze on the waste.' And he, too, half from real good-nature, half, not to be outdone in liberality by his tenant, not only granted the requested permission, but reduced the rent so much that the produce of the vine seldom fails to satisfy their kind landlord.

Now, Hannah showed great judgment in setting up as a dairywoman. She could not have chosen an occupation more completely unoccupied, or more loudly called for. One of the most provoking of the petty difficulties which beset people with a small establishment in this neighbourhood is the trouble, almost the impossibility, of procuring the pastoral luxuries of milk, eggs and butter, which rank, unfortunately, amongst the indispensable necessaries of housekeeping. To your thoroughbred Londoner, who, whilst grumbling over his own breakfast, is apt to fancy that thick cream, and fresh butter, and new-laid eggs grow, so to say, in the country – form an actual part of its natural produce – it may be some comfort to learn that in this great grazing district, however the calves and the farmers may be the better for cows, nobody else is; that farmers' wives have ceased to keep poultry; and that we unlucky villagers sit down often to our first meal in a state of destitution, which may well make him content with his thin milk and his Cambridge butter, when compared to our imputed pastoralities.

Hannah's Alderney restored us to one rural privilege. Never was so cleanly a little milkmaid. She changed away some of the cottage finery, which, in his prosperous days, poor Jack had pleased himself with bringing home – the China tea-service, the gilded mugs, and the painted waiters – for the more useful utensils of the dairy, and speedily established a regular and gainful trade in milk, eggs, butter, honey and poultry – for poultry they had always kept.

Her domestic management prospered equally. Her father, who retained the perfect use of his hands, began a manufacture of mats

and baskets, which he constructed with great nicety and adroitness; the eldest boy, a sharp and clever lad, cut for him his rushes and osiers; erected under his sister's direction, a shed for the cow, and enlarged and cultivated the garden (always with the good leave of her kind patron the lord of the manor) until it became so ample that the produce not only kept the pig, and half-kept the family, but also afforded another branch of merchandise to the indefatigable directress of the establishment. For the younger boy, less quick and active, Hannah contrived to obtain an admission to the charity-school, where he made great progress, retaining him at home, however, in the haymaking, and leasing season, or whenever his services could be made available, to the great annoyance of the schoolmaster, whose favourite he is, and who piques himself so much on George's scholarship (your heavy sluggish boy at country work often turns out quick at his book) that it is the general opinion that this much-vaunted pupil will, in process of time, be promoted to the post of assistant, and may, possibly, in course of years, rise to the dignity of a parish pedagogue in his own person. So that his sister, although still making him useful at odd times, now considers George as pretty well off her hands, whilst his elder brother, Tom, could take an under-gardener's place directly, if he were not too important at home to be spared even for a day.

In short, during the five years that she has ruled at the Shaw cottage, the world has gone well with Hannah Bint. Her cow, her calves, her pigs, her bees, her poultry have each, in their several ways, thriven and prospered. She has even brought Watch to like buttermilk, as well as strong beer, and has nearly persuaded her father (to whose wants and wishes she is most anxiously attentive) to accept of milk as a substitute for gin. Not but Hannah hath had her enemies as well as her betters. Why should she not? The old woman at the lodge, who always piqued herself on being spiteful, and crying down new ways, foretold from the first she would come to no good, and could not forgive her for falsifying her prediction; and Betty Barnes, the slatternly widow of a tippling farmer, who rented a field, and set up a cow herself, and was universally discarded for insufferable dirt, said all that the wit of an envious woman could devise against Hannah and her Alderney; nay, even Ned Miles, the keeper, her next neighbour, who had whilom held entire sway over the Shaw Common, as well as its coppices, grumbled as much as so good-natured and genial a person could grumble, when he found a little girl sharing his dominion, a cow grazing beside his pony, and vulgar cocks and hens hovering around the buckwheat destined to feed his noble pheasants. Nobody that had been accustomed to see that paragon of keepers, so tall and manly, and pleasant-looking, with his merry eye, and his knowing smile, striding daily along, in his green coat, and his gold-laced hat, with Neptune, his noble Newfoundland dog (a retriever is the sporting word), and his beautiful spaniel Flirt at his heels, could conceive how askew he looked when he first found Hannah and Watch holding equal reign over his old territory, the Shaw Common.

Yes! Hannah hath had her enemies; but they are passing away. The old woman at the lodge is dead, poor creature; and Betty Barnes, having herself taken to tippling, has lost the few friends she once possessed, and looks, luckless wretch, as if she would soon die too! And the keeper? Why, he is not dead, or like to die;

but the change that has taken place there is the most astonishing of all – except, perhaps, the change in Hannah herself.

Few damsels of twelve years old, generally a very pretty age, were less pretty than Hannah Bint. Short and stunted in her figure, thin in face, sharp in feature, with a muddled complexion, wild, sunburnt hair, and eyes, whose very brightness had in them something startling, over-informed, super-subtle, too clever for her age – at twelve years old she had quite the air of a little old fairy. Now, at seventeen, matters are mended. Her complexion has cleared; her countenance has developed itself; her figure has shot up into height and lightness, and a sort of rustic grace; her bright, acute eye is softened and sweetened by the womanly wish to please; her hair is trimmed, and curled and brushed, with exquisite neatness; and her whole dress arranged with that nice attention to the becoming, the suitable, both in form and texture, which would be called the highest degree of coquetry, if it did not deserve the better name of propriety. Never was such a transmogrification beheld. The lass is really pretty, and Ned Miles has discovered that she is so. There he stands, the rogue, close at her side (for he hath joined her whilst we have been telling her little story, and the milking is over!) – there he stands – holding her milk-pail in one hand, and stroking Watch with the other; whilst she is returning the compliment, by patting Neptune's magnificent head. There they stand, as much like lovers as may be; he smiling, and she blushing; he never looking so handsome, nor she so pretty in all their lives. There they stand, in blessed forgetfulness of all except each other; as happy a couple as ever trod the earth. There they stand, and one would not disturb them for all the milk and butter in Christendom. I should not wonder if they were fixing the wedding-day.

Going to the Races

A MEMORABLE day was the third of last June to Mary and Henrietta Coxe, the young daughters of Simon Coxe, the carpenter of Aberleigh; for it was the first day of Ascot Races, and the first time of their going to that celebrated union of sport and fashion. There is no pleasure so great in the eyes of our country damsels as a jaunt to Ascot. In the first place, it is, when you get there, a genuine English amusement, open alike to rich and poor, elegant as an opera, and merry as a fair; in the second, this village of Aberleigh is situated about fourteen miles from the course, just within distance, almost out of distance, so that there is commonly enough of suspense and difficulty – the slight difficulty, the short suspense – which add such zest to pleasure; finally, at Ascot you are sure to see the king, to see him in his graciousness and his dignity, the finest gentleman in Europe, the greatest sovereign of the world. Truly it is nothing extraordinary that his liege subjects should flock to indulge their feelings of loyalty by the sight of such a monarch, and that the announcement of his presence should cover a barren heath with a dense and crowded population of all ranks and all ages, from the duchess to the gipsy, from the old man of eighty to the child in its mother's arms.

All people love Ascot Races; but our country lasses love them above all. It is their favourite wedding jaunt, for half our young couples are married in the race week, and one or two matches have seemed to me got up purposely for the occasion; and of all the attentions that can be offered by a lover, a drive to the Races is the most irresistible. In short, so congenial is that gay scene to love that it is a moot point which are most numerous, the courtships that conclude there in the shape of bridal excursions, or those which begin on that favoured spot in the shape of parties of pleasure. And the delicate experiment called 'popping the question', is so often put in practice on the very course itself that when Robert Hewitt, the young farmer at the Holt, asked Master Coxe's permission to escort his daughters, not only the good carpenter, but also his neighbours, the blacksmith and the shoemaker, looked on this mark of rustic gallantry as the precursor of a declaration in form; and all the village cried out on Hetta Coxe's extreme good luck, Hetta being supposed, and with some reason, to be the chief object of this attention.

Robert Hewitt was a young farmer of the old school; honest, frugal and industrious; thrifty, thriving and likely to thrive; one of a fine yeomanly spirit, not ashamed of his station, and fond of following the habits of his forefathers, sowing his own corn, driving his own team and occasionally ploughing his own land. As proud, perhaps, of his blunt speech and homely ways as some of his brother farmers of their superior refinement and gentility. Nothing could exceed the scorn with which Robert Hewitt, in his market cart, drawn by his good horse Dobbin, would look down on one neighbour on his hunter, and another in his gig. To the full as proud as any of them was Robert, but in a different way, and perhaps a safer. He piqued himself, like a good Englishman, on wearing a smock-frock, smoking his pipe, and hating foreigners, to our intercourse with whom he was wont to ascribe all the airs and graces, the new fashions, and the effeminacy, which annoyed him in his own countrymen. He hated the French, he detested dandies, and he abhorred fine ladies, fine ways, and finery of any sort. Such was Robert Hewitt.

Henrietta Coxe was a pretty girl of seventeen, and had passed the greater part of her life with an aunt in the next town, who had been a lady's maid in her youth, and had retired thither on a small annuity. To this aunt, who had been dead about a twelvemonth, she was indebted for a name, rather too fine for common wear – I believe she wrote herself Henrietta Matilda; a large wardrobe, pretty much in the same predicament; an abundant stock of superfine notions; some skill in mantua-making and millinery; and a legacy of a hundred pounds to be paid on her wedding-day. Her beauty was quite in the style of a wax doll: blue eyes, flaxen hair, delicate features, and a pink and white complexion, much resembling that sweet pea which is known by the name of the painted lady. Very pretty she was certainly, with all her airs and graces; and very pretty, in spite of her airs and graces, did Robert Hewitt think her; and love, who delights in contrasts, and has an especial pleasure in oversetting wise resolution, and bending the haughty self-will of the lords of the creation, was beginning to make strange havoc in the stout yeoman's heart. His operations, too, found a very unintentional coadjutrix in old Mrs Hewitt, who, taking alarm at her son's frequent visits to the carpenter's shop, unwarily expressed a hope that if her son did intend to marry one of the Coxes, he would have nothing to do with the fine lady, but would choose Mary, the elder sister, a dark-haired, pleasant-looking young woman of two-and-twenty, who kept the house as clean as a palace, and was the boast of the village for industry and good humour. Now this unlucky caution gave Robert, who loved his mother, but did not choose to be managed by her, an additional motive for his lurking preference, by piquing his self-will; add to which, the little damsel herself, in the absence of other admirers, took visible pleasure in his admiration; so that affairs seemed drawing to a crisis, and the party to Ascot appeared likely to end, like other jaunts to the same place, in a wedding. It is true that the invitation, which had been readily and gratefully accepted by her sister, had been received by Miss Hetta with some little demur. 'Going to the Races was delightful! But to ride in a cart behind Dobbin was odious. Could not Mr Hewitt hire a phæton, or borrow a gig? However, as her sister seemed to wish it, she might perhaps go, if she could find no better conveyance.' And with this concession the lover was contented; the more especially as the destined finery was in active preparation. Flounces, fur-belows, and frippery of all descriptions, enough to stock a milliner's shop, did Hetta produce for the adornment of her fair person; and Robert looked on in silence, sometimes thinking how pretty she would look; sometimes, how soon he would put an end to such nonsense when once they were married; and sometimes, how odd a figure he and Dobbin should cut by the side of so much beauty and fashion.

Neither Dobbin nor his master were fated to be so honoured. The evening before the Races there happened to be a revel at Whitley Wood. Thither Hetta repaired; and there she had the ill fortune to be introduced to Monsieur Auguste, a young Frenchman, who had lately hired a room at B—, where he vended eau de cologne, and French toys and essences, and did himself the honour, as his bills expressed, to cut the hair and the corns of the nobility and gentry of the town and neighbourhood. Monsieur was a dark, sallow, foreign-looking personage, with tremendous whiskers, who looked at once fierce and foppish, was curled and perfumed in a manner that did honour to his double profession, and wore gold rings in his ears and on his fingers, a huge bunch of seals at his side, and a gaudy brooch at his bosom. Small chance had Robert Hewitt against such a rival, especially when, smitten with her beauty or her hundred pounds, he devoted himself to Hetta's service, made fine speeches in most bewitching broken English, braved for her sake the barbarities of a country dance, and promised to initiate her into the mysteries of the waltz and the quadrille; and, finally, requested the honour to conduct her in a cabriolet the next day to Ascot Races. Small chance had our poor farmer against such a Monsieur.

The morning arrived, gloomy, showery, and cold, and at the appointed hour up drove the punctual Robert, in a new market cart, painted blue with red wheels, and his heavy but handsome horse Dobbin (who was indeed upon occasion the fore horse of the team) as sleek and shining as good feed and good dressing could make him. Up drove Robert with his little sister (a child of eleven years old, who was to form one of the party) sitting at his side; whilst equally punctual, at Master Coxe's door, stood the sisters ready dressed; Mary in a new dark gown, a handsome shawl, and a pretty straw bonnet, with a cloth cloak hanging on her arm; Hetta in a flutter of gauze and ribbons, pink and green, and yellow and blue, looking like a parrot tulip, or a milliner's doll, or a picture of the fashions in the *Lady's Magazine*, or like anything under the sun but an English country girl. Robert looked at her and then at Mary, who was vainly endeavouring to persuade her to put on, or at least to take, a cloak, and thought for once without indignation of his mother's advice; he got out, however, and was preparing to assist them into the cart, when suddenly, to the astonishment of everybody but Hetta, for she had said nothing at home of her encounter at the revel, Monsieur Auguste made his appearance in a hired gig of the most wretched description, drawn by an equally miserable jade, alighted at the house and claimed Mademoiselle's promise to do him the honour to accompany him in his cabriolet. The consternation was general. Mary remonstrated with her sister mildly but earnestly; Master Coxe swore she should not go; but Hetta was resolute; and farmer Hewitt, whose first impulse had been to drub the Frenchman, changed his purpose when he saw how willing she was to be carried off. 'Let her go,' said he, 'Monsieur is welcome to her company; for my part, I think they are well matched. It would be a pity to part them.' And, lifting Mary rapidly into the cart, he drove off at a pace of which Dobbin, to judge from his weight, appeared incapable, and to which that illustrious steed was very little accustomed.

In the meanwhile Hetta was endeavouring to introduce her new beau to her father, and to reconcile him to her change of escort; and the standers-by, consisting of half the men and boys in the village, were criticizing the Frenchman's equipage: 'I could shake the old chaise to pieces with one jerk, it's so ramshackle,' cried Ned Jones, Master Coxe's foreman. 'The wheel will come to pieces long before they get to Ascot,' added Sam, the apprentice. 'The old horse has a spavin in the off-fore leg, that's what makes him so lame,' said Will Ford the blacksmith. 'And he has been down within the month. Look at his knees!' rejoined Jem, the carter. 'He's blind of an eye,' exclaimed one urchin. 'He shies,' cried another. 'The reins are rotten,' observed Dick, the collar-maker. 'The Frenchman can't drive,' remarked Jack, the drover, coming up to join the crew; 'he'd as nearly as possible run foul of my pigs.' 'He'll certainly overturn her, poor thing,' cried one kind friend, as, overcome by her importunities, her father at length consented to her departure. 'The chaise will break down,' said another. 'Break! He'll break her neck,' added a third. 'They'll be drenched to the skin in this shower,' exclaimed a fourth; and amidst these consoling predictions the happy couple departed.

Robert and Mary, on their side, proceeded for some time in almost total silence! Robert too angry for speech, and Mary feeling herself, however innocent, involved in the consequences of her sister's delinquency; so that little passed beyond Anne Hewitt's delighted remarks on the beauty of the country, and the hedgerows, bright with the young leaves of the oak, and gay with the pearly thorn blossoms and the delicate brier-rose; and her occasional exclamations at the sudden appearance of some tiny wren, or the peculiar interrupted flight of some water-wagtail, as he threw himself forward, then rested for a moment, self-poised in the air, then started on again with an up-and-down motion, like a ball tossed from the hand, keeping by the side of the cart for half a mile or more, as is frequently the way with that sociable bird. Little passed beyond trifles such as these until Robert turned suddenly round to his companion with the abrupt question: 'Pray, Miss Mary, do you like Frenchmen?' 'I never was acquainted with any,' replied Mary; 'but I think I should like Englishmen best. It seems natural to prefer one's own countrymen.' 'Aye, to be sure!' replied Robert, 'to be sure it is! You are a sensible girl, Mary Coxe; and a good girl. It would be well for your sister if she had some of your sense.' 'Hetta is a good girl, I assure you, farmer Hewitt; a very good girl,' rejoined Mary, warmly; 'and does not want sense. But only consider how young she is, and her having no mother, and being a little spoilt by my poor aunt, and so pretty, and everybody talking nonsense to her, no wonder that she should sometimes be a little wrong, as she was this morning. But I hope that we shall meet her on the course, and that all will go right again. Hetta is a good girl, and will make a good wife.' 'To a Frenchman,' replied Robert drily; and the conversation turned to other subjects, and was kept up with cheerfulness and good humour till they reached Ascot.

Anne and Mary enjoyed the Races much. They saw the line of carriages, nine deep – more carriages than they thought ever were built; and the people – more people than they thought the whole world could hold; had a confused view of the horses and a distinct one of the riders' jackets; and Anne, whose notions on the subject of racing had been rather puzzled, so far enlarged her knowledge and improved her mind as to comprehend that yellow, crimson, green and blue, in short, all the colours of the rainbow, were trying which should come first to the winning-post. They saw Punch, a puppet show, several peepshows, and the dancing dogs; admired the matchless display of beauty and elegance, when the weather allowed the ladies to walk up and down the course; were amused at the bustle and hurry-scurry, when a sudden shower drove them to the shelter of their carriages; saw the duke of Wellington; had a merry nod from the lively boy, Prince George; and had the honour of sharing, with some thousands of his subjects, a most graceful bow and most gracious smile from his Majesty. In short, they had seen everything and everybody, except Hetta and her beau; and nothing had been wanting to Mary's gratification but the assurance of her sister's safety; for Mary had that prime qualification for a sightseer, the habit of thinking much of what she came to see and little of herself. She made light of all inconveniences, covered little Anne (a delicate child) with her own cloak during the showers, and contrived, in spite of Robert's gallant attention to his guest, that Anne should have the best place under the umbrella, and the most tempting portion of the provisions. So that our farmer, by no means wanting in moral taste, was charmed with her cheerfulness, her good humour, and the total absence of vanity and selfishness; and when, on her ascending the cart to return, he caught a glimpse of a pretty foot and ankle, and saw how much exercise and pleasure had heightened her complexion and brightened her hazel eyes, he could not help thinking to himself. 'My mother was right. She's ten times handsomer than her sister, and has twenty times more sense – and, besides, she does not like Frenchmen.'

But where could Hetta be? What had become of poor Hetta? This question, which had pressed so frequently on Mary's mind during the Races, became still more painful as they proceeded on their road home, which, leading through cross-country lanes, far away from the general throng of the visitors, left more leisure for her affectionate fears. They had driven about two miles, and Robert was endeavouring to comfort her with hopes that their horse's lameness had forced them back again, and that her sister would be found safe at Aberleigh, when a sudden turn in the lane discovered a disabled gig, without a horse or driver, in the middle of the road, and a woman seated on a bank by the side of a ditch – a miserable object, tattered, dirty, shivering, drenched, and crying as if her heart would break. Was it, could it be Hetta? Yes, Hetta it was. All the misfortunes that had been severally predicted at their outset had befallen the unfortunate pair. Before they had travelled three miles, their wretched horse had fallen lame in his near foreleg, and had cast the offhind shoe, which, as the blacksmith of the place was gone to the Races, and nobody seemed willing to put himself out of the way to oblige a Frenchman, had nearly stopped them at the beginning of their expedition. At last, however, they met with a man who undertook to shoe their steed, and whose want of skill added a prick to their other calamities. Then Monsieur Auguste broke a shaft of the cabriolet by driving against a post, the setting and bandaging of which broken limb made another long delay; then came a pelting shower, during which they were forced to stand under a tree; then they lost their way, and owing to the people of whom Monsieur inquired not understanding his English, and Monsieur not understanding theirs, went full five miles round about; then they arrived at the Chequers public-house, which no effort could induce their horse to pass, so there they stopped perforce to bait and feed; then, when they were getting on as well as could be expected of a horse with three lame legs and a French driver, a waggon came past them, carried away their wheel, threw Monsieur Auguste into the hedge, and lodged Miss Henrietta in the ditch. So now the beau was gone to the next village for assistance, and the belle was waiting his return on the bank; and Poor Hetta was evidently tired of her fine lover and the manifold misadventures which his unlucky gallantry had brought upon her, and accepted very thankfully the offer which Anne and Mary made, and Robert did not oppose, of taking her into the cart and leaving a line written in pencil on a leaf of Mary's pocket-book, to inform Monsieur of her safety. Heartily glad was poor Hetta to find herself behind the good steed Dobbin, under cover of her sister's warm cloak, pitied and comforted and in a fair way to get home. Heartily glad would she have been, too, to have found herself reinstated in the good graces of her old admirer. But of that she saw no sign. Indeed, the good yeoman took some pains to show that, although he bore no malice, his courtship was over. He goes, however, oftener than ever to the carpenter's house; and the gossips of Aberleigh say that this jaunt to Ascot will have its proper and usual catastrophe, a merry wedding; that Robert Hewitt will be the happy bridegroom, but that Hetta Coxe will not be the bride.

A Castle in the Air

'CAN anyone tell me of a house to be let hereabouts?' asked I, this afternoon, coming into the room, with an open letter in my hand, and an unusual animation of feeling and of manner. 'Our friends, the Camdens, want to live amongst us again, and have commissioned me to make inquiries for a residence.'

This announcement, as I expected, gave general delight; for Mr Camden is the most excellent and most agreeable person under the sun, except his wife, who is even more amiable than her amiable husband. To regain such neighbours was felt to be a universal benefit, more especially to us who were so happy as to call them friends. My own interest in the house question was participated by all around me, and the usual enumeration of vacant mansions, and the several objections to each (for where ever was a vacant mansion without its objection?) began with zeal and rapidity.

'Cranley Hall,' said one.

'Too large!'

'Hinton Park?'

'Too much land.'

'The White House at Hannonby – the Belvedere, as the late people called it?'

'What! Is that flourishing establishment done up? But Hannonby is too far off – ten miles at least.'

'Queen's-bridge Cottage?'

'Aye that sweet place would have suited exactly, but it's let. The Browns took it only yesterday.'

'Sydenham Court?'

'That might have done too, but it is not in the market. The Smiths intend to stay.'

'Lanton Abbey?'

'Too low; grievously damp.'

By this time, however, we had arrived at the end of our list; nobody could remember another place to be let, or likely to be let, and confessing ourselves too fastidious, we went again over our *catalogue raisonné* with expectations much sobered, and objections much modified, and were beginning to find out that Cranley Hall was not so very large, nor Lanton Abbey so exceedingly damp, when one of our party exclaimed suddenly, 'We never thought of Hatherden Hill! Surely that is small enough and dry enough!' And it being immediately recollected that Hatherden was only a mile off, we lost sight of all faults in this great recommendation, and wrote immediately to the lawyer who had the charge of letting the place, whilst I myself and my most efficient assistant, sallied forth to survey it on the instant.

It was a bright cool afternoon about the middle of August, and we proceeded in high spirits towards our destination, talking, as we went, of the excellence and agreeableness of our delightful friends, and anticipating the high intellectual pleasure, the gratification to the taste and the affections, which our renewed intercourse with persons so accomplished and so amiable, could not fail to afford; both agreeing that Hatherden was the very place we wanted, the very situation, the very distance, the very size. In agreeing with me, however, my companion could not help reminding me rather maliciously how very much, in our late worthy neighbours', the Norrises, time, I had been used to hate and shun this paragon of places; how frequently I had declared Hatherden too distant for a walk, and too near for a drive; how constantly I had complained of fatigue in mounting the hill, and of cold in crossing the common; and how, finally, my half-yearly visits of civility had dwindled first into annual, then into biennial calls, and would doubtless have extended themselves into triennial marks of remembrance, if our neighbours had but remained long enough. 'To be sure,' added he, recollecting, probably, how he, with his stricter sense of politeness, used to stave off a call for a month together, taking shame to himself every evening for his neglect, retaining 'at once the conscience and the sin'! 'To be sure, Norris was a sad bore! We shall find the hill easier to climb when the Camdens live on the top of it.' An observation to which I assented most heartily.

On we went gaily; just pausing to admire Master Keep, the shoemaker's, farming, who having a bit of garden ground to spare, sowed it with wheat instead of planting it with potatoes, and is now, aided by his lame apprentice, very literally carrying his crop. I fancy they mean to thresh their corn in the woodhouse, at least there they are depositing the sheaves. The produce may amount to four bushels. My companion, a better judge, says to three; and it has cost the new farmer two superb scarecrows, and gunpowder enough for a review, to keep off the sparrows. Well, it has been amusement and variety, however! And gives him an interest in the agricultural corner of the county newspaper. Master Keep is well to do in the world, and can afford himself such a diversion. For my part, I like these little experiments, even if they be not over gainful. They show enterprise: a shoemaker of less genius would never have got beyond a crop of turnips.

On we went – down the lane, over the bridge, up the hill – for there really is a hill, and one of some steepness for Berkshire, and across the common, once so dreary, but now bright and glittering, under the double influence of an August sun, and our own good spirits, until we were stopped by the gate of the lawn, which was of course locked, and obliged to wait until a boy should summon the old woman who had charge of the house, and who was now at work in a neighbouring harvest-field, to give us entrance.

Boys in plenty were there. The fine black-headed lad, George Ropley, who, with his olive complexion, his bright dark eyes, and his keen intelligent features looks so Italian, but who is yet in all his ways so thoroughly and genially English, had been gathering in his father's crop of apples, and was amusing himself with tossing some twenty amongst as many urchins of either sex who had collected round him, to partake of the fruit and the sport. There he stood tossing the ripe ruddy apples; some high in the air for a catch, some low amongst the bushes for a hunt; some one way, some another, puzzling and perplexing the rogues, but taking care that none should go appleless in the midst of his fun. And what fun it was to them all, thrower and catchers! What infinite delight! How they laughed and shouted, and tumbled and ran? How they watched every motion of George Ropley's hand; the boys and the girls, and the 'toddling wee things', of whom one could not distinctly make out whether they were the one or the other! And how often was that hand tossed up empty, flinging nothing, in order to cheat the wary watchers! Now he threw an apple into the midst of the group, and what a scramble! Then at a distance, and what a race! The five nearest started; one, a great boy, stumbled over a molehill and was flung out; two of the little ones were distanced; and it was a neck and neck heat between a girl in a pink frock (my acquaintance Liddy Wheeler) and a boy in a tattered jacket, name unknown. With fair play Liddy would have beaten, but he of the ragged jacket pulled her back by her new pink frock, rushed forward, and conquered, George gallantly flinging his last apple into her lap to console her for her defeat.

By this time the aged portress (Dame Wheeler, Liddy's grandmother) had given us admittance, and we soon stood on the steps in front of the house, in calm survey of the scene before us. Hatherden was just the place to like or not to like, according to the feeling of the hour; a respectable, comfortable, country house, with a lawn before, a paddock on one side, a shrubbery on the other; offices and a kitchen garden behind, and the usual ornaments of villas and advertisements, a greenhouse and a veranda. Now my thoughts were *couleur de rose*, and Hatherden was charming. Even the beds intended for flowers on the lawn, but which, under a summer's neglect, were now dismal receptacles of seeds and weeds, did not shock my gardening eye so much as my companion evidently expected. 'We must get my factotum, Clarke, here tomorrow,' so ran my thoughts, 'to clear away that rubbish, and try a little bold transplanting: late hollyhocks, a few pots of lobelias and chrysanthemums, a few patches of coreopsis and china-asters, and plenty of scarlet geraniums will soon make this desolation flourishing. A good gardener can move anything nowadays, whether in bloom or not,' thought I, with much complacency, 'and Clarke's a man to transplant Windsor Forest without withering a leaf. We'll have him tomorrow.'

The same happy disposition continued after I entered the house. And when left alone in the echoing, empty breakfast-room, with only one shutter opened, whilst Dame Wheeler was guiding the companion of my survey to the stable-yard, I amused myself with making in my own mind comparisons between what had been, and what would be. There she used to sit, poor Mrs Norris, in this large, airy room, in the midst of its solid handsome furniture, in a great chair at a great table, busily at work for one of her seven small children; the table piled with frocks, trousers, petticoats, shirts, pinafores, hats, bonnets, all sorts of children's gear, masculine and feminine, together with spelling books, copy books, ivory alphabets, dissected maps, dolls, toys and gingerbread for the same small people. There she sat, a careful mother, fretting over their naughtiness and their ailments; always in fear of the sun, or the wind, or the rain, of their running to heat themselves, or their standing still to catch cold; not a book in the house fit for a person turned of eight years old! Not a grown-up idea! Not a thought beyond the nursery! One wondered what she could have talked of before she had children. Good Mrs Norris, such was she. Good Mr Norris was, for all purposes of neighbourhood, worse still. He was gapy and fidgety, and prosy and dozy, kept a tool chest and a medicine chest, weighed out manna and magnesia, constructed fishing-flies, and nets for fruit-trees, turned nutmeg-graters, lined his wife's workbox, and dressed his little daughter's doll; and had a tone of conversation perfectly in keeping with his tastes and pursuits, abundantly tedious, thin and small. One talked down to him, worthy gentleman, as one would to his son Willy. These were the neighbours that had been. What wonder that the hill was steep, and the way long, and the common dreary? Then came pleasant thoughts of the neighbours that were to be. The lovely and accomplished wife, so sweet and womanly; the elegant and highly informed husband, so spirited and manly! Art and literature, and wisdom and wit, adorning with a wreathy and garlandy splendour all that is noblest in mind and purest in heart! What wonder that Hatherden became more and more interesting in its anticipated charms, and that I went gaily about the place, taking note of all that could contribute to the comfort of its future inhabitants.

Home I came, a glad and busy creature, revolving in my mind the wants of the house and their speediest remedies: new paper for the drawing-room; new wainscoting for the dining parlour; a stove for the laundry; a lock for the wine cellar; baizing the door of the library; and new painting the hall; to say nothing of the grand design of Clarke and the flower-beds.

So full was I of busy thoughts, and so desirous to put my plans in train without the loss of a moment, that although the tossing of apples had now resolved itself into a most irregular game of cricket, George Ropley being batting at one wicket, with little Sam Coper for his mate at the other, Sam, an urchin of seven years old, but the son of an old player, full of cricket blood, born, as it were, with a bat in his hand, getting double the notches of his tall partner, an indignity which that well-natured stripling bore with surprising good humour, and although the opposite side consisted of Liddy Wheeler bowling at one end, her old competitor of the ragged jacket at the other, and one urchin in trousers, and one in petticoats, standing out; in spite of the temptation of watching this comical parody on that manly exercise, rendered doubly amusing by the scientific manner in which little Sam stood at his wicket, the perfect gravity of the fieldsman in petticoats, and the serious air with which these two worthies called Liddy to order whenever she transgressed any rule of the game — Sam will certainly be a great player some day or other, and so (if he be not a girl, for really there's no telling) will the young gentleman standing out — in spite, however, of the great temptation of overlooking a favourite divertissement, with variations so truly original, home we went, hardly pausing to observe the housing of Master Keep's wheat harvest. Home we went, adding at every step a fresh story to our Castle in the Air, anticipating happy mornings and joyous evenings at dear Hatherden; in love with the place and all about it, and quite convinced that the hill was nothing, the distance nothing, and the walk by far the prettiest in this neighbourhood.

Home we came, and there we found two letters: one from Mr

Camden, sent per coach, to say that he found they must go abroad immediately, and that they could not therefore think of coming into Berkshire for a year or more; one from the lawyer left in charge of Hatherden, to say, that we could not have the place, as the Norrises were returning to their old house forthwith. And my Castle is knocked down, blown up – which is the right word for the demolishing of such airy edifices? And Hatherden is as far off, and the hill as steep, and the common as dreary as ever.

Rosedale

I DON'T know how it happened when we were house-hunting the other day that nobody ever thought of Rosedale. I should have objected to it, both as out of distance – it's a good six miles off – and as being utterly unrecommendable by one rational person to another. Rosedale! The very name smacks of the Minerva Press, and gives token of the nonsense and trumpery thereunto belonging. Rosedale Cottage! The man who under that portentous title takes that house cannot complain of lack of warning.

Nevertheless Rosedale is one of the prettiest cottages that ever sprung into existence in brick or on paper. All strangers go to see it, and few 'cots of spruce gentility' are so well worth seeing. Fancy a low irregular white rough-cast building thatched with reeds, covered with roses, clematis and passion-flowers, standing on a knoll of fine turf, amidst flower-beds and shrubberies and magnificent elms, backed by an abrupt hill, and looking over lawny fields to a green common, which is intersected by a gay highroad, dappled with ponds of water, and terminated by a pretty village edging off into rich woodlands. Imagine this picture of a place tricked out with ornaments of all sorts, conservatories, roseries, rustic seats, American borders, Gothic dairies, Spanish hermitages, and flowers stuck as close as pins in a pin-cushion, with everything, in short, that might best become the walls of an exhibition room, or the back scene of a play. Conceive the interior adorned in a style of elegance still more fanciful, and it will hardly appear surprising that this 'unique bijou', as the advertisement calls it, should seldom want a tenant. The rapid succession of these occupiers is the more extraordinary matter. Everybody is willing to come to Rosedale, but nobody stays.

For this, however, it is not difficult to assign very sufficient cause. In the first place, the house has the original sin of most ornamented cottages: that of being built on the foundation of a real labourer's dwelling; by which notable piece of economy the owner saved some thirty pounds, at the expense of making half his rooms mere nutshells, and the house incurably damp, to say nothing of the inconvenience of the many apartments which were erected as afterthoughts, the addenda of the work, and are only to be come at by outside passages and French window doors. Secondly, that necessary part of a two-storey mansion, the staircase, was utterly forgotten by architect, proprietor and builder, and never missed by any person, till the ladder being one day taken away at the dinner-hour, an Irish labourer, accidentally left behind, was discovered by the workmen on their return, perched like a bird on the top of the roof, he having taken the method of going up the chimney as the quickest way of getting down. This adventure occasioned a call for the staircase, which was at length inserted by the bye, and is as much like a stepladder in a dark corner as anything well can be.[1] Thirdly and lastly, this beautiful abode is in every way most thoroughly inconvenient and uncomfortable. In the winter one might find as much protection in the hollow of a tree – cold, gusty, sleety, wet; snow threatening from above like an avalanche; water gushing up from below like a fountain; a house of card-paper would be the solider refuge, a gipsy's tent by far the more snug. In summer it is proportionably close and hot, giving little shade and no shelter; and all the year round it is overdone with frippery and finery, a toyshop in action, a Brobdingnagian baby-house.

Every room is in masquerade: the saloon Chinese, full of jars and mandarins and pagodas; the library Egyptian, all covered with hieroglyphics, and swarming with furniture crocodiles and sphinxes. Only think of a crocodile couch, and a sphinx sofa!

---

[1] This instance of forgetfulness is not unexampled. A similar accident is said to have happened to Madam d'Arblay in the erection of a cottage built from the profits of her admirable Camilla.

They sleep in Turkish tents, and dine in a Gothic chapel.[1] Now, English ladies and gentlemen in their everyday apparel look exceedingly out of place amongst such mummery. The costume won't do. It is not in keeping. Besides, the properties themselves are apt to get shifted from one scene to another, and all manner of anomalies are the consequence. The mitred chairs and screens of the chapel, for instance, so very upright, and tall, and carved, and priestly, were mixed up oddly enough with the squat Chinese bronzes; whilst by some strange transposition a pair of nodding mandarins figured amongst the Egyptian monsters, and by the aid of their supernatural ugliness really looked human.

Then the room taken up by the various knick-nackery, the unnamed and unnameable generation of gew-gaws! It always seemed to me to require more housemaids than the house would hold. And the same with the garden. You are so begirt with garlands and festoons, flowers above and flowers below, that you walk about under a perpetual sense of trespass, of taking care, of doing mischief; now bobbing against a sweet-brier, in which rencontre you have the worst; now flapped in the face by a woodbine to the discomfiture of both parties; now revenging these vegetable wrongs by tripping up an unfortunate balsam, bonnets, coatskirts and flounces in equal peril! The very gardeners step gingerly, and tuck their aprons tightly round them before they venture into that fair demesne of theirs, which is, so to say, overpeopled. In short, Rosedale is a place to look at, rather than live in; a fact which will be received without dispute by some score of tenants, by the proprietor of the county newspaper, who keeps the advertisement of this matchless villa constantly set, to his no small emolument, and by the neighbourhood at large, to whom the succession of new faces, new liveries, and new equipages driving about our rustic lanes, and sometimes occupying a very

---

[1] Some of the pleasantest days of my life have been spent in a house so furnished. But then it was of fitting dimensions, and the delightful persons to whom it belonged had a house in London, and a mansion in the country, and used their fancy villa much as one would use a marquee or a pleasure-boat, for gay parties in fine weather. Rosedale, unlucky place, was built to be lived in.

tasty pew in the parish church, has long supplied a source of conversation as unfailing and as various as the weather.

The first person who ascertained, by painful experience, that Rosedale was uninhabitable, was the proprietor, a simple young man from the next town, who unluckily took it into his head that he had a taste for architecture and landscape gardening and so forth; and falling into the hands of a London upholsterer and a country nurseryman, produced the effort of genius that I have endeavoured to describe. At the end of a month he found that nobody could live there; and with the advice of the nurseryman and the upholsterer began to talk of rebuilding and new modelling; nay, he actually went so far as to send for the bricklayer. But fortunately for our man of taste, he had a wife of more sense than himself, who seized the moment of disappointment to disgust him with improvements and improvers, in which feat she was greatly aided by the bills of his late associates; put a stop at once to his projects and his complaints; removed with all speed to their old residence, an ugly, roomy, comfortable red-brick house in the market-place at B—; drew up a flaming advertisement; and turned the grumbling occupant into a thriving landlord. Lucky for him was the day in which William Walker, Esquire, married Miss Bridget Tomkins, second daughter of Mr Samuel Tomkins, attorney at law! And lucky for Mr Samuel Tomkins was the hour in which he acquired a son-in-law more profitable in the article of leases than the two lords to whom he acted as steward both put together!

First on the list of tenants was a bride and bridegroom come to spend the early months of their nuptial life in this sweet retirement. They arrived towards the end of August with a great retinue of servants, horses, dogs and carriages, well-bedecked with bridal favours. The very pointers had white ribbons round their necks, so splendid was their rejoicing, and had each, as we were credibly informed, eaten a huge slice of wedding-cake when the happy couple returned from church. The bride, whom everybody except myself called plain, and whom I thought pretty, had been a great heiress, and had married for love the day she came of age. She was slight of form and pale of complexion, with a profusion of brown hair, mild hazel eyes, a sweet smile, a soft voice, and an air of modesty that clung about her like a veil. I never saw a more lovable creature. He was dark and tall and stout and bold, with an assured yet gentlemanly air, a loud voice, a confident manner and a real passion for shooting. They stayed just a fortnight, during which time he contrived to get warned off half the manors in the neighbourhood, and cut down the finest elm on the lawn one wet morning to open a view of the high-road. I hope the marriage has turned out a happy one, for she was a sweet gentle creature. I used to see her leaning over the gate watching his return from shooting with such a fond patience! And her bound to meet him when he did appear! And the pretty coaxing playfulness, with which she patted and chided her rivals the dogs! Oh, I hope she is happy! But I fear, I fear.

Next succeeded a couple from India, before whom floated reports golden and gorgeous as the clouds at sunset. Inexhaustible riches; profuse expenditure; tremendous ostentation; unheard-of luxury; ortolans; beccaficos; French beans at Christmas; green peas at Easter; strawberries always; a chariot and six; twelve black footmen; and parrots and monkeys beyond all count. These were amongst the most moderate of the rumours that preceded them; and every idle person in the country was preparing to be a hanger-on; and every shopkeeper in B— on the watch for a customer; when up drove a quiet-looking old gentleman in a pony-chaise, with a quiet-looking old lady at his side, and took possession, their retinue following in a hack post-chaise. Whether the habits of this Eastern Crœsus corresponded with his modest début, or his magnificent reputation, we had not time to discover, although, from certain indications, I conceive that much might be said on both sides. They arrived in the middle of a fine October, while the china-roses covered the walls, and the china-asters, and dahlias, and fuchsias, and geraniums in full blow, gave a summer brilliancy to the lawn; but scarcely had a pair of superb Common Prayer books, bound in velvet, and a Bible with gold clasps, entered in possession of the pew at church, before 'there came a frost, a nipping frost', which turned the china-asters and the china-roses brown, and the dahlias and geraniums black, and the nabob and the nabobess blue. They disappeared the next day, and have never been seen or heard of since.

Then arrived a fox-hunting baronet, with a splendid stud and a splendid fortune. A young man, a single man, a handsome man! Every speculating mamma in the country fixed her eyes on Sir Robert for a son-in-law; papas were sent to call; brothers were enjoined to go out hunting, and get acquainted; nay, even certain of the young ladies themselves (I grieve to say it!) showed symptoms of condescension which might almost have made their grandmothers start from their graves. But what could they do? How could they help it, poor pretty things? The baronet, with the instinct of a determined bachelor, avoided a young lady as a sparrow does a hawk, and discovering this shyness, they followed their instinct as the hawk would do in a similar case, and pursued the coy bird. It was what sportsmen call a fine open season, which being translated means every variety of wintry weather except frost – dirty, foggy, sleety, wet. So such of our belles as looked well on horseback took the opportunity to ride to cover and see the hounds throw off; and such as shone more as pedestrians would take an early walk, exquisitely dressed, for their health's sake, towards the general rendezvous. Still Sir Robert was immoveable. He made no morning calls, accepted no invitations, spoke to no mortal till he had ascertained that there was neither sister, daughter, aunt, nor cousin in the case. He kept from every petticoat as if it contained the contagion of the plague, shunned ballrooms and drawing-rooms, as if they were pest-houses, and, finally, had the comfort of leaving Rosedale without having even bowed to a female during his stay.

The final cause of his departure has been differently reported; some hold that he was frightened away by Miss Amelia Singleton, who had nearly caused him to commit involuntary homicide (is that the word for killing a woman?) by crossing and recrossing before his hunter in Sallow Field Lane, thereby putting him in danger of a coroner's inquest; whilst others assert that his land-lord, Mr Walker, happening to call one day, found his tenant in dirty boots on the sphinx sofa, and a Newfoundland dog dripping with mud on the crocodile couch, and gave him notice to quit on the spot. For my part, I regard this legend as altogether apocryphal, invented to save the credit of the house, by assuming that one of its many inhabitants was turned out, contrary to his own wish. My faith goes entirely with the Miss Amelia version of the history; the more so, as that gentle damsel was so inconsolable as to marry a former beau, a small squire of the neighbourhood, rather weather-beaten, and not quite so young as he had been, within a month after she had the ill luck not to be run over by Sir Robert.

However that may have been, 'thence ensued a vacancy' in Rosedale, which was supplied the same week by a musical family, a travelling band – drums, trumpets, harps, pianos, violins, violin-cellos, trombones and German flutes – noise personified! An incarnation of din! The family consisted of three young ladies who practised regularly six hours a day; a governess who played on some instrument or other from morning till night; one fluting brother; one fiddling ditto; a violin-celloing music-master; and a singing papa. The only quiet person among them, the 'one poor halfpenny-worth of bread to this monstrous quantity of sack', was the unfortunate mamma; sole listener, as it seemed, of her innumerous choir. Oh, how we pitied her! She was a sweet, placid-looking woman, and younger in appearance than either of her daughters, with a fair open forehead, full dark eyes, lips that seemed waiting to smile, a deep yet cool colour, and a heavenly composure of countenance, resembling in features, expression, and complexion the small Madonnas of Raphael. We never ceased to wonder at her happy serenity until we found out that the good lady was deaf, a discovery which somewhat diminished the ardour of our admiration. How this enviable calamity befel her, I did not hear, but of course that din! The very jars and mandarins cracked under the incessant vibration; I only wonder that the poor house did not break the drum of its ears; did not burst from its own report, and explode like an overloaded gun. One could not see that unlucky habitation half a mile off, without such a feeling of noise as comes over one in looking at Hogarth's enraged musician. To pass it was really dangerous. One stage-coach was overturned, and two post-chaises ran away in consequence of their uproarious doings; and a sturdy old-fashioned country gentleman, who rode a particularly anti-musical, startlish, blood-horse, began to talk of indicting Rosedale as a nuisance, when just at the critical moment, its tenants had the good fortune to discover that, although the hermitage with its vaulted roof made a capital concert-room, yet that there was not space enough within doors for their several practisings, that the apartments were too small, and the partitions too thin, so that concord was turned into discord, and harmonies went crossing each other all over the house – Mozart jostled by Rossini, and Handel put down by Weber. And away they went also.

Our next neighbours were two ladies, not sisters, except, as one of them said, in soul; kindred spirits determined to retire from the world, and emulate in this sweet retreat the immortal friendship of the ladies of Llangollen.[1] The names of our pair of friends were Jackson and Jennings: Miss Laura Jackson (I wonder whether Laura really was her name! She signed herself so in prose and in verse, and would certainly for more reasons than one have disliked an appeal to the Register! Besides she ought to know; so Laura it shall be!) – Miss Laura Jackson and Miss Barbara Jennings, commonly called Bab. Both were of that unfortunate class of young ladies, whom the malicious world is apt to call old maids; both rich, both independent, and both, in the fullest sense of the word, cockneys. Laura was tall and lean, and scraggy and yellow, dressing in an Arcadian sort of way, pretty much like an opera shepherdess without a crook, singing pastoral songs prodigiously out of tune, and talking in a deep voice, with much emphasis and astounding fluency all sorts of sentimentalities all

---

[1] I need not, I trust, disclaim any intention of casting the lightest shade of ridicule on the remarkable instance of female friendship to which I have alluded in the text. A union enduring, as that has done, from youth to age, adorned by rank, talent, and beauty, cemented by cheerfulness and good humour, and consecrated by benevolence and virtue, can fear no one's censure, and soars far beyond my feeble praise. Such a friendship is the very poetry of life. But the heartless imitation, the absurd parody of the noble and elevating romance is surely fair game, the more so, as it tends like all parodies to bring the original into undeserved disrepute.

the day long. Miss Barbara on the other hand was short and plump and round-faced and ruddy, inclining to vulgarity as Laura to affectation, with a great love of dancing, a pleasant chuckling laugh, and a most agreeable habit of assentation. Altogether Bab was a likeable person in spite of some nonsense, which is more than could honestly be said for her companion.

Juxtaposition laid the cornerstone of this immortal friendship, which had already lasted four months and a half, and, cemented by resemblance of situation and dissimilarity of character, really bade fair to continue some months longer. Both had been heartily weary of their previous situations: Laura keeping house for a brother in Aldersgate Street, where, as she said, she was overwhelmed by odious vulgar business; Barbara living with an aunt on Fish Street Hill, where she was tired to death of having nothing to do. Both had a passion for the country. Laura, who, except one jaunt to Margate, had never been out of the sound of Bow Bell, that she might ruralize after the fashion of the poets, sit under trees and gather roses all day long; Bab, who, in spite of yearly trips to Paris and Brussels and Amsterdam and Brighton, had hardly seen a green field except through a coach window, was on her side possessed with a mania for notability and management. *She yearned to keep cows*, fatten pigs, breed poultry, grow cabbages, make hay, brew and bake, and wash and churn. Visions of killing her own mutton flitted over her delighted fancy; and, when one evening at a ball in the borough her favourite partner had deserted her to dance with her niece, and Miss Laura, who had been reading Miss Seward's letters, proposed to her to retire from the world and its vanities in imitation of the illustrious recluses of Llangollen, Miss Barbara, caught above all things with the prospect of making her own butter every morning for breakfast,[1] acceded to the proposal most joyfully.

The vow of friendship was taken, and nothing remained but to look out for a house. Barbara wanted a farm, Laura a cottage; Barbara talked of cows and clover, Laura of nightingales and

---

[1] Vide *Anna Seward's Correspondence.*

violets; Barbara sighed for Yorkshire pastures, Laura for Welsh mountains; and the scheme seemed likely to go off for want of an habitation, when Rosedale in all the glory of advertisement shone on Miss Laura in the *Morning Post*, and was immediately engaged by the delighted friends on a lease of seven, fourteen, or one-and-twenty years.

It was a raw, blowy March evening, when the fair partners arrived at the cottage. Miss Laura made a speech in her usual style on taking possession – an invocation to friendship and rural nature, and a deprecation of cities, society and men – at the conclusion of which Miss Barbara underwent an embassade; and, having sufficiently admired the wonders within, they sallied forth with a candle and lanthorn to view their ruralities without. Miss Laura was better satisfied with this ramble than her companion. She found at least trees and primroses, whilst the country felicities of ducks and chickens were entirely wanting. Bab, however, reconciled the matter by supposing they were gone to roost, and, a little worn out by the journey, wisely followed their example.

The next day saw Miss Laura obliged to infringe her own most sacred and inviolable rule, and admit a man – the apothecary – into this maiden abode. She had sat under a tree the night before listening not to, but for, a nightingale, and was laid up by a most unpastoral fit of the rheumatism. Barbara in the meanwhile was examining her territory by daylight, and discovering fresh cause of vexation at every step. Here she was in the country, in a cottage 'comprising', as the advertisement set forth, 'all manner of convenience and accommodation', without grass or corn, or cow or sheep, or pig or chicken, or turkey or goose; no laundry, no brew-house, no pigstye, no poultry-yard! not a cabbage in the garden! not a useful thing about the house! Imagine her consternation!

But Barbara was a person of activity and resource. She sallied out forthwith to the neighbouring village, bought utensils and livestock; turned the coach-house into a cow-stall; projected a pigstye in the rosery; installed her ducks and geese in the orangery; introduced the novelty of real milk-pans, churns, and butter-prints amongst the old china, Dutch tiles, and stained-glass of that make-believe toy, the Gothic dairy; placed her brewing vessels in 'the housekeeper's room', which to accord with the genius of the place had been fitted up to represent a robber's cave; deposited her washing-tubs in the butler's pantry, which, with a similar regard to congruity, had been decorated with spars and shells like a nereid's grotto; and, finally, in spite of all warning and remonstrance, drove her sheep into the shrubbery and tethered her cows upon the lawn.

This last stroke was too much for the gardener's patience. He betook himself in all haste to B— to apprise Mr Walker; and Mr Walker, armed with Mr Samuel Tomkins and a copy of the lease, made his appearance with breathless speed at Rosedale. Barbara, in spite of her usual placidity, made good battle on this occasion. She cried, and scolded, and reasoned, and implored. It was as much as Mr Walker and Mr Samuel Tomkins, aided by their mute witness the lease and that very clamorous auxiliary the gardener, could do to out-talk her. At last, however, they were victorious. Poor Miss Bab's livestock were forced to make a rapid retreat; and she would probably have marched off at the same time had not an incident occurred which brought her visions of rural felicity much nearer to reality than could have been anticipated by the liveliest imagination.

The farmer's wife of whom she had made her purchases, and to whom she unwillingly addressed herself to resume them; seeing, to use her own words, 'how much Madam seemed to take on at parting with the poor dumb things', kindly offered to accommodate them as boarders at a moderate stipend, volunteering also lessons in the chicken-rearing and pig-feeding department, of which the lady did to be sure stand rather in need.

Of course Barbara closed with this proposal at a word. She never was so happy in her life; her cows, pigs and poultry, *en pension*, close by, where she might see them every hour if she liked, and she herself, with both hands full, learning at the farm, and ordering at the cottage, and displaying all that can be imagined of ignorance and good humour at both.

Her mistakes were innumerable. Once, for instance, she carried away by main force from a turkey, whose nest she had the ill-luck to discover, thirteen eggs, just ready to hatch, and after a severe combat with the furious and injured hen, brought them home to Rosedale as fresh-laid under a notion, rather new in natural history, that turkeys lay all their eggs in one day. Another time she discovered a hoard of choice double-dahlia roots in a tool-house belonging to her old enemy the gardener, and delivered them to the cook for Jerusalem artichokes, who dressed them as such accordingly. No end to Barbara's blunders! But her good-humour, her cheerfulness, her liberality and the happy frankness with which she laughed at her own mistakes, carried her triumphantly through. Everybody liked her, especially a smug little curate who lodged at the very farmhouse where her pigs and cattle were boarded, and said twenty times a day that Miss Barbara Jennings was the pleasantest woman in England. Barbara was never so happy in her life.

Miss Laura, on her part, continued rheumatic and poorly, and kept closely to her bedchamber, the Turkish tent, with no other consolations than novels from the next town and the daily visits of the apothecary. She was shocked at Miss Barbara's intimacy with the farm people, and took every opportunity of telling her so. Barbara, never very fond of her fair companion's harangues, and not the more reconciled to them from their being directed against her own particular favourites, ran away as often as she could. So that the two friends had nearly arrived at the point of not speaking when they met one afternoon by mutual appointment in the Chinese saloon. Miss Barbara blushed and looked silly, and seemed trying to say something which she could not bring out. Miss Laura tried to blush rather unsuccessfully. She, however, could talk at all times, her powers of speech were never known to fail; and at the end of an oration in which she proved, as was pretty evident, that they had been mistaken in supposing the company of each all-sufficient to the other, as well as in their plan of seclusion from the world, she invited Miss Barbara, after another vain attempt at a blush, to pay the last honours to their friendship by attending her to the hymeneal altar, whither she had promised to accompany Mr Opodeldoc on the morning after the next.

'I can't,' replied Miss Barbara.

'And why not?' resumed Miss Laura. 'Surely Mr Opodel—'

'Now, don't be angry!' interrupted our friend Bab. 'I can't be your bridesmaid the day after tomorrow, because I am going to be married tomorrow myself.'

And so they left Rosedale and I shall leave them.

Children of the Village
The Two Dolls

A LUCKY day it was for little Fanny Elvington when her good aunt Delmont consented to receive her into her family, and sent for her from a fine old place, six miles from hence, Burdon Park, where she had been living with her maternal grandfather, to her own comfortable house in Brunswick Square. Poor Fanny had no natural home, her father, General Elvington, being in India with his lady; and a worse residence than the Park could hardly be devised for a little girl, since Lady Burden was dead, Sir Richard too sickly to be troubled with children, and the care of his grand-daughter left entirely to a vulgar old nurse and a superfine housekeeper. A lucky day for Fanny was that in which she exchanged their misrule for the wise and gentle government of her good aunt Delmont.

Fanny Elvington was a nice little girl, who had a great many good qualities, and, like other little girls, a few faults; which had grown up like weeds under the neglect and mismanagement of the people at the Park, and threatened to require both time and pains to eradicate. For instance, she had a great many foolish anti-pathies and troublesome fears, some caught from the affectation of the housekeeper, some from the ignorance of the nurse: she shrieked at the sight of a mouse, squalled at a frog, was well-nigh ready to faint at an earwig, and quite as much afraid of a spider as if she had been a fly; she ran away from a quiet ox, as if he had been a mad bull, and had such a horror of chimney-sweepers that she shrank her head under the bedclothes whenever she heard the deep cry of 'Sweep! Sweep!' forerunning the old clothesman and the milkman on a frosty morning, and could hardly be persuaded to look at them, poor creatures! dressed in their tawdry tinsel and dancing round Jack-of-the-Green on May Day. But her favourite fear, her pet aversion, was a negro; especially a little black footboy who lived next door, and whom she never saw without shrinking, and shuddering, and turning pale.

It was a most unlucky aversion for Fanny, and gave her and her aunt more trouble than all her other mislikings put together, inasmuch as Pompey came oftener in view than mouse or frog, spider or earwig, ox or chimney-sweep. How it happened nobody could tell, but Pompey was always in Fanny Elvington's way. She saw him twice as often as anyone else in the house. If she went to the window, he was sure to be standing on the steps; if she walked in the Square garden, she met him crossing the pavement; she could not water her geraniums in the little court behind the house, but she heard his merry voice singing in broken English as he cleaned the knives and shoes on the other side of the wall; nay, she could not even hang out her canary bird's cage at the back door, but he was sure to be feeding his parrot at theirs. Go where she would, Pompey's shining black face and broad white teeth followed her; he haunted her very dreams; and the oftener she saw him, whether sleeping or waking, the more her unreasonable antipathy grew upon her. Her cousins laughed at her without effect, and her aunt's serious remonstrances were equally useless.

The person who, next to Fanny herself, suffered the most from this foolish and wicked prejudice, was poor Pompey, whose intelligence, activity and good humour, had made him a constant favourite in his master's house, and who had sufficient sensibility to feel deeply the horror and disgust which he had inspired in his young neighbour. At first, he tried to propitiate her by bringing groundsel and chickweed for her canary bird, running to meet her with an umbrella when she happened to be caught in the rain, and other small attentions, which were repelled with absolute loathing.

'Me same flesh and blood with you, missy, though skin be black,' cried poor Pompey one day, when pushed to extremity by Fanny's disdain, 'same flesh and blood, missy!' a fact which the young lady denied with more than usual indignation. She looked at her own white skin, and she thought of his black one; and all the reasoning of her aunt failed to convince her that, where the outside was so different, the inside could by possibility be alike. At last, Mrs Delmont was fain to leave the matter to the great curer of all prejudices called Time, who in this case seemed even slower in his operations than usual.

In the meanwhile Fanny's birthday approached; and, as it was within a few days of that of her cousin Emma Delmont, it was agreed to celebrate the two festivals together. Double feasting! Double holiday! Double presents! Never was a gayer anniversary. Mrs Delmont's own gifts had been reserved to the conclusion of the jollity; and, after the fruit was put on the table, two huge dolls, almost as big as real babies, were introduced to the little company. They excited and deserved universal admiration. The first was a young lady of the most delicate construction and the most elaborate ornament; a doll of the highest fashion, with sleeves like a bishop, a waist like a wasp, a magnificent bustle, and petticoats so full and so puffed-out round the bottom that the question of hoop or no hoop was stoutly debated between two of the elder girls. Her cheeks were very red, and her neck very white, and her ringlets in the newest possible taste. In short, she was so completely *à la mode* that a Parisian milliner might have sent her as a pattern to her fellow tradeswoman in London, or the London milliner might have returned the compliment to her sister artist over the water. Her glories, however, were fated to be eclipsed. The moment that the second doll made its appearance, the lady of fashion was looked at no longer.

The second doll was a young gentleman, habited in the striped and braided costume which is the ordinary transition dress of boys between leaving off petticoats and assuming the doublet and hose. It was so exactly like Willy Delmont's own attire that the astonished boy locked at himself, to be sure that the doll had not stolen the clothes off his back. The apparel, however, was not the charm that fixed the attention of the young people. The attraction was the complexion, which was of as deep and shining a black, as perfect an imitation of a negro, in tint and feature, as female ingenuity could accomplish. The face, neck, arms and legs were all covered with black silk; and much skill was shown in shaping and sewing on the broad, flat nose, large ears and pouting lips, whilst the great white teeth and bright, round eyes relieved the monotony of the colour. The wig was of black worsted, knitted and then unravelled, as natural as if it had actually grown on the head. Perhaps the novelty (for none of the party had seen a black doll before) might increase the effect, but they all declared that they had never seen so accurate an imitation, so perfect an illusion. Even Fanny, who at first sight had almost taken the doll for her old enemy Pompey in little, and had shrunk back accordingly, began at last to catch some of the curiosity (for curiosity is a catching passion) that characterized her companions. She drew near – she gazed – at last she even touched the doll, and listened with some interest to Mrs Delmont's detail of the trouble she found in constructing the young lady and gentleman.

'What are they made of, aunt?'

'Rags, my dear!' was the reply. 'Nothing but rags,' continued Mrs Delmont, unripping a little of the black gentleman's foot and the white lady's arm, and showing the linen of which they were composed.

'Both alike, Fanny,' pursued her good aunt, 'both the same colour underneath the skin, and both the work of the same hand – like Pompey and you,' added she more solemnly. 'And now choose which doll you will.'

And Fanny, blushing and hesitating, chose the black one; and the next day her aunt had the pleasure to see her show it to Pompey over the wall, to his infinite delight; and, in a very few days, Mrs Delmont had the still greater pleasure to find that Fanny Elvington had not only overcome and acknowledged her prejudice, but had given Pompey a new half-crown, and had accepted groundsel for her canary bird from the poor negro boy.

NOTE. About a month after sitting to me for his portrait, the young black gentleman whom I have endeavoured to describe (I do not mean Pompey but the doll) set out upon his travels. He had been constructed in this little Berkshire of ours for some children in the great county of York; and a friend of mine, travelling northward, had the goodness to offer him a place in her carriage for the journey. My friend was a married woman, accompanied by her husband and another lady, and, finding the doll cumbersome to pack, wrapped it in a large shawl and carried it in her lap, baby fashion. At the first inn where they stopped to dine, she handed it carelessly out of the carriage before alighting, and was much amused to see it received with the grave officious tenderness usually shown to a real infant, by the nicely dressed hostess, whose consternation, when, still taking it for a living child, she caught a glimpse of the complexion, is said to have been irresistibly ludicrous. Of course my friend did not undeceive her. Indeed, I believe she humoured the mistake wherever it occurred all along the north road, to the unspeakable astonishment and mystification of chambermaids and waiters.

The Rat-catcher
A Sketch

BEAUTIFULLY situated on a steep knoll, overhanging a sharp angle in the turnpike road, which leads through our village of Aberleigh, stands a fantastic rustic building, with a large yew tree on one side, a superb weeping ash hanging over it on the other, a clump of elms forming a noble background behind, and all the prettinesses of porches garlanded with clematis, windows mantled with jessamine, and chimneys wreathed with luxuriant ivy, adding grace to the picture. To form a picture, most assuredly, it was originally built, a point of view, as it is called, from Allonby Park, to which the byroad that winds round this inland cape, or headland, directly leads; and most probably it was also copied from some book of tasteful designs for lodges or ornamented cottages, since not only the building itself, but the winding path that leads up the acclivity, and the gate which gives entrance to the little garden, smack of the pencil and the graver.

For a picture, certainly, and probably from a picture, was that cottage erected, although its ostensible purpose was merely that of a receiving-house for letters and parcels for the Park; to which the present inhabitant, a jolly, bustling, managing dame, of great activity and enterprise in her own peculiar line, has added the profitable occupation of a thriving and well-accustomed village shop; contaminating the picturesque old-fashioned bay-window of the fancy letterhouse by the vulgarities of red herrings, tobacco, onions, and salt butter – a sight which must have made the projector of her elegant dwelling stare again – and forcing her customers to climb up and down an ascent almost as steep as the roof of a house, whenever they wanted a pennyworth of needles, or a half-pennyworth of snuff – a toil whereat some of our poor old dames groaned aloud. Sir Harry threatened to turn her out, and her customers threatened to turn her off; but neither of these events happened. Dinah Forde appeased her landlord and managed her customers: for Dinah Forde was a notable woman; and it is really surprising what great things, in a small way, your notable woman will compass.

Besides Mrs Dinah Forde, and her apprentice, a girl of ten years old, the letterhouse had lately acquired another occupant, in the shape of Dinah's tenant or lodger – I don't know which word best expresses the nature of the arrangement – my old friend, Sam Page, the rat-catcher; who, together with his implements of office, two ferrets, and four mongrels, inhabited a sort of shed or outhouse at the back of the premises, serving, 'especially the curs,' as Mrs Forde was wont to express herself, 'as a sort of guard and protection to a lone woman's property'.

Sam Page was, as I have said, an old acquaintance of ours, although neither as a resident of Aberleigh, nor in his capacity of rat-catcher, both of which were recent assumptions. It was, indeed, a novelty to see Sam Page as a resident anywhere. His abode seemed to be the highway. One should have as soon expected to find a gipsy within stone walls, as soon have looked for a hare in her last year's form, or a bird in her old nest, as for Sam Page in the same place a month together; so completely did he belong to that order which the lawyers call vagrants, and the common people designate by the significant name of trampers; and so entirely of all rovers did he seem the most roving, of all wanderers the most unsettled. The winds, the clouds, even our English weather, were but a type of his mutability.

Our acquaintance with him had commenced above twenty years ago, when, a lad of some fifteen or thereaway, he carried muffins and cakes about the country. The whole house was caught by his intelligence and animation, his light, active figure, his keen grey eye, and the singular mixture of shrewdness and good humour in his sharp but pleasant features. Nobody's muffins could go down but Sam Page's. We turned off our stupid deaf cakeman, Simon Brown, and appointed Sam on the instant. (NB This happened at the period of a general election, and Sam wore the right colour, and Simon the wrong.) Three times a week he was to call. Faithless wretch! he never called again! He took to selling election ballads, and carrying about handbills. We waited for him a fortnight, went muffinless for fourteen days, and then, our candidate being fairly elected, and blue and yellow returned to their original non-importance, were fain to put up once more with poor old deaf Simon Brown.

Sam's next appearance was in the character of a letter-boy, when he and a donkey set up a most spirited opposition to Thomas Hearne and the post-cart. Everybody was dissatisfied with Thomas Hearne, who had committed more sins than I can remember, of forgetfulness, irregularity, and all manner of post-man-like faults; and Sam, when applying for employers, made a most successful canvass, and for a week performed miracles of punctuality. At the end of that time, he began to commit, with far greater vigour than his predecessor, Thomas Hearne, the several sins for which that worthy had been discarded. On Tuesday he forgot to call for the bag in the evening; on Wednesday he omitted to bring it in the morning; on Thursday he never made his appearance at all; on Friday his employers gave him warning; and on Saturday they turned him off. So ended this hopeful experiment.

Still, however, he continued to travel the country in various capacities. First, he carried a tray of casts; then a basket of Staffordshire ware; then he cried cherries; then he joined a troop of ruddlemen, and came about redder than a Red Indian; then he sported a barrel-organ, a piece of mechanism of no small pretensions, having two sets of puppets on the top, one of girls waltzing, the other of soldiers at drill; then he drove a knife-grinder's wheel; then he led a bear and a very accomplished monkey; then he escorted a celebrated company of dancing dogs; and then, for a considerable time, during which he took a trip to India and back, we lost sight of him.

He reappeared, however, at B— Fair, where one year he was showman to the Living Skeleton, and the next a performer in the tragedy of the Edinburgh Murders, as exhibited every half-hour at the price of a penny to each person. Sam showed so much talent for melodrame that we fully expected to find him following his new profession, which offered all the advantage of the change of place and of character which his habits required; and on his being again, for several months, an absentee, had little doubt but he had been promoted from a booth to a barn, and even looked for his name amongst a party of five strollers, three men and two women, who issued playbills at Aberleigh, and performed tragedy, comedy, opera, farce and pantomime with all the degrees and compounds thereof described by Polonius, in the great room at the Rose, divided for the occasion into a row of chairs called the Boxes, at a shilling per seat, and two of benches called the Pit, at sixpence. I even suspected that a Mr Theodore Fitzhugh, the genius of the company, might be Sam Page fresh christened. But I was mistaken. Sam, when I saw him again, and mentioned my suspicion, pleaded guilty to a turn for the drama; he confessed that he liked acting of all things, especially tragedy, 'it was such fun.' But there was a small obstacle to his pursuit of the more regular branches of the histrionic art – the written drama: our poor friend could not read. To use his own words, 'he was no scholar;' and on recollecting certain small aberrations which had occurred during the three days that he carried the letterbag, and professed to transact errands, such as the misdelivery of notes, and the non-performance of written commissions, we were fain to conclude that, instead of having, as he expressed it, 'somehow or other got rid of his learning,' learning was a blessing which Sam had never possessed, and that a great luminary was lost to the stage simply from the accident of not knowing his alphabet.

Instead of being, as we had imagined, ranting in Richard, or raving in Lear, our unlucky hero had been amusing himself by making a voyage to the West Indies, and home by the way of America, having had some thoughts of honouring the New World by making it the scene of his residence, or rather of his peregrinations. And a country where the whole population seems moveable would, probably, have suited him; but the yellow fever seized him, and pinned him fast at the very beginning of his North American travels; and, sick and weary, he returned to England, determined, as he said, 'to take a room and live respectably'.

The apartment on which he fixed was, as I have intimated, an outhouse belonging to Mrs Dinah Forde, in which he took up his abode the beginning of last summer, with his two ferrets, harmless, foreign-looking things (no native English animal has so outlandish an appearance as the ferret, with its long limber body, its short legs, red eyes and ermine-looking fur), of whose venom, gentle as they looked, he was wont to boast amain; four little dogs, of every variety of mongrel ugliness, whose eminence in the same quality nobody could doubt, for one had lost an eye in battle, and one an ear, the third halted in his fore-quarters, and the fourth limped behind; and a jay of great talent and beauty, who turned his pretty head this way and that, and bent and bowed most courteously when addressed, and then responded in words equally apt and courteous to all that was said to him. Mrs Dinah Forde fell in love with that jay at first sight; borrowed him of his master, and hung him at one side of her door, where he soon became as famous all through the parish as the talking bird in the Arabian tales, or the parrot Vert-vert, immortalized by Gresset.

Sam's own appearance was as rat-catcher-like, I had almost said as venomous, as that of his retinue. His features sharper than ever, thin, and worn, and sallow, yet arch and good-humoured withal; his keen eye and knowing smile, his pliant active figure; and the whole turn of his equipment, from the shabby straw hat to the equally shabby long gaiters, told his calling almost as plainly as the sharp heads of the ferrets, which were generally protruded from the pockets of his dirty jean jacket, or the bunch of dead rats with which he was wont to parade the streets of B— on a market-day. He seemed, at last, to have found his proper vocation; and having stuck to it for four or five months, with great success and reputation, there seemed every chance of his becoming stationary at Aberleigh.

In his own profession his celebrity was, as I have said, deservedly great. The usual complaint against rat-catchers, that they take care not to ruin the stock, that they are sure to leave breeders enough, could not be applied to Sam; who, poor fellow, never was suspected of forethought in his life; and who, in this case, had evidently too much delight in the chase himself to dream of checking or stopping it whilst there was a rat left unslain. On the contrary, so strong was the feeling of his sportsmanship, and that of his poor curs, that one of his grand operations, on the taking in of a wheat rick, for instance, or the clearing out of a barn, was sure to be attended by all the idle boys and unemployed men in the village – by all, in short, who, under the pretence of helping, could make an excuse to their wives, their consciences, or the parish officers. The grand battue, on emptying farmer Brookes's great barn, will be long remembered in Aberleigh; there was more noise made, and more beer drunk, than on any occasion since the happy marriage of Miss Phœbe and the patten-maker. It even emulated the shouts and the tipsiness of the B— election – and that's a bold word! The rats killed were in proportion to the din – and that is a bold word too! I am really afraid to name the number; it seemed to myself, and would appear to my readers, so incredible. Sam and farmer Brookes were so proud of the achievement that they hung the dead game on the lower branches of the great oak outside the gate, after the fashion practised by mole-catchers, to the unspeakable consternation of a cockney cousin of the good farmer's, a very fine lady, who had never in her life before been out of the sound of Bow Bell, and who, happening to catch sight of this portentous crop of acorns in passing under the tree, caused her husband, who was driving her, to turn the gig round, and, notwithstanding remonstrance and persuasion, and a most faithful promise that the boughs should be dismantled before night, could not be induced to set foot in a place were the trees were, to use her own words, 'so heathenish', and betook herself back to her own domicile at Holborn Bars, in great and evident perplexity as to the animal or vegetable quality of the oak in question.[1]

Another cause of the large assemblage at Sam's rat hunts was,

---

[1] Moles are generally, and rats occasionally, strung on willows when killed; not much to the improvement of the beauty of the scenery. I don't know anything that astounds a Londoner more than the sight of a tree bearing such fruit. The plum-pudding tree, whereof mention is made in the pleasant and veracious travels of the Baron Munchausen, could not appear more completely a *lusus naturæ*.

besides the certainty of good sport, the eminent popularity of the leader of the chase. Sam was a universal favourite. He had good fellowship enough to conciliate the dissipated, and yet stopped short of the licence which would have disgusted the sober; was pleasant-spoken, quick, lively, and intelligent; sang a good song, told a good story, and had a kindness of temper, and a lightness of heart, which rendered him a most exhilarating and coveted companion to all in his own station. He was, moreover, a proficient in country games; and so eminent at cricket especially that the men of Aberleigh were no sooner able, from his residence in the parish, to count him amongst their eleven than they challenged their old rivals, the men of Hinton, and beat them forthwith.

Two nights before the return match, Sam, shabbier even than usual, and unusually out of spirits, made his appearance at the house of an old Aberleigh cricketer, still a patron and promoter of that noble game, and the following dialogue took place between them:

'Well, Sam, we are to win this match.'

'I hope so, please your honour. But I'm sorry to say I shan't be at the winning of it.'

'Not here, Sam! What, after rattling the stumps about so gloriously last time, won't you stay to finish them now? Only think how those Hinton fellows will crow! You must stay over Wednesday.'

'I can't, your honour. 'Tis not my fault. But, here I've had a lawyer's letter on the part of Mrs Forde, about the trifle of rent, and a bill that I owe her; and if I'm not off tonight, Heaven knows what she'll do with me!'

'The rent – that can't be much. Let's see if we can't manage –'

'Aye, but there's a longish bill, sir,' interrupted Sam. 'Consider, we are seven in family.'

'Seven!' interrupted, in his turn, the other interlocutor.

'Aye, sir, counting the dogs and the ferrets, poor beasts! For I suppose she has not charged for the jay's board, though 'twas that unlucky bird made the mischief.'

'The jay! What could he have to do with the matter? Dinah used to be as fond of him as if he had been her own child! And I always thought Dinah Forde a good-natured woman.'

'So she is, in the main, your honour,' replied Sam, twirling his hat, and looking half shy and half sly, at once knowing and ashamed. 'So she is, in the main; but this, somehow is a particular sort of an affair. You must know, sir,' continued Sam, gathering courage as he went on, 'that at first the widow and I were very good friends, and several of these articles which are charged in the bill, such as milk for the ferrets, and tea and lump sugar, and young onions for myself, I verily thought were meant as presents; and so I do believe at the time she did mean them. But, howsoever, Jenny Dobbs, the nursery maid at the Park (a pretty black-eyed lass – perhaps your honour may have noticed her walking with the children), she used to come out of an evening like to see us play cricket, and then she praised my bowling, and then I talked to her, and so at last we began to keep company; and the jay, owing, I suppose, to hearing me say so sometimes, began to cry out, "Pretty Jenny Dobbs!"'

'Well, and this affronted the widow?'

'Past all count, your honour. You never saw a woman in such a tantrum. She declared I had taught the bird to insult her, and posted off to lawyer Latitat. And here I have got this letter, threatening to turn me out, and put me in gaol, and what not, from the lawyer; and Jenny, a false-hearted jade, finding how badly matters are going with me, turns round and says that she never meant to have me, and is going to marry the French Mounseer (Sir Henry's French valet), a foreigner and a papist, who may have a dozen wives before for anything she can tell. These women are enough to drive a man out of his senses!' And poor Sam gave his hat a mighty swing, and looked likely to cry from a mixture of grief, anger and vexation. 'These women are enough to drive a man mad!' reiterated Sam, with increased energy.

'So they are, Sam,' replied his host, administering a very efficient dose of consolation, in the shape of a large glass of Cognac brandy; which, in spite of its coming from his rival's country, Sam swallowed with hearty good-will. 'So they are. But

Jenny's not worth fretting about; she's a poor feckless thing after all, fitter for a Frenchman than an Englishman. If I were you, I would make up to the wido : she's a person of property, and a fine comely woman into the bargain. Make up to the widow, Sam; and drink another glass of brandy to your success!'

And Sam followed both pieces of advice. He drank the brandy, and he made up to the widow, the former part of the prescription probably inspiring him with courage to attempt the latter; and the lady was propitious, and the wedding speedy; and the last that I heard of them was the jay's publishing the banns of marriage, under a somewhat abridged form, from his cage at the door of Mrs Dinah's shop (a proceeding at which she seemed, outwardly, scandalized; but over which, it may be suspected, she chuckled inwardly, or why not have taken in the cage?); and the French valet's desertion of Jenny Dobbs, whom he, in his turn, jilted; and the dilemma of lawyer Latitat, who found himself obliged to send in his bill for the threatening letter to the identical gentleman to whom it was addressed. For the rest, the cricket match was won triumphantly, the wedding went off with great *éclat*, and our accomplished rat-catcher is, we trust, permanently fixed in our good village of Aberleigh.

The Lost Keys,
or a Day of Distress

IT was a glorious June morning; and I got up gay and bright, as the
Americans say, to breakfast in the pretty summer-room overlooking the garden, which, built partly for my accommodation and
partly for that of my geraniums, who make it their winter
residence, is as regularly called the greenhouse as if I and my
several properties – sofas, chairs, tables, chiffoniers, and ottomans – did not inhabit it during the whole of the fine season; or as
if it were not in its own person a well-proportioned and spacious
apartment, no otherways to be distinguished from common
drawing-rooms than by being nearly fronted with glass, about
which out-of-door myrtles, passion-flowers, clematis and the
Persian honeysuckle form a most graceful and varied framework,
not unlike the festoons of flowers and foliage which one sees
round some of the scarce and high-priced tradesmen's cards, and
ridotto tickets of Hogarth and Bartolozzi. Large glass folding-
doors open into the little garden, almost surrounded by old
buildings of the most picturesque form – the buildings themselves
partly hidden by clustering vines, and my superb bay-tree, its
shining leaves glittering in the sun on one side, whilst a tall pear-
tree, garlanded to the very top with an English honeysuckle in full
flower, breaks the horizontal line of the low cottage roof on the
other; the very pear-tree being, in its own turn, half-concealed by a
splendid pyramid of geraniums erected under its shade. Such
geraniums! It does not become us poor mortals to be vain – but
really, my geraniums! There is certainly nothing but the garden
into which Aladdin found his way, and where the fruit was
composed of gems, that can compare with them. This pyramid
is undoubtedly the great object from the greenhouse; but the

common flower-beds which surround it, filled with roses of all sorts, and lilies of all colours, and pinks of all patterns, and campanulas of all shapes, to say nothing of the innumerable tribes of annuals, of all the outlandish names that ever were invented, are not to be despised even beside the gorgeous exotics, which, arranged with the nicest attention to colour and form, so as to combine the mingled charms of harmony and contrast, seem to look down proudly on their humble compeers.

No pleasanter place for a summer breakfast – always a pretty thing, with its cherries, and strawberries, and its affluence of nosegays and posies – no pleasanter place for a summer breakfast-table than my greenhouse! And no pleasanter companion, with whom to enjoy it, than the fair friend, as bright as a rosebud, and as gay as a lark – the saucy, merry, charming Kate, who was waiting to partake our country fare. The birds were singing in the branches; bees, and butterflies, and myriads of gay happy insects were flitting about in the flower-beds; the haymakers were crowding to their light and lively labour in a neighbouring meadow; whilst the pleasant smell of the newly mown grass was blended with that of a beanfield in full blossom still nearer, and with the thousand odours of the garden so that sight, and sound, and smell, were a rare compound of all that is delightful to the sense and the feeling.

Nor were higher pleasures wanting. My pretty friend, with all her vivacity, had a keen relish of what is finest in literature and in poetry. An old folio edition of that volume of Dryden called his *Fables*, which contains the glorious *rifacimenti* of parts of Chaucer, and the best of his original poems, happened to be on the table; the fine description of Spring in the opening of the *Flower and the Leaf*, led to the picture of Eden in the *Paradise Lost*, and that again to *Comus*, and *Comus* to Fletcher's *Faithful Shepherdess*, and Fletcher's *Faithful Shepherdess* to Shakespeare and *As You Like It*. The bees and the butterflies, culling for pleasure or for thrift the sweets of my geraniums, were but types of Kate Leslie and myself roving amidst the poets. This does not sound much like a day of distress; but the evil is to come.

A gentle sorrow did arrive, all too soon, in the shape of Kate

Leslie's pony phaeton, which whisked off that charming person as fast as her two long-tailed Arabians could put their feet to the ground. This evil had, however, substantial consolation in the promise of another visit very soon; and I resumed in peace and quietness the usual round of idle occupation which forms the morning employment of a country gentlewoman of small fortune: ordered dinner – minced veal, cold ham, a currant pudding and a salad – if anybody happens to be curious on the score of my housekeeping; renewed my beau-pots; watered such of my plants as wanted most; mended my gloves; patted Dash; looked at *The Times*; and was just sitting down to work, or to pretend to work, when I was most pleasantly interrupted by the arrival of some morning visiters – friends from a distance – for whom, after a hearty welcome and some cordial chat, I ordered luncheon, with which order my miseries began.

'The keys, if you please ma'am, for the wine and the Kennet ale,' said Anne, my female factotum, who rules, as regent, not only the cook and the undermaid and the boy, but also the whole family, myself included, and is an actual housekeeper in every respect except that of keeping the keys. 'The keys, ma'am, if you please,' said Anne; and then I found that my keys were not in my right-hand pocket, where they ought to have been, nor in my left-hand pocket, where they might have been, nor in either of my apron pockets, nor in my workbasket, nor in my reticule – in short that my keys were lost!

Now these keys were only two in number, and small enough in dimensions; but then the one opened that important part of me, my writing-desk, and the other contained within itself the specific power over every lock in the house, being no other than the key of the key-drawer; and no chance of picking them – for alas! alas! The locks were Bramah's! So, after a few exclamations, such as: 'What can have become of my keys?' 'Has anyone seen my keys?' 'Somebody must have run away with my keys!' I recollected that, however consolatory to myself such lamentations might be, they would by no means tend to quench the thirst of my guests. I applied myself vigorously to remedy the evil all I could by applications to my nearest neighbours (for time was pressing, and our horse and his master out for the day) to supply, as well as might be, my deficiency. Accordingly I sent to the public-house for their best beer, which, not being Kennet ale, would not go down; and to the good-humoured wives of the shoemaker and the baker for their best wine. Fancy to yourselves a decanter of damson wine arriving from one quarter, and a jug of parsnip wine, fresh from the wood, tapped on purpose, from the other! And this for drinkers of Burgundy and Champagne! Luckily the water was good, and my visiters were good-natured, and comforted me in my affliction, and made a jest of the matter. Really they are a nice family, the Sumners, especially the two young men, to whom I have, they say, taught the taste of spring water.

This trouble passed over lightly enough. But scarcely were they gone before the tax-gatherer came for money – locked up in my desk! What will the collector say? And the justice's clerk for warrants, left under my care for the chairman of the Bench, and also safely lodged in the same safe repository. What will their worships say to this delinquency? It will be fortunate if they do not issue a warrant against me in my own person! My very purse was left by accident in that unlucky writing-desk; and when our kind neighbours, the Wrights, sent a melon, and I was forced to borrow a shilling to give the messenger, I could bear my loss no longer, and determined to institute a strict search on the instant.

But, before the search could begin, in came the pretty little roly-poly Sydneys and Murrays, brats from seven downwards, with their whole train of nurses, and nursery maids, and nursery governesses, by invitation, to eat strawberries; and the strawberries were locked up in a cupboard, the key of which was in the unopenable drawer! And good farmer Brookes, he too called, sent by his honour for a bottle of Hollands – the right Schiedam; and the Schiedam was in the cellar; and the key of the cellar was in the Bramah-locked drawer! And the worthy farmer, who behaved charmingly for a man deprived of his gin, was fain to be content with excuses, like a voter after an election; and the poor children were compelled to put up with promises, like a voter before one; to be sure, they had a few pinks and roses to sweeten their disappointment; but the strawberries were as uncomeatable as the Schiedam.

At last they were gone; and then began the search in good earnest. Every drawer not locked, every room that could be entered, every box that could be opened, was ransacked over and over again for those intolerable keys.

All my goods and chattels were flung together in heaps, and then picked over (a process which would make even new things seem disjointed and shabby), and the quantities of trumpery thereby disclosed, especially in the shape of thimbles, needle-cases, pincushions, and scissors, from the different work-baskets, work-boxes, and work-bags (your idle person always abounds in working materials), were astounding. I think there were seventeen pincushions of different patterns, beginning with an old boot and ending with a new guitar. But what was there not? It seemed to me that there were pocketable commodities enough to furnish a second-hand bazaar! Everything was there except my keys.

For four hours did I and my luckless maidens perambulate the house, whilst John, the boy, examined the garden; until we were all so tired that we were forced to sit down from mere weariness. Saving always the first night of one of my tragedies, when, though I pique myself on being composed, I can never manage to sit still; except on such an occasion, I do not think I ever walked so much at one time in my life. At last I flung myself on a sofa in the greenhouse and began to resolve the possibility of their being still in the place where I had first missed them.

A jingle in my apron pocket afforded some hope, but it turned out to be only the clinking of a pair of garden scissors against his old companion, a silver pencil-case – and that prospect faded away. A slight opening in Dryden's heavily bound volume gave another glimmer of sunshine, but it proved to be occasioned by a sprig of myrtle in *Palamon and Arcite* – Kate Leslie's elegant mark.

This circumstance recalled the recollection of my pretty friend. Could she have been the culprit? And I began to ponder over all the instances of unconscious key-stealing that I had heard of amongst my acquaintance. How my old friend, Aunt Martha, had been so well-known for that propensity, as to be regularly sought after whenever keys were missing; and my young friend, Edward Harley, from the habit of twisting something round his fingers during his eloquent talk (people used to provide another eloquent talker, Madame de Staël, with a willow twig for the purpose), had once caught up and carried away a key, also a Bramah, belonging to a lawyer's bureau, thereby, as the lawyer affirmed, causing the loss of divers lawsuits to himself and his clients. Neither Aunt Martha nor Edward had been near the place; but Kate Leslie might be equally subject to absent fits, and might, in a paroxysm, have abstracted my keys; at all events it was worth trying. So I wrote her a note to go by post in the evening (for Kate, I grieve to say, lives above twenty miles off), and determined to await her reply, and think no more of my calamity.

A wise resolution! But, like many other wise resolves, easier made than kept. Even if I could have forgotten my loss, my own household would not have let me.

The cook, with professional callousness, came to demand sugar for the currant pudding, and the sugar was in the store-room, and the store-room was locked; and scarcely had I recovered from this shock before Anne came to inform me that there was no oil in the cruet, and that the flask was in the cellar, snugly reposing, I suppose, by the side of the Schiedam. So that, if for weariness I could have eaten, there was no dinner to eat – for without the salad who would take the meat! However, I being alone, this signified little; much less than a circumstance of which I was reminded by my note to Kate Leslie; namely, that in my desk were two important letters, one triple, and franked for that very night, as well as a corrected proof-sheet, for which the press was waiting; and that all these dispatches were to be sent off by post that evening.

Roused by this extremity, I carried my troubles and my writing-desk to my good friend the blacksmith: a civil intelligent man, who sympathized with my distress, sighed, shook his head, and uttered the word Bramah! And I thought my perplexity was nearly at its height, when, as I was wending slowly homeward, my sorrows were brought to a climax by my being overtaken by one of the friends whom I admire and honour most in the world – a person whom all the world admires – who told me, in her prettiest way, that she was glad to see me so near my own gate, for that she was coming to drink tea with me.

Here was a calamity! The Lady Mary H., a professed tea-drinker, a green-tea-drinker, one (it was a point of sympathy between us) who took nothing but tea and water, and, therefore, required that gentle and ladylike stimulant in full perfection. Lady Mary come to drink tea with me; and I with nothing better to offer her than tea from the shop – the village shop – bohea, or souchong, or whatever they might call the vile mixture. Tea from the shop for Lady Mary! Ill luck could go no further; it was the very extremity of small distress.

Her ladyship is, however, as kind as she is charming, and bore our mutual misfortune with great fortitude; admired my garden, praised my geraniums, and tried to make me forget my calamity. Her kindness was thrown away. I could not even laugh at myself, or find beauty in my flowers, or be pleased with her for flattering them. I tried, however, to do the honours by my plants; and, in placing a large night-scented stock, which was just beginning to emit its odour, upon the table, I struck against the edge, and found something hard under my belt.

'My keys! My keys!' cried I, untying the ribbon, and half-laughing with delight, as I heard a most pleasant jingle on the floor; and the lost keys, sure enough, they were, deposited there, of course, by my own hand; unfelt, unseen, and unsuspected during our long and weary search. Since the adventure of my dear friend, Mrs S., who hunted a whole morning for her spectacles whilst they were comfortably perched upon her nose, I have met with nothing so silly and so perplexing.

But my troubles were over – my affliction was at an end.

The strawberries were sent to the dear little girls; and the Schiedam to the good farmer; and the warrants to the clerk. The tax-gatherer called for his money; letters and proof went to the post; and never in my life did I enjoy a cup of Twining's green tea so much as the one which Lady Mary and I took together after my day of distress.

Farewell to Our Village

WAS it the gentle Addison, as quoted by Johnson, or Johnson himself, that tender heart enclosed in a rough rind, who said that he could not part without sorrow from the stump of an old tree that he had known since he was a boy? Whoever said it gave utterance to one of the deepest and most universal feelings of our common nature. The attractions of novelty are weak and powerless in comparison with the minute but strong chains of habit, and the moment of separation is that of all others, in which, with an amiable illusion, we brighten and magnify the good qualities of the object we leave, whilst we forget or overlook whatever at another time may have displeased us. The last tone is a tone of kindness; the last look a look of regret.

The very words consecrated to parting embody this sentiment: farewell! adieu! goodbye! Why they are benedictions, tender solemn benedictions! How poor and trivial when measured with their intensity seem the ordinary phrases of meetings: good day! good morrow! how d'ye do? how are you?[1] These are felt at once to be mere formal ceremonials, sentences of custom, spoken bows and curtseys, as cold and as unmeaning as the compliments at the beginning of a note or the humble servant at the end of a letter. Even between the most assured friends there is the same remarkable distinction in manner and in word. We shake hands at meeting, at parting we embrace.

The poets, faithful chroniclers of human feeling, have not failed to resort frequently to a source of sympathy so general and so

---

[1] Mr Spenser's little poem, 'One day Good-bye met How d'ye do?' is a pretty illustration of this difference.

true: witness the parting of Hector and Andromache in the 'tale of Troy divine'; and many of the finest passages in the finest writers, from Homer to Walter Scott. Nay, the feeling itself has made poets, as in the case of Mary, Queen of Scots, whose beautiful verses, 'Adieu plaisant pays de France!' may be reckoned amongst the tenderest adieux in any language. Perhaps, at no instant of her most unhappy life did that unfortunate beauty experience a keener sensation of grief than when sighing forth that farewell! I doubt, indeed, if farewell can be spoken without some sensation of sorrow.

Nevertheless, it is a word that must, in the course of events, find utterance from us all; and just now it falls to my lot to bid a late and lingering goodbye to the snug nook called *Our Village*. The word must be spoken. For ten long years, for five tedious volumes,[1] has that most multifarious, and most kind personage, the public, endured to hear the history, half real, and half imaginary, of a half-imaginary and half-real little spot on the sunny side of Berkshire; but all mortal things have an end, and so must my country stories. The longest tragedy has only five acts; and since the days of Clarissa Harlowe no author has dreamed of spinning out one single subject through ten weary years. I blush to think how much I have encroached on an indulgence, so patient and so kind. Sorry as I am to part from a locality, which has become almost identified with myself, this volume must and shall be the last.

Farewell, then, my beloved village! The long, straggling street, gay and bright in this sunny, windy April morning, full of all implements of dirt and noise, men, women, children, cows, horses, waggons, carts, pigs, dogs, geese and chickens; busy, merry, stirring little world, farewell! Farewell to the winding, uphill road, with its clouds of dust, as horsemen and carriages ascend the gentle eminence; its borders of turf, and its primrosy hedgerows! Farewell to the breezy common, with its islands of cottages and cottage-gardens; its oaken avenues populous with rooks; its clear waters fringed with gorse, where lambs are

---

[1] Originally published in five volumes.

straying; its cricket ground where children already linger, anticipating their summer revelry; its pretty boundary of field and woodland, and distant farms; and latest and best of its ornaments, the dear and pleasant mansion where dwell the neighbours of neighbours, the friends of friends; farewell to ye all! Ye will easily dispense with me, but what I shall do without you, I cannot imagine. Mine own dear village, farewell!

MARY RUSSELL MITFORD
THREE-MILE CROSS
9 April, 1832

FOR THE BEST IN PAPERBACKS, LOOK FOR THE

In every corner of the world, on every subject under the sun, Penguin represents quality and variety – the very best in publishing today.

For complete information about books available from Penguin – including Pelicans, Puffins, Peregrines and Penguin Classics – and how to order them, write to us at the appropriate address below. Please note that for copyright reasons the selection of books varies from country to country.

In the United Kingdom: For a complete list of books available from Penguin in the U.K., please write to *Dept E.P., Penguin Books Ltd, Harmondsworth, Middlesex, UB7 0DA*

In the United States: For a complete list of books available from Penguin in the U.S., please write to *Dept BA, Penguin, 299 Murray Hill Parkway, East Rutherford, New Jersey 07073*

In Canada: For a complete list of books available from Penguin in Canada, please write to *Penguin Books Canada Ltd, 2801 John Street, Markham, Ontario L3R 1B4*

In Australia: For a complete list of books available from Penguin in Australia, please write to the *Marketing Department, Penguin Books Australia Ltd, P.O. Box 257, Ringwood, Victoria 3134*

In New Zealand: For a complete list of books available from Penguin in New Zealand, please write to the *Marketing Department, Penguin Books (NZ) Ltd, Private Bag, Takapuna, Auckland 9*

In India: For a complete list of books available from Penguin, please write to *Penguin Overseas Ltd, 706 Eros Apartments, 56 Nehru Place, New Delhi, 110019*

In Holland: For a complete list of books available from Penguin in Holland, please write to *Penguin Books Nederland B.V., Postbus 195, NL–1380AD Weesp, Netherlands*

In Germany: For a complete list of books available from Penguin, please write to *Penguin Books Ltd, Friedrichstrasse 10 – 12, D–6000 Frankfurt Main 1, Federal Republic of Germany*

In Spain: For a complete list of books available from Penguin in Spain, please write to *Longman Penguin España, Calle San Nicolas 15, E–28013 Madrid, Spain*

FOR THE BEST IN PAPERBACKS, LOOK FOR THE

THE PENGUIN LIVES AND LETTERS SERIES

A series of diaries and letters, journals and memoirs

William Allingham: A Diary, 1824–1889 Introduced by John Julius Norwich

Arnold Bennett: The Journals Edited by Frank Swinnerton

Lord Byron: Selected Letters and Journals Edited by Peter Gunn

The Daughters of Karl Marx: Family Correspondence 1866–98 With a Commentary and Notes by Olga Meier

Earthly Paradise Colette

The Letters of Rachel Henning Edited by David Adams with a Foreword and Drawings by Norman Lindsay

Lord Hervey's Memoirs Edited by Romney Sedgwick

Julia: A Portrait of Julia Strachey By Herself and Frances Partridge

Memoirs of the Forties By Julian Maclaren-Ross, with a new Introduction by Alan Ross

Harold Nicolson: Diaries and Letters: 1930–64 Edited and Condensed by Stanley Olson

The Pastons: The Letter of a Family in the Wars of the Roses Edited by Richard Barber

Queen Victoria in her Letters and Journals A Selection by Christopher Hibbert

The Quest for Corvo: An Experiment in Biography By A. J. A. Symons

Saint-Simon at Versailles Selected and Translated from the Memoirs of M. le Duc de Saint-Simon by Lucy Norton

Osbert Sitwell: Left Hand, Right Hand! Abridged and Introduced by Patrick Taylor-Martin

Evelyn Waugh: Diaries Edited by Michael Davie